ABOUT THE AUTHOR

Ian Breckon was born in 1970. His first novel, *Knight of Swords,* was published in 2009.

* * *

PRAISE FOR *KNIGHT OF SWORDS*

'A story of multiple deceptions and concealed identities . . . Mysterious, beguiling, playful – yet making perfect sense'

Gerard Woodward

'An exciting and lyrical new voice in fiction. Breckon's work is thought provoking and intelligent'

Mo Hayder

First published in Great Britain in 2011 by Old Street Publishing Ltd
Trebinshun House, Brecon LD3 7PX
www.oldstreetpublishing.co.uk

ISBN 978-1-906964-30-6

10 9 8 7 6 5 4 3 2 1

A CIP catalogue record for this title is available from the British Library.

Typeset by Old Street Publishing Ltd.

Printed and bound in Great Britain.

ALL THE STARS ELECTRIC BRIGHT

ALL THE STARS ELECTRIC BRIGHT

IAN BRECKON

OLD STREET PUBLISHING

"… those who say Fascism, say first of all *beauty*."

BENITO MUSSOLINI, 28TH OCTOBER 1923

1

10th May 1930

Fast from Milan on Autostrada 8, they took off into the hills without dropping speed, accelerating into the hairpin bends as the landscape opened ahead of them in a swinging V of perspective and rushed away, shattered, fragmented, gone. The Alps were on the northern horizon. Rocky spurs jutted above the climbing road, and precipices swooped beneath. The car was a shock of yellow and black, sun flashing from its windshield, leaving the road shimmering behind it.

Perched on the rear seat, Emilio Calvi spread his arms and tried to hold himself steady. Another curve, the wheels drifting before the tyres bit. His stomach clenched. He focused on the dashboard, the speedometer needle flicking 90, then on the strands of black hair dancing from Nina's headscarf. The roof of the car was down, and a breeze curled around the windscreen, showering him with dust. Emilio kept his mouth tight shut and breathed through his nose, willing the journey's end.

Nina's stockinged feet heel-toed the pedals in a tight dance step. Beside her in the front passenger seat sat Arturo Gallo, a muscle clenching in his jaw. Nina's gloved hand reached blindly for the gear stick, fingers brushing his thigh, and both of them tensed. The rush of the wind shredded his words.

"… want to kill *yourself*," he said through his teeth. "… understand it … if you wanted to murder *me*, even … but it's not fair to involve Emilio!"

Emilio, crucified against the folded tarpaulin at the back of the cockpit, pretended to hear nothing. *What am I doing here?* he thought, crushed in the back of his best friend's lover's car, hurtling towards a party he did not want to attend.

He could have been at home in their shared apartment in Milan, as the sun went down and the noise of the traffic rose from the street below the balcony. He had spent an hour putting his suit on and taking it off, knotting his tie in different ways to try and hide the greasy spots, deciding not to go and then changing his mind. By six o'clock he was resolved; his jacket was smoothed over the back of a chair, and he was heading for the studio to begin an evening's painting. But just at that moment Arturo had arrived home. "Put that on," he'd ordered, pointing to the jacket. "Let's go. We're late."

Downstairs the Fiat had been waiting at the kerb with the engine idling. Nina, immaculate in white, sat ready in the driving seat. They pecked cheeks, and as Emilio scrambled across the luggage into the rear seat she had given him the hint of a wink, as if to say, *Don't worry, this isn't about you.*

No consolation in that. Sicker with every gut-hauling bend, Emilio sat tensed for the lurching loss of control, the fatal collision. The waspish Fiat seemed an arsenal of lacerating blades.

Ahead of them the road divided. Nina slowed only momentarily before hauling the wheel around to the right.

"Do you even know where we're going?" Arturo said. "I mean, do you have *any* idea …?"

Nina made no reply. Emilio craned to the left, trying to glimpse her face in the wing mirror. He saw only the whip of her headscarf, the twin dark circles of her driving glasses, the taut line of her smile. Sunlight illuminated her bare shoulder, and her scent mingled with the dust and the car's oily breath.

The sun was dropping towards the mountains as they

crested the summit and started the descent. The trees grew thicker, fencing the road and interlacing overhead to form a tunnel. The boxy black Lancia ahead was invisible at first – Nina spotted it suddenly and stamped on the brake, bringing the Fiat up with a skate and a jolt just short of the rear bumper.

"*Jesus*," Arturo breathed, hands flying instinctively to his head, fingers twitching an abbreviated cross over his chest. The two men exhaled. A face appeared in the oval rear-view window of the car ahead.

"Isn't that Rossi's car?" Arturo said, leaning forward into the windscreen. "He must know the way. We could just follow him …"

But Nina dragged the wheel to the left and accelerated, curling out and around the sedan in a spray of grit. The Lancia seemed to reel back as they passed, the faces of the men in the front blanked with surprise as Nina raced the Fiat down the open road ahead, towards the lakeshore and the villa by the water's edge. Behind them, a plume of dust spiralled and died slowly into haze.

The Villa Berardi faced the lake. Its roof was peaked low and heavy at the eaves in the local style, its walls white-cream with shutters and doors picked out in neat pistachio. From the broad terrace the gardens dropped in lawns and gravelled paths to the water. The lowering sun turned the Alps on the far shore into a banked grey haze.

The new wing of the house jutted from the flank of the main building: a stretched U of white concrete, clean-lined and unadorned. Berardi, the owner and host of the party, stood at the upstairs window of the new dining room. Hands gripped at the small of his back, he watched, frowning, as the cars approached along the lakeshore road.

Somewhere else in the house, his wife was shouting for

him. Servants raced up and down flights of stairs as Berardi stood and gazed into the narrowing delta of the cars' approach, the shrinking zone of emptiness that every moving body throws ahead of itself. Already he could feel the insult of their colours and their sounds, jabbing into his world of ordered stillness and sober monochrome.

Light from the window surrounded him, delineated him, made him solid and immobile. He would have liked to be a statue, poised mid stride while the world pivoted around him. He dreamed of a universe of interlocking steel rings and smoothly sliding polished ball bearings, with himself at the centre, the unmoved mover.

"Maurizio! Maurizio!" Mariagrazia was calling, her voice ringing through the house like an electric bell, "Maurizio, the guests are arriving! Where are you?" His wife still behaved as if she lived in a three-room apartment in the railway suburbs of Milan, not this lakeside mansion surrounded by mountain calm and glacial light.

Now she entered his field of vision, moving across the gravel of the drive in her bright new costume. All around her, servants lined the margin of the lawn. With her, of course, was the architect Conti. Look at him, Berardi thought. Flapping his hands. Like a *prick*.

Outside, the first car was gliding in – the little sports Fiat. Berardi heard the fall of the engine, the dying roar and the crunch of gravel as the car drew to a halt.

His wife was waiting to greet her guests. Her new cocktail dress was turquoise, lemon and black. She and Berardi were slipping through their fifties, declining into old age and inertia. Her defence was to grasp at youth, colour, art, love, and to make them her own; to construct around herself a barricade of noise and activity. His, conversely, was to find the stillness at the heart of noise. This new wing of the house had been specially commissioned and built to his orders. Not a machine for living as much as a machine against dying, against the slow death of creeping irrelevance. Shorn of all adornment, of all the frills and flourishes that catch and drag at time's current, it would fix time and hold it still, in the quivering instant of exactly *now*.

Berardi moved through the dining room and out onto the mezzanine above the picture gallery with measured step. He was still an imposing man: the cropped skull and solid jowls above the black bow tie, the physique of a boxer slowly losing to fat. His world was made of rationalised productivity quotas, of syndicates, consortiums and cartels. A world of fixed orbits and clear hierarchy. A member of the Central Industrial Committee, President of the Bertino Corporation, board member and leading shareholder in eight other major firms, Berardi was the owner of newspapers, steel mills, precision machinery plants, football teams, department store chains and shipping companies. His father had built racing bicycles, but Berardi had made his first fortune in the war, supplying electric timers for military and industrial explosives. And now he was the owner and financial director of the Berardi Gallery, Via Manzoni, Milan. The name was at his wife's insistence; he would have preferred anonymity.

This party, too, had been Mariagrazia's idea. She was the creative force behind the gallery; she was the inspired one. Berardi had always felt a foreigner among artists; he was far happier alone with his collections. But his wife had persuaded him – the party would be a fitting gesture, and perhaps even advantageous. F.T. Marinetti, founder of the Futurist movement, lately appointed to the Royal Academy of Italy, would be attending as guest of honour. He would provide the schedule of events; he would direct the show. The evening would belong to Marinetti, but the new wing of the house would be a showcase. A bold new venture – and in uncertain times, Berardi knew, only the bold survive.

But how could he enjoy all this without lowering himself into the broth and froth of the world?

He came to a halt before the French windows that opened onto the balcony. Beside him on a tall plinth was a marble bust. Berardi gazed at the domed head, the jutting jaw and the distinctive frowning profile. He reached out and laid a palm over the stone, as if to draw power from it.

Downstairs, he stood between the pillars of the main porch and watched his guests as they moved among the cars. Renzo Martino Rossi, at least, he was glad to see – a man he could regard as an equal. Rossi was even older than Berardi himself, a veteran. Two other men had arrived with Rossi in the Lancia, and the three young people in their fast little car. Berardi had seen them only days before, at the opening of the gallery exhibition, but even so he found it hard to connect the faces and the names. There was the photographer woman, Giannina Della Torre, whom he remembered talking to at the opening – remembered her voice more than anything, that flat nasal drawl that all the young women affected nowadays. She stood by the open door of her Fiat, stooping to remove her headscarf and survey her neat black bob in the wing mirror. Her two companions, the painters Emilio Calvi and Arturo Gallo, stretched their legs and shrugged at the shoulders of their jackets. One was more promising than the other, but for now Berardi couldn't remember which. Both Young Turks anyway.

They approached now, into the long shadow of the house while their hot machines ticked and gleamed behind them. From the porch, Berardi raised his arm in greeting – half wave, half Roman salute.

From the lobby with its sweeping staircases they moved in single file through the rooms of the main building, Berardi leading them like a tour guide. They entered the salon, where potted palms rose almost to the inlaid ceiling. French doors opened onto the terrace and the sunlit blaze of the lake.

Through a blue drawing room – piano, stuffed chairs – and along a corridor, they passed from the main house into the new wing. The space above them rose dramatically. The room still felt new, with a slight smell of fresh concrete and plaster.

"And this is the art gallery," Berardi said. "As you can see, I keep my private collection here. Some of your own works amongst them, in fact."

The sun angled in through the upper windows, leaving the paintings beneath the mezzanine in darkness. There were a couple of Depero abstracts, an early Prampolini, along with some older works by Rossi – *Aerial Simultaneity* and *Automobile Speed + Noise.* The more traditional paintings, a small Modigliani nude among them, had been relegated to the shadows. Already some of the works were becoming valuable, but it was nevertheless a bold collection. Berardi had bought the pictures not for their material worth, but because he wanted to own them. They reflected the aspect of himself that he most prized.

The guests circulated in a slow half-step. Typical that the artists should all arrive before all the others; he supposed they had little else to do but go to parties, especially if dinner was involved. He checked that line of thought: important to be genial now, to be the perfect host. Still, the prospect of having to make conversation with them alarmed him. It was one thing to collect their work, admire it even, and quite another to understand them. Mariagrazia was doing a fine job anyway, flitting between them like some fabulous tropical creature, praising and congratulating.

Berardi paused beside one of the paintings: Arturo Gallo's *Dynamism of the Seaplane.* Here was colour and form in bold conjunction, a harmony that pushed close at chaos. And there was Gallo himself: an angular loping figure in a well-cut grey suit and co-respondent shoes. Berardi saw his knife-shaped face, his insolent mouth.

The figures passed through the gallery, appearing momentarily framed by their own pictures – as if he had brought them here to add to his collection. Not only the artworks but the artists themselves, with their strange seething inspirations, the obscure dramas of their private lives. Here again was the young woman who had arrived with Gallo – Signora Della Torre. Her father, he recalled, had been a man of substance, a major Party backer in the early days. A man of Berardi's own type. How could a man like that have produced such a daughter – that tall slender figure, that sharply questing profile and those mocking, languorous eyes? She was quite beautiful, in the modern style. Married, of course, although she used her maiden name. Was there some scandal there, perhaps something that should not be mentioned? She had something of a reputation anyway. But then, every young woman under thirty seemed to have a reputation these days. He had bought a couple of her photographs, strange swirling grey abstractions, apparently taken from the cockpit of an aircraft, that gave him a disconcerting sense of profound loss.

Her other companion, Calvi, was a different type altogether, withdrawn and quiet-seeming, musing between the pictures with the eager attitude of a zealous young school-teacher. But there was an intensity about him that was almost forbidding. A strange trio. Berardi wondered what had drawn them together.

All these people, all these modern young people, inhabited the space far better than he himself. He had designed the new wing of the house, overseen its construction, but still it unnerved him slightly. Its austerity was a challenge he was not sure he could meet. Perhaps, after all, he belonged back in the old house, amidst the faded neo-classicism? The new extension, like the paintings in the gallery, was a vision of what he wanted to become, but feared he could not. He studied the faces of his guests, saw them looking back at the pictures they had created, the vibrant worlds they had conjured into form and colour. Did they too feel lessened, confronted with the visualisation of their dreams?

Rossi appeared, beaming, at his side. "I must say, I have little idea what to expect from this evening, Berardi. All very mysterious, no?" Berardi made a vague sound of assent. He had little idea what to expect either. "All these vague promises and suggestions … and this mention of a *special guest* too! Well, when Marinetti arrives …"

When Marinetti arrives … Berardi tasted acid in his throat, the first swells of his recurring indigestion. Marinetti alone could draw this crowd, the promise of his presence could summon them to this isolated place and give form to the evening ahead.

"If you'll follow me through here, ladies and gentlemen," he announced loudly, "we can go up to the dining room."

Climbing the black spiral steps, the party rose to the dining room. It stretched before them to the curve of windows at the far end. The wall facing the lake was an expanse of glass panes. The architect Gino Conti, a smallish man in a large suit, was duly commended.

"I hope," Berardi said, turning to address the group, "that His Excellency Marinetti will be able to join us very soon. He did tell me that he might be held up briefly in Milan, but he has, in any case, left detailed instructions …"

"*Very* detailed instructions!" his wife added.

"So, there should be no delay in commencing as soon as he arrives. In the meantime, perhaps you would all care to adjourn to the terrace for drinks?"

But the guests were already moving past him, drawn

along the length of the room, past the stacked furniture and folded screens heaped in the middle, to the windows. The view claimed them: the blue of lake and sky, the mountains in a haze between. Framed in the great square panes, the world outside the house felt composed, specially presented, to them alone. The guests stared into the blueness of it. They felt as if they were looking back at a perfected vision of the world, from the furthest promontory of the future.

In the main house, Nina followed the maid along the corridor towards her room. She had absented herself from the gathering, claiming a slight headache and a need to "freshen up".

The maid left her at the door. Nina locked it behind her and crossed the room to open the tall shutters. The sound of more guests arriving drifted from the back of the house – the noise of another car, the rattle and pop of a motorcycle.

Besides the large bed, the washstand, the dressing table and a folding lacquered screen, the room held little, but it possessed a simple elegance. The polished wooden floor reflected the lit western sky. Nina kicked off her shoes and flexed her toes. Sitting at the dressing table, she opened her slim handbag. As she took out her mirror case, her fingers brushed the torn edge of an envelope deeper inside the bag. Laying the mirror case on the table, she drew out the letter.

It had arrived that morning, sealed inside another envelope from her brother in Turin. She had read it first over her morning coffee, eyes darting across the page, unable to digest the words, or to fit this news into her life. Now she read it again. The familiar handwriting in blue ink, but an address on Avenue Pedro de Mendoza, Buenos Aires: *I needed to wait until I knew that my situation here was secure. I know that you must have condemned me many times for what I did, but there were reasons which I can only explain to you in person. Please forgive me for all the distress that my departure, and my long absence, must have caused …*

A knock at the door.

"Who's there?" she said, trying to keep the alarm from her voice as she folded the letter and slipped it quickly back inside her handbag.

"It's me. Arturo."

She crossed to the door and turned the key, then walked away as he entered the room. He stood, closing the door behind him, then leaned back against the wall with his hands in his pockets.

"Remind me why we aren't speaking," he said. Something in his voice, his stance, caught her. His crafty charm. From the first she had been attracted to that. Just for a moment she could have forgiven him everything.

"I seem to remember that one of us wasn't too keen on coming here."

He shrugged. "I could have got a lift with somebody else." *I don't need you.*

But he does, Nina thought. He needs me here tonight, and he knows it. He was bluffing: he knew he'd won. She could not back out of it now.

"I don't see your objection anyway," he said. "It's a party, that's all. I thought you liked parties."

"You know exactly what my objection is," she said, more sharply than she had intended. Immediately she was sorry. She didn't want harshness, didn't want to provoke another argument. "Let's not talk about it any more."

Arturo shoved himself away from the wall, nonchalantly strolled across the carpet and dropped to sit on the edge of the bed. "Nice lodgings they've given you," he said, idly scanning the room. "They've put me with Emilio, upstairs. I know a servants' room when I see one. Still, maybe I could join you here tonight …"

"Let's consider that later."

"Or I could climb up to the balcony there. Past midnight, with a rose between my teeth ..."

"You'd find me heavily sedated and wearing a sleeping mask."

"All the better for me then!"

The familiar grin lit his face. But in his tone, his posture, seated there on the bed with his hands dangling, there was a tension he was trying to conceal. Nina felt the thrill of her power over him: he still feared what she might do. She thought of the letter in her bag. It was a weapon he did not know she possessed.

"You know this evening's important to me," he said, hesitant. "I know you don't take me very seriously these days, but please ..."

She glanced at him, alert for irony, but his face was clear and guileless. He was one of the least relaxed men she had ever known, yet there was a strange grace to him, a loping, awkwardly-angled confidence. It was touching to see him so vulnerable now. For all his attempted cunning, there was nothing Arturo was capable of hiding from her. She cherished this: the frankness of his gaze taking her in, the generosity of his spirit; his restless, ranging energy, always so close to the surface, close to aggression but closer to a childlike enthusiasm.

She *had* taken him seriously, she wanted to say. She wanted to still, but already he was twisting himself into a different shape – the shape the world demanded. How could she not despise that? These last months they had scaled opposing heights, trying to gain leverage over each other; now their hands were linked across a precipice, their bodies braced for balance. She said nothing, and the moment stretched long between them, the bitterness of their dispute clouding the air. Then he let out an exasperated gasp.

"Why do you always have to make everything so complicated?" he said, punching the mattress beside him. "Why do you have to be this complicated person?"

"It's my complicated past, I'm afraid."

"Me, I'm not complicated. I'm a simple man ..." She began to laugh, despite herself. "A simple man, from a line of simple men. To me, life is transparent. My needs are very simple. But you – you have an aristocratic strain. You need all this Byzantine complexity. Everything invested with drama."

"So are you worried I'll *invest this evening with drama*?"

"Just ... don't stab anybody with a fork at dinner."

"I promised, didn't I?" Then, quieter, turning away: "Just allow me some space. Let me do this my own way and I'll try to help you."

She would try. She would take his hand and lead him into that fabulous world that his ambition had conjured. Even though it was a world she had grown to detest, and to fear. But when that world had claimed him, would she really be able to walk away and leave him there?

He paced silently, stepping up behind her, close but not touching.

"Shall we stop arguing, then?" he said.

"No apologies."

"Fine."

At his first touch she tensed, then relaxed, a flicker running up from the base of her spine. She felt his lips brush her bare shoulder, the rasp of fine stubble on his chin. He kissed the back of her neck, reaching around her body, fingers smoothing her breast. But something in her would not give way.

"Enough of that," she whispered. She lifted his hand clear, turning in the circuit of his arm. Facing him now, she saw the sun's glow in his irises, deep darting green.

"For such a simple man, you have very complicated eyes."

She turned her head just in time to shift his kiss from lips to cheek.

"Give me five minutes," she told him, "and I'll join you outside."

Walking backwards, arms still spread, he reversed himself from the room. Nina locked the door behind him. Secure in her solitude, she closed the shutters against the sun and took the letter from her bag again.

With all that happened between us I know you may find it impossible to trust me, but for the sake of our son please do not ignore this letter. Matters have taken a serious turn, and you are no longer safe in Europe. For your own sake and our son's, you must leave as soon as possible. I will arrange passage and all the necessary documents for you both.

Everything is prepared here for you and Marco. I have a house with room for all of us to be together again. I cannot promise happiness, but can promise to give all that I have.

Please let me know what you decide. Your brother knows how to contact me.

With love, always – Amedeo.

P.S. Tell no one of this letter, and please burn it immediately after reading.

Nina pressed her hands to her face, the paper crushed against her cheek. She had ignored the final direction, not wanting to lose the words so soon. Without them she might have doubted the reality of what she had read. Now she shuddered, alert to the danger. *You are no longer safe in Europe.* She laid the folded letter in a heavy glass ashtray on the side table. A match to the paper, and it caught fire, curling into itself and wrapping the blue flame and the twist of smoke until nothing remained but soft ash.

It had been over eighteen months since she had last seen

her husband, and not a word from him. She pictured him, his calm reserve, his inscrutable smile, and felt a stab of sudden anger. Even now, he still had the power to reach into her life. *For your own sake and our son's …* But where was the danger? What was the threat? Several weeks must have passed since he wrote the letter. Was it already too late? She should have refused to come tonight. By now she could have been packed and ready to leave, to make her escape … Nina caught herself. Panic, like a cold finger, was pressing at the base of her neck.

She was safe here. Nothing could touch her, surely, in this place. She twisted the bracelet on her wrist, holding the pendant with the inscribed symbols between her fingers. The night lay ahead of her. There would be music, perhaps dancing, there would be Marinetti's special performance, and the meal, about which they had heard much speculation but knew so little. Her lips shaped silent words. Praying did not come easily to her. Just one night, another few hours of heedlessness, before she had to make her decision. She would put the matter from her mind. She would tell nobody.

Returning to the dressing table, she flipped open the circular mirror. The packet fell onto the tabletop, the blade of a safety razor neatly slipped inside. Already feeling the first rushes of anticipatory adrenaline, Nina opened the packet and tapped the throat of it into a funnel. In the disc of the mirror, her eyes were thorn-black in a careful squint.

Powder spilled from the packet in a measured pile. The steel blade made a keen sound against the glass as she scraped. Cocaine shaped in a neat line, she slipped the slim metal tube from the back of the mirror case, inhaled smoothly, feeling the numbness of it, then the glow inside.

11th April 1919

From the back seat of her father's pearl-grey Isotta-Fraschini, shunting steadily through the traffic on Via Dante, she saw a pattern of upraised straw boaters, pale circles against the darkness of suits and dresses. The car's leather upholstery and glass muted the sounds of the street, but she heard the noise growing from overhead and pressed her face into the angle of the window. A slot of sky showed through the lattice of tram wires, between the high cornices of the buildings.

"Here he comes again!" somebody shouted, pointing, and the heads of the crowd turned as one. A burst of sound, men clutching hats to heads. The shadow fell first, then the machine passed over, so close it seemed to Nina that if one of the men outside jumped he might touch it. The aeroplane was painted in bold colours, long strokes of red and blue curling under the wings and along the fuselage. A second passed, then a third, each swooping up to dance around the black spires of the Duomo.

Nina's father glanced from the window on his side of the car, but the planes had whirled out of sight again. Out of the corner of her eye, she saw him reach into his waistcoat to check his watch. He was due to attend a meeting at his bank. Between them, her French governess sat staring straight ahead, while Gino, broad-backed in his grey serge uniform, gripped the steering wheel, ready at any moment to turn the big car away from whatever trouble might break ahead of them. Her father eased back in the seat, the leather creaking, and she felt his tension like an electric charge. He was alert to the dangers of crowds, to their strange irrational surges.

Five months since the war ended, and now it was springtime and the long mourning was lifting. Still the city pulsed with the energy of alarm, of panic and riot. The war had changed everything; Italy had been victorious, but nothing felt like victory. Sealed behind glass, she felt remote from the city, as she had felt remote these last four years. Remote even from her own grief. But now here was the world, pressing up against the windows.

The traffic in the street was immobile. Horse drays and motor lorries were jammed tight against the yellow trams and the automobiles, and the big Isotta-Fraschini was blocked in on all sides. The engines were running, chugging, and the trench of the street was hazed with fumes. Between the stilled vehicles the pedestrians moved, perching in the middle of the street, waiting for the planes to appear again. Nina read the expectancy on their faces. She felt it herself – a terrible marvellous dread. A man stepped onto the footboard on the driver's side of the car, craning upwards, and Gino told him to get down.

"I'm going to be late if we're stuck here much longer," her father said. "Gino, when the traffic moves take the car on across the Piazza and park it by Via Mercanti. Nina and Mademoiselle can stay with you. I'll walk to the meeting."

"Can't I walk too, Father?" Nina asked, leaning forward to speak across the governess. "The Galleria's not far away, I can be there in two minutes, then I could look at the shops until you get back ..."

"No," her father replied. "Stay in the car. We can go shopping later."

He tapped the shoulder of the chauffeur again, an unspoken communication passing between them, then bid the two women goodbye and stepped out into the street. The crowd consumed him at once.

Through the car window, Nina saw the people on the

pavement reflected in the big glass panes of the shops, bright flashes of sunlight on the polished brass of a carriage lamp or the flank of an automobile. She had not been to Milan since the war started. Four years ago – maybe five – but it felt a different life altogether. She had been a little girl then, holding her mother's kid-gloved hand. Now she remembered it clearly: a café table in the Galleria, eating sorbet from a tiny glass dish, her legs swinging. Her mother's hat decked with black ostrich feathers.

That was the old world, and it was gone, like the plumed horsemen, riding down Corso Re Umberto on their fine horses in a blizzard of tricolour confetti, to face the machine-guns and the gas shells and the flame-throwers. It had been blasted apart, on the mountains of Caporetto and the plains of the Piave. But what had replaced it? Nina did not know. She stared from the car and marvelled at it, and the world shouted back, incoherent.

Noise from overhead, and the crowd reflected in the shop windows jolted into motion as the plane flashed across the glass, appearing in six or eight places at once. Nina angled her head upwards as the machine roared away down the gulf of the street.

"*Qu'est-ce qu'ils font là-haut, ces idiots?*" her governess said. White flecks filled the sky. For a moment it seemed like snow, then confetti, and then Nina saw that they were sheets of paper. As they fluttered down, the crowd began to jump and shout, scattering between the traffic to snatch the paper out of the air.

"*Regardez-les! Comme c'est vulgaire!*"

A sheet billowed against the windscreen of the car, and Gino reached out to pluck it free. Over his shoulder, Nina read the bold header:

FUTURIST AERIAL THEATRE

Flight as the Artistic Expression of a New Lyrical Consciousness

"Can I see it, Gino?" She leaned forward, reaching for the paper in his gloved hand. He shrugged and passed it back to her. The sound of the engines was growing again, swelling from the sky. Nina read, scanning quickly.

We Futurist aviators are today creating a new artistic form, capable of expressing the most complex states of mind ... From the skies, with the darting speed of our machines, we shout our sensations and the lyrical power of our desires ... From the furnaces of war we bring the new sensibility of the FUTURE, breathless, beautiful and bizarre ...

Nina knew nothing of war. She had spent those years at the house in Orbassano, or at her convent school, sealed away in green, unknowing calm. Her family were patriotic, Jewish and bourgeois; the nuns at the school secretly supported the Austrians, while proclaiming indifference. None of it was real to her: battles were fought on the pages of breakfast-table newspapers, across a map stuck with little pins and flags in her father's study. A war on paper, and then a death on paper too, carried by a uniformed orderly. *Captain Gabriele Della Torre gave his life for Italy.* So many had died at Caporetto that their family grief dissolved into the grieving of a nation. Her brother had joined a phantom army, the sacrificial martyrs of victory.

Nina gripped the printed sheet, and the words bled. She saw herself, aged eleven, on a warm spring day in 1915. In her grey smock and buttoned boots, she was running out across the gravel path and down the steps to the garden. Behind her in the courtyard, her eldest brother Gabriele was standing in his smart kepi and gleaming boots, while the photographer framed his image against a sunlit wall.

She ran across the damp sheen of grass to the big sycamore

tree in the corner of the garden. Gripping the saddle of the lower branches, the wood smoothed by many hands, she began to climb. Climbing higher, she could see the house and the yard and the driveway beyond. They would think she was just being capricious – like the time Gabriele called her a coward and she threw herself into a bank of stinging nettles to prove him wrong. But that had been a performance, and this was real. She climbed until the limbs bent beneath her and the young leaves no longer hid her. The air was still, and she could smell the sap of the wood. Far below, they were all running across the lawn – Gabriele in his new uniform, waving his riding crop.

"Come down! Come down before you hurt yourself! Little girls shouldn't climb trees!"

"I'm not a little girl!" she shouted back, her voice cracking. "And I don't want you to go!"

The new sensibility of the FUTURE, breathless, beautiful and bizarre … she read the words again. The planes whirred behind the glass. A plunging vertigo gripped her, a heady nausea: she could not remain in the car any longer. She could not remain behind glass, in closed rooms, trapped in slow suburban gloom and mourning. The aeroplanes were unsealing the city. They were ripping open all the doors and abolishing the past.

Nina reached for the door handle, turned it, stepped out onto the street – she was diving forward, into the world. The planes wheeled together in the sky like a vertical carousel, and the crowd began to applaud, horns and whistles blaring out.

"Get back inside," Gino said. "Signorina, please get back in the car …"

Heat rushed to her face, and she felt the pulse in her neck as she stared upwards, part of the crowd now. One by one the planes reached the zenith of the arc and peeled aside, swooping into long dives over the spires and the domes, the roof tiles and the chimney pots. One plane flung itself directly upwards. Nina sensed the human intelligence, the mind at the controls of the machine, and her spirits rose with it. She too was floating high in the air, alone with the planes dancing around her. For the first time she felt truly alive.

Abruptly, the engine cut off, and the machine hung in silence over the city. Slowly it turned and began to drop. The crowd hushed. A woman screamed; somebody laughed nervously.

Then the engine roared again and the machine hauled itself out of its plunge, and for a brief instant, before her governess pulled her back into the safety of the car, Nina felt herself lifted and carried, as the crowd were all carried, with the street and its stilled traffic and everything else the city contained, rushing upwards into the void.

2

10th May 1930

Outside the French doors of the salon, the guests gathered on the terrace, sitting on slim steel and wicker chairs or standing along the balustrade to admire the early evening light over the lawns and gardens beneath them. Servants brought buckets of ice water and bottles of chilled Asti Spumante.

Emilio lingered in the salon, pretending a close interest in the modernistic furnishings. The dizziness of the journey had passed, but he still felt an oppressive tightness across his shoulders and down his back. To plunge forward was the thing, reckless and impetuous. But he held back, unwilling to make that step.

He flicked his gaze between the men outside, scanning the lapel of every suit for the glint of a Party badge. He saw none: the suits betrayed no allegiance but to wealth and quality tailoring. But then there was no need. The lustre of power and influence was all around him. Even this salon, with its glass-beaded lampshades and rectilinear armchairs, its slanted oval mirrors and geometric rugs, spoke of authority. Emilio felt waves of nervous tension passing through him.

He remembered the sealed hospital ward at Monza, remembered himself kneeling beside the bed of the condemned man, clasping his hand. The promises he made then, barely a week ago: *I will not compromise myself with them. I will not accept their favours or their patronage. I will not collaborate with the regime; I will not give my assent to what they have done.* Now, by his mere presence in this house, he was betraying it all.

Arturo stood at the far side of the terrace, his profile like something snipped from tinplate. As he watched him, Emilio envied his lack of conscience more than ever, his overpowering, single-minded ambition. He could have come here with Nina alone, but claimed he needed Emilio's support. He needed the sense of solidarity. But solidarity to what end?

"Well, hello," Nina said, appearing beside him. He flinched, hand darting instinctively to the knot of his tie; there was a lively amusement in her eyes. Standing at Emilio's shoulder, she glared out at the gathering. Arturo was beside the balustrade with his back to them, shoulders heaving at some remark of Berardi's. "How inviting that looks," she said flatly.

"I was just about to go outside and join them," Emilio lied. He had a sudden urge to touch her arm, to demonstrate the complicity between them. Neither had wanted to come tonight; they were here for Arturo's benefit. But she was Arturo's lover, and the strange energies of their relationship were closed to him. Besides, Nina was wealthy herself, and these sorts of surroundings would be familiar to her. Emilio, in his creased suit, his armpits prickling with nervous heat, was the outsider in this place.

"You know, I wanted to apologise for my behaviour earlier," Nina said. "On the way here, I mean. Driving like that – it was very irresponsible. I'm sorry I was so awful."

"Oh, no, it was nothing …" There was something unnaturally alert about her, a strange electric thrill in her voice. Why did she pretend not to enjoy these events? How little he knew her, in reality. Her world was quite different from his own, her feelings and reactions almost those of a different species.

Nina tensed and grabbed his arm. "Is that Fosca out

there?" she said, motioning towards a woman out on the terrace. "Oh *shit* I think it is." The woman was in her late forties, stout, with a frizzed lobe of orange hair showing grey at the roots.

"If I'd known she'd be here I certainly wouldn't have come," Nina said, and let her forehead drop to rest lightly on Emilio's shoulder. "Help me, will you?" she said. "We'll have to go out and socialise."

He felt the pressure of her touch, the realness of her body beside him. He knew she was flattering him, giving him this opportunity to feel protective.

"I wish we could find somewhere private and just talk, you and me. It seems like months since we've talked," she said. But the eagerness in her voice belied her words.

"Wait a minute, there's something on your face ..."

Nina shifted her head slightly, eyes rolled upwards, as Emilio brushed at her cheek with a fingertip.

"Gone now," he said. "Just some powder or something."

She took his arm again and he walked her out into the sunlight.

"So what's the problem with this Fosca person?" Emilio said in an undertone as they approached the other guests.

"She's intolerable, that's what," Nina whispered, leaning closer. Emilio felt her breath warm in his ear, the scent of her body, her hip moving against his as they walked. "She used to pretend to be Jewish, but nowadays she claims to be an occultist or a spiritual medium or something. Be careful what you say to her – she's a vicious gossip."

As they reached the group of guests in the middle of the terrace, Fosca launched herself towards them, arm extended. She wore a heavy assortment of polished wooden beads around her neck and a gold clasp shaped like a serpent on her bare upper arm.

"Giannina, my darling!" she proclaimed, her hand

clasping at Nina's shoulder and drawing her in for a swift double peck. "So pleased you could come! And this is your … friend?"

She slid an appraising glance up and down Emilio, grimacing tightly – with approval or disdain, he couldn't tell.

"Emilio Calvi," Nina said coolly. "The painter."

"Well, of course, we met earlier, didn't we?" said Fosca. "But, Giannina, where *is* your husband? It's been so long since I last saw him!"

"Oh, he disappeared," Nina said.

"Disappeared … ? Oh my goodness. Nothing bad, I hope? Nothing … *personal*?"

"No, just disappeared."

"Hnnn … And your dear little boy?"

"Montreux. School."

"I see. Convenient!"

They stood for a moment, with the space chilling between them. Emilio took a deep breath. "We should …" he said, and he began to draw Nina away.

"Speak to you both later!" Fosca exclaimed.

They veered off towards the group lining the balustrade, where Arturo stood with Berardi.

"Sorry about that," Nina said under her breath. She disengaged her arm from Emilio's and took a glass of Spumante from a passing tray.

"You have this," she said, passing it to him. "I don't like fizzy drinks. They make me sneeze."

Emilio sipped at the drink, feeling the bubbles mass on his tongue.

"I suppose," Nina said, "I should go and talk to my surly sweetheart." She looked over at Arturo, still wrapped in talk with Berardi. "We'll speak more later, promise."

Across the lake, a seaplane was sliding down the sky. The

sound of the engine – the reverberant radial drone – echoed off the far mountains, quiet at first but insistent, filling the spaces in the conversations of the people gathered on the terrace. One by one they fell silent, moving instinctively towards the balustrade. Sun gleamed off the broad surfaces of the wings. The hush was reverent.

Bright foam trailed behind the plane as it skimmed the water, wingtips shaking, the noise of the engine louder, then dropping to a low rumble. The plane slowed and settled, the propellers turning arcs.

Arturo squinted down at the aircraft floating on the lake. It seemed much smaller than it did in flight, and far from impressive.

"It's a Savoia-Marchetti," Berardi said. "They have a station on the far shore there. Incredible, isn't it – an aircraft like that was flying over the jungles of Brazil before the world had even heard the name Lindbergh!"

"Incredible, yes!" Important to acknowledge these little patriotic asides. Arturo looked at Berardi, hoping that a significant moment of recognition might pass between them. *Dynamism of the Seaplane,* the picture that now hung in his private gallery, was the first of his works that Berardi had bought. Surely he must have noticed this happy concordance of art and inspiration, of artist and subject?

But Berardi turned away to talk to the man at his other shoulder: a middle-aged man, slim and too well dressed, with a neat moustache and bulging startled eyes. Arturo recognised him – Rossi's friend, the composer Lino Osvaldi.

"For a moment there," Osvaldi was saying, "I thought that might be Marinetti swooping down to join us!"

"Ah, no ..." Berardi said. "I believe he's driving up here by automobile."

"In his own good time, as usual," Osvaldi said. "Still, what could be more Futurist than to always arrive *in the future*, eh?"

The conversations had resumed, the seaplane forgotten, a dwindling white freckle on the vastness of the lake. Nina touched Arturo on the arm.

"You look uneasy, darling," she said quietly, then louder: "Perhaps we should go for a walk in the gardens?"

Down the steps from the terrace and along the gravel path they walked together, she a step or two ahead, Arturo prowling behind. The sound of the people talking beside the balustrade drifted above them, mingling with bright airy jazz from a gramophone.

"I spoke to that pig Fosca," Nina said, over her shoulder. She walked with a studied ease, but the pitch of her voice betrayed her. "She had the gall to ask me where *my husband* was! I've spoken to her on at least two occasions since Amedeo left, and she still pretends not to know."

The garden stretched before them, neat clipped lawns and box hedges divided by paths and short flights of steps, brickwork hazed with moss and creeping flowering vines. Towards the shore, above a file of slender palms, a little belvedere stood on a grassy rise, plasterwork imitating pillars and a classical dome.

"Either Berardi has inherited his garden," Arturo said, "or he harbours secret anti-modern tastes … All very *passéist*, I'd say." He lit his last American cigarette, then crumpled the empty packet and wedged it behind a marble Cupid.

Nina paused, one heel twisting in the gravel.

"Aren't the mountains beautiful?" she said. Arturo glanced at them with vague surprise.

"Are they? *A thing is beautiful only when it responds to a need.* What need do the mountains respond to?"

"The need to stop Switzerland sliding into the sea? Who said that anyway? It isn't your quote."

"That architect back there. Conti. That, and a lot of

other Germanic-sounding pronouncements. He studied in Dresden, I think, and Rotterdam. He talked a lot about austerity and audacity … all the *awe* words."

"He must have impressed you deeply."

"Not much. He gets white stuff in the corners of their mouth when he talks. And he speaks like he's just run up the stairs carrying something soft on his tongue."

She looked back at him with wry appreciation, then continued along the path towards the belvedere. He watched her moving against the landscape, trying to see her as a stranger might. She wore a sleeveless white dress, flesh-toned stockings, high-heeled pumps in grey suede, strapped black. Her hair was bobbed and lightly waved, a black hook rising to either cheek, like parentheses framing her face. She had posed naked for him once, and later he'd painted her portrait. What need, he wondered, did Nina's beauty respond to?

He had known what she was about to do when he left her room. He had grown accustomed to these clandestine rituals. A few times, near the beginning, he'd taken the drug with her, but she never seemed especially keen to share and after a while he learned to leave her alone. The cocaine was, he wanted to believe, merely a vestige of the person she used to be, a fragment of a lost life – one which did not contain him. Arturo wondered how many other little chemical blisses, each their own private mystery, the house would see before the evening was done.

Ahead, Nina reached the belvedere and paused, transfixed once more by the view of the lake. Arturo knew the drug and its duration; he knew the rush, and the glassy calm of the dying fade. It wasn't so much the drug itself he hated, but the passivity that it forced on him; he became the observer, merely the foil to her states of mind. Now, in this state, her behaviour seemed unreal. She was acting herself.

He needed her to be charming that night, for his own

selfish reasons. Somewhere in the expanses of the evening ahead there would be a man that he must meet and talk to, a man of power and influence. The man would offer an important commission, a more than lucrative commission – an opportunity that would cement Arturo's reputation and secure his future. Berardi had told him about it, on the night of the gallery opening. He had told him, leading him aside from the crowd to speak in confidence, and in his eyes was an unmistakable promise. The offer had been maddeningly vague, but after so many years of scraping and striving, success seemed almost close enough to taste.

He stepped inside the belvedere, finding the twilight gathered there. Rough brickwork hid under the fake Palladian plasterwork shell. Artifice surrounded him, the whole garden a nineteenth-century millionaire's recreation of an eighteenth-century classical ideal.

Nina stood in the last of the sunlight. Shadow filled the bowl beneath the mountains; a few sparks of snow were still illuminated on the higher peaks. What would we look like from the house, Arturo wondered, if anyone were to lean over and peer along the line of the garden? Two youngish people, maybe lovers, posed in an agreeable setting. Appearances tell us virtually nothing. But if we could just break the thin ice of appearances and reach beneath, into the chill of genuine awareness – what then?

"Will we remember this moment in the future, do you think?" Nina said. Arturo leaned against a pillar, hands in his trouser pockets, shrugged. "I often ask myself that," Nina went on, tipping her head back. The sun coloured the curve of her throat. "Whether we'll look back one day and remember this very moment, right now, and what we were thinking and feeling."

"I've never really thought about it," Arturo said. "I do sometimes wonder if I ever pictured this moment, back in the past somewhere. If I ever thought that I might be here, one day, doing this."

In his imagination the future was empty and blue as the air above the lake, greyish now as evening set in, the colour of infinity. Even here, amidst the placidity of this scene, as they stood doing nothing, time was splitting before their charge. They were at the speeding edge of the present, the constant *now*, opening a spreading V of past time behind them.

"I got a letter this morning," she said abruptly. "From my husband."

He remained silent, refusing her cue. What was this, now? There was a tacit agreement between them that this subject was not to be discussed. Her husband, her son, the world she inhabited before meeting him – these were things that had no part in their lives together now. "That's no concern of mine," he said eventually.

"It could be … But clearly you're quite incapable of caring."

"The past should be abolished," he declared, more angrily than he had intended, throwing the words out towards the lake. He heard Nina's dry laugh.

"Wouldn't that be convenient!" she said. "You know, your tempers used to amuse me once. What have you got to be cross about, anyhow? You're doing what you wanted, aren't you? We're all here for your benefit, aren't we? For your marvellous career, your glittering future …"

"What's that supposed to mean?" He took in Nina's ironic air. She had been goading him, daring him ever since they left the terrace. He had the violent urge to grab her, slam her up against the wall with his body and grind her white dress against the mossy bricks. He took a stride towards her, swinging his hand, his fingers hooked, groping between her thighs. Nina stepped back, swatting his hand away.

"Crude," she said. "Beastly person." But there was a bright

mischief in her eyes. Abruptly his anger slackened. He had no wish, suddenly, to play her game.

"I might have to go and find somebody else to amuse me," Nina said. "Sullen people bore me, as I'm sure you know by now. I only came here because you insisted, remember?"

"And you agreed not to drink too much, take cocaine or insult anybody, including me!"

"Oh dear," she replied, turning and walking away, "is this *our argument* swelling up again? I thought we'd bled that dry already."

Arturo kicked at the base of a pillar. Perhaps *their argument* was all that held them together. But he could not act alone, could not trust himself to navigate the night unaided. For Nina, this party was merely entertainment, and not greatly entertaining entertainment at that, but she possessed what he did not. She had been born into wealth, and moved in the society of powerful men with the familiarity of a sleepwalker. Her ease with luxury entranced him, but still he resented her. These last two weeks, polluted by constant argument and temporary reconciliation, had caused his confidence to falter. She meanwhile, seemed not to care. She didn't, he reflected, have to care.

"Tennis?" Nina said, from away to his right.

Behind the belvedere and across a lawn, between clipped square hedges, there was a tennis court laid out. Nina followed the hedge along to its break, skimming her fingers over the cropped foliage as Arturo crossed the lawn. Was she even actually annoyed, he wondered, or was her anger a charade as well? She seemed happy enough now.

"Sorry," he said in an airy tone. "I shouldn't have done that, back there."

"Be a darling and shut up, would you? I'd almost forgotten all about it."

"About that letter from Amedeo ..."

"It was nothing," she said over her shoulder. "Nothing, really. I shouldn't have mentioned it."

They patrolled the margins of the court, scuffing at the red clay. The net was taut and white, freshly stretched – somebody must have been playing recently. Arturo walked to the baseline and squatted on his haunches. Beyond the rectangle of earth-red was another of green, and beyond that one of blue – a swimming pool lined with mosaic tiles. Palms lifted round shabby heads between the stands of tall cane, and far away, invisible in the sky, another plane was droning away towards Switzerland.

Arturo scrubbed at the nape of his neck, feeling a punchy energy rising through him. A game would be good now. He could take off his jacket and his two-tone shoes, work up a sweat, lashing the ball back and forth. He could run, yelling, and leap the net. But Nina moved on from the red rectangle into the green, crossing the small lawn towards the swimming pool.

He remembered her at the gallery opening in Milan, the crowd milling between the sculpture-pedestals, while outside in the electric-lit night the long, polished cars drew up one by one. "*Let's get away from here,*" she had whispered. "Let's go to the Americano Bar and drink cocktails, or something, or anything ... These people ... I can feel my eyeballs shrinking just looking at them all."

Outside the gallery she had let out a gasp, almost a shout of relief, stamping her feet along the pavement and under the archway into the piazza, the noise echoing. He took her arm, running with her to the tram stop on Via Manzoni, and when the tram glided in – nearly empty at that hour – they sat together in the hidden corner behind the driver, in the sputtering sodium yellow glow, and kissed ferociously. At Piazza Cavour an elderly couple got on the tram and sat opposite; Nina turned her face to the reflection in the window, and passed a tissue to Arturo so he could wipe the smeared lipstick off his mouth.

Now she stood beside the pool. In the stillness of the evening, the water barely moved. Fifty hours had passed, more or less, since Arturo sat with her in that tram after the gallery opening, but the feeling that consumed him then – that voracious passion, shared so totally, or so it seemed – was utterly mysterious to him now. The woman beside the pool was not, could not be, the same woman he was with then. It was not a new sensation; he had felt it many times during the eight months of his relationship with her. He looked at his watch; half-past seven already, and barely more than an hour left before dark. The air seemed almost to hum with the onrush of night.

"I suppose I should say sorry, shouldn't I?" she said. "I don't mean to be cruel to you. It's just … well, this is supposed to be a party. It's supposed to be *jolly* …"

The word seemed to hang before them, fluttering over the water like some rare and ludicrously plumed bird.

"And I mean, it'll be no good if we're sniping at each other all night, will it?"

Arturo watched her carefully, gauging the change in her mood. The drug was ebbing from her now, its slow seep drawing her down and making her pliable. He sauntered closer, a lazy swing in his step. Lifting his arm as he passed behind her, he let his fingers drift across her shoulders; Nina tensed at his touch, then gave a relieved shudder as she relaxed.

"You're right," he said softly. His fingers traced down her arm, his hand moving for hers. "Maybe a quick dip would do us good …"

"What?" she had time to say, then his arm was around her waist, scooping her up and back.

For a moment they fell together. The perfect composition

of the garden and the evening was shattered by her scream and their sudden movement. Somewhere birds shrieked and lifted from the trees; the air itself seemed to dart wildly away.

Her arms were tight around his neck, clinging to him, her feet kicking out for balance and her body rigid between, but he had judged his attack well – a foot braced at the brink of the pool pavement, both arms holding her suspended over the rippled water. Her brocade evening bag dangled on its long strap.

"Beast!" she said as he lifted her back upright, breathless and grinning. She punched his shoulder with delight. "I'd have pulled you in after me, you know!" Her face was full of colour, the rush of her blood bringing a last quick surge of chemical euphoria.

"You should trust me more," he said as they stumbled together, back from the water's edge. "I'm not actually insane, after all."

"I sometimes wonder," she said, arms looping his neck again, her head dropping close to his shoulder.

They moved together, clumsy at first, stiff-legged and lurching, but beginning to sway into a sort of rhythm. Arturo drew her body to him; her scent lifted on her body's warmth, and he breathed her in. He knew that she was clinging to the dying glow of the drug now, nursing it like a sinking flame in a breeze.

"What is this?" she said vaguely, raising her head, "a foxtrot, or what?"

"Call it a waltz," he replied, and they swung together again, each counting time just beneath their breath, lips moving silently, the only sound the click of their heels on the tiles. She missed a step, trod on his toe, giggled like a girl.

"Can't do this without music," she said. "Sing something!"

"You want me to *sing* a waltz?"

She reeled away from him, grabbing his hand and drawing

out to arm's length. "'Tiger Rag!'" she said, and kicked her foot back.

They began to dance again, shuffling at first until they caught the rhythm. Arturo's knees flexed, his shoulders winged; Nina shimmied and twisted on her toes, and the sound of the imagined band swelled around them – the clarinets and the saxophones, the snares and the bouncing bass.

"Ah-*wooop*! Dah – badab – *dah* – dab!" Arturo sang, clicking his fingers to the music. "Ah –*wooop*! Hold-ah that *ti*-ger!"

Nina broke away, her hand dropping from his as she fell laughing into a half-crouch. "So funny!" she said. "You look so funny! Moving your hand like that … it looked like you were *polishing* something!"

Arturo was laughing too, but then caught himself. He glanced around warily, checking if anyone had seen them. What an imbecile he must have looked, dancing about! He shrugged his shoulders into his jacket, tugged at the lapels, ran a hand through his hair. Nina's amusement subsided into stifled chuckles. She wasn't even looking at him any more. Numbness was stealing her away.

He turned on his heel and took a few paces from her. Behind him, he heard the rasp of a match.

"Offer me a cigarette, will you," he said. "I'm out."

"If you don't mind smoking women's cigarettes," she said, speaking through the smoke. She tossed her packet of Serraglio to him.

"I'll smoke anything." He took a cigarette, frowning at its gold filter, lit it with a flourish and passed the pack back.

"You know, I don't understand why you're so agitated," she said. "You're the young hope here. You and Emilio."

"Don't be ridiculous."

"It's true. I'm not important. I'm just decoration. Nobody

really cares what I get up to. Why don't you just relax, go back there and impress everybody?"

"I want to stay here for a while," Arturo said. Around the angle of the pool there were chairs and a table, white wicker bright in the last of the sun. He sat down, legs crossed, smoking.

"Fine," Nina said. The old hauteur had risen around her again, sealing her off. "You'll have to excuse me. I need to go back inside."

She walked away, fluttering a brief wave. Arturo breathed smoke from his nose, tasting it at the back of his throat. Stretching his legs out before him, he lounged back in the wicker chair. With Nina gone he felt better able to appreciate her. On the night of the gallery opening, the tram had taken them, eventually, to a smoky working-men's bar near Porta Garibaldi, where they played billiards and drank sour grappa and he had talked her out of dancing on the bar. He would have got into a fight with somebody if a couple of railwaymen had not bundled them both into a taxi.

He gazed down the line of his crossed legs, through the break in the hedge and over the sloping lawn. The sun felt reddish, but he could see the plane out there on the water, tiny as a floating bird. Berardi's comment came back to him, about the famous flight to Brazil. Not only Brazil ... He tipped his head back, his vision dyed crimson. Take me to Caracas. Take me to New York ... Tokyo ... Peking ...

Eight months before, when he began his affair with Nina, Arturo was stuck halfway through his painting of the seaplane. It had been sitting on his easel for weeks when she first visited the studio. Periodically he would take it down and turn it to the wall, sick of the sight of it. She saw it fresh, though, and then he was able to see it freshly through her eyes. He realised that it had stopped being merely a picture, merely an arrangement of shapes and colours on a flat surface, some time ago: that realisation enabled him to finish the painting, and exhibit in the Syndicate show, where Berardi saw it and paid nine hundred lire for it. And because of that, Arturo had become a valued guest at his house. Because of that painting, which for weeks had seemed utterly hopeless, Berardi had taken him aside at the gallery opening and whispered his promise about the commission. Such an arbitrary series of connections; it was chilling to consider.

The painting had taken so long to finish because he was trying to put so much into it. He had kept the image in his mind for more than ten years, preserving it until he felt he had the skill to portray it with all its power intact.

It was a memory from the last summer of the war, when he was sixteen years old. The previous autumn the front line, once far off in the mountains, had drawn so close to the family home in Treviso that the concussion of the artillery bombardments shuddered the windows in their frames. At night they heard the shells thudding like the footsteps of an approaching giant. They had moved to a dilapidated summer villa on the coast at Miramare, south of Rimini, but Arturo thought only of the war happening beyond the northern horizon. He could feel it, like a heat on his face or a stir in the air. In November he would be seventeen and eligible for enlistment.

The empty days stretched around him. He walked on the beach, waiting for the war to claim him. It was everything he wanted – an escape into the world, a liberation from his narrow existence. Morbidly adolescent, he liked to imagine himself dead, flung heroically on some blasted mountainside, illuminated by the unearthly flare of the star-shells. Sometimes he saw ships passing, grey hulls slipping along the horizon line, and one morning he found the beach lined with washed-up gas masks, flopping in the surf like obscene underwater creatures. These events seemed like messages to him.

One day in late August, the plane appeared out of the perfect blue of an Adriatic noon. It blinked into existence as suddenly as a semaphore, canting down in a wide arc over the waves. Arturo saw it with extreme clarity: a seaplane fighter with the sun in the blur of its propeller. He saw the pilot in the open cockpit, the snout of the machine-gun, the slim, boat-keeled fuselage painted not only with the green-white-red roundel but also with a great crimson mouth and two rows of hooked white teeth – the jaws of a snarling shark with a black eye above. He ran fast along the wet sand beside the water, the wind loud around him as the plane touched down, jetting foam behind it. He ran, staring after the plane and not wanting to lose it, tracking it as it skimmed the waves until it vanished into the haze off Rimini.

That was what he had tried to paint more than ten years later in the studio in Milan. Because there had been no war for Arturo: on the fourth of November, just two weeks before his seventeenth birthday, the Armistice was signed with Austria and the fighting came to an end.

To capture that on one-and-a-half square metres of stretched and primed canvas was impossible. It was not only the scene itself that he was trying to paint, not only the speed and dynamism of the plane, its colours and the shapes it threw across the water, but everything that surrounded it: his almost sexual longing for the perfect heroism of war, and the denial of its promise. He was trying to paint a portrait of his own youthful desire for the sublime in all its forms.

It had all been so much easier when he first started painting. So much easier to try and paint like Cézanne, lugging his canvases out into the countryside to pummel the colour into slab-forms of hills, into trees like bunched fists. There was something primitive in the love of paint, its smell and texture and oily residue; the cobalt, cadmium, magenta and chrome; the umber and ochre; the good manly muck of it. And it was satisfying, in those days, just to paint – to let the hills be green and the sky be blue, and not worry about what the pictures meant.

Those weeks in Milan, as he laboured over the seaplane picture, he'd come close to abandoning painting altogether. The paint was just dirt and rotten metals in a suspension of grease – inert, coloured mud, daubed on cloth. He wanted to paint in ozone and steel, in petroleum vapour and sea-spray. He wanted to slash the mess on the canvas to shreds and never paint anything again.

But when Nina had seen it standing on the easel – seen it and known nothing of all the scrapings-back and the scrubbings-out, the battle that had raged across its surface – everything seemed different. Aside from Emilio, who worked quietly and diligently on the far side of the studio, nobody else had seen the picture. Nina gazed at it for a moment, pursed her lips, nodded and said that she liked it. She liked it, that was all, but it was enough. Arturo had started reworking the painting that night. He worked through until morning, and by the afternoon it was finished. His memory of the plane coming down off Rimini had faded, burned off like mist, and all the dilemmas had gone with it. Instead there were formal problems to be resolved. A matter of colours, shapes and harmonious proportions.

He finished the painting, he got the work done. It had fallen short of his ambitions, but it sold, and sold well. Before that, he'd had to sell two canvases a month just to pay his share of the rent, or borrow the money off Emilio. He had believed in the sincerity of art. Despite the cynical front, he believed that he had a true sensibility. The sale of the seaplane painting made him realise that he was a workman, a decorator: the disillusionment had been strangely liberating.

Why did he feel so different now? These last few weeks had plunged him back into just that state of terrible frustration that he had inhabited before Nina's arrival. Only now she was unable to free him from it; in fact she seemed determined to keep him there. Back in the studio in Milan, another painting waited, unfinished, on the easel – another painting he had struggled and sworn over. He needed to finish it, he needed to get it done and time was short, but rather than helping him, Nina had done everything she could to stop him. She had even picked up a knife and tried to slash the canvas … She had become mysterious to him, her trust and belief in him had been withdrawn. And, when he needed that trust and belief the most, the lack of it pained him.

He sat up, irritation flaring in his body. *Fucking woman.* Away to his left, he could just make out her distant figure, a dash of white moving between the far hedges towards the house. His hand tightened on the arm of the wicker chair. She would leave him like that for good one day soon, just walk away into some other life in which he did not exist. Was there anything he could say or do to stop that? For a second he tensed, ready to follow her, chase her through the gardens. But his pride would not allow it.

Pride – that, at least, he still possessed. But the ache of tenderness was there too, riding out over the anger. He saw the cigarette she had dropped before she left, her gold-tipped Serraglio still smouldering on the paving beside the pool. The faint marks left by their shoes as they performed their silent dance.

Come back to me.

23rd March 1923

All morning the parades had moved through the city, spilling out from Piazza Duomo and filling the streets with their noise, but in the painting studio of the Accademia Brera, behind old iron window-grilles, the only sound was the quiet dabbing and scuffing of brushes on canvas. The nude woman sat in the middle of the room. Around her the easels stood in a ring, eleven young men studying, frowning, raising thumbs and brushes to measure and plot the curves of her body. A loud, aggressive scratching came from the far corner, then abruptly stopped. Emilio glanced up from his work; heads turned, smiling briefly.

Professor Cattaneo moved between the easels in slow, steady perambulation: a tall figure in a suit of heavy tweed, smoking a pipe. Beside each student he paused, the pipe descending – a grunt of approval, or the sharp intake of despairing breath.

"More fluidity in your line, I think, Signor Bruccoli … your figure looks constipated!" He took the brush, swiped an easy flourish in the air. "Like so …"

The sound of scratching again, of the wooden tip of a brush handle scouring canvas. It made Emilio's teeth hurt. Bruccoli stifled a giggle.

The figure on Emilio's canvas only barely approximated a human form: there was a shape there, but it shifted in and out of definition as he worked, the colours blurring into grey, then outlined in bold black. He lowered the brush and stared at the model. She sat in a sort of tired *contraposto*, her flesh heavy and sexless. Behind her was the clutter of the painting studio: empty wooden stretcher-frames stacked against the walls, folded easels, dusty plaster busts of Charlemagne and Marcus Aurelius. It was hard to imagine a less dynamic subject.

Emilio sighed, then scrubbed an angry grey zigzag across the canvas. He pictured the rest of the building, beyond the walls of the studio: the colonnaded courtyard outside, the great baroque chambers of the gallery on the floor above. Mantegna, Botticelli, Caravaggio: Cattaneo had taken them up there in the first week at the Academy, guiding them between the works of the masters, his pipe-stem eloquent as he instructed them in what to love.

And Emilio did love the Brera; he loved the massive quiet of the place, the scents of oil paint and sawn wood and the reek of rabbitskin glue rising from the vaulted workshops in the cellars. But it was oppressive. The weight of the past was everywhere; the place was engulfed by History. It did not inspire him; it served only to fog his brain. He longed to be outside, in the brilliant air, the spring sunlight pale above the steel-veined streets, tracing silver around the gables and pediments.

Then, from the far corner, the same rapid, grating scratch …

"Signor Gallo, do you have an itch?" Cattaneo stalked across the studio, removing his pipe. The scratching stopped, and Arturo's head appeared above his canvas. Across one of his cheekbones was a bright streak of vermilion; it looked deliberate, the war-paint of a savage. Cattaneo surveyed Arturo's easel, his face pinched into an expression of dismay.

"Signor Gallo, does the entire history of Western art mean nothing to you at all?" Stifled laughter circled the room. "What is this?" the professor went on, jabbing with his pipe-stem. "What is the purpose of these jagged lines? The poor model looks as if she's being electrocuted!"

They were all getting up now, stools and easels shunting. At Cattaneo's almost imperceptible nod, the model relaxed, stretched up from her position and wrapped herself in a shawl. Emilio trailed the other students as they grouped around Arturo's easel. The figure was fractured across the rectangle of canvas, shot through with streaks of colour and explosive scratch-lines. The painting was ugly, even brutal. Emilio thought it was brilliant.

Arturo sat back from his easel with a look of defiant satisfaction, the paintbrush gripped between his teeth like a dagger.

"You do these things to try my patience, I know," the professor said. From the beginning, Arturo had been his favourite. Colour, form, composition – he had mastered them all, then thrown them away deliberately, wantonly.

"And you, Signor Calvi," Cattaneo said, turning to Emilio now. "You are also infected with this virus, this … *rebellious strain.* Oh, I know your type all too well." He tamped his pipe with fresh tobacco, lit it, breathed smoke. "You misread a little Nietzsche, a little Bergson, inhale the more pungent of Signor Marinetti's eructations and reckon you can overturn public taste and morality. I'm afraid the public is no longer that stupid!" He enjoyed these provocations, Emilio knew – brief tastes of the fervour he possessed himself, back in his unimaginable youth. "All your hero Marinetti assaults these days is pasta …"

"He's not my hero," Arturo said, prickling. "I've never met the man, let alone *inhaled* him."

"Your vitriol is commendable, I suppose," Cattaneo went on, through the smoke. "But if you explode tradition, what will you put in its place? That childish Dada nonsense? Surely not those absurd Futurists again? Didn't they all die in the war? Oh no, wait, there's still Martino Rossi – and he's taken to painting flowers, I see …"

"Very *modern* flowers!" Emilio broke in. "Then there's Prampolini, Depero … there's Bruno Moresco!"

"And there's *us*," Arturo announced, rapping his knuckles on the easel.

Emilio had first met Arturo Gallo under a blur of fists and swinging cudgels, in the turmoil of a street riot. It was August 1922, late evening, and the city was vivid with violent energy. The General Strike had collapsed; strike-breakers drove the tramcars, and on the side of every tram was chalked *FREE SERVICE! VIVA FASCISMO!* In Corso Venezia a man in a business suit and spats was sweeping the crossing, a little tricolour flag tied to the end of his broom. On street corners and in piazzas, motor-lorries were drawn up with their engines running, packed with black-shirted youths. As he walked through the centre of the city, Emilio felt broken glass crackle and squeal beneath his feet.

In Piazza della Scala a crowd pressed towards the Palazzo Municipale. Blackshirts occupied the council rooms, brandishing their flags from the windows and shouting, "*Viva Italia*! Death to Lenin! Down with Democracy!" The blackshirts called themselves war veterans, but most looked younger than Emilio himself. There were even women amongst them, Amazonian in their piratical black headscarves. Together they radiated mob-threat, a restless, indiscriminate violence; they were the tentacles of a vast octopus, ready to uncurl and strike.

Emilio didn't see exactly how the first fight broke out. He saw the crowd shudder and split, the red flags tossed and torn, then the flung stones cracking down onto the pavement as a line of mounted men – *carabinieri* in grey uniforms – advanced from the far end of the piazza. The noise of iron-shod hooves was loud; behind him the crowd was gone. He ran, hearing the horses at his back, before leaping beneath the crowded portico of the theatre.

"Hold this," a voice said, and somebody passed Emilio a bottle. He took it mutely, by reflex, the glass slippery in his sweating hand. A match flared, there was a ripple of flame, and the bottle was blazing. "Throw it, idiot! Throw it!"

Emilio stepped out from the portico and hurled the bomb away from him, feeling the heat of it up his arm. It arced and shattered, and fire bloomed across the cobbles of the piazza. Back through the portico, he pushed between surging bodies. A fist struck his shoulder; he staggered and fell, then a cudgel smacked the wall above him. Covering his head, animal terror buckling him, Emilio rolled into a crouch. Hands gripped him and dragged him clear, then he was on his feet again, running.

"I saw you! I saw you throw that bomb! It was fantastic!" His rescuer looked familiar, but in his stunned fear Emilio could not place him. "You're Calvi, right? From the Brera?"

"No, no. You must be mistaken …" But he recognised the face now, knew the voice. They ran together through the blur of streets, and Emilio was no longer afraid, no longer panicked but exhilarated. He still felt the rush of excitement – the petrol bomb in his fist, the heat of the flames.

Emilio knew all about Arturo Gallo. Since the first year at the Brera, he had heard the stories about him – the catalogue of his renown. How, at the age of thirteen, he was expelled from the School of the Barnabite Fathers for pissing in the font. How he was arrested for brawling in the Galleria, for throwing a woman's shoe through the window of a cake shop on Via Montenapoleone, for attempting to set fire to a police kiosk on Via Paolo da Cannobio, for brandishing a loaded revolver in the Café Jamaica.

For a long time Emilio had not cared for Arturo Gallo at all. He saw arrogant pride in him, and an affected cynicism that only masked a need for acclaim. Emilio himself was a far better draughtsman, but felt no need for admirers. He had no boastworthy achievements of his own, no glories. Both his parents had died of influenza in the great epidemic of 1919, leaving him orphaned in the suburban house of a Milanese uncle. The sound of Gallo's voice, that dry, clever twanging from across the painting studio, irritated him. But on the night of the riot, Arturo seemed a different man altogether. Or perhaps he himself had changed, and could appreciate what before had been invisible to him.

Past midnight, they sat on the wall beside the canal sharing a flask of grappa and watching the soldiers move into the city. Armoured cars prowled the piazzas, their megaphones crying out to the abandoned streets. "Citizens of Milan! Do not compel the troops to discharge their most painful duty to the Fatherland!"

Back in Arturo's attic room, sleepless and exhausted amongst the unwashed plates and the curling tubes of paint, they covered the floor with books and magazines splayed open at the full-page reproductions: Boccioni's *Riot in the Galleria*, Balla's *Noise Speed Motorcycle*, Bruno Moresco's *Explosion in a City Street*. Arturo found a pamphlet of Marinetti's old Futurist manifestos and they passed it between them, declaiming the alarming phrases: "*Kill solemnity everywhere! ... Spit on the altar of art! ... Break down the mysterious doors of the Impossible!* They were laughing like men drunk on oxygen.

From that day, they were partners. Emilio's painting changed: no more still-lifes or landscapes, no more carefully plotted nudes. Instead he was out in the streets with Arturo, watching the crowds and the demonstrations, the syncopated rhythms of urban existence, wanting to saturate his painting with the same noise, velocity and sensation. For three years, he realised, he had been choking on the ash of the past; he had been all but mummified by loss and death. But now here, all around him, was colour, light, action. He tried to change his personality as well, become more dynamic, more abrupt, more rude and abrasive; more Futurist. Life, Arturo declared, should be lived as if at the wheel of a speeding car. Emilio rode a bicycle and hated cars, but still he found the concept exhilarating.

Emilio was aware that there were problems with Futurism. The exuberant pre-war spirit even now seemed faintly antique. Then there was Signor Marinetti himself, figurehead of the movement; everyone knew that he'd been one of the first and most active Fascists, even if recently his outlandish enthusiasms had proved too much for the Party. Emilio's uncle was a staunch socialist, and he tried to conceal his new allegiance at first. But his uncle had merely laughed when he discovered it. Marinetti, he said, was a joke.

"A rich bohemian dilettante! *War's the sole hygiene of humanity*? Is he still coming out with ludicrous stuff like that? Surely this country's had enough of idiots like him, after all we've been through ..." Emilio shrugged, uncomfortable, and said nothing. Great artists would always be mocked and misunderstood.

One painting above all others defined his mood. Arturo had a small monochrome reproduction of it: Boccioni's triptych, *States of Mind*. They admired it together, trying to conjure the colours of the original from the murky greys of the reproduction. The first panel, *The Farewells*, was a scene in a railway station, smoke churning around figures distorted with the anxiety of departure. Next, *Those Who Go* showed the travellers in speeding motion, the future opening before them in a rush of oblique lines. In the last panel, *Those Who Stay*, bent figures retreated into the vertical rain of passive obscurity. *Those Who Stay*, of course, were Cattaneo and the other students at the Brera; Arturo and Emilio, naturally, were *Those Who Go*. It was a manifesto in paint, a brilliant, uncompromising statement of belief.

But where were they going, in reality, after their studies ended? For Arturo the question was less rhetorical; for him there were the two years' compulsory *Servizio Militare* that he had been deferring during his time as a student. Emilio, exempted by asthma, was spared that. For all the evenings spent talking and drinking in Arturo's room, in the garret of a high-shouldered house with a sniper's view over the tram carousel of Piazza Susa, he had never devised any real plans. Yet the future – the real future, rather than the one they imagined in their art – was waiting for them both.

One day soon, Emilio knew, he would feel nostalgic for this life – even for the poverty of it. He would look back on these years at the Academy as a wild and irresponsible childhood. The long night walks through the city with Arturo, the evenings in bars and cafés trying to make their drinks last; the hot chestnut polenta, bought from the street-barrow on Via Brera for one lira a slice in thin paper that left grease printed on the fingers; the sense of being apart from the rest of society, of being an artistic elite, of possessing a spirit refined beyond material cares. All of it would soon be past, fondly remembered, irretrievably lost.

The students in the painting studio had returned to their easels. Flora, the model, emerged from behind her screen and shed her robe once again. But before anybody could begin, a new sound came from the street outside: a muffled rattle of drums, a ragged cheering, a chant.

"What fresh nonsense is this?" Professor Cattaneo said, angling his pipe up at the ceiling. But already the students were getting up again from their stools, dashing across the studio to the alcoves and pulling themselves up to the high windows.

"Is there some reason for this boisterous celebration? And must you hang from the walls like a pack of apes?"

"It's the anniversary, signore," Bruccoli cried. He leapt plumply up onto his stool, and assumed a martial posture, "… of *the glorious founding of Italian Fascism*!" Fists on his hips, he jutted his jaw. There was a clatter of laughter from the other students.

Arturo reached down and seized Emilio by the hand, dragging him up into the alcove. He levered open the window and grabbed the bars of the grille outside. The noise was suddenly very loud, punching into the closed air of the studio: drums beating and the brassy yell of bugles. The parade was passing directly below them, but through the narrow opening they saw only the raised banners jaunting by in a ripple of green, red and white.

"*Blackshirts of the revolution*!" Bruccoli growled from his stool, blowing out his cheeks and knuckling the air. "*Our flags stream beneath the Italian sky! Like a genius sculptor, I shall mould you with the inflexible force of my will*!"

"Shut up, Bruccoli. They'll hear you!"

Emilio stared out into the street, into the heart of the noise and the colour. He knew little about politics. His uncle's socialist faith, respectable as it seemed, was hardly inspiring. All those late-night debates in the dining room between Renato and his gathered comrades, that utopian theorising and intractable wrangling – how could that move him? But fascism was unnerving and hypnotic. In the months since the riot, it had swept all opposition before it, propelling Benito Mussolini to the head of government. Part of Emilio agreed with his uncle – it was disastrous, the country swayed above a terrifying abyss – but he was excited too. He was glad to live in these times. He remembered the sensation of throwing the petrol bomb. That was force. That was inspiration.

Beside him, Arturo was twisting himself higher into the gap of the window. Emilio knew his friend's recklessness, the vivid ferocity of his imagination, and felt a sudden sense of danger: he reached out, ready to seize Arturo and drag him back if he tried anything. But the parade had moved on. Bruccoli clambered down off his stool.

"Come along, gentlemen, back to work," Cattaneo was saying. "The parades pass, but art endures!"

Emilio dropped to the ground, leaving Arturo hanging at the window. "But what if the parade *is* the art?" he said.

"What if," Arturo called from above him, "we *are* the parade?"

Back at his easel, Emilio squeezed a long glistening tongue of paint onto his palette. He loaded his brush, swiped colour onto the canvas. Quickly, before the sensation left him, he began daubing bold strokes onto the canvas – sweeps of green, white and red filling the space above and around the seated figure.

The parade enters the house.

And I am the parade!

3

10th May 1930

The sun was low to the west, just capping the mountaintops. Full and gold on the face of the house, it filled every window with reflected fire. The party gathered on the terrace had grown now, and every few minutes the French doors from the salon emitted more people. Mariagrazia Berardi, in her loud party dress, dashed to greet and to guide, while the waiters rattled the bottles in the ice buckets and the gramophone sent music sighing and crackling between the guests.

Emilio ranged across the paving, skirting the central table with the bottles and the attentive waiters. He was enjoying himself now, several glasses of Asti Spumante lifting his mood. Drifting, he caught quick eddies of laughter and wafts of conversations that seemed to lead one into the next, somehow connected. People introduced themselves, but he forgot their names at once. He knew almost nobody there, but found a kind of luxury in his anonymity.

Idling near the balustrade, he pictured the scene abstracted, as he might portray it in a painting. *Anticipation*, he would call it: the terrace a trapezoid, suspended in a yellow Asti Spumante glow. Diagonals of black suit lapels and white shirt-fronts, and the iridescent dresses of the women, faces repeated in different attitudes, all of it split by jagged shards of multicoloured laughter. And through it all, like a vivid red pulse, Marinetti's name.

With every new arrival, heads turned in quick expectation

– but it was never him. They were waiting for Marinetti to arrive and give form to the coming night. His name was a promise, constantly repeated. Emilio had never met the man, but the name had resonated through these last eight years of his life. The founder of Futurism, the dynamic genius of modern Italy. Marinetti might seem a less alarming figure now than he had once been, but he still had the glamour of legend about him. The prospect of finally meeting him, of being introduced, even talking to him, was daunting. It was like a devout Catholic meeting the Pope. He wondered if he actually wanted to meet Marinetti at all. Perhaps the reality could only be disappointing?

At the far corner of the terrace there was a man standing alone. His face was familiar, even in profile, but it took Emilio several long seconds to recognise him. All the portrait photographs of Bruno Moresco showed the artist with neatly clipped moustache and thick black hair brushed straight back: there was something gypsyish about him; something slightly military as well, like a bandit chief. But the figure at the end of the terrace – and it *was* certainly Moresco – had nothing of that manner. Clean shaven, his face appeared stripped; his hair was still thick, but wilder now. He looked like a hermit, or the grim survivor of some unknown disaster.

Emilio took a step forward. He would go and introduce himself. Since his days at the Brera, Moresco's painting had been one of his keenest inspirations. Back in 1923, he had bought a book of his work, cut the reproduction pictures out of it and pinned them on the wall of his studio. Yet he hesitated to approach; the man's solitude was profound and slightly awesome. He was standing like a sentinel at the furthest edge of the crowd.

"… can't think why he even came," somebody said. Emilio stiffened; the voice came from directly behind him. "… like the ghost at the feast! Actually, I thought he'd died."

"Maybe better if he had," another man said. "He hasn't done any decent work in years." They were speaking quietly, with conspiratorial relish. "And you know, they say he's a …"

The last words were lost in a whisper. Emilio turned, about to confront the two speakers. This is Bruno Moresco, he wanted to say: one of the greatest artists of his generation … and who were they, what had they done, what possible right had they earned, to speak like that of him? But they had already moved away, and when he glanced back, the artist had disappeared from view. Emilio looked around at the others on the terrace. All seemed engrossed in their own conversations; all seemed to be having a splendid time. He suddenly felt foolish, and tried not to let it show.

"But should we really call Signor Marinetti *Your Excellency*?" somebody said. It was Fosca, the woman Nina had been so eager to avoid. "Now that he's a member of the Royal Academy? I mean, it's surely important to know!"

She was talking to a cluster of others. Emilio recognised Martino Rossi, Signora Berardi, and a thin-necked man in glasses whom he vaguely recalled as Assanti, a journalist for one of the Milan papers.

"Oh, I'm certain he wouldn't protest …" Martino Rossi replied.

"And can anyone tell me who the *special guest* is to be? I've heard somebody of great importance is coming … besides Marinetti himself, of course. Could it be …? I really thought it might be *Him*. You know!"

Rossi laughed, and Mariagrazia shook her head stiffly. "No, no!"

"Oh my dear," said Assanti, the journalist, "did you really think that *He* might be here? He's far too busy, I assure you, running the country. Especially now, with the economic troubles …" A quick warning cough from Mariagrazia, and he bit his words.

But even the suggestion caused a slight, chilled hush of reverence. Emilio found himself glancing upwards, as if he might see that masterful face bearing down upon them.

Then, unwilled, the memory came to him. The oily glimmer of a long corridor, smelling of urine and detergent; his dull nausea as he walked under the swinging electric bulbs. A policeman sat by the door of the ward, scanning a newspaper. Inside, the room was closed and reeking, the windows sealed and barred. Emilio dragged a chair to the bedside, shocked into silence, the greeting dying in his mouth. His uncle's face was still bruised, his skull wrapped in greasy, stained bandage.

"*What did they do to you*?" he whispered.

In reply, his uncle's cracked smirk; blood on his broken teeth.

It was the evening of Berardi's gallery opening, and Emilio had been preparing to go out when he received the message from the hospital. He had no idea what had happened. Even then, as he sat at the bedside, he could not determine the facts. Yet his uncle's broken face was the only fact that mattered. Uncle Renato, who had raised him and supported him, had been his only family since the death of his parents.

Renato's lips moved as he tried to speak: "*Special Tribunal.*"

"I can help you … Maybe I can speak to some people …" But his uncle's head shook fiercely.

"But what can I do? Tell me what I should do!"

"Promise," his uncle told him. The anger was still live in him, the grim commitment. "Promise me you won't give in to them. You won't believe their lies."

It was painful to watch him speaking; there was fresh blood at the corners of his shattered mouth. "Of course. Of course I won't."

"No!" Renato's hand leapt from the bed, seizing his own, the grip vicious. "On your knees. Promise me!"

And Emilio had promised, sliding from the chair to

kneel beside the bed like a penitent. *No compromises. No collaboration. No assent.*

"They'll try to tell you," his uncle said, still gripping his hand, "that I gave in and confessed. Confessed my crimes. Maybe they'll tell you I died in my sleep. They come at night, sometimes … But I need to know that you will never believe them, never give in to them. That you will never take what they offer you – that would make you one of them."

When Emilio left the ward, the policeman was gone. It was a Blackshirt militiaman who locked the door after him. All the way back down the corridor, under the swinging bulbs, he felt the fire of the man's eyes on his back. Outside, coming down the steps, a man in a white coat offered him a cigarette, which he refused.

"He should have known," the man said, "carrying on like that. What did he expect, eh?" It was one of the doctors, Emilio realised. The man lit his own cigarette, falling into step beside him. "You can't beat the system! You can't beat the regime! What was he thinking?" He shook his head sadly as he spoke, then glanced at Emilio with an accusatory expression. "And you, you're his nephew. What were you doing? Couldn't you have done something to stop him?"

"Me?" Emilio said.

The doctor struck him lightly on the lapel, raising his eyebrows. "Some people need help, don't they? Their minds are … not right. They fall into bad ways of thinking. Don't you understand that?"

Emilio shuddered quickly, turning away and pacing towards the hospital gate. That tone in the doctor's voice, half sympathy, but the other half contempt. It would be no responsibility of theirs, he implied, if Renato died under their roof. Around the corner, out of sight, Emilio fell against a wall and stood braced for several minutes, breathing deeply, his guts heaving.

Arturo and Nina were gone when he got back to the apartment, still out at the gallery opening. When he saw them again the next day, he lied, told them his uncle had fallen ill, but would recover soon. Was he ashamed of what had happened, or of what he had said? Perhaps it wasn't just shame; perhaps also he didn't want the brutal fact to enter their lives. He had concealed it from them, from everyone.

If Arturo were here now, he might tell him … but Arturo was too preoccupied with his own ambitions. Where was he anyway? He had been so keen that Emilio attend the party with him, to give him support, and now he'd vanished. Nina, though – Emilio would draw her aside, tell her everything. But he remembered her strange, distracted mood earlier. Would she even understand what he was saying?

"Have you seen Signora Della Torre?" he asked Fosca. The woman stared back at him, baffled.

"Giannina? Why no," she replied. "Haven't *you*?" She smiled coldly. "But where is Marinetti?" she said, turning back to the group, "He should really have arrived by now … "

"Excuse me," Emilio said, to nobody, and moved away.

With the memory of his uncle's words fresh in his mind, the guilt of being at this house, amongst these people, was suddenly agonising. Swallowing, dry throated, he drank down the last of his wine. The dregs fizzed sourly, and a passing waiter took the empty glass from his hand and replaced it with a full one. He scanned the gathered guests, searching for Nina, willing her to appear. A breathless agitation gripped him.

Then he saw her. She was walking slowly along the path from the gardens. Leaning on the balustrade, he willed her closer, but she turned and walked away to her left, disappearing inside the house.

A short man dressed in a suit of abrasive tweed and what looked like a hessian tie stepped up beside Emilio. A black pipe jutted from his face, and his hair was stiff and spiky. Emilio recognised Volpi, the young man who had arrived in Rossi's car.

"Who was that stick of celery?" Volpi said out of the side of his mouth. His accent was quite thick, maybe from the Romagna.

"Who? Oh … that was Nina Della Torre."

"Ah, so that's her, is it? The woman who does those funny blurred photographs? I hear she's something of a tart. Attractive, I suppose, even with that big nose. Mind you, I wouldn't give her one myself – I don't go for these fast modern girls."

Volpi had a fleck of lettuce trapped between his front teeth. The sight made Emilio's stomach lurch. He remembered that Volpi made crude aggressive sculptures out of jagged steel, which explained the sour reek of welding flux mixed with the stale pipe smoke in the heavy weave of his suit. His hands looked huge and useful, and there was a compact force about him.

"Actually, you know, the Signora is a very good friend of mine." The statement hung limply in the air.

"Oh, I see," Volpi said, with a wink over his pipe.

Nina moved silently through the house. The shade was a relief after the scrutiny of the sunlight. She had entered by a side door in the new extension, and now she was in the gallery, the paintings dull and silent, their colours quelled.

She paused before Arturo's paintings. One of them was the seaplane picture, which had been half finished on the easel that first time Nina visited his studio. The other, *Aerodynamic Womanhood*, was a camouflaged nude portrait of Nina herself. She felt the heat prickle her skin. The picture was abstracted out of recognition, but the sinuous line against the fractured planes of sky blue sketched her profile. She had never liked the picture, or its crass title, but on some level it was honest, a bold simple statement carried through from start to finish, and she could respect that.

From the gallery she passed through into the main house. Long drapes hung motionless, and tall shutters were folded partway across the windows to block the glare of the low sun. Shadows stretched across the geometric rugs, and the noise of the party spilled in from the terrace. The sound of motors came from the drive: the guests were still arriving.

At first Arturo had demanded nothing from her. He performed for her, but until recently had never expected her to perform in return. Now, he seemed to need Nina more for what he believed she could do for him. Had he always seen her as a useful connection, nothing more? Could he have known, when they first met, of the world she moved in, the people she knew?

But no, he could not, and it hadn't been like that at all. She thought of their first meeting, at the party in Viventi's studio the previous September. She had been dressed in one of her husband's old dinner suits, taken in with pins; Arturo as a pirate from a Sabatini novel. The mutual intrigue was obvious, but at the time she wasn't quite in the mood for it. The studio was large and loud with people, and they had gone together to a little kitchen off the main room. He sat on the table and picked up a guitar, strumming at it discordantly; he was playing "Cubist jazz", he said. She found him funny, slightly alarming, faintly repellent, deeply attractive.

A man wearing a gorilla suit got drunk and hung out of the studio window, roaring at the people in the street below and throwing fruit. Then he threw a bottle, and a gang came storming up the stairs to get him. The door was barricaded, there was angry yelling on the landing, panic and hilarity in the upper room. Nina sat with Arturo in the kitchen.

They passed a bottle between them, but in the end she left without saying goodbye, slipping out in the aftermath of the fight and taking a taxi home by herself. They had told each other little about themselves, barely even exchanged names. She was a photographer, he a painter; neither was more than barely acquainted with their host, who for all they knew might have been the gorilla.

Then, three days later, he appeared in the frame of her lens. Midday at Porta Venezia, and she stood on the traffic island while the trams swung around her. Hunched over the viewfinder, the brim of her hat shading her face, she didn't think he would recognise her. But there he was, moving through the crowd, pausing mid-step to look again, then closing in on her, duck-walking the last few paces until his clowning smirk filled the camera's eye.

"Hello," she'd said, into the box between her palms, through the glass and the mirrorplate. Pressed the shutter button: a portrait.

She was not in love with Arturo. She had guarded herself against that. But she loved what he represented to her: the easy freedom of their life together. He didn't judge her. She was sick of being judged, by her family and her husband's remaining friends. A wayward wife, a bad mother. Arturo would never criticise that side of her life.

When he made his first big sale, selling the painting to Berardi shortly after they met, he went out and bought himself a new tailor-made suit and a pair of two-tone shoes. It had seemed a touching extravagance – appearing in the doorway all spruce and gallant in new fabric and gleaming leather ... When had his certainty and self-confidence begun to slip? Before she met him, she knew, though she had not seen it at first. Already the doubt had gnawed him, the suspicion that art alone was not enough.

She remembered their fight, in the studio in Milan. "You

don't want me to succeed, do you?" he had shouted. "You always want to be superior!"

She had snatched up a palette knife, striking at the painting on the easel, that awful painting, unfinished and unfinishable. The thin blade of the knife bent against canvas so thick with dried paint, layer upon layer of paint, that the tip barely bit.

"What are you doing?" he had shouted, incredulous. "You want to destroy me!"

"I want to save you!" she yelled back.

He slapped her then, but pulled the full force of the blow before his palm struck; she barely registered it. Incandescent in his anger, he slammed his fist into the wall, fracturing the plaster. He kicked out, overturning the bucket of paint-scummed turpentine beside the easel.

"Now look what's happened," he said, as the wash of bitter fluid soaked into the dusty rug. She stood with her hand to her cheek, feeling the scald of his palm printed there.

"I didn't mean it," she found herself saying. "I'm sorry."

But she had meant it. She hated what he was trying to become, and did not want to help him to that end. His hunger for success and acclaim made her despair. She had known that hunger; had seen it often enough in those men who used to hang around her husband. She knew their subtle begging for favours, their charmless desire for reward. Why could Arturo not have stayed as she had found him, with all his honesty and his discontent?

Beyond the salon and the blue drawing room, Nina paused in the passageway as the latest arrivals entered the front hall: two men, one of them a valet or chauffeur. She heard Berardi's voice as he greeted the second man, but didn't catch the name. He stood in the hall while the valet removed his light wool overcoat. She was certain she had seen the man before somewhere: a doleful face, with sagging cheeks already darkened with stubble. He reminded her of a sad dog. A party badge was pinned to his lapel. So this was the *special guest*, she thought.

Berardi led the man through into the salon, and once the hall was empty Nina continued. Twin staircases rose to the upper landing; she climbed, feeling the breeze from the front porch. Across the broad landing, the upstairs corridor was in deep gloom, lined with closed doors, packed with the stored heat of the day. Nina halted, catching herself, her mind blank.

She stood at the head of the stairs, knowing that she had come into the house to get something, but unable to remember exactly what. Her camera, perhaps? Was she going to her room to fetch her camera and take some pictures before the light went? She was not going to her room to take more cocaine. She felt the lack of it keenly, but she no longer needed it – and to take more now would be a very bad idea. She knew that she could ride out the craving. It was no different from the craving for coffee or cigarettes. For sex. It would pass. She remembered the addiction all too well, remembered her condition in the months after she returned from Paris. Craving was too weak a word for what she had felt then; it was a screaming in the blood. In those days she had injected it, needing the sensation of numbed exhilaration it brought. No more of that. She breathed deeply, and let the need subside. Her face felt tight and hot, and at the back of her skull was the suggestion of a headache. Just a few minutes, she told herself, ten or fifteen, to recover equilibrium, to let the last washes of the drug fade and normality reassert itself, then she would go back downstairs.

Nina opened the bathroom door onto shuttered darkness. She pulled the cord, and electric light burst harshly over the white porcelain and the enamel. There was a smell in the room, sharp and acid – bleach perhaps – that stirred her memory. Locking the door behind her, she pulled a chair to the sink and sat. A crank of the tap, a long metal gargle, and cool water spooled down into the basin. She dangled her fingers in it, then dabbed at her brow. Leaning forward, elbows on the sink edge, she pressed her fingers to her temples and tried to focus on the sound of the flowing water.

Beside the sink was a set of shelves in wickerwork. Nina scanned the pots and jars – reducing salts for the bath, skin tonic, peroxide vanishing cream, Venetian Special Astringent, peach tint Poudre D'Illusion – all feminine lotions and potions. This was clearly Mariagrazia's domain.

The smell, she realised, was of developing fluid, the scent she had carried in traces on her fingers for days at a time when she first started her photography, before she began to use rubber gloves and sprung wooden tongs. But it was a smell she liked, and she liked the way it marked her. It was proof that those images, these neatly framed photographs, did not emerge from nothing but were brought forth by a strange alchemy. This was the attraction of photography: it allowed her to be a medium between the world and the image, the art and the reality it captured and distorted. There was something maternal, almost mystical about it. She did not bring this work into the world in an act of brute creation, but rather as a guiding presence, a decoder of meanings already present – in the action of light on form, in the motion of bodies in space, of vapour and the settling haze of distances. The darkroom in her apartment in Milan was a sealed and private place. She would never let Arturo in there.

If she went to Argentina, she would be leaving all of that behind. She would have to leave Arturo as well, of course. The full impact of Amedeo's letter, and all its implications, was upon her now. She had tried to neutralise it, she realised, with the racing drive and the drug. In the months since her husband's disappearance she had lost herself in the possibilities of freedom, with no consideration of what the price might be. And all that time, she knew, she had been tapped and followed, her name inscribed on government forms, in plain brown folders in secret offices, her life picked apart. She felt herself caught in a vast machine whose size she could not begin to imagine.

She felt a sudden surge of hatred for Amedeo. He had kept so much of his life from her – his secret dealings and political manoeuvrings – with the unspoken implication that it was none of her concern. But now he was gone, and she remained, implicated and endangered by what he had done.

Back along the corridor towards the landing, she felt a momentary nostalgia for childhood – the quiet house, its stored heat, and the sense of being out of bounds. The deliciousness of trespass. Each closed door she passed held the promise of discoveries.

Approaching the landing and the head of the stairs, she heard voices rising from the hall below: Mariagrazia, Fosca and another woman, somebody's wife or mistress. They were climbing the stairs towards her. Stepping backwards into the safety of the corridor, Nina reached out and found a door handle behind her. As the women reached the landing, she slipped through the door and closed it silently.

She heard the women coming along the corridor, Fosca and Mariagrazia sounding as if they were both talking over one other. Fosca's voice rose clearly as they passed the door: "… but there is *something* about them … an indifference, perhaps, that I find off-putting. But cynicism is quite the fashion nowadays …"

Her voice faded along the corridor, wreathed in the mumbles of the other two women. There was the click of a door opening, then closing, and the voices cut off.

Turning swiftly on her heel, Nina confronted the room into which she had escaped. Just another bedroom, bigger than her own but with little else to distinguish it. She should leave while the corridor outside was clear. Instead she advanced, quiet across the rug, into the centre of the room.

The bed was big and bland, just like the ones in expensive hotels, and nothing about the room itself or its furnishings looked distinctive – even so, there was a patina of use about things, an aura of home. A male home: nothing in there bore any sign of Mariagrazia's presence. The room must be Berardi's own chamber. The air was scented very slightly with *eau-de-cologne*, cigar smoke, peppermint mouthwash.

Nina made a tour of the room, trailing a finger over the surfaces, laying a brief claim to this space and its calm security. Cigar stubs in a glass ashtray. Half-moon reading-glasses neatly folded on the nightstand. A couple of books on a side table – Spengler's *Decline of the West*, and *Principles of Corporative Economics* – both filmed with dust. Next to the bed, on a straw-bottomed chair, was a slim volume of D'Annunzio's poetry. Nina imagined Berardi in bed, propped on pillows, glasses on the tip of his nose and lips moving silently as he recited the verses to himself.

A door led through to the next room. Nina could make out the voices of the women on the other side. Connecting bedrooms.

She tensed as the voices got louder, approaching the door. They could walk through at any moment, but somehow Nina knew they would not. This room, with its masculine air, was a sanctuary that Mariagrazia would not feel free to invade.

Fosca's voice through the door: "Another Jew, of course, a big financier. And she *claims* he just disappeared, didn't even let her know where he'd gone! Left a tidy allowance for her and the child, naturally. Well, with the way she'd been behaving, nobody was surprised. And now she calls herself a photographer ..."

Nina took a step back. The voice had gone again, Fosca moving back into the depths of the room. For a moment she had the urge to fling the door open and confront them … but the thought died.

"*Puttane*!" she said, stifling the word in her throat. A seething energy ran through her. She wanted an object to unleash it on, but the room lacked obvious candidates. She snatched the pillow from the bed and hurled it towards the door, tensing almost instantly, dreading the thud it would make against the wood panel. But the missile fell short, dropping without a sound onto the rug. Nina took a step forward to retrieve it, then froze dead.

A gun lay on the bare mattress where the pillow had been. Nina sat on the bed, all thoughts of Fosca gone. The gun was a slim black automatic, scarcely larger than the palm of her hand. She picked it up, read the words stamped along the barrel: PISTOLA AUT – BERETTA-6.35. BREV.1919.

It was the sort of gun a woman would carry in her handbag. She could take it, right now, and nobody would know. Holding the pistol in a two-hand grip, she aimed it towards the connecting door.

The only gun she had ever fired was a heavy English revolver belonging to her old lover, Bianchi. Once in the woods near the airfield he tried to teach her to shoot. Standing behind her, he had enclosed her with his arms, his hands wrapping hers as she held the revolver, pointing at a tree twenty paces away. It was a cold day in early autumn. The gun went off like a cannon, kicking up into her shoulder and startling the birds screaming in all directions.

"Don't jerk at the trigger like that," Bianchi had said, his voice in her ear, his moustache prickling her cheek. "Squeeze it back into your palm, and slacken your right elbow to absorb the recoil …" Dazed, she watched the hammer rise and heard the cylinder click round, then the explosion again.

A yellow gash opened in the tree's black bark; Nina leaned back into Bianchi as he hugged her to his chest.

This little Beretta automatic was nothing like Bianchi's Webley, but it still held a lethal potential. Nina sighted down the barrel, imagining the jolt and the muzzle flash. But the figure that appeared before her, the victim her imagination conjured, was not Fosca. It was her husband's features that she saw transfixed by the pistol sight, his clever smile erased by fear. She felt the sweat prickle at the nape of her neck.

Unnerved, she quickly put the pistol down and placed the pillow back over it.

Leaving the room, she waited in the corridor before the landing, listening to the other women going back down the stairs. Fosca's sly mocking laughter rose up to her as they passed through the entrance hall below.

Nina walked quietly to the banisters and looked down. The women had gone, but she wanted to compose herself before following them. The landing was broad, and filled with a warm glow from the diamond-paned skylight high overhead. The wall opposite the stairs was in shade, the electric lamps still unlit in their sconces. A display of photographic prints hung along the wall, each framed behind glass.

She paced slowly across the landing, looking at the pictures, leaning closer as the images formed out of the dimness. First there was a portrait of Berardi and Mariagrazia standing together, rather stiffly, between parted draperies. Next a picture of Berardi and several other well-dressed men – business associates, Nina supposed – holding cigars. There was a photograph of Berardi sitting with Marinetti on a wall beside some railings, both men in summer suits and straw boaters, Marinetti looking uncomfortable and slightly bloated in the face, as if his collar was too tight. Then there was a picture of Berardi standing with the Prime Minister, Benito Mussolini – the Duce.

The next group of prints followed a theme. There was a picture of Mussolini in tight vest, jodhpurs and shiny leather boots, mounted on a stallion. Mussolini, bare-chested like a circus strongman, straddling a tractor, fists on hips, before a mass of cheering farm labourers. Mussolini hedged with flags and glittering bayonets, pinning a medal on a child in military uniform. The Duce as Great Sportsman, as Man of the People, as Military Leader.

Here he was in tailcoat and starched white collar, white spats, silk hat, frowning gravely from a gathering of elderly dignitaries. Here again, in a business suit, posed on the vehicle ramp of the Fiat factory in Turin, surrounded by workers and industrialists, chin clasped in his fist as he gazed knowledgeably upwards: Mussolini the Great Statesman, the Man of Industry, the Man of Destiny, the Saviour of Italy.

Nina passed along the line, eyeing each image briefly. She had seen them many times before, in newspapers. magazines, posters, newsreels … the central protagonist of the national drama. Once she had seen the man himself, in the flesh – she was in Rome, and he was making a speech from the balcony of the Palazzo Chigi. She had been watching from an apartment on the far side of the piazza, over the moving masses of the crowd. The figure in the distance had seemed comical, his big, bald head jerking and jutting, his hands gesticulating wildly. She could no longer remember what he was speaking about – some domestic battle won, for grain perhaps, or the lira. His words carried to her in snatches, his voice a high-pitched squawk: necessary sacrifice, unending struggle, blood, Italy, unity …

When he was finished, when he stood posed there on his balcony and the crowd below erupted into a roar of approval, Nina found herself applauding with them. It had bemused her at the time, the commandeering of her body and her emotions by the energy of the masses below her. She felt the electricity of history, of destiny; all the grand abstractions suddenly as invigorating as raw oxygen. So she had cheered, and saluted, and cried out his name, her voice one amongst thousands.

Arturo's unfinished painting, the scarred and battered canvas that she had failed to destroy with a palette knife, was a portrait of the Duce. That bald skull and jutting jaw, hacked out of congealing paint. He wanted to call the painting *The Genius of the Leader*, he said. He wanted to enter it for the Fascist Party gold medal in the Venice Biennale competitions. Was it the subject itself that had offended Nina so much? The banality of it, perhaps, and what that banality represented: an artificial synthesis of flags and salutes and bold empty gestures. Whatever had moved her that day in Piazza Chigi, whatever emotion had gripped her and propelled her into applause, she knew that Arturo had never felt anything of the sort. Nina had felt the power of the totalitarian state, and it was a terrible thing, inhuman and irresistible. To try and engage with that was to be consumed by it. Real art, she knew, could never truly celebrate power; it should only oppose.

The final photograph showed Mussolini standing with a group of men, gathered informally under a tree in the countryside somewhere. The men wore caps and coats; there were dogs at their feet. Perhaps a shooting party. The Duce was turning away to one side, seeming distracted. Berardi was to his right, hands in pockets, and to his left two figures stood apart in the shade of the tree. Nina moved closer, squinting into the grain of the photograph, but knew she was not mistaken. The first of the two men wore a light overcoat, his face closed. It was the same face she had seen in the hall downstairs. The second man, smiling confidently beneath his rakish trilby, was Amedeo Sorani. Her husband.

10th January 1925

The apartment held a noisy, sociable heat, pressed up against the sealed windows and the plush patterned walls. Outside, fog loomed hugely over the skeletal chestnut trees in the Public Gardens, and all along Corso Venezia cars with spectral headlights brought the partygoers from the theatre. Guests arrived in twos and threes, the men in evening dress, the women feathered and furred. The lobby was hung with coats, and in the drawing room the cigar smoke reeled into arabesques above the nested armchairs.

Nina, perched at the head of a chaise-longue, was in conversation with an Englishman in an eyepatch. Through a haze of boredom, she listened politely and nodded appropriately.

"Essentially," the Englishman said, his accent mangling the words, "I still consider myself a Freudian, although one must admit that the ideas of Jung have a certain appeal, shall we say, a certain dramatic magnetism ..."

"Mmmm," said Nina. The Englishman's patch jogged and twitched as he talked, and Nina's eyes skated across him and away down the length of the interconnecting rooms. A sequence of open double doorways, one inside another, framed at their deepest recess her husband, Amedeo. He stood with a knot of other young men, his hair gleaming. Then the intervening crowd shifted, and he was gone.

"I personally," the Englishman was saying, "would be inclined to think in a Jungian way about the state of my own country, whereas in your own ..."

Nina smiled and wondered whether her feathered

headband went with the beaded black chiffon after all. A bit much, perhaps. She had never been quite convinced by the fashion for plumes anyway – you didn't see men wearing feathers on their heads. Then again, perhaps it might be better if they did?

"How fascinating," she said, cutting into the weave of words, "but you must please excuse me, I think my husband is calling."

"Your husband?" said the Englishman, stepping back smartly. "Ah, but of course, forgive me for detaining you!"

"*Charmed*," she said, in English – a long syllable and a final chop – then made her escape. That was easy, she thought, slipping through a door into the next room, and wished she had done it sooner. Flutes of white wine were arrayed on a sideboard; Nina drained one quickly and took another, feeling the chill inside her.

In the far corner, two women in long gowns and feathers examined each other. "It's by Maison Paquin, my dear," one said. "Direct from Paris, and the very latest. I also saw the new collection by Lanvin, but it seemed to me not as good. The quality of the fabric …"

Beside the open doors, the violins outlined a melody from tonight's performance: Boito's *Mefistofele*. Nina made her way across the room, through the slow stir of thickened air. Amedeo's voice carried to her; his polished laugh.

Earlier, she had been sitting with him in their box at the theatre, too distracted to concentrate on the music, staring instead into the threadbare upholstery. Every now and again he had lightly touched her hand, as if these token gestures of intimacy were enough to sustain their roles. After the performance, a car was waiting take them together across town to the party, but she knew he would have preferred to go alone. Her husband's worldliness felt stifling sometimes.

But why should she complain? She was a married woman

and a mother whose needs were provided for. A woman whose husband was young, handsome, rich and well connected, both socially and politically. Whose husband might suggest driving to Monte Carlo for the weekend, or taking the train to Paris, or going skiing at St Moritz. All of it easy, all of it free.

"... Stravinsky, of course," somebody said. "Stravinsky cannot be discounted, although, naturally, as a Russian he has a certain sensibility ..."

"... so you know Fosca di Marzio already, then? Oh, but you should meet her! Very good friends with Signora Sarfatti, you know. Who is *very good friends* with the prime minister, if you know what I mean, so ..."

Since childhood she had been raised to expect this. Home, marriage, children, family. And it had all happened so easily. That day, soon after her seventeenth birthday, when she had entered her father's drawing room to find the young man, this visitor from Milan, rising artfully bashful from his seat – she had known then, at first sight. It had all been arranged so smoothly. The ceremony at the synagogue, the handsome man leading her beneath the canopy; the spilt wine and the shattered glass. Then she was a married woman, eighteen years old, nothing to fear in the world. At the time she had felt an all-encompassing bliss so beautiful she could scarcely believe it real.

The world belonged to him, it seemed. He had presented it to her on a silver tray, with a modest shrug, almost as if he had created it himself. Everywhere doors opened before him, before his easy smile and unhurried gesture. Only the nights were wrong – the sex awkward and abrupt, his body rigid as she lay against him and he turned his face away from her. She had become pregnant within six months of the wedding, and tried not to notice the relief blazing through his joy.

"This is all I keep hearing," a man's voice said, "– *totalitarian* this and that … what does it mean? We're living in a world of rampaging neologisms!"

"… there wasn't room, but I got a lift with Severino. He's got a new car, a Lancia, very plush, but as we got in I'm afraid Violetta was a little sick on the back seat …"

Nina thought of her son, Marco. Nearly two years old now, he was at home in the nursery of the apartment on Via Monforte. A healthy boy, a blessing to their families. Amedeo loved him, and Nina loved him too, she supposed – loved the feel of him, the clutch of his tiny hand closing around her finger. Yet when she was not with him, she doubted that love. Sometimes she even doubted the reality of her child. After the birth, she began to see an evasiveness in her husband's eyes, a look of apology, as if to say, this is all I can do for you, and you cannot ask for more. *I'm very fond of you*, he had told her once, *I'm very fond of you and I care for you deeply*. From those words, the unreality of their marriage had rushed outwards, claiming everything.

She was not even sure quite what her husband did. He was a financier, a money dealer – like her father. There were meetings in Paris and Rome, lengthy absences, oblique suggestions. He had connections in politics, with the new government – the *regime*, as they were beginning to call it. "Important to be on the inside," he would tell her smoothly. "*We're* on the inside. All the best people are – your father and I and many others." Would her brother have been there too, if he had survived? "A tragedy that he never lived to see these days," Amedeo had said. "He would have been proud of this country, of what we're doing. It's for him, and all the others who died. They would have supported us in the Party. There's no doubt of that."

She thought of her brother, lying in a stony trench on a mountainside above the Isonzo river, huddled beside his men in the grey dawn after the gas had rolled over them.

One of the million dead, the sacrifice. Would he have given his assent to this new Italy her husband and his friends were helping to build?

"... no, they've done nothing worthwhile since the war, for all their noise. Bruno Moresco still produces some good work, but the younger ones are very poor imitators, for the most part. There are far more interesting artistic movements in this country, and they don't make such inflated claims either ..."

"... and when she finally arrived, she was wearing this appalling thing that looked like a sack. She claimed it was by Soeurs Callot, but you should have seen their faces ..."

"*Hello? Hello, can you hear me?*"

The words came from behind a partly open door. In the stilled and gloomy room beyond the voice spoke again. *Are you there? Can you hear me?* Nina pushed the door wider and peered through.

"Oh, I'm sorry," she said automatically, the words catching in her throat, seeing the group huddled around the table, the glass upended between them. Closing the door, she walked quickly away, draining the last of her wine.

"Nina, there you are!" A hand on her arm, jogging her out of the trance.

"Amalia! I didn't know you were here," Nina said. "I just interrupted a séance, I think."

"Really?" her friend said. She was slightly older, well-dressed, with heavy pearls at her throat and a blue-tipped cigarette in a slim holder. "I don't understand why people should go to such trouble to contact the dead. Most of them can't even bear to speak to their own parents." She drew Nina over to a corner beside a fireplace, handing her a fresh drink.

"I see your husband is in his element," she said, with a sideways glance.

"Is he? We separated as soon as we arrived. I've hardly spoken to him all night."

"You know what I mean," Amalia said. "His new friend's rather interesting – have you met him yet?" Nina shook her head, peering into the further room; she had a brief glimpse of a face, sallow and sullen-looking. "He's with one of the Ministries," Amalia whispered. "His name's Scoglia, Scaglia … something like that. One to watch, they say." Nina saw her husband through the noise and the space of rooms and smoke and people. She saw the other men, with their gleaming hair.

Amalia leaned closer, the powder that she wore to hide her freckles showing matt and grainy in the firelight. "Well, we really shouldn't let Amadeo monopolise the interesting people, should we? I mean, if he won't introduce us himself …"

Nina sipped from her glass, tasted the burn of whisky. "Oh, I'm sure it's better to leave them alone," she said quickly. "They're probably discussing something quite atrociously dull …"

But Amalia was already moving, drawing Nina along beside her as she passed through the connecting door and into the next room. Together they advanced towards the men in the far corner. As she approached, Nina tried to catch the thread of what they were saying, but heard only a blur of masculine voices through the cigar smoke. Her feet locked suddenly. Another gust of laughter, and Amedeo glanced across the room and caught sight of her; just for a second, before he composed his expression, she caught the look of disapproval on his face.

"Hello there!" she said, unnaturally loudly, pretending she'd seen nothing. "Look who I've found! It's Amalia Giuliani …"

The two men stepped apart slightly to allow them in, while Amedeo made the introductions. His friend, Signor Scaglia, bowed solemnly to Amalia, then took Nina's raised hand and held it lightly to his lips. It was a mechanical gesture, almost impolite in its formality. Nina disliked him at once.

"What were you men talking about?" Amalia said, a hand on Amedeo's sleeve. "It sounded so fascinating."

"Oh, nothing," he replied. "Nothing, really …" Nina gazed into the fireplace. She was smiling so intently her face hurt.

"Oh, but perhaps you can't tell us," Amalia said, addressing Scaglia now. "Perhaps you were discussing *affairs of state*?" She drawled the words, making them sound ridiculous. The man coughed lightly, shaking his head.

"Signor Sorani, perhaps I should leave you to these ladies," Scaglia said. He gave a curt farewell nod to Nina and Amalia, but Amedeo clasped his shoulder.

"Federico, please," he said. "My wife and her friend only wanted to say hello, that's all …" He turned to Nina, and gave her a smile of dazzling insincerity. "I won't be back until very late tonight, my dear," he said, leaning to kiss her lightly on the cheek. "Do look in on Marco before you go to bed, won't you?"

"May we presume, then," Amalia said as they moved away across the room, "that he won't be returning to your house tonight?" Her voice was rich with sympathy.

"I suppose not."

"If you want," she said, "we could go somewhere together. I have cocaine, if you need it. A cabaret, perhaps. *He'll* be doing the same, won't he, with his 'friends' …"

"Thanks, but I shouldn't. I need to go home and see to Marco."

"Oh, the mother's role. You'll feel different after your third, believe me. You shouldn't be so conscientious – you've done your duty, haven't you?"

"Even so," Nina said, trying to keep her tone light. She drank back the remains of the whisky cocktail, then took another glass of chilled wine.

They moved through the rooms together, the party

flowing around them. Nina felt her surroundings becoming unstable. The walls seemed to retreat before her, the ceilings and carpeted floors to warp towards a vanishing point. She had the urge to reach out and clasp at surfaces – the heavy texture of the wallpaper, the marble lintel of the fireplace, the polished wood of the doorframe – to touch something real and of substance. Somebody screamed and then fell over, spilling wine on the Persian rug. The Englishman with the eyepatch loomed briefly. A man beside the fireplace started to declaim poetry; three more jumped up and smothered him with cushions. "Whose party is this anyway?" somebody else was calling out. "Does anybody know who owns this place, or what?"

"I'm drunk," Nina said, but nobody seemed to be listening.

Amalia introduced her to a bearded man in a velvet jacket, who remained seated as he limply shook her hand.

"Count Vladimir is a genuine Count," Amalia was saying. "Although dispossessed, of course."

"Oh, poor Count," Nina said, and lightly patted the man's head. "Poor, poor Count!"

Some time later, when the noise of the party had blurred into a rushing underwater sound in her ears, Amalia backed her into a corner and kissed her on the mouth for what seemed like a very long time.

From the balcony, Corso Venezia was a fathomless gulf strung with floating globes. Nina shivered, and pulled the borrowed coat tight around her shoulders. It was a man's overcoat of thick, black wool; she had found it draped over the back of an armchair beside the balcony doors. Already the moisture in the air was forming a tracery of water-drops on the shoulders and lapels, catching the light from inside the building, glittering like strings of tiny pearls.

Amalia had gone without saying a word. Amedeo had no doubt gone too, with his friends. Inside, the party was ebbing away, blurred spaces appearing between people, charged with smoke.

Beneath her nodding feathers, Nina stared out into the wet night. *Nothing more is expected of me. Everything is provided for me. I have done my duty.*

She reached into the pocket of her borrowed coat and brought out a slim silver case. Inside were four Manoli Filters and a book of matches beneath the clip. She took a cigarette, smelled sweet sulphur in the flare of the match. The smoke filled her, calmed her. She flicked the spent match away and it fell, spinning. Voices echoed up from the invisible street below. From somewhere indoors, Nina heard the booming voice of the Englishman.

"You don't understand!" he was saying. "With your *Fascismo*, Italy has accomplished the final fusion of life with art. Stale representational democracy has been banished, replaced with the pure abstract force of the dictatorship. Your *Duce* is the final triumph of the id over the superego, the victory of the unconscious, the total liberation of human desire!"

"Signor Barnaby," another man broke in, "perhaps I might call you a taxi? It's very late …"

The voices fell silent. A motor-lorry droned past, its great headlamps heaving aside the dark for a few moments before the night closed in again.

Nina smoked, the touch of the cigarette against her lips reminding her of Amalia's kiss. What a strange world this was. Her son was at home, watched by nursemaids, but she had no desire to go to him. Her husband was in a club somewhere, and would not come home tonight. Perhaps this time he would not come home at all. Men have their needs. She was not one of his. I am a married woman, Nina thought, whose husband gives her everything. Whose husband needs nothing she can give.

She exhaled smoke and the night swallowed it. The cold pinched her face, creeping in through the clenched lapels of her coat to claim her body and its heat. She would have liked to melt into the air, to lift high above the city where no words had purchase upon her. She felt that she could almost relax now, not make a conscious choice but just lay herself out on the night's tide and let it carry her, beyond pain or caring. She would feel no sensation of falling, no fear of the impact below, only a blissful dissolution. She let her body tilt against the balcony rail. Below her, the fog streamed past like a river.

The tram was sudden, plummeting down the street on its hanging wires, fast and almost silent. Nina, off balance, snatched at the rail and gripped tight as the machine passed beneath her; there was a crack of noise, an arc of light, electric sparks showering through the mist.

She stood on the balcony, hugging herself deeper into the borrowed coat, shuddering and fearful. For a moment shock pricked her skin, then exhaustion rose through her. It was past time to go home.

4

10th May 1930

Deep within the house a telephone bell was ringing, the metallic bleat bringing the maids hurrying down the stairs and along the hallways. In the salon, the long white drapes were pulled to cut the sun's burnished glare. A table was set with dishes of canapés as the guests started to filter in from the terrace.

"They look safe enough," said Martino Rossi, prodding at the pastries. "But one never knows with Marinetti. They may explode!"

Emilio took a selection of the canapés, trying to recapture the thread of his argument. He had been speaking to Rossi, but there was a crush around the table and he had been distracted. "But as I was saying," he began again, enthusiastically, "surely it isn't possible to judge a work of art by the same criteria that one would judge a person, or a country, or a political system. Notions of good and bad don't apply in the same way …"

He glanced up from his napkin, but instead of finding Rossi beside him, Emilio discovered that he had addressed himself to Bruno Moresco. Moresco gazed at him, his face waxy and corded, and then raised an eyebrow. The rest of the crowd around the table had fallen away and Emilio was alone with him now.

"I mean," he said, "the aesthetic value, the true worth of a painting, should stand above …" His mind reeled, trying to connect what he was saying with some train of thought that might make sense, but it was no good. He couldn't think of a single impressive or even sensible thing to say. Moresco stared at him in vague fascination. As if I were an insect, Emilio thought.

"Don't you think?" he concluded weakly.

Moresco's face split, the muscles contracting to show his teeth. Laughing at me, Emilio thought. He's laughing at me.

"Excuse me," Moresco said, then walked away into the brilliance of the terrace.

Emilio was unable to move. That laugh, that mocking smile, had felt almost like a physical assault. Others must have seen and heard the exchange. A touch on his arm, Martino Rossi's quiet voice released him.

"Please forgive him," he said. "Bruno hasn't been well recently. He's … He doesn't mean to be offensive."

"No, no, really I wasn't offended at all," Emilio replied. Hunching, the insult still burning through him, he concentrated on eating the pastries. Rossi was leaving him too now. He scanned the room, but there was no sign of Arturo or Nina.

The salon had filled, most of the guests circling the central table. Emilio navigated the complexities of the room, steering through the reefs of potential embarrassment and intrigue. He had almost reached the refuge of the furthest corner, when suddenly Volpi blocked his path.

"I need to talk to you about something," Volpi said. He was smiling, clearly trying to appear agreeable, but his expression was strained. "You know about the performance later, don't you?"

"What?" Emilio said, pastry crumbs on his lips. "Oh, no, I don't know anything. It's Marinetti's performance, I think. I mean, he's the one arranging everything …"

"Yes, of course," Volpi said with obvious impatience. A

nervy annoyance animated his body, and he looked like he wanted to break something. "I've written a piece that I want to perform," he hissed. "I want to read it, I mean. It's a poem. I want to *declaim* it."

Volpi reached into his jacket, bringing out a folded sheet of paper.

"I can't show it to anyone yet," he said in a harsh whisper. "It's Ultra-Futurist. I call it 'A Hymn to Violence, the Iron Necessity of the Human Will'."

"Oh!" said Emilio, glancing rapidly across the room and back, a canapé half eaten in his hand. Volpi rustled the paper.

"I want to declaim it tonight, to Marinetti and the others. I think it … that it's … I believe it's worthy of the attention. You *know* what I mean."

Volpi was glaring at him, a sick acidic hunger in his expression.

"Well," Emilio said. A lump of spiced salami was perched on his back molar, and he swallowed heavily. "Perhaps you should speak to somebody else about it? Lino Osvaldi, for instance – he's part of the performance …"

"Osvaldi? That dandy? What can he do?" Volpi glared at Emilio. "You know Marinetti, don't you? You're on intimate terms?"

"No, not at all," Emilio said, surprised. "I've never even met him."

"Never met him? But you're Gallo, right? Arturo Gallo?"

"No," Emilio said. "I'm Calvi, Emilio Calvi."

Emilio noticed Nina entering the room from the hall. A waiter handed her another glass of Spumante. She raised the glass briefly to Emilio before disposing of it on a side table.

"I really think you should speak to Marinetti about it yourself," Emilio managed to say. "When he arrives … if he arrives."

"Yes, I'll do that," Volpi said heavily. "I'll certainly do that."

A slight nod, and Emilio freed himself from Volpi's glowering presence. He closed with Nina in three long strides.

"Where have you been?" he said quickly, trying to keep the accusation from his voice.

"I was only upstairs arranging my things. Have you seen Arturo? I need to speak to him. I was a bit short with him earlier and I think he may have taken it badly." She appeared brittle and uneasy.

"I haven't seen him either," Emilio began, but Nina's attention was distracted. He felt her tense, saw her throat tighten.

"What's that man doing here?" she asked.

Over by the fireplace, Berardi stood talking to a sallow-faced man in a pin-striped suit. A party badge glinted from the man's lapel.

"He's the *special guest*, apparently," Emilio told her. "Only it's very disappointing, because nobody actually knows who he is."

"I think I know him," Nina said. A quick shiver ran through her.

"Why, Giannina, there you are!" called Mariagrazia, advancing on them in her clashing party frock. Fosca and a blonde, distracted-looking girl followed in her wake. "We've been searching for you everywhere."

"Oh, but I was looking for Signor Calvi, that's all. And now I've found him!" Emilio felt her hand tighten on his arm. The blonde girl following Mariagrazia was younger even than Nina. She had short hair slicked down flat and a blank masklike face. Beautiful in a vacant sort of way, Emilio thought. Her eyes seemed focused on something invisible to others.

"We were just admiring these works of Fosca's," Mariagrazia said, gesturing towards a collection of ceramics displayed on the sideboard. "As you can see, I keep them in a prominent position!"

"You're too kind, really," said Fosca. The pots gleamed in green and grey. Some were lumpy hemispheres, others warped ovoids, shallow and vaguely vaginal. Together they regarded the pots.

"You know, Fosca," Nina said, "you should get one of those … what are they called? *Wheels* … you should get a *potter's wheel.* Then your pots wouldn't go so wobbly."

"Oh, hah hah," Fosca replied. "Humour!" Emilio coughed behind his hand.

"They're artistic ceramics, dear," said Mariagrazia with a light frown. "One isn't supposed to eat off them."

"This one," said Fosca, as she stroked one of the dishes with a fingertip, "is called *Cosmic Motherhood.* It's an expression of the sacred maternal instinct. But I expect you know all about that don't you, Nina!"

"Naturally," Nina said.

"Or do you, I wonder? Come to think of it, I don't suppose you can feel so very maternal, when you're sending your little boy away to another country at such a young age! If I had a child I don't think I could bear to be parted from him."

It took Emilio a moment to realise quite what Fosca had said. Nina's mouth opened as if she was about to speak. Fosca herself smiled sweetly.

A maid in a black and white uniform bobbed at Mariagrazia's side. "Excuse me, Signora," she said. "A telephone message came for you a few minutes ago." She passed her mistress a folded slip of paper. Mariagrazia glanced at it then walked towards the hall with the maid trailing after her. Emilio turned to Nina, only to see her stalking away across the room. The blonde girl continued to say nothing, staring fixedly at a point in space.

"Oh dear," Fosca said, "I do hope I haven't offended poor Nina. She does seem so … *highly strung* these days."

Emilio could find no reply. He should be angry; he should

say something. But what did he know of Nina's private life? What did he know about any of them? Fosca circled a fingertip on the rim of her ceramic dish.

"Signor Calvi, I'm sure you would agree that the qualities prized in a man might not be thought as desirable in a woman?"

"I've never really thought about it," Emilio said. He leaned back against the sideboard and scanned the room. Volpi was prowling nearby.

"I mean that caustic sort of wit that your friend Nina loves so much," Fosca went on, drawing closer. "It may seem all very clever and so on, but as one gets older it can appear a little crude. I say that as her friend, you know."

"Of course," Emilio said, in what he hoped was an abrupt tone. Across the room, he saw Arturo entering from the terrace. Nina walked straight up to him and took him by the arm, steering him from the crowd.

"But I know you men can find that sort of thing off-putting," Fosca said, almost whispering in Emilio's ear now. "We women have a certain mystique, don't you agree, that we should guard carefully?"

"Hmmm,' Emilio said flatly. Fosca was whispering something about nurturing and intuition. "You men," she kept saying. "We women ..." On the far side of the room he saw Arturo and Nina together in front of a window, lined in white light against the long drape.

On the mantelpiece above the fireplace, a spray of lilies was doubled by a huge plate mirror. Maurizio Berardi gazed through the flowers into the reflected room beyond, anxious for any outbreaks of chaos or absurdity. The party was beginning to take on form, but still it lacked its centre.

"Is His Excellency often this late?" the man beside him said. "I mean, I've come considerably out of my way to be here this evening, I've made a considerable effort, and if Marinetti isn't going to turn up …"

"Oh, he will," Berardi said. "He will very soon."

He resisted the impulse to check his watch. In reality, Marinetti's delayed appearance was proving very difficult. Without His Excellency as the focus for what was supposed to be happening, Berardi felt the weight of expectation settling upon him. Irritation mounted from his gut. His clothes were too tight, and he was beginning to break a sweat.

The man beside him was casting dull glances around the room, appraising it. Not easy company, this Commendatore Scaglia. At close quarters the man was far from prepossessing: his cheeks were blue with fine stubble, and he had a faint unwashed odour. He might once have been handsome, but the gravity of his position had dragged him downwards. Is that, Berardi wondered, how I appear to others? Do I too have this air of hefty unease? The Commendatore had not smiled once since he arrived at the house. His Party badge, too, added a note of vulgarity. Berardi had wanted to swiftly pluck it from his lapel and slip it into the man's pocket. As if he needed to advertise his loyalties like that! There were many here who had done far more for the Party than Scaglia, and they felt no need to make a show of it. It was regrettable, this desire for display. Like that other political big-shot – what was his name? – who was rumoured to wear his military medals in bed, pinned to his pyjamas! Berardi imagined the Commendatore in his silk sheets, sweltering under a chestful of regalia. But perhaps, in these difficult times, it was important to make public shows of loyalty, even crude ones?

Berardi caught a flash of lemon and turquoise in the mirror: his wife Mariagrazia. Across the room, the architect Conti tipped his head back, mouth open in laughter. For the last two hours Berardi had been covertly monitoring the movements of these two, dreading some humiliating public demonstration of affection. But they were keeping their distance – for now.

Martino Rossi approached, in conversation with Assanti, the journalist. "Talking of Depero, I got a letter from him just last week," Rossi said. "He's in New York, you know. Designing covers for *Vanity Fair*, no less! He says he wants to become a *Futurist couturier*!"

The journalist frowned. "Well, I don't expect he'll be there much longer," he said. "America's finished. Their economy won't recover."

"I wouldn't be so sure ..." Rossi said. "They've recovered from crashes in the past. I don't see this one as being different ..."

"No, he's right," said Commendatore Scaglia, roused from his scrutiny of the room. "America's on the way down. They've been making a big noise since the war, but they'll be coming to us for help, you wait and see." He had their attention now; he seemed to grow in height and bulk now he had an audience. "There's no future for democracy in the twentieth century," he declared. "America, France, England: they'll all be looking to us soon. And as for Germany ..."

"Ah yes, I was in Germany just recently," Assanti broke in. "It's entirely chaotic there!" He waved a hand, as if to invoke the chaos of Germany.

"The world economic crisis," Scaglia went on, his finger raised, "has shown the world that only *our* way can succeed. State control, public works, the rigorous suppression of anti-statist liberties ..."

"Absolutely!" the journalist said with enthusiasm. "Apparently even the United States are planning to introduce a fascistised labour charter ..."

"But surely," Berardi said, "this depression affects us too? As a businessman, as an industrialist, these are hard times for Italy." Berardi wished he had explained to Scaglia that politics was not to be discussed. Next they would be talking about the naval treaties, or the pact with Austria ... The Commendatore fixed him with a steely glare.

"Courage is needed," he said. "Courage, and Italy will lead the way. Defeatist talk can only lead to loss of morale, and anything that lessens national morale is *treason*!"

Berardi felt the tension massing in his body, the trapped irritation now filling his throat with hot bile. He saw Emilio Calvi loitering nearby and grabbed him, steering him into the group beside the fireplace.

"But this is the artist I wanted you meet," he announced to Scaglia.

"Actually I think you've made a mistake," the young man said, looking startled. "I'm not Arturo Gallo. I'm Emilio Calvi."

"Yes, yes, I know that," Berardi said. "Signor Calvi, may I introduce Commendatore Federico Scaglia?"

"Very pleased to meet you," Emilio said warily, shaking hands. The Commendatore gave him a curt bow from the neck. Berardi groaned inside: the young man appeared to have no idea what was going on. Hadn't his friend told him? This whole thing had been planned badly, and now it was all unravelling into farce.

"In fact, if you'll excuse me, Commendatore," he went on, laying a palm lightly on Emilio's shoulder, "I need to speak with Signor Calvi alone for a moment."

"Of course," Scaglia said, unsmiling, as Berardi guided Emilio towards the door. In the mirror, Berardi saw the Commendatore's quizzical parting glance.

They walked out into the hall, Berardi leading the way and Emilio following. The door swung shut behind them, and the noise from the salon cut off. Mariagrazia intercepted them before they reached the stairs, the maid still trailing behind her.

"Maurizio, where are you going?" she called.

"I was taking Signor Calvi upstairs to show him the view from the roof," Berardi told her. "I'll only be a few minutes."

"There was a call from Milan," his wife said as he started up the curving stairway. "From the Hotel Trianon. They say Marinetti left them an hour ago, and should be with us shortly."

"Excellent," Berardi said.

"You won't be gone too long, will you?" Mariagrazia asked. "Your guests might miss you!"

"I'm sure you can keep them all amused for ten minutes."

He took the rest of the stairs at a jog.

"I've never actually met Marinetti before," said Emilio from behind him.

"You surprise me. I understood that he likes to meet all the younger artists. But I suppose these days with him living in Rome it's more difficult. Extraordinary to think he's married and has children!" Berardi wondered what sort of children they might be. He imagined strange little creatures made of tinfoil and electricity.

They reached the landing, and he crossed to the line of photographs displayed on the wall. "There he is. The man himself," he said, gesturing at the picture of himself and Marinetti. "Though that was taken some years ago now."

They passed along the line of pictures, Emilio pausing to look at each one. Berardi studied him, evaluating him. There was a naïve placidity in the young man's eyes. Perhaps he was shy, but Berardi hoped not. He had little use for shyness in his world.

"Mussolini," Emilio said, pointing.

They stood together, shoulder to shoulder, looking at the pictures.

"You know what I admire most about him?" Berardi said. "His ability to compromise. An ability not easily captured in a photograph, but the secret of his power nevertheless."

"Yes, I suppose so ..." Emilio replied.

"I am a businessman before all else, you see," Berardi went on, turning towards the corridor. "In my world, those unwilling to make compromises are either fools or failures. That's the true genius of the man: he can make a deal with anybody, while at the same time giving the impression of unyielding strength."

And it was only an impression; the reality, he knew, was very different. The irritation he had felt listening to Scaglia in the salon rose up in him again. Berardi was far from a defeatist: he could put on as bold a front as anyone. But the last six months had tested him. Already four of his factories were running at a loss due to the cancellation of foreign orders, but he was not permitted to scale back production. Any visible sign that the economic crisis was affecting Italy was forbidden, and so the goods piled up in the warehouses and the cost was passed onto the producer, onto Maurizio Berardi. Soon he would have to announce wage cuts, and then the workers would feel it too. There was collision ahead, but still everyone had to pretend. Still everyone had to march in step.

Berardi had supported the regime from the beginning – or almost the beginning. Back in '21, he had been dubious of the bold claims of Fascism. He was a new man then, with his war-profit wealth and his burden of grief – his only son killed in battle, his first wife dead of tuberculosis. It had been Mariagrazia, then still his secretary and not yet his second wife, who had won him to the cause. For her, politics was a fleeting enthusiasm, but once he had committed himself he remained loyal. Perhaps this new faith, this allegiance to the future, could salve his wounds. And the regime had done well, nobody could deny that: the menace of Bolshevism crushed, the reeling economy stabilised. Fifty per cent growth in manufacturing output in the first five years of fascist government – surely that was worth a few broken heads? Their methods were severe, but the times demanded it.

Only recently, in these last few months since the New York crash, had Berardi's conviction faltered. Perhaps Bolshevism had never been such a menace to Italy in 1922. Perhaps the economic recovery was merely part of a global trend, rather than the result of one man's governing will. And now, with these storms of financial disaster rolling across the Atlantic, could he really trust the protecting hand of the state? They had assured him that he could; the assurance came from the very top, from Arnaldo Mussolini, the Duce's own economist brother. The angel of economic annihilation would pass over Italy and leave his house intact. Even so, Berardi was not sure. He sensed the loom of terrible events, of tragedy.

Along the corridor, he led Emilio from the main house into the new extension. They emerged onto the mezzanine above the gallery. Overhead the walls rose plain and white to a ceiling with a square atrium skylight.

"That gentleman downstairs," Berardi said over his shoulder, "Commendatore Scaglia. You've heard of him, perhaps?"

"No," Emilio replied. In the volume of space their voices echoed oddly. There was still the faint smell of raw concrete, damp plaster.

Perhaps, Berardi thought, I really have made a mistake with this man? Perhaps – he felt a pinch of distaste – perhaps he was rather simple? "The Commendatore is very highly placed within the regime," he went on, drawing closer. "He used to be with the Interior Ministry, but he's recently been appointed vice-president of the National Institute of Fascist Culture. That means, of course, that he could soon be awarded a seat on the Grand Council itself …" He was speaking quietly, with a musing man-to-man tone that he hoped the younger man would appreciate. "He came to the gallery on the day before the private viewing … saw your work and liked it a great deal. He was, ah … very favourably impressed. Something of an admirer, one might say."

He paused meaningfully, but Emilio made no reply. Was he even listening? Did he understand anything?

"The commission, of course, is for the Institute. They want to present a work of art, a painting, to the Duce himself, on his birthday. The money's good, very good, but more than that … well, I hardly need say. The prestige for the artist concerned would be more valuable still!

"I was thinking perhaps," he said, "– although I wouldn't like to interfere with any ideas you might have – of something on the theme of the evolution of Italian industry. My father, you know, used to make bicycles. Racing cycles. I was thinking of that series of paintings you did of cyclists …"

Emilio frowned, staring at the blank wall in front of him. He sees it now, Berardi thought; in his mind, the pictures are forming.

"You want me to take the commission?" Emilio said.

"Yes. Yes, of course. That's the idea."

"But …" From the dining room next door came a clatter of wood and steel. "I'm sorry, but I understood you'd offered it to Arturo Gallo?"

How had this happened, Berardi wondered. Had he not made himself clear at the gallery opening? Yet it seemed that Gallo had misunderstood, had thought the commission was intended for him.

"I might have mentioned it," he said. "But I did not offer it. No, I believe you are better suited."

Emilio said nothing. Berardi brought his spread hands together, in what he realised too late was almost a throttling gesture. His fingers knitted. Clearly he had not been sufficiently direct: he had suggested, he had insinuated, and hoped the message would be passed on. He was accustomed to dealing with men of business and industry, men who did not need to have things spelt out to them, who recognised opportunity and seized it. But artists had odd qualms, inhibitions, and he was unable to make sense of Calvi's reaction. Berardi felt himself wading through murky and uncertain waters.

They were entering the dining room, its long space now the scene of activity. Men were fixing painted screens to cover the windows, and stringing electrical wires along the ceiling to a chandelier of jagged glass and steel suspended rather precariously over the long polished table. Calvi still said nothing.

"All this is *as per* Marinetti's instructions," Berardi said. "The décor is fairly restrained compared with the menu itself. *Eau de cologne* as a salad dressing! And the business with the sandpaper! The staff, you know, have been rather shocked by it all!" Emilio refused to be drawn; he merely nodded.

"But you'll find out soon enough," Berardi muttered. He wondered if he had offended the young man with his offer, whether he had said something vulgar. Was that why he gave no sign of gratitude or acknowledgement? It didn't matter, he told himself. Scaglia at least would be grateful to him for arranging it. Soon the Commendatore would have a seat on the Grand Council, and Berardi knew how these things worked. If he wanted concessions from the regime on reducing his productivity quotas, a solid ally on the Council would be worth any amount of pandering to the strange whims of artists. The painting would go to the Duce, perhaps even find a place in his private collection. The prestige of this commission would not be Calvi's alone, but his patron's too. In these difficult times, it paid to be adaptable. Art, and the strange young men who produced it, might just prove a worthwhile investment.

As he reflected on this, he felt a renewed warmth for the man beside him. He clapped an arm across Emilio's shoulders and drew him back towards the stairs. "Come with me a moment," he said. "I want you to see the view from the roof before it gets too dark."

The roof above the dining room was flat and ringed by a low parapet. It looked like a long concrete tongue, stuck out from the side of the main house. In the centre of the area stood a folding canvas beach chair.

"My wife's chair," Berardi said to Emilio as they emerged from the cylinder of the stairhead. "She likes to come up here and take the sun. It wasn't so long ago that women were scrupulous about their pale complexions; now they all want to look like Arabs!"

They walked to the far parapet. Lake and mountains merged into a haze. The western sky was glazed violet, with a single smudge of high cirrus. Snow still gleamed on the highest peaks.

Berardi narrowed his eyes towards the mountains. As a young man, he had been a keen alpinist. By eighteen he had climbed to the higher summits of the Valtelline; he had reached the top of Gran Paradiso two years later. His greatest triumph was back in '03, when he had scaled the Lion Ridge of the Matterhorn. He would have been the same age then as Emilio Calvi was now. But surely climbing was something than this young man would not understand: the work of muscle and sinew, the unyielding bones of the earth beneath your fingers. The ice and black rock were clear in his mind, the sting of clean air and the great distances soaring away beneath. The blue glow of heaven.

Berardi focused on the embers of the sun's fire on the

mountaintops, the other man at his side forgotten. If his own son had survived the war, he would have been twenty-nine now. His son by his first wife: dead at seventeen in the mud of the Piave. If he had lived, Berardi wondered, would he have been any different from all these other young people today? All these vacant and indifferent young people? Anxiety pushed at his heart, speeding his pulse, when he thought of the night ahead. In his ears was the hollow clang of Scaglia's voice: *loss of morale … anything that lessens national morale is treason*!

There was nothing to worry about, he told himself. Marinetti would take charge of everything. The night belonged to him. But still he felt uneasy.

From the east, the direction of the advancing darkness, a noise was growing louder in bursts. Berardi turned, as Emilio had already turned, to scan the hillside. A point of light fell steadily down towards them, flashing on and off: the headlights of a car, swinging around the curves of the road.

"Marinetti?" Emilio asked.

"Yes," said Berardi. "Here he comes."

7th April 1926

He waited in a café-bar on the corner of Via Pontaccio, the Three Stars. Outside, a gang were working on the tram rails in Corso Garibaldi; the oxy-acetylene torch burst sparks across the street, vivid in the greyness of late afternoon. They had come to this place a lot as students, but Emilio had not been back since. It still looked the same – brown wood polished by age, black linoleum on the floor, faded motor-racing posters on the walls. Outside, the street had a new coat of asphalt over the old paving stones; inside, the only differences were the framed official portraits of the king and Benito Mussolini hanging behind the bar, between the ranked bottles.

"Meet me at the Stars," Arturo had said, through the brass and Bakelite of Emilio's uncle's telephone. It was over two years since they had last seen each other, time enough for lives to drift and settle, then this: Arturo, back in Milan after his military service in the colonies, wanting to meet. Perhaps he wanted to pick up where they had left off. He had sent postcards from Africa: sepia-tinted desert vistas, lumpy camels, ragged palms, the fantastic white architecture of Tripoli, a bold new Italian city on a barren shore. But then there had been no word for eighteen months, and Emilio had given up on his friend: he was gone, lost, swallowed by the vast white emptiness of the continent.

He stared down into his coffee cup, the dregs pooled like thick oil. They had arranged to meet at four, nearly an hour ago. The bar was a funnel of cigarette smoke, and Emilio's throat felt tight and hot. Then he looked up, and saw him framed in the doorway.

Arturo waited for a moment, posed against the dissolving street, a girl clasped in the crook of his arm. Then the girl was gone, vanished from the frame and away across the street while the sparks showered and flickered over the new tarmac behind her. The door shuddered as Arturo pushed it open and walked inside.

Emilio watched him as he moved along the bar. He still had the same stalking stride of his student days, but he was different now, lean and compressed. He was darker too, his sharp-angled face tanned by months of African sun.

"You're late!" Emilio began to say, rising uncertainly from his chair. Before the words were out, Arturo pulled him into a fierce embrace, then planted a smacking kiss on each cheek.

"Sorry!" he said, and jerked a thumb back over his shoulder. "I forgot I was supposed to be spending the evening with her."

"Who was she?" Emilio asked, before he could stop himself. "You should have brought her in and introduced her."

Arturo called to the barman for a bottle and two glasses. "Her name's Bianca," he said as he sat down. "Niece of my landlord. Sweet girl, but she does get boring after a while. Anyway, her mother told her never to go into bars with strange men." He lounged back in his chair, heavily sated; Emilio had the strong impression that he'd spent the last twenty-four hours with Bianca, somewhere secluded.

"So ..." he said. Emilio shrugged. The bottle appeared between them. Arturo cracked a grin, the tension falling away.

"You're still at your uncle's place! I only called him to get your address. Imagine my surprise!"

"Imagine mine. How long have you been back?"

"Two weeks. I was demobilised last autumn, but didn't fancy the cold damp winter up here, so I found a job in Bari, working at an auto garage. The boss there served in the 1912 war and liked helping out colonial veterans. Now I've got a room out in Cagnola and a job mending wireless equipment …"

It had been six months, Emilio calculated rapidly, since he came back to Italy. He had time enough for work and women. But there had been no word in all that time. Anyone would feel the insult.

"I wanted," Arturo said, "to get myself set up here before I contacted you. So it wouldn't seem … well, I don't know."

"You said you were wounded?" Emilio broke in. "I was imagining you with one leg or something."

"Only a flesh wound, I'm afraid, and an accident at that. I was lucky though. The surgeon told me another few centimetres and the bullet would have punctured my lung." He slapped his chest, high up on the left side. "Right there," he said. "Nice dramatic scar, too; I'll show you some time. I spent five weeks in the military hospital in Tripoli, and by the time they let me out my term of service was up, so they sent me home."

They drank the earthy red wine as Arturo continued his story. Emilio said little. Emilio, who had never left Italy; Emilio, whose six months' teaching at a cockroach-infested school in Mantua represented the height of his life's adventures; Emilio, whose closest brush with death was a bout of chronic dysentery, which ended his teaching job and sent him back to his uncle's house in the Milan suburbs.

"I only volunteered for service overseas," Arturo said, "because I had the idea that I might be trained as a pilot. It was either that, I thought, or end up being sent to some infantry garrison in Sardinia to spend eighteen months marching up and down and shining my boots. But it turned out that only serving officers get to become airmen. They trained me as a wireless operator instead and posted me to the airfield at Sirte."

A bowl of roasted chestnuts arrived, and Emilio ate while Arturo talked.

"The place was a hellish dump. Picture a great, flat expanse of grit, sand, concrete and cracked tarmac all shimmering in the sun, between the desert and the sea. We were living in these long low huts, corrugated iron, with palm-leaf shelters outside. In summer the temperature was up past fifty, and the petrol vaporised in the drums. Everything ended up smelling of it."

Arturo gulped wine, flipped a chestnut into his mouth and chewed as he talked.

"You know the strangest thing about it?" he said. "All that time I spent there, and I never once saw the people we were supposed to be fighting. The *enemy*. The Arab rebels. The bombers would go roaring off across the dunes, but to us it seemed almost as though we were fighting a war against the desert itself. Because I worked at the wireless station, I'd hear all the messages relayed between Tripoli and Benghazi, all these names of places. *Ghadames*, *Bu Ngem*, *Agedabia*. You imagine these fantastic citadels in the desert, bristling with savages ..."

A chorus of shouts came from out in the street, but Arturo seemed not to notice. He was, Emilio realised, a little drunk already; he must have been drinking with Bianca before he arrived. What does he want with me, he wondered. His life, in the years since Arturo disappeared, had found a sort of level. That reckless enthusiasm that had possessed him during his student days, that diving after life and belief in the future, was almost gone from him now.

After returning from Mantua, Emilio had found work as a commercial illustrator, working for Felippo Bruccoli, his fellow student at the Brera. He had a fiancée too: a short, pretty, flat-faced girl called Maddalena, who worked in a shoe shop near Bruccoli's office. Though he called her his fiancée, they had made no formal engagement to marry; she wanted marriage, he knew, and in a sense he wanted it himself, but something held him back. He loved her, in a thoughtful and sensitive way, without passion but genuinely. She loved him too, although she claimed to love Rodolfo Valentino more. They walked together on Sundays, and often went to the cinema to watch the latest American romances: she had an obsession with an actress called Norma Talmadge, whom she believed she resembled. Emilio's own tastes were for moody German pictures filled with black, angular shadows and silent screams, but he went to see those alone these days. Maddalena had refused to speak to him for a week after *The Cabinet of Dr Caligari*.

Until now, he had almost considered himself happy. Even if, sometimes, queuing in the rain outside the picture house for the latest Douglas Fairbanks or Mary Pickford feature, he would feel suddenly hollow and lost, and would stare bleakly into the gathering dusk … until Maddalena playfully punched his arm and demanded to know why he wasn't talking to her.

But now Emilio saw himself through Arturo's eyes, and found himself sadly lacking. He was embarrassed by himself; embarrassed even, he realised with shame, by Maddalena. What would Arturo think if he met her? Surely *his* women – Emilio imagined those desert sirens, those haughty bohemians, even the lascivious Bianca – surely they would not want to talk about hats for hours, or constantly ask about weddings and children's clothes? Surely they would not, on those few snatched and guilty nights, have turned their mother's portrait to the wall, kissed their crucifix necklace, muttered a nervous prayer of repentance?

"You know what?" Arturo was saying. "I haven't picked up a brush since we left the Brera. I suppose I just abandoned painting as soon as I enlisted. When I was in that hospital in Tripoli, though, surrounded by these big white drapes hour after hour, sleeping or sedated most of the time, I found a novel that one of the doctors had left behind, by Marinetti, of all people. *The Untameables*, it was called. Completely absurd sort of fantasy story, set in a desert somewhere. But when I read it, it all came back to me, all those ideas we had when were at the Brera together … All the ways we were going to revolutionise art. You remember all that?"

Emilio nodded.

"Well," Arturo went on, "when I was passing through Rome I decided to try and find Marinetti and talk to him. I found out where he was living – 30 Piazza Adriana, near the Vatican. Huge place it turned out to be, virtually a palace. I never believed that he was really a millionaire, but it must be true. So there I was, only a week after getting off the ship, still dressed in my old suit that I'd had in mothballs for two years, black grease still caked under my nails, sitting in a salon in Rome drinking cocktails with F.T. Marinetti!"

He allowed himself a satisfied pause, swirling the wine in his glass.

"Anyway, I talked a load of balls about Africa, and he seemed impressed. Told me he'd help me in any way he could if I wanted to start painting again. His apartment was full of work – Depero, Prampolini, Moresco, all those new Futurist artists he's been promoting since the war. By the time I left I was on fire to paint again."

"And did you?"

"No. I thought about it, but I couldn't get started. I thought I needed to come back here, to Milan. I thought, actually, that I wanted to see you again first."

He leaned forward across the table to grasp Emilio by the wrist. "I was thinking, you see, that we could get a studio together, help each other …" He released him again, sitting back thoughtfully. "But what about you? I haven't even asked what you've been doing all this time."

"You remember Bruccoli, from the Academy? I do illustrations for him – film posters, travel brochures. Quite nice things, some of them. Modern. A bit Matisse, you know … It pays, but it's not art, exactly. I've wanted to paint again, properly, as well."

"Then we should do it," Arturo was already saying, a new vehemence in his voice. "Let's agree on it. With the money I make at the electricians' workshop and whatever Bruccoli pays you we should be able to afford a studio."

"Agreed." They clasped hands. Emilio felt illuminated. Art, he suddenly realised, was what he had missed, what he needed. And he had missed Arturo too – that sense of brotherhood, of connection.

"We need another bottle," Arturo declared.

Outside, the welding gang had packed up for the night. Another shout came from the street, then a noisy chorus of discordant voices. The sound of running feet, and a clatter like a kicked steel bin.

"What's happening out there?" Arturo asked the waiter as he brought the bottle. Men were passing the doorway, volleying shouts up and down the street. The waiter, a young man with oily hair, shrugged and set the bottle on the table.

"Didn't you hear the news?" he said. "Somebody tried to shoot Mussolini this morning. It was on the wireless. Happened in Rome. Some woman, English I think. She only grazed his nose, apparently … Luckily he was opening a surgeon's convention at the time …"

"Bad shot," Arturo said, still turned to the door. The waiter went back to the bar. "So I suppose they're roaming about trying to find people to beat up?" Arturo went on. "Antipatriotic elements to stamp on?"

"I had to call my uncle earlier and tell him to stay at home," Emilio said in a hushed voice. "He's a socialist, you know."

"Still? I thought he'd have given that up by now. But let's

drink a toast!" He raised his glass, slopping a little onto the tabletop. "To Futurism, and our future role in it!"

"To Futurism!" Emilio said, and they drink.

Three men walked in from the street, all wearing dark trousers and black shirts. Two were young and looked like students, the third was older and bigger. He had a broken nose, and looked like a boxer. The first two propped themselves at the bar while the boxer went to the player-piano and started jamming coins in the slot.

"Let's see if he can get that thing to play *Giovinezza*!" Arturo said under his breath.

The player-piano started up. A few bars of discordant noise, then the tune revealed itself to be a rendition of the march from *Aida*. The three Blackshirts began beating on the bar-top in time with the music.

"Ah, now this brings back memories!" Arturo knocked back his glass and poured himself another. "Back at the base at Sirte, the flying officers lived in a little cantonment of huts by themselves. They had an ornamental pond, a palm-leaf gazebo and a gramophone, and in the evenings they would all sit out on deck chairs listening to *Aida*. Just imagine it, in all that desolation, Verdi wafting out across the runways and off over the desert! There was something beautiful about it, even there."

Of all the people in the bar, Emilio realised, Arturo seemed to be speaking the loudest, his voice raised over the racket of music. The Blackshirts were singing wordlessly along to the tune from the piano, *Bah-Bah-Bah-bahda-badah-ba-bah* …

"So," he said, giving Arturo a warning look. "What about your wound? How did that happen?"

"Oh, yes" Arturo exclaimed, "Funny story, I suppose. There was this mechanic at the base, from Napoli. I quite liked him, but he didn't like me much. Anyway, this mechanic – Torelli, his name was – got himself an old revolver while he was on leave in Benghazi. He was a typical Neapolitan, if you know what I mean. An anarchist, basically. *What do I care about the rules?* he used to say. *I don't give a shit! I couldn't give a shit for Italy, I'm Neapolitan! I love food and my mother, and fuck all else!* He was great… *What do I care about Fascism?* he said. *I couldn't give a blind man's flying fuck about it! Mussolini can lick my balls!*"

Over Arturo's shoulder, Emilio could see the three men at the bar glancing over at him. He tried to estimate the distance to the door and how quickly he could cover it. Could he drag Arturo with him? Would he stay to help, if they cornered him?

The player-piano juddered to a halt, a zone of silence spreading through the room, which Arturo appeared not to notice. He yawned back in his chair, lifting the glass to drain the dregs and slamming it down on the table again. Emilio, wincing, his palm hovering as if to clamp itself over Arturo's mouth, tried not to look up at the group by the bar. He couldn't help it; looked anyway; saw them staring right back at him. Arturo was still talking.

"And he was on the bunk below me, bragging away as usual, cleaning his evil-looking old Glisenti. I'd just leaned over the bunk to tell him to shut his mouth when there's this sudden *BANG!* Bullet went straight through his skull, the bunk, the mattress and my shoulder. Buried itself in one of the roof beams …"

"Hey, you!" the boxer said, for the second time. Not to Arturo, but to Emilio, who raised a tentative gaze. The Blackshirts had moved away from the bar now, grouping themselves in the middle of the room to cut off the route to the door. Emilio was astonished to see a look of satisfaction on Arturo's face.

"I was telling a story, that's all!" Arturo said, turning in his chair to address the three men, palms raised as if seeking support from the barman, who looked elsewhere.

"We heard what you were saying," one of the younger men said, and all of them moved a step closer. The other men in the bar posed in attitudes of careful inattention. The door rattled briefly as somebody stepped inside, then quickly left again.

"I heard what he said before that, too," said the waiter with the oily hair. "*Bad shot*, he said."

"I wasn't talking to you!" Arturo called. Beneath the table, his knee jogged compulsively. Emilio sensed the punchy energy radiating from him.

"*Let's go*," he whispered to Arturo, who ignored him. The two younger men were flanking the boxer, waiting for him to move. Emilio pictured the scene ahead: a first punch, then a whirl of fists, breaking bottles, hurled chairs … He tried to stand, but his legs were numb.

Arturo sprang up. "Let's not have any misunderstandings here!" he proclaimed. "I wouldn't like to think my patriotism was in doubt. After two years in Africa, fighting for Italy …"

"You?" said one of the younger men, leering.

Emilio tried to ease his legs from under the table. In disbelief, he watched Arturo walk calmly to the player piano and drop a coin into the slot. The three Blackshirts seemed just as bemused. "I think he wants to dance," one said.

"You there!" the barman called to Emilio, "take your friend and get out! I don't want troublemakers in here!"

"Wait a moment!" Arturo said. Behind him, the player piano started crunching out the *Aida* march again. The three Blackshirts shifted on their toes, ready to strike. Emilio managed to stand up, gripping the tabletop.

"I will not," Arturo said, grinning wildly, "have any man question my patriotism, nor cast any slurs upon my character! You three gentlemen may believe me to be something that I'm not, but be assured that you *are mistaken*."

As he spoke, he reached into the inner pocket of his jacket.

Was he about to draw out a gun? Emilio remembered with sickening clarity that Arturo had once possessed an old pistol.

The three men moved at once, seeming to take one huge step forward in unison – a step halted by the card Arturo held raised in his hand.

"As you can see," Arturo was saying, over the clatter of the piano, "I'm just as loyal to the cause as you are!"

Emilio, moving with swift unsteady steps down the length of the room, saw the three men pause, glaring at the card. Arturo showed it to each in turn, then replaced it in his pocket. The big boxer shrugged, rocking back on his heels.

"I don't care what you are!" the barman called. "Get out, now!"

Arms raised as if in surrender, Arturo retreated slowly down the bar with Emilio at his heels. At the door he paused for Emilio to pass him, then turned to address the room.

"*Viva Italia*!" he yelled, then spun on his heel and left, slamming the door behind him.

The street seemed unnaturally hushed, as if awaiting an uproar. Arturo walked fast to the opposite pavement and paused to light a cigarette. Emilio noticed that his hands were shaking. He took a couple of strides, to the end of the asphalt strip. The workmen had left the road churned up around the tram tracks, steel bolts and loose paving stones lying in a heap.

"Filthy bastards," Arturo said, and Emilio realised that he was shaking with anger. "All the times we used to drink in that place. All the money we spent in there, and they tell us to get out like a pair of drunks."

"That was a Party card you showed them, wasn't it?" Emilio said. "I never knew … when did you join?"

"Back in Rome," Arturo said, seething behind his teeth. "Reasons of expediency. Another time … " He turned to glare back towards the bar. A shout of laughter came from inside.

“Wait,” Emilio said, “don’t …” But Arturo had already snatched up one of the blocks of paving stone and was stalking back across the street with it. He cocked it back in his hand, cigarette clamped between his teeth.

“On the summit of the world,” he spat, “once again we hurl defiance at the stars! Ha!”

He lobbed the stone in a great long-arm swing, and it arced across the street towards the window of the bar. Emilio had a brief glimpse of the faces behind the glass, turning in surprise and horror, before the window exploded in a shower of ringing shards.

5

10th May 1930

His Excellency Federico Tommaso Marinetti, the Father of Futurism, the Animator of Italy, the Caffeine of Europe, came sweeping down the drive towards the house in a blood-red, supercharged Alfa Romeo 1750 Gran Sport. The car swung across the forecourt and slid to a halt.

A platform of electric light projected from the open door of the house, broken by the stretched shadows of the people already gathering on the steps to greet the new arrival. Marinetti climbed from the cockpit of the car, unfolding himself from the passenger seat and shedding his long, dust-coloured coat to reveal a double-breasted suit in immaculate black. He straightened his bow tie and drew himself up to his full height. At fifty-three years of age, he was still an impressive figure: his face composed in an imperious frown, his moustache clipped, his bald head domed and gleaming.

All voices fell silent, the guests arranging themselves around Marinetti as he stood posed, one hand raised to command attention, a foot braced on the running board of his car.

"Friends! Futurists! It was in an Alfa Romeo machine just like this one," he declared, "that the racing genius Tadio Nuvolari won the Thousand Mile Cup at Brescia, thereby proving once again to all foreign observers that Italy is no longer, as they might once have imagined, the home of ice-cream vendors, tourist guides, pasta cooks and singing gondoliers, but rather a dynamic nation of sportsmen, daredevil aviators and adventurers!"

There was a spatter of applause, a few cries of agreement. Someone handed Marinetti a glass of Spumante. From the margins of the group, Nina watched with interest. It was typical of Marinetti to start the show the moment he arrived; after all, he'd had over an hour to think about it, in that little hurtling car. The chauffeur was still in the driving seat wearing his cap and goggles, unobtrusive.

"Racing here tonight," Marinetti went on, "at over one hundred kilometres per hour on the Milan Autostrada, my brain was ventilated by the rush of oxygen, as if by the force of a mighty aircraft propeller! In my blood I felt the stirrings of a vibrant creative energy that longed for release. So I urged my driver on to even greater speed, filled with desire to join with you, my friends, at this gathering tonight, where I am convinced that we will witness the birth of a new and dynamic poetic sensibility!"

He lifted his glass, as if in benediction, then tipped back his head and drained the drink. Figures spilled from the open door and the steps, surrounding him, competing to welcome him, and he greeted everyone in turn with a handshake that might have been thought rather traditionalist of anyone but him.

These performances must have been extraordinary once, Nina imagined, in those years before the war when Marinetti used to roar his speeches to the cheering mob in the Milan Galleria. In those years, that is, before Mussolini stole the show. Now, it all seemed so familiar, even if she still felt the charge of his words lingering in the air.

She remembered the last time she had seen him – three years ago, was it, or four? A party in Rome, on one of her visits there with Amedeo. Marinetti was beside the fireplace in the main salon, his voice booming out through the adjoining rooms. Nina remembered his wife as well, a poetic-seeming woman, much younger than Marinetti; they had talked about children, as the woman was expecting her first. Nina had wondered then what it must be like to be married to Marinetti, tried to imagine the private man, the family man, behind the public braggadocio. His wife said she had made him hire a chauffeur, as he was such a terribly bad driver. It was strange to imagine him taking orders like that.

Marinetti was escorted up the steps and into the house. He passed through the hallway, still talking, still gesticulating, Berardi to one side of him and Mariagrazia the other. Nina spied Arturo waiting eagerly at the foot of the stairs; Marinetti greeted him, the two men shook hands, and Arturo was drawn along with the cavalcade as it moved towards the salon. She remembered a circus she had seen as a child in Turin, a ringmaster with his waxed moustaches and his great bawling voice. Marinetti is our ringmaster, Nina thought. And we are his circus: his clowns and performing animals, his high-wire artists.

Outside, the chauffeur started the car, the fumes swirling and eddying between the lingering guests. As he slowly pulled away towards the parking area, the crowd was sucked back into the brightly lit house, leaving the dusk to the insects and the dying haze of exhaust smoke.

The moon was over the lake as Nina climbed the stairs to the roof terrace. At the top she saw Emilio seated on the far parapet, gazing into the gathering gloom. She wanted to surprise him, but he looked up at the click of her heels on the concrete.

"I spotted you watching from up here, while we were all out at the front," she said. "I'm surprised you weren't there. You know, greeting the chief."

"I thought … I thought I'd wait a while and let the fuss die down. I'll go and introduce myself to him later."

Nina shifted the deck chair to the centre of the terrace and sat down, stretching her legs. She suspected that Emilio had no actual desire to meet Marinetti. The reality of the man could only be a disappointment after so many years' distant adulation. She lit a cigarette and leaned back in the chair, breathing out smoke. The sky to the west was still a deep blue, a few stars showing high up. Emilio was in semi silhouette as he sat on the wall with a foot up on the parapet.

"You look like one of those old romantic poets," Nina said to him. "You know, contemplating the twilight hour. Rather passéist, don't you think? Don't you remember the slogans? *Let's Murder the Moonlight!* and all that?"

Emilio raised his head and sucked in a deep breath.

"Twilight," he declared, "is a period of dim illumination caused by light diffused from a reflection of the sun's rays. That's all there is to it. My father was a chemical engineer, you know. He took great relish in pointing out the facts behind all poetic fancies."

"It still looks nice anyway," Nina said. "Even if we're not supposed to think so any more." Sounds of insect life rose from the gardens, a rhythmic buzz. Lying back in the canvas chair, she stared up at the sky. Around the edges of the roof terrace there were tall metal poles. She had not noticed them earlier. Looking back over her shoulder, she saw the coil of electric cable and the wooden crates beside the stairs.

"It looks like they hang strings of lights from the poles," she said. "How wonderful – they could have music up here, and dancing …" She imagined the scene: the long terrace illuminated by electric bulbs, like a stage projecting out into the blackness of night. Or like the upper deck of a ship: some great white liner, far out on the ocean, floating music out over the water. The cylindrical stairhead looked like nothing so much as a funnel; in fact, the whole extension resembled the superstructure of a ship. She shuddered, suddenly picturing an expanse of empty sea surrounding her, with no chance of escape or rescue.

"Was Arturo down there?" Emilio asked. "With Marinetti, I mean?"

"Of course he was," Nina said. "Basking in the reflection of his rays, in fact. Which was one of the reasons I came up here, to tell the truth. It gets quite tiring being ignored."

She had barely had time to talk to Arturo before Marinetti's arrival. Not enough time, anyway, to say the things she had planned to say. She had wanted to tell him about the letter, explain the choice she had to make. But Fosca's barbed comment about children had slipped in beneath her defences, so that she was almost speechless when they met. Besides, he was so wrapped by his own concerns ... *Don't get emotional*, he had told her.

She stood up, drawing her shawl tight about her shoulders, and crossed the terrace to stand beside Emilio and look down into the garden.

"I'm sorry about earlier on," said Emilio. "With Fosca, I mean ... I should have spoken up for you."

"It would only have encouraged her. Did she say anything about me, after I'd gone?"

"Not really," Emilio said, hesitant. "I wasn't paying much attention. They were asking, she and Mariagrazia, about some book they'd read: *Italian Feminism and the Rebirth of* ... something, I don't remember. They wanted my opinion on the sacred duties of women and the spiritual femininity of the race. They told me that women have to emancipate themselves from materialism and a false sense of competition with men, and uphold their rights to the sacred maternal sublime. I don't think they really wanted my opinion, though."

"The stupid cows, of course they didn't," Nina said. "It's just an attack on me. Fosca thinks *you're my lover* – obviously I must have a lover, being such an impossibly wanton woman. Witches! Neither of them have children, that's why they hate me. *I* have a child. I *am* a mother! I hope their *race* dies out altogether!"

Emilio flinched at her vehemence.

"… But I imagine Fosca's given up sex altogether these days. That would fit with her latest fad. No doubt she'll become a nun soon – wouldn't that be a logical conclusion to it all!" She began to laugh. "Fosca a nun, can you picture it!"

Her laughter died away into a desperate sigh, and she hugged the shawl more tightly around herself.

"Berardi wants me to take the commission," Emilio said. "You know, the one Arturo thought he was going to get."

"Oh," Nina said. A moment passed, and she wondered what Emilio expected her to say.

"I don't know what to tell him," Emilio went on.

"He's probably heard that Arturo hasn't finished a painting for months," Nina said.

"There's the portrait he's working on, for the Biennale."

"Oh, that fucking portrait! Which he'll never finish, even if Marinetti promises him a room all to himself at Venice to exhibit it in."

"You shouldn't be so hard."

"And you shouldn't be so loyal. He blames me, you know. He thinks it's my fault he can't work. Probably blames you too. Blames everyone but himself."

"Even so," Emilio said, "I need to tell him about the commission, it wouldn't be fair otherwise. Maybe if he spoke to Berardi himself, he could explain things. Perhaps you could mention something to him?"

"Me? I don't think it'd do much good with things as they are between us at the moment."

Emilio mumbled an apology, and Nina took his hand. "I know he's your friend," she said. "And I don't want to offend you. But sometimes I think you look up to Arturo like an older brother. He doesn't need that, and it doesn't do you any good. If you want the commission, take it. Maybe the shock would do him a favour, who knows?"

"I don't want to feel like I'm in competition with him," Emilio said.

But you are, Nina thought. *You always have been. And you keep losing.* She said nothing.

"Why do you think he's stuck with his work, anyway?" Emilio asked.

"Isn't it obvious? It's his own fault. He's trying to do something he doesn't believe in. He thinks that it's expected of him, and he'll be rewarded for it. But it's shallow, it's meaningless … At least you've always held onto what you believe, haven't you?" She squeezed his hand lightly. "You've still got a sense of the ideal …"

She stiffened suddenly. "Who's offering this commission?"

"Oh, that man we saw downstairs. The *special guest.* Commendatore something-or-other. I didn't catch his name. He's quite important, Berardi told me."

"Scaglia," Nina said quietly. "Commendatore Scaglia." She was completely sober now.

"Did you say you knew him?"

"My husband did once. A long time ago."

Sounds were rising from downstairs – a metallic clatter, a scraping of chairs.

"You should go and get dressed for dinner," she said quietly. "And if you see Arturo … tell him I need to speak to him."

"I will," Emilio said. His thumb traced a circle on the back on her hand. He began to get up, then leaned in quickly and kissed her on the brow. Before she could react, he was pacing away towards the funnel of the stairhead.

Nina exhaled, the tension easing from her body. She felt

the warmth of Emilio's kiss printed on her skin. She had considered his feelings so little over all these months. Once she had believed that he resented her, perhaps was even jealous of her. But the relations between them had become blurred and uncertain now. Arturo would not get the prized commission. It would be Emilio instead. Her anger at Arturo faded: in his disappointment, she would offer him forgiveness.

She should go downstairs and get ready for dinner. How many times had she experienced this moment, the prelude to some great party, before Amedeo left? Seeing Scaglia again had brought it all back to her. She had planned to avoid him, to ignore him and hope he did not recognise her. The link to her husband, to his disgrace, was unsettling. Since Amedeo's disappearance she had taken to using only her maiden name, Della Torre, rather than her married name, Sorani. It was possible that the Commendatore would fail to make the connection. But he frightened her, and she had believed she was safe here.

Now, with this same man offering the commission to Emilio, the commission that Arturo had wanted so badly, she felt herself being drawn into his orbit. This what was she had wanted to escape: rooms full of important men, contracts and commissions and underhand dealings, connections and commerce and the awful necessity of good behaviour.

It was stupid to imagine that she could ever truly be free of it. Had she not used some of those other old acquaintances, Amedeo's network of influential people, to further her own artistic career? Art had been her refuge in the months since her husband's disappearance, the new life she believed she had constructed for herself. But now, like all dreams, this had ended, led back with sickening vertigo to the same place that she had left. She hated it, but it also felt like home.

She was facing west towards the last of the twilight. Somewhere out there across the spines of the mountains lay Montreux. Nina pictured her son Marco, asleep in his dormitory room. The thought that he was in danger, that she had endangered him by her negligence, anguished her. Fosca's easy insult had struck home.

But now she had an opportunity to change all that: an address in a foreign city, on a distant continent. She could take back her son and together they could sail away across the ocean, into a different future … No. She would escape, but not to Argentina, not to her husband. She would drift, fabulously cosmopolitan, between the capitals of the world, her son growing into youth, into adulthood, under her care alone. But it was an impossible fantasy. If Amedeo cut off her allowance, paid by his bank in Milan, there would be no money. She could not erase him from her life so easily.

She stood up and breathed deeply. *Courage.* Squaring her shoulders, she walked upright towards the stairs.

Emilio, edging open the door, spied first a pair of two-tone shoes jutting over the end of the bed nearest the window, then the rest of Arturo stretched along the mattress. A soda water siphon and a glass were on the bedside table.

"Oh, here you are," Emilio said. "Nina was looking for you." Arturo was already wearing his black evening trousers and dress shirt, but his collar was unfastened. The two halves stuck up from behind his neck in stiff white mandibles. Emilio sat on the edge of the other bed, beside the door, and opened his portmanteau. The room was an oddly-angled box, plain white walls and a ceiling sloping down to the single low window.

Arturo picked up the siphon and squirted a foaming jet into the glass. "If I drink any more of that disgusting fizzy wine," he said, "I'll choke on it." He knocked back the water and yawned. From the house below them came the muffled sound of slamming doors.

"Did she send you to find me, by the way?"

"Not in so many words," Emilio said. "She was looking for you, that's all." A tightness in his throat; there were words he needed to say but could not.

"She's being very difficult tonight. I might have guessed she would be … Oh, you don't have a spare front collar stud, do you? I've lost mine. I was just thinking I'd have to go sneaking about the house trying to steal one."

Emilio opened his portmanteau. A haze of camphor fumes rose from within. Black wool and white cotton, folded tight.

"Here," he said, and tossed the stud across the room. Arturo snatched it deftly.

"*Merci*!"

Unfolding his dinner suit, Emilio frowned at the shiny cuffs and worn lapel. It was second-hand, of course – aside from a trip to the theatre a year ago, he had never worn the thing. He worried that it might have shrunk, or come apart at the seams. At least the shirt was new: board-stiff and heavy with starch.

"Did you speak to Marinetti then?" he asked as he got undressed.

"Oh, we exchanged the usual salutes," Arturo replied. "There were too many people about to talk more. What did you think of him, then?"

Emilio pulled the shirt on over his head. Engulfed in the starchy whiteness, he told Arturo that he had not been there for the introductions. "I thought I'd wait a while," he said. His head emerged. Arturo was giving him a sideways look. Emilio, flustered, busied himself with his cufflinks.

"I was talking to Berardi a little while ago. He mentioned the commission."

"Oh, the commission," said Arturo, refilling his glass with a *shhh* of the siphon. "Yes, I need to ask him about that. There's somebody here I should speak to, apparently."

Emilio heard the mattress creak beneath him as he got up. *Tell him now*, he thought.

"Ridiculous, isn't it," Arturo asked, "that we still have to get dressed up like this for dinner? All this expensive tailoring just to take on vital nutrients. In the future ..." he paused, grinning.

"*In the future*," Emilio declared, raising a finger, "diners will wear paper clothes, that can be easily discarded after the meal!"

"No ... edible clothes! Dinner dress will be made of sweet plant fibres, easily digestible as dessert! Everyone will eat the clothing of the diner to their left ..."

Emilio snapped his braces over his shoulders. It was an old game.

"But it's all so exhausting though, you know," Arturo sighed. He flung a tie around his neck and knotted it with a casual flourish. "All this dancing around people, courting their favour. A denial of the self, is what it amounts to."

Emilio watched Arturo as he stood before the mirror above the small washbasin. He recognised the mood, had seen it often enough. His friend's egotism often amused him, but often annoyed him too.

"Didn't Marinetti say that he'd get you on the list for the Biennale competition?" He joined Arturo at the mirror, tie loose around his neck. The starched collar of his shirt was very tight and stiff, the wings digging into his jaw.

"He did. Trouble is, he probably said much the same to a score of others. At least they can't enter the paintings actually on show in the exhibition. So, what we have to ask ourselves is, how many spaces remain, and who's going to fill them? Me? You?"

"Oh, he never said anything to me about it."

"Should have done. You're better than half of the others, at least. We both are."

Arturo glared over Emilio's shoulder at his reflection. Squinted, frowned, shoved his hair back off his forehead. His long face looked wolfish, especially savage beside Emilio's placid oval.

For all his friend's naked ambition, Emilio still believed in Arturo's artistic integrity. It was not just ambition to be wealthy, but to be respected as a painter. To *win* respect. The vices that drove him were pride and vanity, not greed. Emilio concentrated on fastening his tie. His fingers were awkward and shook slightly as he gripped the silk.

"Did you speak to that man, Scaglia," Arturo said, pacing away across the room. His hard soles banged on the floor. "The special guest. Apparently he's the one with the commission that Berardi offered me."

"No, I didn't," Emilio said, Berardi's voice in his mind. *I may have mentioned it … I certainly never offered it.* "I think Nina knows him. Or her husband did." His fingers slipped, and the bow of his tie tumbled loose.

"Does she, indeed?" Arturo stopped pacing. In the mirror, Emilio watched him turning thoughtfully in the centre of the room. "Well, that's certainly convenient. Amazing the people that woman knows! That's the thing, you see – she's used to this society. Haven't I always said she'd be the key to getting in with the best people?"

There was an ugly relish in his voice. "No," Emilio said quietly. "No, you haven't." He took up the ends of the tie again, trying to wrestle it into a bow. "Surely you don't think of her in that way?"

"No," Arturo said, his tone softening, thoughtful. "No I don't really … But what are you doing with that tie? Trying to throttle yourself?" He stepped over to the mirror, turned Emilio by the shoulder. "Here, let me do it!"

They stood close before the washbasin, Arturo's fingers deft as he folded the silk, looped it and tied it. Emilio could smell his cologne, sharp above the earthy scent of tobacco.

"It's all about hierarchy," Arturo said, frowning as he worked. "You've got to keep in with the leaders, otherwise they'll forget you exist and give the prizes to someone else."

"Maybe you don't need the prizes," Emilio said, his throat constricted as Arturo pulled at the tie. "Maybe it's better to just ..." A shrug. "... follow your own ..."

"Oh, shut up," Arturo laughed. "Look – you've got a stain on your lapel. Stay still–" He licked his thumb, and then rubbed it over Emilio's jacket.

"What I mean is," Emilio began. He should tell Arturo about the commission now – but Arturo was still smiling, that charming rogue's smirk, and he felt the bond between them as an almost physical thing.

"What you mean is," Arturo said, "that we're the best, you and me. We deserve to succeed. Haven't we worked for it?" A last twist and tug of the tie, then he clasped Emilio by the shoulders and stepped back. "There, now you look civilised." He gave him a light slap on the cheek, then turned and paced back to the bed. Emilio slipped a comb from his inside pocket and started running it through his hair.

"How long have we been doing this now?" Arturo said. "Five years? Five years painting, waiting for the breakthrough. I'm sick of obscurity, Emilio. I want big sales, exhibitions, prizes. I want international gallery shows in Berlin and New York. Paris, Tokyo, wherever. You, too – how long are you going to keep on scraping by on five thousand a year illustrating tourist brochures for the Amalfi coast, or whatever it is you do for Bruccoli these days? I could have been earning more by now if I'd stuck at being an electrician! And here we are surrounded by rich complacent bastards that we have to entertain somehow ..."

Emilio turned from the mirror, comb raised. "Oh, come on," he said. "Surely you don't mean Marinetti?"

"No, not Marinetti. He's genuine enough … Will you stop waving that comb at me?"

"I'm not waving it," Emilio said.

"You are. You look like a duellist or something." Arturo stood up, cheeks puffed, brandishing the soda siphon like a weapon. Emilio, comb levelled, circled around him. Their feet shuffled on the carpet.

"But we have to believe in him, don't we," Arturo said as they moved. "We all have to believe in the wondrous powers of Marinetti the Great."

"I've heard you defending him often enough," Emilio replied, sparring with his comb. "You defended him against Bruccoli just the other week."

"Bruccoli's a homosexual; what does he know about taste?"

Emilio darted forward, flicking the comb under Arturo's nose. Arturo dodged back, unleashing a jet from the soda siphon – the water fumed out, soaking the front of Emilio's shirt.

A knock at the door, and both of them stood, unmoving. A second knock; Emilio crossed to the door in two strides and opened it halfway.

In the hallway, a maid was waiting. She bobbed a little. "Sorry to disturb you, Signore," she said, noticing Emilio's wet shirt. She was young, maybe sixteen, blonde and quite pretty, with a local accent. "Signora Della Torre sent me," the maid said, "with a message for a Signor Gallo …" She glanced into the room: Arturo circling in the background. "The Signora requests that Signor Gallo join her in her room, if he has a moment to spare."

"Thanks," said Emilio. "I'll pass it on."

"Sorry about your shirt," said Arturo, after Emilio closed the door. "I've got a spare one that should fit you. It might be a bit crumpled, though." He dragged his small suitcase from under the bed.

"About the commission," Emilio began, trying to sound casual. Arturo, bent over the open suitcase, just grunted. "Well," Emilio went on, fiddling with the comb again. "I was talking to Berardi about it earlier. He seemed to think ... that is, he was suggesting that I should take it."

"Oh," said Arturo, standing up. He dropped the folded shirt on the bed beside him. "Well," he said blankly, after a pause. "Congratulations."

Emilio had turned back to the mirror as he spoke, but in the glass he caught Arturo's brief grimace of angry resentment. He swiped the comb across his head once more, pretending he'd seen nothing.

Arturo walked quickly to the door, his feet loud. "I suppose I should go and see what she wants," he muttered. He opened the door and went out into the corridor.

"Listen, come with me, will you," he said a few seconds later, stepping back into the room. "If I'm alone with Nina she'll only make a hysterical scene and I'm not in the mood. Besides, I can't stand watching you fussing with your hair like a woman."

Emilio dropped the comb onto the nightstand, then followed him out of the room.

Behind a tall folding screen, black lacquer patterned with geometric gold, Nina leaned forwards and drew the dress off over her head. She stood in her camisole, flimsy fabric dangling from her outstretched hand. Beside her, the maid unpacked the next dress, unwrapping it carefully from its tissue-lined box. Inside the box lid, the label read *Marcelle André / Couture-Lingerie / 43. Rue Boissy d'Anglais – Paris (Madeleine).*

"What I don't understand," said Arturo, from the other side of the screen, "is why you couldn't have decided what to wear *before* coming. Then you wouldn't need to pack so much."

"Don't be silly, darling," Nina said, as the maid helped her with the side fasteners. "How could I know what sort of party it would be before I got here? Anyway, I like packing."

The dress secured, she emerged from behind the screen. Arturo was leaning against the wall. "Well," she said brightly. "What do you think of this one?" She moved to the mirror, turning in the lamplight; the dress was lavish, an evening gown with a long scalloped skirt.

"Looks reasonable, I suppose," Arturo said, and lit a cigarette. He looked very stern and sober in his dinner suit, although the two-tone shoes he still wore gave him a raffish air.

Nina swayed on her toes, the skirts of the dress swishing heavily. "Oh, I don't know," she said. "I think maybe it's a bit staid. Do you think it makes me look older? It makes my bust look huge. And it would be terrible for dancing."

She stepped back behind the screen, gesturing to the maid to help her out of the dress. "Such a shame we don't have a gramophone up here," she called out, "then we could all dance. Get into the party spirit!"

"I'm always in the party spirit," Arturo said, breathing smoke. "Give me a comb and some tissue and I'll play you a tune."

Emilio sat awkwardly in a cane chair beside the bed. The damp shirt clung to his chest, and his collar was biting. Nina's room was larger than the one he shared with Arturo, lit softly by a lamp on a tall stand, the air scented faintly with perfume. Behind the screen, tissue rustled and fabric whispered. From where Emilio was sitting, the mirror reflected a sliver of the scene – Nina's left arm and leg, the curve of her spine as she bent forward, the maid's back as she moved around her. Emilio remembered the painting studio at the Brera: the model behind her folding screen, shedding her clothes in secret, emerging nude before the measuring gaze of the assembled men. He shifted in the cane chair, wondering if perhaps he might be able to see more. Is it me she's performing for, he wondered, or Arturo?

The next dress was dazzling: a long sheath of pale silk embroidered all over with multicoloured sequins – sprays of red, gold and blue from shoulder to hemline. Nina moved to the mirror, the sequins catching the light in waves across her body.

Emilio cleared his throat. "Very colourful," he said.

"Don't you like it?" Nina said. "I think it's very *up-to-date.*" She swirled around the room, her feet quickstepping as the sequins swung and glittered. Passing Arturo, she took the cigarette from between his lips, inhaled quickly and then replaced it again. He remained motionless. Beside the screen, the maid was clasping a wreath of tissue paper.

"I suppose you think it looks frivolous?" said Nina, returning to the mirror. "You could be right. I wouldn't want anyone to think me less than serious."

"Looks like a costume for the cabaret," Arturo said.

Nina shrugged. "Well, in that case I'd better try another one." She stepped back behind the screen, and Arturo grinned at Emilio.

The third dress was all black – sheer chiffon set with tiny glass beads, over a black silk slip. Nina posed, one hand on her hip, head cocked. Emilio remembered their exchange up on the roof terrace, and the possibilities that had seemed to float between them then. *She thinks that you're my lover.* He remembered the warmth of her hand, her face when he kissed her.

"Well?" she said.

Emilio nodded, made an assenting sound in the back of his throat.

"Sure, why not," said Arturo.

In the mirror Nina turned from side to side, lips pursed. "I think so," she said. "But it needs something else."

She scooped a rope of pearls from the table beside the bed,

held them suspended against her chest. "This fastening's so difficult," she said. "Emilio, help me would you?"

He stood up. Hovering behind her, he took the two ends of the necklace, a gold screw thread and cap, tiny and delicate. His fingers brushed the nape of her neck, the line of downy hair, and he tried not to notice Arturo's smirk. He fumbled, sensing the colour rising to his cheeks, inhaled long and slow, lips shaping a curse.

With a click, the screw thread caught. Nina turned on her heel, the pearls swinging.

"Thank you darling!" she said. In her eyes, an unmistakeable gleam of mischief. She touched his cheek with a fingertip. "But your shirt's soaked!" she said. "What's happened to you?"

"Emilio had an accident with a soda siphon," Arturo said.

"Arturo did it," Emilio said quickly. "He's lending me one of his shirts."

"Or perhaps," Arturo said, "Nina could lend you one of her dresses?"

"Oh yes!" Nina cried. "They might fit you! You'd look so *beautiful*!" Arturo made a snorting sound, and the two of them burst out laughing.

Emilio said nothing, hot with discomfort. Nina subsided onto the cane chair, a hand pressed over her mouth. With her other hand she reached out and drew Arturo to her.

"Emilio in flashing sequins!" Arturo said, and squeezed Nina's hand. Emilio turned his back on them. He was their game now, their victim. It was hard to laugh along with it.

"Look at us," Nina said. "Look at us together." She took Emilio by the arm and drew him close, Arturo on her other side. The tall mirror showed their reflection: two men in smart black dinner dress, and a woman between them in pearls and chiffon. The room behind framed them, lined them with an electric glow.

“Don’t we look magnificent?” She drew them both closer, pressed in tight, and Emilio felt her shudder of delight. Across the room, he saw the maid waiting beside the screen, a shy smile spreading across her face. How fine we must appear to her, he thought. For a moment, his discomfort was gone – in the mirror’s glassy image, everything was perfection. Three young people in a brilliant modern world.

“Now,” Nina said. “Let’s see what the evening holds.”

14th July 1928

Together, you walked around the machine. He wore his grave expression.

"Tell me what we're looking at," he said.

You named the parts, as he taught you to do, checking each one: wheels, rudder, elevators, ailerons, exhausts, wing struts and bracing wires. Past the hangars and the boundary fences birds were singing, and from somewhere up in the haze of the morning another plane was already droning across the sky. You smelled damp, new-cut grass, engine oil, waxed leather and varnish.

There was a deliberate stiffness in the way he was standing. A few mechanics loitered beside the hangars, but there was nobody else to observe you. His attitude seemed one of professional distance, as if he were unwilling to get too close to you. He gazed up into the sky, hands clasped behind his back. His leather flying suit creaked.

"Very well, Signora," he said. "You may board the aircraft."

Two stirrup-steps cut into the fuselage; you gripped the strut and hauled yourself up on your left foot, then stepped over the side of the plane and down into the pit of the forward cockpit. You clipped the webbing straps around you, then checked the instruments: tachometer, compass, barometer, fuel gauge.

Fuel on. Throttle closed. Switches off. You checked and called back, making the hand signals. He stepped out of sight under the raised coffin nose of the plane, the propeller thudding as he pulled it around to draw the fuel into the cylinders.

"Throttle set," you told him. "Contact."

He swung the propeller and the engine caught. A jolt ran through the wooden ribs of the machine, then the engine banged and coughed greasy white smoke from the exhausts. He vaulted up into the rear cockpit as the plane lurched into life. At the end of the runway he turned smoothly and began to accelerate, the undercarriage jolting and bouncing off the turf as the speedometer needle swung past fifty knots. Throttle full open, the tail rose and the plane was horizontal, vibrating like a plucked string – then you were airborne, the field with its hangars and fences and the parked vehicles along the perimeter swooping away beneath you and the sky opening overhead.

His name was Eugenio Bianchi, formerly Captain Eugenio Bianchi of the 56th Reconnaissance Squadron. Once he had flown raids over enemy lines, led bombing missions over the mountains to Austria and Slovenia and mapped the oases of Tripolitania from the air. Now he taught wealthy businessmen and their wives to fly planes for recreation.

"It's quite the latest thing, you know," the woman at the Americano Bar had said. "Ever since the Lindbergh flight, it's been more popular than golf, or even skiing. This summer it could even be more fashionable than *sunbathing* ..."

"And the pilots at these schools are *real heroes*," her friend agreed. "So *handsome*!"

In your mind was the memory of the planes swooping and diving over the city, back in the years before your marriage. The future's promise written across the sky.

The first lesson was in the classroom of the flying school. Bianchi paced before the blackboard, striking marks with chalk. His manner was brusque and abrasive. You recited the parts of an aircraft. Instructions for take-off. Fuel, throttle, magnetos. You could have allowed yourself to be insulted by his distaste for the situation, but instead you held his stare, finding a relish in his discomfort. The chalk scratched furiously, darts and circles. He was tired of all this, his attitude said, tired of bored housewives pretending to be pilots on their husbands' money. You maintained a studious calm. The chalk snapped, the broken piece skittering away across the floor, and he stood locked still for a moment, then you both grinned.

When he took you flying that first day, you saw nothing but the cascading clouds, heard nothing but the roar of the wind pressing you down into the cockpit. Gravity hauled at your body, dragged at your cheeks beneath the tight band of the goggles, and your stomach punched and dived. Back on the ground, you climbed from the machine, exuberant, light-headed and triumphant. You wanted to embrace him but your legs gave beneath you and you fell onto the springy turf.

He called his plane a ship, which amused you at first. The aircraft, like its pilot, was a product of the war – a two-seater Ansaldo SVA. The school had smaller, lighter training aircraft, but Bianchi claimed that he preferred to take his pupils up in a machine that he respected. The plane was powerful and hard to control, and you knew that he meant to intimidate you. You would not let him. You would prove that you too could be the master of his machines.

He told you that the sky is not a void, that a plane does not hang in empty space, but floats suspended in a medium. The air is muscled with moving currents, huge invisible forces pushing and pulling, that the pilot must learn to recognise. He taught you the new geography of flight: the sheering winds of a mountain range, the solid rising heat of a city at noon.

Down on the airfield, on the gravel strip behind the hangar buildings, your chauffeur waited beside the car to take you home. Each time, as the car pulled away you looked from the rear window and saw him gazing after you. Four lessons, then you sent the chauffeur home alone, and went with Bianchi, riding pillion on his motorcycle. In his apartment the shutters threw stripes across the bed. His moustache prickled as he kissed you – a lingering breathless moment, delicate in its awkwardness, then he swept you up and onto the bed beneath him.

You told him that this was not the first time you had been unfaithful: he had not broken you, had not corrupted you. But when you made love, his eyes were open and you couldn't look at him. It felt like he was studying you, gauging your responses, learning your body. There were times you wished he would just hump away, carelessly and thoughtlessly, with an easy need for gratification, spill himself all over your belly then fall asleep and snore. It might have been easier that way to keep a distance from him. It felt shameful to want him so much, to need with such intensity. You wanted to be saturated with him.

At five hundred metres the plane levelled out. Between the competing forces of the air, the rising and falling masses of heat and cold, wind and cloud, you were suspended in a flimsy cage of wood and wire. The controls in the two cockpits were linked – through the stick in your hands and the bar beneath your feet, you felt the movements of his body. You followed his motions with your own, learning the reflexes. Bianchi's voice came to you through a tube from the rear cockpit. He was passing the controls to you.

Your feet were heavy on the rudder bar; the plane slid sideways in the air, engine racing. The machine seemed alive in the wind, and you were swimming, your whole body moving to maintain balance and direction, nerves stretched taut along the steel tendons that ran from the stick in your hand to the limbs of the plane. His instructions from the rear cockpit were calm and clear, speaking from nowhere, from inside your own head, the voice of God.

"Keep the nose up. Level the fuselage. Steady. Stabilise with the rudder …"

You needed his affirmation. His voice thrilled you and lifted you, carried you in the air. You could have been anybody now; you could have been nobody at all. It didn't matter that you had a name and a home and a husband and a son, that you were a respectful wife and a good mother. Up there you were nothing but a single consciousness flung out across the sky, without name without sex without flesh without earthly ties. And he was there with you, was part of you.

In the dim heat of the afternoons you lay across him, tracing your lips over his skin. Pooled in the hollow of his throat was a gold chain with a medallion – Our Lady of Loreto, he told you, patron saint of aviators. Not your religion, he knew. Sometimes it seemed strange that he asked so little about you; he wanted to know nothing about your life outside his own, had no curiosity about your husband, your son, or your family. He would not admit even the vulnerability of interest. Before darkness fell you left him and went back to that other life; you never saw him at night, never saw him sleeping.

Once, racing along the open road from the aerodrome on the back of his motorcycle, you passed an open-topped Lancia coming in the other direction; for a second, you saw your husband in the rear seat between two other men. In a frozen moment, it seemed that something like an understanding passed between you, then the car was gone and you pulled yourself tighter against the curve of his back.

Rising above the thin scrim of cloud you saw the Alps along the northern horizon, the peaks and ridges in perfect definition. You could have dived down into those frozen valleys, those troughs of snow and ice, soared up again along the diagonals of the rock slopes, ridden the moving masses of air as they swept down from the higher peaks.

Cloud funnelled into a great cylinder, ramparts of white vapour massing and dispersing around you, and the wind was first icy against your cheek, then a soft caress. He took the controls again, and the horizon dropped and wheeled about you, the weight of your own body dragging against the canvas webbing straps as you hung inverted and the ground sped over your head, mottled by huge moving shadows.

In the dimness of his room he told you stories about his life, and you lay with your ear pressed to his chest, hearing the voice quiet and deep from inside him. He talked about war with an unnerving candour – the exhilaration of darting through the sky pursued by death. He told you about flying over the desert on night reconnaissance missions, hunting for the encampments of the Arab rebels by the glow of their fires; about slipping into sleep, alone in the cockpit, lulled by the steady caress of the night air, then lurching awake, dazed beyond fear, lost in the vertigo. He talked about the accident that invalided him out of the service – the ground racing up from thick cloud and snatching him out of the sky.

With your head tilted you followed the length of his body, the curves and planes of muscle under taut skin, and imagined yourself gliding across a night landscape – a terrain of flesh. You reached down and cupped your hand over his penis: the soft flesh shrank from your touch, then swelled in your palm. A groan ran through him – you felt it in his chest. You dipped your head and plotted him with your kisses, marked him with your tongue, explored the tastes and scents of his body: desert musk, clear oil, salt of sweat; the metallic flavour of sperm.

Below you, the city wheeled into view: Milan, impossibly complex in brick and tile, intricate as a thumbprint on the earth. You swooped down towards it, a long gliding descent, then a solid column of air punched upwards: the heat of the city, of the roof tiles and the chimneys and the lives packed together down there rising in a thermal updraught and lifting the plane with it.

You felt the swoon running through the machine – the controls were live in your hands, the rudder bar kicking under your feet as the city tilted beneath you. The plane bucked and shivered, then began to fall, and just for a fleeting, panicked second, you thought that you really were alone; that he had vanished and left you to struggle unaided against the mighty forces of the sky.

Hauling back on the control stick, legs braced against the rudder, you dragged the plane up out of its dive. The air was shimmering all around you, the wind hard as a knife blade against your cheek. Tears welled at the rim of your goggles, and the wind whipped them away. You could let yourself drop now – you could release the controls and let the plane tumble out of the sky, let it fall like a dead leaf onto the city below, let it burst and flame over the rooftops, and it would not matter. He had the power to give you fear, and to release you from it.

"Very good," his voice said. "You performed the manoeuvre well."

6

10th May 1930

The music – if it could be called music – had a hollow, echoing quality. Each keening note hung, oddly sustained, issuing from one of the speakers placed at intervals around the small auditorium. At the front, Lino Osvaldi crouched behind a collection of piled boxes, his brow creased in concentration as he conjured the electric noises. Opposite was a gleaming black piano: the pianist sat stiffly, fingers spread on the keys. Above them, on a platform resembling a pulpit, Marinetti stood with hands on hips and chin jutting, staring up at the ceiling. A carafe of water and a glass were set beside him. There was a smell of hot metal wiring and dust.

Four rows of chairs faced the low stage. Some of the audience sat calmly, arms folded, waiting for the performance to begin; others whispered, fanned themselves rapidly with the printed sheets found on each chair.

SIMULTANEOUS FUTURIST
AEROPERFORMANCE
FREEWORD AERIAL POETRY BY THE
ACADEMICIAN MARINETTI
INTERPRETED IN DANCE BY
THE FUTURIST AERODANCER
ADRIANA GIOVENE
AND IN SOUND HARMONICS AND MUSIC BY
NOISE-MACHINIST OSVALDI AND
PIANO ENGINEER BENEDETTI

Cigarette smoke hung in a grey canopy, shot through with the gleam of spotlights. On his pulpit, Marinetti sipped water and winged his shoulders.

A low, flatulent roar burst from the speakers, bringing the audience to attention. The noise rose to a shriek like tearing steel, then dropped and stabilised into a turbine drone. Chairs grunted and squealed as those nearest the speakers moved further away. There was a trill of bright piano keys, then a sonorous chord. The speakers whined and hummed as Osvaldi adjusted the instruments on the desk in front of him.

Then the dancer appeared.

She took the centre of the stage, poised on her toes, slim and gleaming in skin-tight silver that left only a pale disc of face exposed. Above her head, a wavering corona of copper wires shimmered with every movement of her body, merging into a metallic halo. From her arms descended sheets of translucent material, fine silver fabric or gauze, streaming in the air as she moved. With a smooth circling movement she tilted her body to the horizontal, one leg stretched straight behind her and arms extended to either side, revolving slowly.

It was the blonde girl who had been with Fosca in the salon, Nina realised. She must be a professional dancer to move like that: a ballerina perhaps. Nina watched in fascination. The girl's body was poured fluid, liquid metal.

Sudden violent motion, the flex and spring of piston limbs. Around the dancer's head the wires shimmered and clashed as the piano issued a minor key nocturne over the steady electric drone. Emilio, sitting in the third row, remembered a film he had once seen. He remembered the great silver dirigible, the lady sky-pirate descending to earth in her electric capsule... He frowned, trying to remember what the film was called. From the pulpit, Marinetti's words rolled out over the heads of the audience, his voice filling the room.

"*Night flier, in an immense basin of transparent darkness gliding diving soaring at three thousand metres! Wings more resonant and lively than harps harmonies rhythms modulated by each vibration fill the frayed black void with astonishing new music!*"

The girl dropped onto braced knees, her head weaving. One leg stretched out straight; an arm described a sinuous curving line: a descending spiral. It was beautiful, Nina thought, and felt her spirits lifted, as if the light of the future was bathing her. Beside her Arturo leaned forward from his seat, his expression unfathomable. He had looked so handsome as they came downstairs together, immaculate in his black suit and white waistcoat, his jaunty shoes. He had been offhand about the commission, and she was grateful for that.

Thuds and squelches came from the speakers, punctuated by angled piano chords.

"*Below, great cities blaze with flashing signs, moonlight abolished as ten thousand electric stars declare incessant war against old firmaments and antique constellations. Suspended in the infinity of a new extraterrestrial spirituality my thought is the immense burst of a new rising sun!*"

Still the old power in his delivery, Berardi noted. That unrivalled vocal blast, one moment mimicking the strident staccato of newsboys yelling the morning headlines along the street, the next rising to the fervour of the demagogue, fists hammering the air. But his fury was all performance, all simulation. He never lost control. A little breathless, perhaps, his age counting against him, but he never broke sweat. Twenty years, and he was still coming out with the same stuff.

Berardi remembered him in the years following the war, when everything was in the balance. The graffiti on the walls of Milan: MARINETTI DUCE. He could have been that.

A leader to rival Mussolini, or so they had once believed. He was always the better public speaker. Seeing him now, burlesqued, carnivalised, he considered how close they were, the artist and the politician. But what kind of country would this be with Marinetti in charge? What kind of bizarre zoo would they be living in?

His stomach growled, and Berardi jogged a wrist from the cuff of his suit to check his watch. In the dining room upstairs, the servants would be setting the table for dinner. Beside him, Commendatore Scaglia was slumped in his seat, a bored frown on his face. Try not to think about him, Berardi told himself. Try to be unmoved, austere. Like a machine.

On stage, the dancer pivoted down into a crouch as the pinwheel beams circled above her. She rose slowly, expanding upwards, spinning in one outstretched hand a golden globe the size of a beach ball. Marinetti sipped again from his glass of water, squinting down at the papers on the table beside him.

"*Dawn,*" he declared, hands jutting in time with his words, *"streaming dances of drops sunrise surprise showers the deifying softness of perfume fluttering aerial gardens motorised by my frenzied gesture!*

"Pale chastity of sky triangulated by virile airforce squadrons as the world drinks the oxygen of machines into its insatiable lungs."

With the ball spinning at her fingertips the dancer glided across the stage, then launched herself back towards the pulpit. White light burst, glaring into the faces of the audience and silhouetting her. Nina, lost in the dazzle, found herself remembering the sensation of flight. She was airborne, leaning from the rear cockpit of a slim Fiat monoplane with a box camera between her palms. The world below her reeled and raced. Useless to try to focus; she could only capture the speed of it, the blur of the earth and the city sprayed across the lens. Now, as she sat in the auditorium, she felt that same sense of nausea, sudden but delicious. Her hands knotted in her lap, twisting the strap of her brocade bag.

A swift glissando rang from the piano, tuneful for a moment, before discordant electric noise crashed through it.

"*Simultaneous as time-space-dream-desire*" Marinetti declaimed, *"angels of speed darting swift explosive firebrands, the fury of their engines a great blowtorch that sears chars melts the metal points of the last stars!"*

Emilio felt the heat massing around him, the press of bodies in the smoky darkness. His shirt – Arturo's borrowed shirt – was bunched around his midriff, and the collar was chafing. He shifted sideways in his seat, uncomfortable, perspiration forming. To his right he could see Nina, her face in profile, eyes heavy-lidded. What was she thinking? He curled his fingers into the palm of his hand, remembering her touch when they sat together on the parapet. Her pale flesh in the twilight; her white dress clinging. The noise of the electrical instruments seemed to vibrate in his blood. His scalp felt tight and his breathing shallow.

He turned again to watch the stage, the flex of the girl's body as she moved, the sheen on her face. Silver and black, like the moving pictures. He was inside the film, the living light flowing over him. As the dancer stretched he saw the nubs of her nipples beneath the tight silver costume, the flat plane of her belly and the curves of her hipbones, her pubic mound under taut fabric. Around him rose waves of heat, enclosed desire condensed by the frequencies from the speakers. Sweat broke on his brow.

The dancer's movements were fast now, aggressively geometric. Her feet pounded at the stage, elbows jutting, then her body arced back as if electrocuted. A siren wail from the speakers, cut with jagged piano notes. With her head thrown back and the halo of wires shuddering, she advanced with measured step, tensed as if to spring.

"*Control towers radio attack dive!*" Marinetti called, his fist raised. "*Formation assaults of electric bombardment searing scourging atomising with laughing fury of machine-joy dead matter of passéist prefuturism, revealing naked splendour of machine-soul machine-love machine-war.*"

Deep foghorn drones from the noise machines as the pianist started hammering out notes, fast and percussive. On stage, the dancer was flinging her body into spiralling pirouettes. Back in the third row, Volpi sat hunched, his left knee jogging. He folded and refolded the napkin on which he had written a message to Marinetti, the sweat from his palms bleeding the ink into the tissue.

"*Skin metalised, blood electrified, gears of hearts nerves arteries lubricated by scorching ionic floods of LIFE.*"

All at once, piano chords and electrical noises merged into sonorous harmony, a sound like a vast rusty saxophone. Emilio imagined a machine like an X-ray, but probing deeper. A machine that could illuminate all the workings of the human psyche – the fluxes of desire, the wiring of the soul. He pictured everyone in the auditorium, revealed before the sublime force of the machine-melted into one single organism, pulsating in unity. He wanted to rise from his seat and spread his arms, to embrace everyone around him. Life – that was it. *Life, the future, and all its possibilities.*

Above the hanging smoke, the dancer stretched on her toes, head thrown back and arms spread wide, revolving slowly under a hail of lights.

"*Vulcanised by searing solar winds the mechanical geometric power of Fascist Futurist simultaneous dynamism assaults the gulfs between planets between stars between galaxies green white red victory incessant unending.*

"At the speed of a gyroscopic compass whirling at twenty thousand revolutions per minute we will liberate ourselves from space and time and ascend, ascend, ASCEND!"

The noise peaked into a long reverberating wail as the dancer stood still with arms raised: a tall, silver Y. She blinked. The front of her costume, heavy with sweat, hung slack between her raised breasts.

There was a long hush as the smoke settled. Somebody coughed; a chair scraped. Should they applaud? Was applause the correct response, or was it passé?

Berardi began to clap, then the rest of the audience joined him. There were a few whistles. Someone shouted, "*Bravo! Bravo!*" In the back row, Volpi was on his feet and pushing his way forward, shunting chairs aside.

"What's happening now?" Fosca asked loudly. "Are we all leaving so soon?"

Volpi reached the front and pressed the folded napkin into Marinetti's hand. Behind him, people were standing and starting to thread their way towards the doors. The stage was empty now, the dancer departed behind a heavy curtain. The speakers let out a brief whine and a pop as Osvaldi turned off the machines.

"One moment, one moment please," Marinetti called. He plunged down into the crowd, arms raised, commanding attention.

"What's this?" said Fosca. "What's happening? Isn't it over?"

"A moment, if you please," Marinetti continued, into the spreading hush. "In the true spirit of Futurist spontaneity, my friends, I would like to present an addition to our performance tonight..."

At the front of the auditorium, Volpi unfolded his sheet of paper. His naked teeth gleamed.

"Signor Arnaldo Volpi... Aerosculptor and free-word

poet," Marinetti continued, peering down at the wadded napkin, "will now declaim his latest composition ..." He stepped to one side. The audience, caught between leaving and staying, shuffled restlessly.

"*It is necessary to kill,*" Volpi said, in a flat, metallic voice, staring at his paper. He paused, cleared his throat, began again.

"*It is necessary to kill. Like a wild ferocious savage. We shall mow down with machine-guns. Which sing of death. The last defenders of a decrepit civilisation ...*"

His voice snapped and twanged as his free hand sawed wildly at the air.

"*Grrrrash!*" he said. "*Dadadadada! Krrsshh! Destroy! Destroy!*"

The audience, their attention caught, craned forward to watch.

"*In the name of the Duce,*" Volpi yelled, fist raised, stamping his feet "*Ahead, destroy! Like soldiers we march. Like soldiers we fight! Grrraaah! Yaaah! Rrrrratatatatat!*"

Marinetti's expression was impossible to judge. Was it annoyance, or perhaps amusement? Commendatore Scaglia, for his part, was sitting forward in his front row chair and smiling broadly.

"*The will is forged in the flames of war. Expressed in furious machine-gun joy. Dadadada! Krrshhh! Graaah! I want to make love to the weapons of our victory! Kneel before our cleansing steel! In the name of the Duce, for the glory of Italy. Rise! Ahead! Destroy! Destroy!*"

Volpi's arms dropped to his sides. A smoke-grained silence, then Scaglia got up and began to clap loudly.

Released, the crowd swirled out into the brightly lit gallery outside the auditorium. Some climbed to the mezzanine; others lingered near the open glass doors, hoping for a fresh night breeze. There was a sense of uncertainty among them, a stalking suspicion that the performance had not yet ended, that this was not an intermission but rather a shifting of gear – that something unknown would be expected of them. Their voices sounded thin and abrasive after the resonance of the music.

From the door, Mariagrazia called them to attention. "Dinner will be served in around twenty minutes! If you'd like to have another drink, your patience will soon be rewarded!"

The dancer, Signorina Giovene, her costume changed for a simple grey dress, stood near the auditorium door, surrounded by admirers. She appeared now very young, and slightly prim. Her yellow hair looked freshly painted. To the comments and congratulations she said barely anything, merely inclining her head politely, only once responding to a question: "Yes, La Scala."

A cry carried across the gallery, and Fosca sank to a crouch on the mezzanine stairs, palm to her brow. A small crowd at once formed around her.

"No, no, it's nothing," she said. "A momentary faint. My nerves, I think. The frequencies during the performance, perhaps. The music, or noise, I should say. I feel these things very sensitively … A glass of water, yes …"

Martino Rossi, face creased with concern, stooped to take her pulse, as Mariagrazia fanned her with a fluttering handkerchief. Someone suggested lack of food might be to blame.

"Oh no, no not that, I eat very little anyway. For reasons of health and fitness. Just a little yoghurt, some fruit. And no alcohol at all. Oh, but I feel such a strong sensation, a conflict in the room. I really can't explain …"

People turned to look, as if they might see some kind of aura, a malicious violet cloud spreading amongst them.

"Is she all right?" the dancer asked.

"Perfectly, I should say," Nina told her.

Across the gallery, a glass of fizzing liquid in his hand, Emilio would have preferred to be alone, silently in communion with the paintings. Stilled speed, abstract velocity, the severe beauty of clear geometries. Why were these pictures here, trapped in a private collection where hardly anyone could see them? They shouted of youth and vitality, mounted an assault on the banality of life ... They were supposed to ignite in the oxygen of the public gaze. Instead they were caught in this airless space. Emilio felt the other guests pressing around him, fogging the atmosphere with the imperfections of humanity: here was a suit too tight in the shoulders; here a cheek too thickly powdered, mossy in the electric light. The scurf of a pink scalp showing through thinning hair.

In a corner, Emilio saw one of Nina's prints, small and monochrome, easily missed amidst the blaring canvases. A photomontage, or photographic collage: silhouette shapes of aeroplanes repeated and superimposed in a spiral, like silky grey cut-outs. Very different from a man's art, Emilio thought to himself: the machines dissolving, blurring and metamorphosing. The title of the picture was *Aeroplanes in Love with the Sun.*

Her more recent photographs were in the show in Milan – cityscapes taken from above, from the cockpit of a plane, streets and buildings melded together by speed and motion, yawing into vertiginous spirals. A vortex of grey gaseous shapes. There was something poetic about them, something sublime and almost deathly in their annihilation of solid form and colour. The exhibition catalogue had mentioned "aerial spirituality". Arturo had found the phrase hilarious.

"Signor Calvi?" a voice said, and Emilio turned, startled, almost spilling his drink. The man beside him had appeared so suddenly that he might have risen from the ground. "We should talk, I believe."

Commendatore Scaglia, Emilio realised, disconcerted

by the man's uncanny arrival. He had been trying to avoid thinking about him.

"Perhaps Signor Berardi has told you something of me?"

Emilio nodded.

"I've seen your work in the exhibition in Milan, and I was most impressed," he said. "Clearly you're very, uh, talented."

Emilio could only smile politely, reflexively.

"But tell me," the Commendatore continued, "what do you think about the role of the artist in today's society?"

Emilio opened his mouth to reply, but could find nothing to say. Scaglia was observing him carefully now – this was a test. But how to answer? He remembered Berardi's words: Scaglia was highly placed, a rising star of the regime, soon to have a seat on the Grand Council … Emilio had known that he would have to speak to him at some point, but now the moment had arrived he felt ambushed, unprepared and uncertain. He had promised not to have this conversation.

"Let me tell you my views on the matter," the Commendatore said. "It seems to me that art should speak to us from the heart and from the soul, rather than from the head, don't you agree?"

"Well, yes …"

"I mean of course the heart and soul *of the nation*, not the individual. It must …" he made a grand and airy gesture, "reach for the profound and the universal. Would you not say?"

Emilio felt the Commendatore's presence beginning to engulf him. He tried to take a step back, but realised too late that he was standing in a corner. Scaglia's forehead gleamed with tiny beads of sweat, a liquid constellation. Emilio stared at them, repulsed, before the glinting Fascist Party badge on the man's lapel drew his attention instead.

"Painting today," the Commendatore continued, his voice gaining in depth and resonance, "requires something more than a purely artistic temperament, I believe. It needs an understanding of the responsibilities of art, or culture. Particularly now, in these difficult times. When I look around at these paintings here," – he stared about him, as if seeing the pictures on display for the first time – "these paintings, ah … tell us something about who we are, no? About what we represent as a nation and a culture. It's important for artists to recognise that obligation."

"Yes," Emilio replied, trapped under the heavy freight of words. To find a clear path out of the conversation, he needed to think, but clarity of thought was beyond him. He remembered his uncle's bruised face, his smashed mouth, yet all he could manage in response was a passive and indistinct agreement.

"When we admire the art of the past," Scaglia was saying, "the paintings of Da Vinci, or Tiziano, or … or other artists … what we should admire is not the art but the *Italianness*, the patriotic intent on display. Do you not agree? Good, good. What's needed is stern and wholehearted devotion to the cause, to the nation. An art that speaks of our national aspirations, of our national will and our glory as a people, as a *race*. The national will, of course, as manifest in the leader, and the party. A painting that expresses these things must be good, no matter what aesthetic considerations might lie outside of these concerns. A painting that does not is, well … fairly worthless. Do you understand me?"

"I think so, Commendatore." He was short of air. Scaglia was consuming all the oxygen in the room.

"Good! Some artists today, I know, still hold to these outdated views about individuality and so forth … I feared you might be one of them."

Emilio, about to deny holding any such views, managed to stop himself. He gave a wordless shrug.

"I believe," the Commendatore said, his expression more intent, "that you might be related to a certain person – a Signor Renato Pampilio?"

Emilio's throat constricted. He nodded. "Yes, he's my uncle."

"Hmm. And this uncle of yours has … run into some difficulties with the law recently, yes?"

Difficulties, Emilio thought, incredulous.

"Come along with me, somewhere a little more private," the Commendatore said. He laid a hand, unexpectedly heavy, on Emilio's shoulder and steered him, unresisting, towards the darkness of the terrace.

Outside the French doors, Marinetti stood with head thrown back, pluming smoke. The knot of people around him maintained a respectful distance: Berardi stood closest, with the journalist Lorenzo Assanti and a woman who must be his wife. Arturo loitered on the periphery, tense with attempted nonchalance.

There was no breeze; the darkness hung heavy as a curtain. The still air crackled with flying insects, and the smell of the lakeshore rose from somewhere, clammy and swampish.

"Have you met my wife, Excellency?" the journalist was saying, "My wife, Luciana Volani Assanti …"

The woman inclined her face in Marinetti's direction, bobbing a curtsy.

"A very fine show already, if I may say so," she said, "and dinner promises a great deal! Can you tell us anything about what you have planned?"

"No, no, I can disclose nothing," Marinetti said, with a suppressed chuckle. Clearly he was enjoying himself immensely.

Arturo smoked with short, abrupt gestures. What, he wondered, did Marinetti's mind contain? A brilliant collision of images, words, sensations – cities, machines, fast cars and aeroplanes, fantastic factories and blazing lights, the glowing steam of genius? It was more than twenty years since he had written his first manifesto, his declaration of war against traditionalism, conservatism, pacifism, the ossified morality and desiccated grandeur of the past … Older and heavier now, metal cracked and rusted, mired knee-deep in the glue of domesticity, matrimony, respectability, but always battling onwards, indomitable.

His Excellency Marinetti … He still glared from the portrait photographs, challenging the insult of the camera. These days, though, he appeared in the plumed hat and braided coat of the Royal Academy. Arturo had seen the pictures, and had hardly believed it possible. Yet perhaps it made a perverted sort of sense: there was an audacious wit in becoming everything he once professed to despise: the family man, the patrician, the Academician. But where were all those others now, who had supported him since the old days, had believed in and followed where he led them? They circled, moths around his flame, batting against the impregnable glass.

"But come on," the journalist was saying, "we're not children! Surely you can tell us something? The idea is, if I'm not mistaken, to reform the national cuisine?"

"Something of that nature, yes," Marinetti said. "And you people have been especially selected to be the first to have your palates revolutionised!"

"Oh, very good!" said the journalist's wife.

"Down with pasta! Down with bread!" Arturo called out, but in the laughter nobody noticed.

A sudden charge in the air, then a faint prickle of the scalp. All seemed to notice it at once and turned to stare at the sky. For a moment, nothing, then the light flared over the horizon, a harsh illumination.

"Heat lightning!" somebody said. There was another burst to the northwest, the shapes of the mountains revealed in a snapshot from the depths of the night, huge and threatening.

"Electrical war has been declared over Switzerland!"

Marinetti announced, raising himself up to address the night. "A new era of Helvetic electrodynamism has been born!"

The display drew others out from the gallery, and the space around the doors was crowded..

"I knew it!" said Fosca, now fully recovered from her ordeal. "The energy! I felt it!"

"Oh, but I do hope there won't be rain," said Mariagrazia. "Not with the roof terrace lit up specially!"

In the next flash of light, Arturo saw Emilio walking with another man. The Commendatore. They passed through the lit rectangles thrown from the windows of the gallery and salon, and disappeared. Arturo had not spoken to Emilio since the news about the commission. He could not help resenting him. His first and best chance for success and advancement, snatched from him by his closest friend. Perhaps there had been a mistake? Had Emilio been mistaken for him? No, of course not: it was just luck, the same bad luck that had kept him in poverty and anonymity all these years. Arturo hoped he wouldn't have to speak with Emilio. He had never been able to hide his feelings.

"Hello," said Nina, appearing beside him. Smiling, she slipped her hand into the crook of his elbow.

"Signora Della Torre," Marinetti called out, "I'm so glad you could come tonight!"

"Arturo here persuaded me." She winked quickly at him. "I believe he wanted to talk to you …"

"Yes … about the competitions," Arturo said, after a pause.

"The Biennale competitions, of course. It quite slipped my mind. Well, we have a moment now …"

"Excuse me, won't you," Nina said, releasing Arturo to Marinetti's presence and taking a few steps back. She hoped he would be grateful. If only all of her obligations could be discharged so effortlessly. She surveyed the crowd, feeling a need to attach herself to somebody agreeable. Fosca was loitering nearby; she turned away and noticed Renzo Martino Rossi near the doors. He smiled at her and waved, and she moved in his direction.

As she crossed the terrace, she caught sight of Emilio. Beside him, a palm clasping his shoulder, was Commendatore Scaglia. Both were in black and white evening dress, and Nina paused, reminded of another evening years before. Emilio was a little shorter than her husband, but he had a similar slim build, and Scaglia was heavier now than he had been. Yet for a moment the similarity was uncanny. Nina felt suddenly very cold.

Scaglia left Emilio and walked in her direction. She felt immobilised, trapped in mid step. If he glanced up, would he recognise her? She tried to muster some suitable words of greeting, something innocuous. He passed her, close enough to touch, and his eye met hers. His gaze caught, lingered, and skated away.

Then he was gone, into the house. She breathed deeply. Rossi was beside her now, making some joke about the lightning that Nina did not catch. She took a cigarette from his silver case, stooped to the twisting flame of his match. Her hands shook as she inhaled.

Emilio stood with his back to the light at the far side of the terrace, beside the stone steps that dropped to the lower lawn. Legs braced, hands clasped at the base of his spine, he tried to appear calm. Scaglia had gone, but the man's parting words filled his mind. *Think on what I've said, won't you?*

But already the details of their conversation were becoming confused. What, exactly, *had* the Commendatore said? And what had he, Emilio, replied? They had discussed the commission, of course, the painting required as a present for "a most important personage", that must be completed "with great dynamism". But it was the other subject which clenched at Emilio's heart. They had also discussed – or almost discussed – Emilio's uncle. Scaglia had promised him nothing, and Emilio had made no promises either. Even so, he felt a deep cringe of shame. While his uncle lay hospitalised, beaten, condemned for an invented crime, Emilio had talked with Scaglia, listened to his ridiculous views and passively given his agreement. How could he have done that? How little it would have taken to refuse.

It would be most unfortunate, the Commendatore had said, *if a matter like this were to damage the career prospects of one of this country's most talented young artists* … Nauseous, Emilio remembered the swell of pride he had felt at those words. *It might be possible, were you amenable to helping with this commission, for me to arrange some accommodation for your relative* … So, by one easy act, everything could be redeemed and set straight.

This is how it happens, he realised: a door opens and you step through. You enter the room beyond and there they are, the men of weight and influence waiting to reward and congratulate. They sit at a polished table, fingering their bankbooks. With money he could live a different life; with money everything could belong to him. His own apartment, his own car and a chauffeur to drive it. Commissions and prestige. Plush carpets, good hats, polished shoes, a man to brush his suit, another to run his bath; wireless sets that spoke his name, exhibition catalogues with photographs of his work. Luxury and security, the flush panelling of a well-fitting world, and his place within it. Emilio finally understood just how close he was to success, to acceptance. He saw the door and the distance across the threshold. How did he come to be here? How was he drawn to this point, unknowingly? After so long, was this not his due?

Emilio knew about advertising, had produced enough of it, working all these years for Bruccoli. *The Ligurian Riviera, The Amalfi Coast, The Delights of Sicily* … all rendered in brilliant jewelled gauche the colour of sunlight. Art was different. His painting was distinct from all that. It was truth rather than illusion. But Scaglia didn't want truth, he didn't want sincere expression. Scaglia wanted propaganda: advertising for the regime Emilio's uncle detested.

He remembered what he had said to Bruno Moresco in the salon: *the aesthetic judgement, the true worth of a painting … notions of good and bad don't apply* … Now he understood Moresco's scorn. Moresco, the veteran, with all his experience and regret, had known what Emilio could not. So many of the pictures in the gallery behind him were nothing more than propaganda, advertisements for youth, for speed and force. For the genius of F.T. Marinetti.

He knew that the commission would pay more than he had ever earned – though he had no idea, in fact, exactly what sum was being offered. He had forgotten to ask. But money could not be the reason he took it. It could only be for his uncle.

Emilio pictured the islands in the burning south. Lipari, Salina, Panarea. He had no idea where they would take him. A penal colony: lines of men marching under a haze of volcanic dust, guards in sweat-stained uniforms, the bored brutality of the truncheon and the solitary cell. Was that how it was? His mouth was ashen.

Another flash spiked the sky, illuminating a distant alpine valley. Emilio, squinting up at the vague shapes of the mountains, imagined some terrible conflict taking place – cannon venting blasts of energy, a clash of vast machines, the turmoil of huge unearthly forces. A low growl of thunder rolled down from the heights, charging the air with ozone, an invisible tide that broke over the terrace and the people huddled outside the gallery doors. Emilio closed his eyes and felt it pass over his face, like a film of warm silk, tingling against his skin.

8th December 1928

He woke suddenly, dragged back from the speeding precipice of a dream to lie stiff on the bed. Panic still whirled the room, the grey ceiling above him utterly unknown. The images in his head were already fleeting away, but he recalled them before they faded completely. Where was he? New York? City of rearing steel skyscrapers and plunging canyon streets in perpetual night; noise of screeching car tyres and shattered glass; the blare of jazz and the incessant clatter of Thompsons.

Emilio pivoted on the mattress, swung his legs out and down, sat. It was morning, and he was in his narrow bedroom in Milan. The sky spat rain at the window, and from the courtyard below came the boom and clang of the big steel bins. His room smelled damply of paint and turpentine, with a scent of coffee drifting in from the hall. Standing, Emilio splashed his face from the basin on the washstand – the cold made him gasp – then pulled a dressing gown on over his nightshirt and went out to the hall.

No sign of Arturo, and his bedroom door ajar. The hallway was still in early gloom, the doors to the salon and the dining room closed and their panes of frosted glass dull grey, no light from the shuttered chambers on the other side. Emilio walked along the hall to the kitchen. A pot steamed silently on the stove, the smell of coffee rising in a plume and fogging the window.

He heard the voice of the woman downstairs, hollering something, then Arturo's voice from the landing, shouting back. "What? *What*?" The apartment door banged open, and there he was in his bulky overcoat, hat pulled down tight, cradling a bag from the bakery and a folded newspaper.

"That woman's getting on my nerves!" Arturo called along the hallway. "Old witch, I can hardly pass her door without her yelling at me!"

"She thinks you're a police spy, that's why," Emilio said, yawning and scrubbing his head.

"Perhaps I am a police spy!" Arturo said from the kitchen. Emilio peered through the doorway: cream pastries spilling from the bag, and Arturo pouring the steaming coffee into the cups. "If I was, I'd report her as a subversive, and get her sent to break rocks!"

Emilio sat down and sipped his coffee. Ever since they moved into the apartment, more than a year ago, the woman downstairs had been complaining to the *portiere* and the landlord about them. She disliked them carrying bulky easels and canvases up and down the stairs, claimed they chipped the banisters and scraped the paintwork and generally lowered the tone of the building.

Their apartment was on the third floor of a turn-of-the-century block at the bottom of Via Lazzaretto. From the tiny iron balcony outside the salon window, perched high on the jutting angle of the building, they could look out over the gulf of the street and the corner directly below, where the clattering trams turned off Viale Vittorio Veneto, and across the wide tree-lined promenade of the Bastione Porta Venezia to the misty green expanse of the public gardens beyond. On clear days, the afternoon sun burst through the big grimy panes of the windows and flooded the rooms with light.

Inside, the walls were painted battleship grey, coated on thickly in the first week to seal in the floral wallpaper and polished gravy-brown wood of the apartment's previous incarnation. Now the big high-ceilinged salon was Emilio and Arturo's painting studio, the furniture all shifted out and replaced by easels and paint pots, sheaves of paint-caked brushes and a covered bucket of turpentine sitting in the middle of the floor beneath the chandelier.

Emilio's was the smallest room. From beside the bed, he could touch the walls on either side with outstretched fingers. It would have been the chamber of the cook or maid, when this was a bourgeois apartment. Arturo had the master bedroom, with a connecting door to the bathroom and its modern fittings and enamel bathtub. The windows of Emilio's bedroom, the tiny kitchen and the bathroom looked out into the central courtyard of the building, a deep square pit, corded with drainpipes. Somewhere down there, between the lines of dangling washing, a bunch of shabby fat-bellied palms thrust upwards from the courtyard floor, but their leaves were grey with dust all year round.

The apartment suited them both well enough. Before moving here, Emilio and Arturo had lived separately and shared a sequence of other studios – a room above a print workshop on Viale Piave, a big garret in an artists' cooperative on Corso Montforte, a strange shed with thin wooden walls beneath the railway arches that shuddered under the passing trains. The apartment was not perfect, but, with its high windows and residential calm, it was the best they could afford. Arturo had found the place and agreed to pay the bulk of the rent – one hundred lire a month to Emilio's sixty – which gave him the use of the master bedroom. He worked whenever and wherever he could, at a bewildering array of jobs – electrical engineer, car mechanic, labourer, cleaner – and was fired and rehired, it seemed, week by week. Emilio struggled by on whatever commissions he could pick up from Bruccoli, designing greeting cards, shop signs and cheap posters. They managed a sort of shabby elegance.

As a child, Emilio had been habituated to solitude. His family moved often, going where his father's work took them. In his first sixteen years, he had lived everywhere from Brindisi to Bologna, from Livorno to Rome, never staying in one place long enough to form genuine attachments. Arturo was his first real friend, although he could never quite understand what he got from their friendship, except perhaps an uncritical audience.

At first Emilio had been dubious about moving in with him, felt he needed to maintain a certain distance outside of the studio, feared his friend's reckless energies. Now, though, after a year, their lives were synchronised. Painting and living had merged into a seamless continuum. Sometimes it was intolerable, a hell of close confinement: Emilio's simmering silences, Arturo's explosive rage. But when things worked, life took on an almost heroic grandeur, in defiance of the surrounding, everyday nullity.

In the studio, their canvases stood side by side, stacked with faces to the wall so as not to distract, not to accuse. Their easels were set up in opposite corners, positioned to get the best of the light from the angled windows, or the feeble gleam of the dusty chandelier. Often they painted in silence, lost in their own separate inspirations. Arturo's mood was easy to judge – half the time he scowled behind his easel, scrubbing at the canvas, hurling brushes to the floor. When the work went well, though, he became expansive, singing, sometimes jumping up to take a turn around the room, whistling. A couple of times he grabbed Emilio and set off on a clumsy foxtrot between the easels. Emilio was more introspective: they complemented one other.

Some days they opened the connecting doors to the dining room and put one of Emilio's American jazz records on the gramophone, painting to the syncopated beat of the music, trying to trap some of that energy into line and colour. A cousin in Berlin sent the records by post, swathed in innocuous brown paper, messages from a strange and exotic other world – Jelly Roll Morton and his Orchestra, The New Orleans Rhythm Kings, The Clarence Williams Blue Five.

Once, in summer, they opened the windows and sat out on the balcony with the horn of the gramophone angled down into the street, blasting "Wolverine Blues" and "Clarinet Marmalade" down at the tramcars and the bewildered pedestrians passing below. Sitting there in the summer sunshine, with the noise of the rasping snares and the skirling horns, Emilio had felt a rush of joy course through him, as if he and Arturo were Nietzchean supermen, high on their summit above the earth. At such moments, everything seemed to make perfect sense.

Today, as he sat in the kitchen, the collar of his coat pulled up to his ears, Arturo seemed far from the carefree individual he had been that afternoon. He was barely twenty-seven, but already his face showed lines around the eyes; already a few silver hairs flecked the black at his temples. He'd had a sleepless night, but the tiredness went deeper than that. The enthusiasm, the ambition, were still there, but they burned deeply like the aching muscles of a distance runner.

"Have a pastry," he said, nudging the bag across the table. "They're the almond ones. Freshly baked. I just went out to buy cigarettes, but then I thought you might like some breakfast." He took a pack of Nazionales from his coat pocket and ripped off the seal. There was an apology in his voice, but it took Emilio a moment to remember why: the noise that had woken him in the early hours.

"You don't understand, do you? You'll never understand!" the woman had been shouting. A door slamming, and Arturo's weary reply, "Fine, off you go then."

Emilio, lurching briefly out of sleep, had barely registered the footfalls along the hall, the blast of the apartment door and the racket on the stairs. The noise had no doubt woken the woman below them as well. It wouldn't be the first time – twice now she'd sent her husband up, bleary and embarrassed in the morning calm, to protest. A small round man in a stiff collar, thin hair plastered weakly to his skull, he seemed more apologetic than accusatory. Perhaps after last night's performance they might all have some peace, for a while at least.

For the last few months, Arturo had somehow contrived to be having simultaneous affairs with two women, both named Ada. Last night's visitor – Ada One – was a short fleshy southerner from Calabria, while Ada Two was a pale freckly girl from some mountain village near Belluno. Come to think of it, Emilio hadn't seen much of Ada Two recently, so perhaps both had chosen to withdraw their favours.

He sipped his coffee. There were no women in his life, of course; nor had there been since that awful afternoon, more than two years ago now, when he'd finally broken up with Maddalena. He still missed her sometimes – but it would never have worked. She detested Arturo, for a start, and Arturo, as he had often said, found her "maddeningly vacuous". Emilio wasn't convinced of that. Had there not been a sincerity in her affection, the way she pressed herself against him on cold evenings, burrowing her face between the lapels of his overcoat? She had never liked his painting though, and when Emilio showed her his work for the first time she had giggled behind her hand. *Vacuously,* he had decided at the time.

No, it could never have lasted: he had chosen a new life. Besides, Emilio now dreamed of a different type of woman. A woman of a sort he had encountered only on the flickering screens of the picture houses. A woman of cool mystery, yet dark and fierce as a dream; a woman to be adored with wild passion. Sometimes he had tried to draw this woman, but never managed it, the result a mere assemblage of jutting angles and crabbed arabesques, or else somebody who looked like Maddalena through a distorting lens. But Emilio was sure this woman of his dreams existed, in some other world, which he would access one day. The world to which art would lead him. The world of his desire. The world of the future.

Outside the misted window, pigeons hacked and squawked along the sill. Arturo launched himself from his chair, clapping his hands and yelling *Ya! Ya!* The pigeons flapped into rapid motion, wings flickering against the glass, and dived away between the washing lines; Arturo subsided back into his seat, exhaling. Ignoring the pastries on the table, he lit a cigarette and dragged at it hungrily.

As he worked his way through the pastry, Emilio watched Arturo snap the newspaper open on the table and scan the columns. The cigarette hung from his fingers, its smoke rising straight up at the ceiling. Emilio felt the burn in his sinuses.

Arturo sighed and dropped the newspaper closed again. Rain spattered against the window, a slow staccato fusillade. On days like this, everything seemed to prey on his nerves. He cracked a long yawn.

"Last night I started thinking," Arturo said at last, "after she left, and I couldn't sleep. I was thinking about the syndicate."

Emilio paused mid chew. The pastry tasted cloying now, too much like a bribe. "I thought we'd already discussed that," he said.

"Yes, but I thought more about it. I think we should join, both of us."

The artists' syndicate, the Fascist Syndicate of the Fine Arts, had been looming over them for more than eighteen months now. They had tried to ignore it. Politics, they had told each other again and again, was the poison of art.

"Didn't we decide that you could join if you wanted to? I don't want to."

"But it wouldn't feel right if I joined and you didn't. We have to do it together."

Emilio was on his feet and pacing to the window. He slipped the latch and shot it open, leaning out into the damp air of the courtyard. Rain freckled his face, and the pigeons erupted in a batter of wings from the next sill.

"Sorry," Arturo was saying as he stubbed out his cigarette. "I know the smoke irritates you ..."

"It's not that." Emilio stared down into the depths of the courtyard, the desolate palms between the empty dripping lines. "I don't want to make state-sponsored art."

"State-sponsored art!" Arturo exclaimed. He leapt up too, striding back and forth – two steps to the stove, two steps back to the far wall, his coat flapping. "For God's sake, Emilio! What's so bad about it? They don't tell you *what* to paint! It's support, that's all, and we need it. I can't go on like this ... The syndicate would give us regular exhibitions, financial aid, a chance of actually prospering. Why, when for once the state takes artists seriously, treats us like any other professional worker, do you have to protest so much?"

Emilio said nothing. The debate had the familiarity of a headache.

"Can't you see this is progress?" Arturo was quieter now, conciliatory. "Aren't we supposed to be in favour of that? And what's the alternative? We carry on living our own private existence, like characters out of *La Bohème* or something? We might as well be wearing smocks and berets. This isn't the nineteenth century any more! Joining the syndicate would mean joining the modern world, the world of the future. This is the new Italy. We should learn to work with it."

"Oh yes," Emilio said grimly. "*Everything for the state, nothing outside the state, nothing against the state.*"

He had known, in his heart, that this moment would come. They had tried to keep the world at bay. The New Italy had passed beneath their high balcony and they had regarded it with wry detachment. It had never entered their souls. Outside in the city the slogans covered the walls, the bellicose songs and speeches blared from the radios and the uniformed masses paraded on the anniversary of the March on Rome. All of it had left them unmoved. But when year after year the parades get bigger and the music gets louder, and you discover that you are the only one not marching in step, what then?

"It isn't modern," he said, turning from the window. "It's a return to the Middle Ages, or the Renaissance. The state as one of those great princes, keeping a stable of tame artists to flatter their vanity and obey their commands ..."

"Exactly!" Arturo pointed a vindicating finger. "And without those great princes, no Michelangelo, no Da Vinci! Think what we could do, Emilio, with the support of the syndicate! No more struggling for exhibitions, no more squabbling for meagre sales! Besides, sooner or later membership will be compulsory. You won't be able to exhibit anything in this country – not a single pot, not a watercolour – without joining the syndicate."

"So you've made up your mind?"

"I would have joined months ago if it weren't for your objections."

Emilio suddenly understood that for Arturo this was a question of personal loyalty. The heat of his argument died inside him: what was his resistance but a stubborn allegiance to an inherited political position in which he had never truly believed? To let go of that now would be a relief, to allow himself to sink into the moving torrent of society, the warm flood of consensus carrying him into the future. Historical inevitability was a soothing concept after all: the surrender of responsibility. Give in to it. Cease to care. Cease to resist. Beyond the strife of ideology, there was friendship.

"Fine," he said. "We'll join. I didn't know you felt so strongly about it."

Arturo simply looked up from the table and nodded. He took a pastry from the bag and began to eat.

So that was settled. The open window poured cold air down Emilio's back, and he shivered. He slammed the window closed behind him, sealing off the world.

7

10th May 1930

Nina missed her footing on the narrow spiral stair to the dining room, caught a heel on the step and grabbed for the rail. A hand at her elbow steadied her at once. Half turning, she thanked the man behind. She suddenly felt dizzy, as if the alcohol had gone to her head after the brief jolt. Yet she had hardly drunk anything – just a few sips of the awful Spumante.

She felt the heat rise to her face. The details of the room blurred into a glimmering haze; she stood still, swaying, her pulse racing.

"Are you unwell?" a voice asked, and she blinked a face into view: Conti, with his wet mouth and inquisitive eyes. Nina shook her head, forced a smile and began to walk. The room was still dreamlike, lit by a metallic glare: the long table glinting and alien, the light bursting down in electric shards from a great chandelier of steel and glass hanging above the table like an exploding artillery shell. Fans spun on either side. Soft carpet muffled her tread, and she imagined her consciousness floating in a balloon tethered above her body. The place settings had name cards written in neat black calligraphy; scanning the table as she passed, she found herself staring at her own name. *Giannina Della Torre*. Me. She sat down.

The surrounding haze was beginning to drift back into focus, but she wanted to resist clarity for a little longer. The slow whirl of the room was blissful and horrible at once. Automatically, she took a cigarette from her evening bag; a match was struck and appeared from her right-hand side. She drew in a deep breath, flavoured with smoke, and held it until she felt the tightness in her throat. She exhaled slowly, letting the room settle back, attain shape and form. The mood had passed, the strange, sickly radiance gone. She watched the others at the table, arranged under the threat of the chandelier, all of them desiring to appear modern, hard-edged and knowing, viciously self-possessed. There were around thirty of them, seated on the small, uncomfortable metal chairs. She knew about half the guests in person, the rest by sight or by reputation. Arturo was down at the far end, near Berardi and Marinetti. Things seemed to be going well for him after her gesture of assistance out on the garden terrace. Scaglia was there too; Nina did not want to look in his direction.

Instead she watched Arturo talking to Marinetti: the way that he pursed his mouth, thumb pressed into the curve of his underlip. A gesture she knew well. She felt herself blushing with the sensuality of memory. A desire took her to be touched, or kissed. Not only, she realised, by Arturo. An indiscriminate lust. The fans above her drove the air across the tabletop, stirring the carefully folded napkins.

Glancing down at the table, Nina saw herself reflected – her face a white oval, haloed in silver fire. The plate set before her was a rectangle of polished steel, slightly dished, warping her image like a fairground mirror. The table itself was metallic; from a few steps away it had seemed a great platform of gleaming aluminium, but now she saw it was an ordinary table spread with a silver cloth, the silver already patchy and flaking. Winking grains of it were pressed into the heel of her palm where it rested on the tabletop. What she had thought were white irises in a vase were actually thin curled cellulose on stems of bright steel, but the effect was sinister and lovely under the fierce light.

Beyond the table, floor to ceiling screens, covered in silver paper, lined the room. They rippled and swayed gently in the draught of the fans. Something else about the table setting was unusual, but it took Nina a moment to notice: there was no cutlery.

"Quite impressive, don't you think?" said the composer Osvaldi, sitting to her left, as he gestured up at the perilous chandelier. He dropped his voice and leaned in to her shoulder. "It's one of Martino Rossi's designs," he said, his eyes bulging expressively. "I believe he calls it *Damoclean Shellburst*!"

"Yes, well," Nina said. "It's certainly very striking."

"Although I'm not altogether sure about these plates, are you? They hardly inspire appetite. Rather more likely to induce indigestion, having to gaze at oneself as one eats... though not in your case, of course!"

Nina ground out her cigarette in a little glass ashtray beside the plastic flowers. She was becoming aware of her hunger, the tight clamp in her belly no longer subdued by the drug. Opposite, beyond the cellulose blooms, she saw Fosca talking to Emilio, her cheeks furrowed with pantomime horror as she narrated some ghastly occurrence. Emilio sent a hopeless glance back across the table.

Fosca had changed into a tight, sleeveless dress, printed with lurid Chinese dragons. Mariagrazia, three places to Nina's right, was wearing a scalloped pink gown, while Signora Assanti, the journalist's wife, wore what looked like a harem dancer's costume wreathed in flimsy chiffon veils. Nina felt underdressed by comparison. Perhaps she should have chosen the sequins?

"All that Asti leaves one rather parched, doesn't it?" Osvaldi said. "A drink of cold water wouldn't go amiss..."

Even as he spoke, columns of waiters in smart white

jackets advanced from the stairs carrying trays of drinks – not Spumante this time, but large cocktail glasses filled with variously coloured liquids. The trays were set down along the table, the diners left to choose for themselves. Several of the glasses were fizzing.

"What do you think, Nina dear?" said Fosca, leering around the plastic lilies. "Are we supposed to choose based on the colour of our outfits, would you say? Fine for you, then. Anything goes with black, doesn't it!"

Beside her, Emilio gingerly lifted a blue glass to his lips. Nina took a glass of what looked like milk – and tasted like milk, she discovered as she sipped it. Milk with a shot of rum, and perhaps a hint of aniseed. Over the rim of the glass she watched the others around the table – choosing, tasting, considering.

"This appears to be green water," said Osvaldi, sounding disappointed. "Oh no, it's not …"

"Mine tastes like *fish*!" said somebody along the table. "Marinetti! Is this fish liqueur?"

Fosca put her glass to one side. "I never could stand rhubarb," she said.

A high-pitched whine cut through the sound of voices. Marinetti stood at the head of the table, running a wetted finger around the rim of his glass. "Friends," he said, powering his voice to the back of the room, "more than twenty years have passed since we first declaimed the bold agenda of Italian Futurism and began the revolutionary struggle against cultural, artistic and political stagnation."

"Hear hear!" somebody called from the far end of the table.

"Great victories have been won in those years. Now, in Benito Mussolini, we have a leader of truly Futurist fervour and temperament, guiding the state into an ever more modernist form."

"*Or something like that*," Osvaldi muttered under his breath.

"But … our restless and dynamic sensibilities shout for new battles! Therefore I announce to you tonight the birth of a new Futurist culinary aesthetic, a revolt against passéist and moribund traditional cuisine, which strangles and corrupts the vital energies of our race!"

There was a short burst of applause. Marinetti raised his hand, then continued.

"In this culinary battle," he said, "the first target for our scorn and violence must be the national addiction to pasta, which has for centuries made Italy seem humorous to foreigners."

"Well, I don't know …" Fosca began.

"Indeed so!" Marinetti declared, his finger jabbing out. "For what is pasta but a drug, a false panacea that fills the stomach with a mass of inert white pulp? Pasta clouds the mind, inducing apathy, languid pacifism and feeble defeatism; a body fed on pasta becomes a museum, decaying and immobile. Against pasta, which is flaccid, soft, lugubrious, we must deploy foods that are virile, active, vigorous. If we want to remake the Italian body as a machine fit for war and conquest, and for the increasingly high-speed airborne world of the future, pastaphilia must be banished to the Italy of the past, along with mandolin-playing sentimentalists and moustachioed waiters."

Laughter, and the sound of somebody banging one of the metal plates on the tabletop.

"As Futurists," he went on, "we look forward eagerly to the day when necessary nutrients, calories and vitamins will be provided by the state in chemical form, or even transmitted by radio waves or light beams. Then cooking will be liberated from the dull and routine necessity of providing daily sustenance, and take its place as a true art form! But with our characteristic impatience and impetuous audacity, we yearn to taste the cuisine of tomorrow today! And so, by combining modern scientific methods of food preparation with the verve and intuition of the artist, our Futurist food-technicians have created dishes of maximum explosive nutritive power, capable of rejuvenating and nourishing the heroic strengths and creative genius of the Italian people. And this evening, my friends, you will be the first to experience them!

"Our intention," Marinetti continued, with a dramatic gesture, "is to let the food we eat, and therefore the lives we lead, be as inspired, lyrical, dynamic, revolutionary, ephemeral and aerobatic as the greatest Futurist paintings or poetry."

More applause, and cheering from the end of the table. Nina saw Arturo rubbing his chin thoughtfully, a smirk flickering.

"Futurist food technicians?" Volpi sneered across the table. "I'd like to meet one!"

"Well, I certainly hope they'll produce something substantial shortly," Fosca replied, "before I starve to *death.*"

Her last word coincided with a synchronised hush, a momentary silence around the table into which the word plummeted. Fosca let out a quick, tight giggle. "Don't you hate it when that happens!" she said.

Now bottles moved down the room – iced white Soave and Vernaccia, full red Barolo and Grignolino – with trays of sparkling glasses.

"I love that sound," Nina said as the waiters poured. "Wine into a glass."

Mariagrazia got up, proposing a toast to the building, and this first meal eaten within it. And so they all stood, the architect, Conti, shrugging with assumed modesty. Glasses were raised and the toast duly drunk – to Conti, to his design, to all modern architecture and the bold new world that it would bring. Conti began to talk about architecture, telling them of theories and practices, his moist lisping voice fluttering a confetti of foreign names: Le Corbusier, Walter Gropius, Adolph Loos ... But before his monologue could gain momentum, a muffled gong sounded, declaring the arrival of the first course.

"Simultaneous Antipasto," Marinetti intoned as the waiters placed dishes along the table. "To quicken the culinary intellect and awaken digestive creativity!"

"Rice balls?" said Osvaldi.

Rice balls indeed, in conical piles, lightly fried and steaming. Nina took a couple, hot between her fingers. She nibbled gingerly at them, then, too hungry to care, gulped them down. One was stuffed with orange marmalade, the other with caviar.

"Marinetti, do you remember," Martino Rossi said as they ate, "the Simultaneity Day you tried to organise? What was it going to be, again? Poetry declamation and simultaneous sack race!"

"Water polo and simultaneous boxing," Marinetti said with a florid gesture. "A shame we never managed it. We should try it again. Political oration and simultaneous high-wire acrobatics!"

"Choir singing and simultaneous fornication?" Conti suggested.

"Pornography and simultaneous Papal denunciation!" said Rossi, grinning.

Nina sat back in her chair, cooling her palate with white wine. Most of the appetisers had quickly been eaten; only rice crumbs and few of the less appealing – liquorice, raw onion – remained. A vestige of the strange mood that had gripped her as she entered the room still lingered. The table and the other diners seemed unreal to her, like the afterimage of a dream that she might dispel with a blink or a wave of her fingers.

Suddenly the light blazed hot orange, as tall lamps in the corners of the room replaced the chandelier's glare. Marinetti was on his feet again to announce the arrival of the next course.

"I have great pleasure in presenting to you," he declared solemnly in the tropical glow, "an entirely new and revolutionary dish, prepared by our chefs to a formula by the extraordinarily talented Renzo Martino Rossi," – a bow from the waist by Rossi – "*AZZURRICE* – a synthesis of the skies and seas of our Holy Mother Italy!"

A reverent hush fell as the plates were set out, each one adorned with a heap of violently blue risotto, churning with seafood. Chevrons of rice cracker formed white sails on a steaming sea.

"I had no idea you were involved in this, Rossi!" hissed Osvaldi.

"Oh, just an idea or two thrown in," Rossi replied. "The blue is merely methylene dye – flavourless, unfortunately, but we added vermouth, a dose of grappa and some eau de cologne."

"How are we supposed to eat it without cutlery?" Fosca asked, gazing down at her plate. "With our hands, like at a children's party?"

"You could do that," Marinetti said. "Or suck it up off your plate, if you prefer. To eat futuristically is to indulge all the senses, touch as well as taste and smell … Not to mention your ingenuity!"

Nina took one of the crackers and used it to scoop up a sticky lump of the blue mass, lifting it carefully to her mouth. At first the taste was much like an ordinary risotto, the rice cooked just right, blended with parmesan, with a fine slice of something – squid, perhaps? Then the spirits hit the back of her throat, burning like seawater in her sinuses. She swallowed heavily, reaching for her wineglass.

"Do you think," somebody was saying, "that I might just have a fork? I mean, I understand the principle, but …"

Her hunger urging her on, Nina ladled up another mouthful. The taste wasn't so bad once you became accustomed to it. Unfamiliar, yes, and with a somewhat alarming chemical tang, but edible. She ran out of crackers and began to use her hands, squeezing the rice together into lumps. The colouring dyed her fingers a dull blue. Across the table, Volpi held the plate up to his face, shunting the rice into his open mouth; a morsel fell onto his shirtfront, leaving a long blue stain.

"Is my mouth blue?" Osvaldi asked, turning to Nina. All around, radiant in the orange light, hands and mouths, cheeks and chins were spotted and daubed with the colour. Fosca waved her fingers before her face, entranced by the sight of them, smiling with blue teeth.

"Remarkable, remarkable," Osvaldi said. "I just hope the colour isn't permanent …"

The waiters were returning with basins of warm water and towels, to sponge and dab and soak. Nina pressed a towel to her mouth, relishing its freshness, and realised that the man sitting to her right had not said a word. She turned to him.

"I don't believe we've been introduced," she said.

The man was sitting far back in his little chair, as if to absent himself from the rest of the table, and had not touched his food. Nina knew of him, even if she'd never spoken to him: Bruno Moresco, one of Emilio's favourite painters. He lounged back, formidable in his dark square suit.

"No," he said, "I suppose not."

They paused. Nina held out her hand, still faintly blue. The slightest gesture of a shake, and he released her. Nina opened her mouth to speak, but stopped. There was something repellent in his languor, the flat boards of his face. Something in the nature of a challenge.

"You don't care for the blue food?" she asked. Moresco looked down at his plate, as if surprised to find it still there.

"No," he said slowly. "I prefer to admire it and leave it unmolested."

Nina shrugged and turned from him. On the opposite side of the table, Fosca was wiping Emilio's cheek with a wadded napkin – an attention to which he was submitting with obvious embarrassment.

"Such an ascetic face you have," Fosca told him. "Almost monastic, in fact. You look like a holy father from an old painting, do you know that?"

"No, I'd never noticed," Emilio replied.

"You do, though. He does, doesn't he, Giannina? Such an aura of holiness, I almost want to kiss your hand. I believe that you must have been a priest in a past life. Do you believe in past lives?"

"No … not really, no."

"Oh, but you should! I myself am a firm believer in reincarnation. In fact, I have proof! You know, I shouldn't tell you this, but ever since I was a little girl I've felt a very strong identification with Lucrezia Borgia …"

"Pfff!" said Conti from across the table.

"How can you mock what you don't understand?" Fosca said to him. "You really are too much of a rationalist. The principles of reincarnation are attested by many of the greatest minds in Italy! Why, the last time I spoke with His Excellency the Duce we had a very interesting discussion on precisely that subject!"

"Of course you did."

"Yes, we did! I mean, who could think that a man like the Duce could have come from nothing? Yes, he is the son of a village blacksmith, but his soul is ancient. I could feel it in his aura. He is undoubtedly a King or an Emperor reborn!"

"Isn't that the odd thing about reincarnation?" said Martino Rossi, still cleaning his hands with a towel, "These people who're hypnotised to remember their past lives always turn out to have been Garibaldi, or Julius Caesar!"

"Or Napoleon!" Osvaldi chuckled.

"But I'm not talking about just anybody! I'm talking about Benito Mussolini!"

"If I had a past life," said Volpi with relish, "it was as a supercharged particle of white-hot energy streaking across the cosmos at violent and unimaginable speed, zealous to be reborn as … me!"

The gong sounded, and the plates of *Azzurrice* were conveyed away. The light switched to a blue-white, reflected near-blindingly off the silver tabletop. From somewhere behind the metallic screens came the weep of a solitary violin …

"Ah, music!" sighed Fosca.

… replaced by the abrasive roar of an engine. After three seconds of engine noise the recording switched again. Lush operatic vocals swelled forth, then vanished. Silence.

"Friends," announced Marinetti, "with typical impetuosity we plunge onwards. It would be tedious, not to mention anti-Futurist, to give too thorough a description of each new food production, but in the case of the next one a few words might be advisable. These waiters now moving amongst you carry both edible substances and tactile devices, together comprising *AEROFOOD*, created from a formula by the genius artist Fillia, sadly absent tonight."

The dishes appeared as he spoke. On each circular white plate were arranged three black olives, an orange kumquat and two slices of salami. To the left of every diner, meanwhile, was a block of wood, the sides covered with red damask, black velvet and sandpaper.

"As I have said, to eat futuristically is to employ all of the senses simultaneously. I suggest, therefore, that while your right hand conveys the edible substances to the mouth, the left explores and appreciates the tactile block, to produce unpredictable sensations of flavour, texture, colour and scent."

Marinetti's words were punctuated by random snippets of Neapolitan operetta, alternating with fragments of a Bach violin sonata, all emanating from two gramophones concealed behind the screens at the end of the room. The engine noise broke in intermittently.

Nina surveyed her plate, contemplating the aesthetics of the arrangement, the asymmetry of coloured ovoids and circles on the white disc. There was something vaguely Japanese about it. Her left hand caressed the block with its tactile surfaces. She tried an olive as she touched the sandpaper, and tasted gritty earth – the flavour of the olive made blacker, somehow. The kumquat delivered a spike of bitter citrus; the velvet seemed to turn the bitterness synthetic.

Nina shut out the jarring noises that crackled from the gramophones, letting the sensations fill her and carry her. Every combination had its own association, playing a part in the theatre of memory. The citrus conjured an image of a shuttered room in a hotel in Juan-les-Pins, one summer years ago. Blades of sunlight streamed between the slats at the window, and she lay face down on the bed while the fan turned above her. Not the keen whirr of the fans above her now in the dining room, but a slow afternoon throb. She'd fallen asleep on the beach and her back had burned; waking from dull medicated sleep, she had found Amedeo beside her, sitting in a chair in his white linen suit. He had spread pale green ointment on her back, hot and then cool on her skin, while a generator droned, coughed, droned in the yard outside.

All around her, hands were touching and caressing, self-consciously fondling the silk and the velvet, as if they had never touched, never tasted, never felt before. There was a laugh of delight. The waiters circled, lifting brass pump-bottles to spray the air above the table with scents of lavender and burnt cork, as the scraps of music crashed, soared and whined.

Nina's hand hovered over the plate again, fingers coming to rest on a salami slice. She felt the oiliness of the meat. As she raised it from the plate, Moresco reached across and took her wrist, his hand closing over her bracelet, the amulet of the *Shaddai* on its slender gold chain. A large hand, heavily veined. His touch was firm and assured.

"Not very devout," he said, in a near-whisper, "to eat pork. Even if you do wear the name of the Almighty on a medallion."

She should have known from his name, but somehow it had not seemed important, so accustomed had she become to thinking nothing of religion – her own or anybody else's. Letting the salami drop back onto the plate, she drew back her hand.

"It was my mother's," she said. "She was observant. I'm not really. I just wear this for luck, I suppose."

"I know of your family, I believe," Moresco said. His hand rested idly on the tabletop now, his fingers twitching at a napkin. "The Della Torres of Orbassano, am I right? Wealthy. Assimilated. My own background was less affluent, so we tended to hold on to whatever we possessed. Even so, it's easy to slip." He took the salami from Nina's plate, folded it between finger and thumb and put it in his mouth. Nina wondered if she should feel offended.

"You should never betray who you are," she said quietly.

She pictured her father, dying at fifty-eight. The summer of '26 in the old house at Orbassano: he lay in the upstairs bedroom with the view of the cedars lining the drive, his face yellow and moist as old candle wax. He said he was cold and wanted the window closed; the room grew hot and filthy with the smell of him. Flies circled in the heavy air over the bed; they made her gut clench to see them. Beside the bed was a steel kidney basin full of bile. The nurse brought her boy into the room, her little Marco, only three years old, and held him up to look at his grandfather. She remembered the child's unguarded expression of sick dread and repulsion. The old man stretched a hand from the bed, but the boy could not understand. He ran crying from the room and down the stairs.

Her father had been a secular man his whole adult life, but there on his deathbed he converted to Christianity and the Catholic faith. In the hallway her brother Giuseppe wiped tears from his cheeks. *Never betray who you are*, he kept saying, *no one should betray their own past.* The priest had to stoop over the bed to hear the old man's words. He held the crucifix tight in hands as he died; when the windows were opened again, Vittorio had prised the cross from his father's grip and flung it outside.

"Betray who you are?" Moresco said. "Perhaps one shouldn't, but people do, don't they? People betray themselves all the time. Haven't we all? Until one day you decide that you've betrayed enough."

Nina had the unnerving sensation that everyone around them could hear his words. The room seemed to have shrunk to a nimbus of pale light around them, the voices of the others at the table only a vague ripple in the air.

"But surely Della Torre isn't your married name," he continued. "In fact, I believe I knew your husband as well. Amedeo Sorani, wasn't it? I use the past tense, but of course he's still alive."

"Yes," Nina said. "He had to leave the country." She

felt petrified. Was her connection to Amedeo really so widely known? Sorani was a sufficiently unusual name to be memorable in the small world of the Milanese Jewish community, and Amedeo himself sufficiently prominent a figure. But wasn't it odd that she and Moresco had been placed together at the table – the only two Jews in the room? Who had sent this man her way, and why?

"Yes, he had to leave," Moresco said. "Although certain others are still with us, unfortunately." He was looking away as he spoke, and Nina followed his gaze towards Commendatore Scaglia, seated at the end of the table. "*He* remains, for example. He came out of the whole thing rather well. He wasn't always a Commendatore, of course." Moresco spoke in a breathy whisper. He had drawn much closer to her as he was speaking, and it occurred to Nina that they must appear locked in some flirtatious exchange.

"I'm sorry, I don't understand what you're talking about."

"No," he said, with a wry frown, "I don't suppose you do."

Nina knew very little about Scaglia. He had been one of those on the edge of her husband's aura – a vague but obscurely important figure. She had always been aware that this man was far more significant than her husband liked to pretend. She had known, too, from her husband's evasiveness whenever his name was mentioned, that Scaglia was more than an acquaintance. She had known, but had pretended not to know, for that was what her husband wanted.

"And now he's been appointed vice-president of the National Institute of Fascist Culture ... Although some people aren't so convinced by him. You'd think anyone who had exposed a plot against the head of state would be immune from suspicion, eh? But now that he's had to demonstrate his loyalties once ... Well, let's just say he isn't in a position to refuse further requests ..."

Suddenly Nina felt very exposed. Anybody could have overheard Moresco's words. She couldn't quite grasp their meaning, but sensed the danger in them. The threat that Amedeo had warned her about – to herself, to her son – was close now.

"When was the appointment?" she asked quickly.

"A little over a month ago. End of March, I believe."

Forty days ago … When would Amedeo have learned of it? The new French airmail route carried letters to Buenos Aires in under ten days. There had been enough time for the news to reach Argentina, and for his return letter to find Nina in Milan. And even before that he would have heard rumours, warnings … *Matters have taken a serious turn, and you are no longer safe in Europe. For your own sake and our son's …*

"Don't be fooled by his title," Moresco said. "The closer you get to power, the more there is to fear. Nobody is immune, and certainly not him. There are rumours, you know, that he's under investigation even now …"

"Please don't tell me anything more. I don't want to know."

Nina turned away. She saw mouths moving, heard voices speaking but could not connect the two. She noticed that she had lit another cigarette and smoked half of it without noticing. Dropping it into the ashtray she reached for her wineglass, but found it empty. Already a waiter was at her shoulder, leaning across with the bottle. But as he refilled her glass, Nina realised that it wasn't wine she wanted, not cigarettes, not food. Cocaine, she thought. *Yes yes yes.*

No. She had to concentrate. After the meal, *immediately* after the meal, she would leave this place. Could she somehow convince Arturo and Emilio to follow her?

"And one day," she heard Conti say, "we shall have cities as clean and functional as razors. And when that day comes …"

His voice cut off as the room was pitched into darkness. Afterimages of colour burst and died, as all speech died, into a ringing, vertiginous black. Nina reached out in fright, and her hand met Moresco's. She clung to him tightly, fingers clasping and interlocked, as the world spun.

12th February 1929

The train left Paris as night fell, pulling out of the Gare de Lyon and south through the suburbs, gathering speed across the flatlands of the Seine. In the dining car, alone at her table, Nina turned to the window and sipped her dry gin soda. There was rain outside, and the reflections of the other tables in the dining car hung suspended within it, yellow and blurred by the water streaming across the glass. Now and again a station passed, and Nina tried to read the nameboards in their little puddles of gaslight beneath the awnings, but the train was an express and moved too fast. It was the same train that she had taken years ago, on her trips to Paris with Amedeo.

There were a few people left in the dining car, lingering over late suppers – the duck terrine and the veal cutlets. All were men. Nina watched them reflected in the window. One man seated across the aisle, neatly dressed with shining pomaded hair, lifted his wine glass every time Nina took a drink, as if he might shortly ask to join her at her table.

On the other side of the window the water beaded and broke, making fast diagonals across the black glass, cancelling the faces of the men in the dining car, all those potential encounters. The train powered southwards, the locomotive, streamlined and bullet-nosed, shovelling smoke back over its shoulder. Paris was far behind in slumbering dusk and the winter chill, and Nina was going home.

She had arrived in Paris in early October, as the last washes of sun lightened the grey stone of the city. Two weeks beforehand, her life had fallen apart. Her husband Amedeo had sent a note telling her that he was gone – not just *leaving* but already *gone*, with a finality that implied the pointlessness of further enquiry. Three days later, her lover Bianchi had died in a motorcycle crash. An hour after dawn on the road to the airfield – a patch of oil spilled on the tarmac. He had lain unconscious for an hour before he was found, and was dead before he reached the hospital. Amedeo had left her an annual allowance of twelve thousand lire, an apartment in Milan and arrangements for the schooling of their son Marco in Switzerland. Bianchi had left her pregnant with his child.

Paris was her only option, but if she was going to be unhappy, she would at least be comfortable. She took a suite in the most expensive hotel she could afford, with high windows overlooking the Luxembourg Gardens. For ten days she delayed making the final decision. In the park, she walked between the bare trees, watching the children playing, and in the evenings she drank until she was drunk enough to cry, then wept for all the lost love, all the bad luck, all the false morality and unfairness of the world. She told herself that if her husband had not left she would have kept the child. Amedeo would have understood; they would have come to some arrangement. But with him gone, and Bianchi gone, she had no choice. Or so she told herself. She thought of her son Marco far away in Montreux; he seemed to grow daily smaller and fainter in her imagination, as if he was shrinking back into a distant infancy, into a memory, into an idea.

On the eleventh day, when she could delay no longer, she took the Metro to Passy and found the address she had been given by a friend in Milan. A private clinic, clean and modern, in a respectable residential street. After the operation, and forty-eight hours of heavily sedated bed-rest and observation, she was released. She walked beside the

Seine in the soft drizzle, feeling cold and sick as the drugs washed out of her. The world was an assault on her senses, and her body felt a raw and alien thing. Back at her hotel, she drank brandy from the bottle until she could vomit. She tried not to think about Bianchi. She tried not to think that she had just killed the last remaining part of him.

She took a cheaper room at a hotel in Montparnasse, on Rue Notre-Dame des Champs. She went to the famous bars and the cafés – the Dôme, the Select, the Rotonde, the Bal Nègre – and found them jammed to the doors with Americans, a few third-rate artists sitting at tables amidst the throng doodling sketches on napkins and selling them to pay their bar bills. Everyone told everyone else that they should have been there ten years ago, or five years ago, or last summer; any time but now. Everyone agreed that Montparnasse was dead, that Paris was dead, that the whole of Europe, most likely, was dead. Probably the only life remaining was in Soviet Russia, or the jungles of the Congo, or in the canals of Mars.

"The only real artists left in Paris are the Surrealists," a woman told her at the Select, "and they're all Communists and hate everybody!"

Nina went shopping. She bought clothes by Patou and Chanel, perfumes by Guerlain, jewellery by Hermès. She went to cabarets and theatres, she danced to live jazz at Le Grand Écart and the Boeuf sur le Toit; she got herself noticed. She got invited to gallery openings, cultural salons and the Vicomte de Noailles' house parties. She was congratulated on having escaped the tyranny of Mussolini's Italy. One woman – the daughter of a textiles magnate – showed Nina the portrait of Leon Trotsky she wore in a brooch. "Some nights I kiss it before I go to sleep," the woman said.

In an attic in Saint Germain she attended a private

screening of Eisenstein's *Battleship Potemkin.* It was an uncut copy of the film, illegally imported and very rare, but she had been up all the previous night dancing and fell asleep halfway through. She only awoke at the end, when the red flag was raised, and half the audience stood up and began singing the *Internationale.*

She took lovers: a Japanese lithographer, an Algerian saxophonist, a disgraced American tennis star. She had dinner with a Romanian grand duke in full military regalia, whose chest blazed with medals and decorations. "The world, my dear, is clearly going to the dogs," he told her, "so we have a duty to enjoy ourselves while we can" – and he iced the rim of her cocktail glass with cocaine.

At the Gaumont Studios in December, she was an extra in a costume epic, shivering in a flimsy robe and pretending to cheer charioteers. That evening she went home with a Polish photographer called Tadeusz, who was connected with the Surrealists and claimed to know everybody. "You want to be an art whore?" he asked her. "In Paris it's easy. You want to meet Picasso? You want to meet Stravinsky?"

"Not really," she said, lying on the bed naked, and lit another cigarette.

She detested Paris in winter: the dripping black streets, steeped in nineteenth-century morbidity, the damp, stewing languor of the cafés, the stumpy prostitutes on the street corners. It snowed, and grey slush piled up in mounds in the gutters. Nina stayed in Tadeusz's studio, injecting cocaine. "Always into the vein," he told her, guiding her hand. "With coca, if you spike the muscle tissue you paralyse it." She guided the needle in, imagining herself paralysed, turned to white marble, numbed to all pain.

Tadeusz had no money to pay for his addiction. She lent him cash that he could never repay. He sold her one of his cameras, a Contessa Nettel, and all his darkroom equipment, and she taught herself how to develop photographic prints. The drug made him impotent, but they would rush out together into the windy streets, crashing through the cafés, ranting in cemeteries, hating and loving each other erratically, like flickering electric bulbs. One night he did not come home. The next morning she heard from the concierge that he had been arrested and was in jail. He had tried to rob two American tourists at knifepoint on the Boulevard St Michel. She packed her bags.

The Paris–Rome express was not as popular as it once was, and Nina was the only passenger in her sleeping compartment. When she returned from the dining car she found the bed already made, blankets and crisp white sheets embroidered with the monogram of the Paris-Lyon-Mediterranée railway company. In the washing cubicle she wiped her face, cleaned her teeth and regarded herself into the mirror.

In Paris, mirrors had surrounded her. Her reflection had stalked her through the bars and the cafés, staring back from stainless steel and glass, from the black convexity of a camera lens. She became accustomed to seeing herself as others saw her, to seeing her own image as separate from herself. She had left that person behind her now. All the dead matter of the past was left back in Paris; she was clean and free from it and the train was speeding her into the future, through the mountains and across the wide plains of Italy in morning sunshine.

She leaned closer to her reflection until her forehead touched the mirror pane.

Sleep held her lightly for an hour or two. Then she woke, uneasy, with the train rocking side to side, moving fast. She sat up, put on her shoes and pulled a coat over her pyjamas. She thought about opening the window in the compartment, but the rain was still streaming against the glass.

Small blue bulbs lit the corridor outside. Nina walked slowly, feeling her way, still drowsy from sleep, passing the closed doors of other compartments with the blinds pulled down to seal in the speeding dreams of others. At the end of the carriage she yanked down the window and the breeze rushed at her. She pulled the lapels of the coat tight, leaned into the angle of the door and lit a cigarette, the last of her Gauloises. The air came in flavoured with rain and wet green and engine smoke, and the noise of the rails was huge in the dark.

Nina gazed out into the night, wanting to stay like this, awake and alert, for the whole journey. Stations passed in the small hours, the deserted platforms and the spreading steel deltas of rail yards empty under the moon: Mâcon, Lyon, Chambéry, the train ghosting slowly through, breathing steam, a slow wail of brakes.

A little after dawn, in the grey of the mountains, the train halted at Modane, the last French town before the Mont Cenis tunnel and the border. Bags were searched; passports checked. The Italian policemen went through their lists of banned items, banned books, banned people. The passengers waited shivering on the platform, threaded with the drifting steam. Nina stood a little apart from the others, wrapped in her coat with a hat pulled down low, the packet of cocaine and the syringes safely hidden in her inside pocket.

In the station buffet, she read an Italian newspaper as she drank her coffee. The front page carried a declaration of the pact between the Vatican and the state. *A Grand Political and Spiritual Victory for the Regime*, the headline read. *Emotion all over the World!* Sipping her coffee, Nina read that Italy was now officially a Catholic country, the Italian people and the Church cemented in insoluble alliance. Sudden weariness fogged her mind; she tossed the paper aside.

At last, the checks complete, the passengers piled back onto the train for breakfast and the last run under the mountains and out into the Italian sunrise. Outside Turin a pair of Blackshirts passed along the carriages, opening all the compartment doors. Nina heard them coming along the corridor, the swish and bump of the doors. When they arrived at her compartment she glanced up; the man framed in the open doorway was young, barely older than twenty. She managed a tired smile.

"Welcome to Italy, Signora," he said.

8

10th May 1930

"Nobody move!" Marinetti's voice called from the darkness, "Everyone must remain seated." But there was movement all around the table, waiters gliding deftly though the gloom. Someone let out a feverish giggle, then the light burst back, dazzling.

"Oh!" Fosca exclaimed, hands raised. Before her, before each of them, a fresh plate was revealed in the shock of illumination.

"*MACHINEMEAT*," Marinetti proclaimed. "About which nothing need be said."

From each square dish rose a gleaming piston of beef rissole, capped with half a red pepper and heavily lubricated with melted honey. At the base sat two shiny spheres of chicken meat.

"I say, what a virile creation," Osvaldi declared.

"What do you think?" Fosca asked Emilio, leaning closer. "It's very impressive, wouldn't you say?"

"Very," Emilio replied, embarrassment coursing through him. He wished Fosca would stop touching his leg under the table every time she spoke to him.

"What sort of machine do you think it's supposed to be?" she asked, whispering fruit into his ear. Emilio shrugged, attempting to draw away from her without actually moving. Why had he been placed next to this woman? He suppressed a shudder, then probed at the pillar of meat with a forefinger.

It wobbled meatily, and his finger came away trailing viscous honey.

Across the table, Osvaldi lifted the red pepper cap, revealing, through the steam, a core of packed green spinach beneath. He tugged at the meat, ripping away a slab from the side of the column. Emilio took one of the chicken balls and dabbed it in the slick of honey. What sort of machine, he wondered, *is* it supposed to be? A machine of meat, or meat made by a machine? Or maybe meat *for* a machine? Machine food. The diet of automatons.

He pictured the City of Tomorrow, the realisation of Conti's dreams: a dining room of cellulose, diners dressed in cellophane, eating Machinemeat. Outside the huge windows rocket-cars passed, fizzing like fireworks, trailing sparks. Buildings of mirrored steel turned silver wheels in the sky – cities in outer space, on the Moon, on Jupiter, rising from plains of sterile white dust. Machinemeat factories, whirring and clicking in the endless lunar night. Emilio dug his fingers into the minced beef, meat juices and honey dribbling into his palm, and imagined new food formulas sent from earth by light beam: dishes transmitted by telephone; volleys of meat-shells fired out to feed the interplanetary populace; steel-meat, aluminium-meat, explosive-meat.

But this was not like that at all. Emilio looked around him at the other diners. The guilty expressions of pleasure, the hands still blue with faded methylene now oiled and greasy, grasping and tearing; the collapsing constructions on the plates, sagging and despoiled, spilling soggy spinach – none of this spoke of a pristine healthy future. This was pure carnality.

And what was Nina thinking, on the far side of the table, as she primly licked her fingers? Moresco was beside her, his face a closed door. Emilio had seen them in the flash of the returning light, had seen her blush as she pulled her hand away from his. He had looked away quickly, conscious of the terrible grip of jealousy. Not just jealousy but something else too: a sudden sense of possibility. Everything, anything, could happen now.

With a shock, he realised again how exclusive this gathering was, how select a company surrounded him. Almost everyone here (excepting Fosca, her sticky hand on his sleeve again) was respected and successful; everyone was admirable. Beside Nina was Bruno Moresco, to Emilio's mind the greatest painter of the day. And to his right was Renzo Martino Rossi, dignified, unquestionably brilliant. And at the head of the table sat Marinetti, the Father of Futurism himself.

How had he come to be here with them, to be counted amongst their number? Could he too be brilliant, successful, admired? Emilio took a sip of wine. Yes. Yes that could be possible. He felt a rising elation. He wanted to call out along the table, laugh loudly at some joke of Osvaldi's, impose his presence on them all. Demonstrate what he could become. He willed Nina to look his way. He felt he could reach across the table, reach out across the silvered expanse and take her hand, the honey gumming their palms, and feel the warmth of her. He could do anything.

All emotion, all feeling, was merely the product of chemical interaction. His father had told him that, lectured him on the subject. Back then, as a child, Emilio had pictured tubes of coloured liquids poured one into another, fluids mixing inside glass. His brain a glass ball full of swirling chemicals, mingling indiscriminately. Was there really no more to it than that? Were his feelings, his personality, all he thought himself to be, only a composition in mixed colours, pigments blurred together, a clash and collision of painted shapes? Nothing in his experience had taught him otherwise. But that did not rule out love, did not rule out devotion. On the contrary, it reinforced them, gave them the legitimacy of science. If he felt these things it was because they were real. And if wine were just another chemical – this heavy red Barolo that he drank down to its dregs, holding up the glass for more – what difference did it make? The effects of it were no less true than the effects produced by sobriety.

It had been only eight months since he had first seen Nina, on the stairs of the apartment building. He had been on his way out to buy a paper, and heard her and Arturo coming up from below, the ring of their voices in the stairwell. She had been wearing a tight beige sweater and a skirt, neatly unobtrusive, and carried a camera in a leather case; she had been photographing the trams at Porta Venezia. They paused on the stairs while Arturo introduced them. A brief exchange, then Emilio carried on down to the street.

Outside, he had found himself hurrying, trying not to run, across to the news kiosk outside the park gates, fumbling with change, and then back again. What had he seen in her? How was she different from any of the other stream of women that Arturo brought home with him, the endless Ritas and Monas? He didn't know, but still Emilio ran back up the stairs gulping breath, pausing before the door of the apartment to steady his nerves before going inside.

They were in the studio. Nina stood in the centre of the room, beneath the dusty chandelier, gazing about her, half smiling. From the doorway, Emilio watched her, twisting the rolled newspaper in his hands into a tight baton. She appraised the room, possessed it. Arturo was doing his bluff act, shrugging and gesticulating, snatching up a brush to point and stab at the painting on the easel. It was the picture of the seaplane. He had been labouring over it for weeks.

"Trying to keep the form," he was saying awkwardly, "while flattening the colours, you see, the depth of the picture. To make it more dynamic..."

"But I like it," she said, simply. "It's very good. I like it. It must be nearly finished?"

And Arturo had grinned, shrugged again, and tossed the brush back down. "Yes," he said. "Almost done."

She turned in a half pirouette and scanned the rest of the studio, the clutter of canvases and smeared tins, bits of cardboard piled in corners. Emilio took a step forward into the room, catching Arturo's loaded glare.

"Those are Emilio's paintings," Arturo said. "We share the studio."

"Yes, I see," Nina said, then turned to Emilio. "I like these too," she said. Behind her back, Arturo made a meaningful gesture. Emilio ignored him.

"Well," Arturo went on, "I suppose we should have that drink I promised you."

And so they drank – the bottle of cheap wine from the kitchen – and wound up the gramophone to play some of Emilio's jazz records.

"I know this one!" she said as they sat listening. "This is Duke Ellington!" She leapt up from the couch and kicked off her shoes. As the music reeled around the room she grabbed Arturo and tried to pull him to his feet. He shook his head, so she turned to Emilio.

"Come on," she said, the glass of wine held high. "Let's dance!"

She took him by the hand and swung his arm. Arturo joined in, and the three of them danced together, shuffling on the rug, the mood infectious. When the record ended they wound up the gramophone and danced again, whooping and jumping, Arturo leaping up onto the couch and back down again with a crash that shook the floor and summoned a volley of thumps from the apartment below.

The music over, the wine gone, they sat together on the couch. Nina sat between the two men, giggling and sharing a cigarette with Arturo, and for a brief while there was only joy between them. When she left, an hour or so later, Arturo followed her out to the landing and closed the door behind him. Emilio tried not to imagine what had passed between them; told himself it was enough to have been included in it, even for a short time.

But it was no longer enough. What was so different now, eight months later? Why did the same chemicals now intoxicate him with false promises? Insanity, too, must be a chemical reaction. Were the delusions of the mad any less real than those of the sane?

A voice broke in, interrupting his thoughts. Martino Rossi, reclining under his paunch: "I meant to commend you," he said.

"Excuse me?" Emilio said.

"I've been meaning to commend you, I said, on your work." Rossi's teeth were still slightly blue. "Those three paintings you have in Berardi's show, the triptych of cycle racers. Very assured."

"Oh," Emilio replied, "They aren't that good." Why the instinctive modesty? He must be greater than that, he thought.

"You should learn to accept praise, young man," Rossi said. "You'll be getting quite a bit of it soon, I expect." He stroked his little moustache. "I hear," he said in an undertone, "that you'll be taking the commission for the National Institute?"

"Yes," Emilio said, trying not to look across to where Scaglia was sitting, swirling white wine in his glass without enthusiasm as he poked at his food.

"The Commendatore," Rossi went on, in a conspiratorial voice. "is also a close friend of the General Secretary of the Party. More importantly, he's going to be on the jury panel for the Biennale prizes – or so Marinetti believes."

A burst of amusement came from along the table.

Everything suddenly seemed to be much noisier, the voices around the table raised against each other. Emilio's lips felt puffy and his tongue thick. When had he said he would accept the commission? He should have told Rossi that he had not taken it yet; that he had made no promise, accepted no responsibility. But now that everyone already knew, how could he turn it down? If he took Scaglia up on his offers – the painting and that other, more nebulous service – would his uncle ever forgive him? Would Arturo? Most of all, would he ever be able to forgive himself?

At the end of the table, seated to the right of Marinetti, Berardi felt excluded from the life of the party. Perhaps it was for the best; at least this way he could preserve a certain decorum. Was he not the host? All of this was his property. The food, the table and the chairs, the walls of the room and everything in it: his.

Volpi's voice erupted: "I don't see why we should pay attention to these foreign styles at all! Italy already has brilliant architecture of her own. We *invented* architecture!"

"Architecture of the *past*!" Conti replied, heat in his voice. "I'm talking about architecture of the future. Gropius …"

"Oh, Gropius! What can a bunch of foreign homosexuals teach us, anyway?"

"You have no idea what you're talking about," Conti said. "No idea at all!"

Berardi had no idea what either of them was talking about. His gut gurgled, fluids shifting, gases surging. Acid splashed at the back of his oesophagus, and he clenched his throat muscles to keep it down. Automatically, his palm went to his top pocket, but he had left the peppermint tablets in his room; he would have to suffer the indigestion unrelieved.

He might be the host, but Marinetti was in control here; it was his circus. How could he remain so calm in the midst of it all? He sat at Berardi's elbow, chatted amiably, smoked a cigarette, made his pronouncements, as if he did this sort of thing every night. Perhaps he did? It occurred to Berardi, not for the first time, that he had no sense at all of what drove Marinetti. He had money – had always had money – and power, prestige and influence far beyond his actual achievements. Why did he continue producing these insane spectacles? There was something unreal about him, something chimerical. He was a self-created man, born of his own imagination. Berardi, on the other hand, was a self-made man, through his own hard work and effort. His achievements were solid and discernible. He should despise Marinetti, who had never had to work a day in his life. Yet he could not despise him – could not quite like him, but still couldn't help respecting him, as one respects what one cannot understand.

"Maurizio darling, Maurizio!" his wife was calling. Berardi caught her rapid gesture. Yes, time for the next course. The majordomo, Greco, was already there, pacing down the length of the room with unobtrusive candour. A solid man, Greco; nothing confusing about him. Berardi nodded to him; the majordomo nodded in reply and retreated.

In looking at his wife, Berardi had also been forced to look at the architect, Conti. His gut seethed, and he gulped heavily. Why, after everything that he had achieved in this life, must he endure men like Conti? A turd, a prick, a … He felt his face redden. For three months now his wife had been trailing around with the architect, making no attempt to hide it. As if Berardi wouldn't guess, or wouldn't mind, what was obviously going on between them! He had kept his composure, said nothing, given no sign that he was in any way moved, but now it was becoming too much to bear.

Later tonight, when events had wound themselves to a conclusion, he would retire to his room alone. He would wash, put on his silk pyjamas, get into his large expensive bed and lie sleepless and gut-aching, trying not to imagine the sounds through the connecting door, the muffled whispers and the giggles, the stifled gasps of amusement and pleasure at his expense. Surely tonight, if they had not already done so already, they would consummate the affair … Why should he endure this? For the sake of decorum, dignity? She could flirt around as much as she liked, cavort about town with that lisping prick of an architect, Berardi's own employee, a man half her age, a man who *dyed his hair*. He didn't care so much about that: Mariagrazia was entitled to her amusements. What grated was that they didn't seem to give a thought to whether he cared or not.

Tonight, would he take the gun from under his pillow, cross the room to the connecting door and open it? Would he stand over the bed, the bed of sin and insult, and level the black Beretta at the entwined bodies? He could do that, he *should* do it. Look, he could say then. This is your death, here in my hand. What do you think about that?

But he would not do it, because he was too old now for that explosion. Life was too precariously balanced. No, he would lie there in silence, then get up and go to his nightstand, take two sleeping-pills with water, lie back and wait for oblivion. He would cease to care, until the next time.

"But who is this next war supposed to be against?" Mariagrazia was saying. "I mean, the way you all talk it's as if battle will erupt at any moment! Against whom? Italy has no enemies! The Turks? The French?"

"I seem to remember," Conti said, "that Marinetti predicted the next war would be between pederasts and lesbians, and that afterwards they would join forces to attack the heterosexuals!"

"Which are you, Conti," Volpi muttered, "a pederast or a lesbian?"

"The next war," Marinetti declared gravely, "could well be fought in outer space. The conquest of the planets, the stars, the galaxies. The patriotic spirit demands constant expansion, ever onward, ever upwards."

"But seriously?" Mariagrazia asked.

"Seriously?" Marinetti mused, sucking his lip. "I expect another great European conflagration within five to ten years. The economic crisis will produce it. War is the vital force of our civilisation, and without it we fall into decadence and decline."

"And do you desire such a war?" Scaglia asked, frowning. "Do you honestly wish for it?"

Marinetti paused, then gave a noncommittal shrug. "Obviously, yes," he said. For the first time since he arrived, he looked a little less than completely sure of himself. Perhaps, Berardi thought, even Marinetti felt the drag of age upon him.

But he recovered his composure swiftly enough as the next course was brought up from the kitchen. Rising from his seat, he cleared his throat and announced: "Ladies and gentlemen, Futurists of the revolution, I present to you *ITALIAN WINGS OVER AFRICA.* A piquant portrayal of the exploits of our glorious colonial airforce. I certainly hope you will enjoy devouring it as much as I enjoyed thinking it up!" His flashing smile, his incandescent charm: these must be the secret of his success.

Watch this man, Arturo thought. *Watch his every move, follow his every word.* The man was Commendatore Federico Scaglia.

On the terrace outside the gallery Marinetti had told him that Scaglia would be sitting on the jury for the Biennale prizes – a jury otherwise polluted with rank conservatism, choked with reactionary sentiment, neo-classicism, passéism in all its manifestations. For all his shortcomings, Scaglia was the best chance for a radical vote. Perhaps, even, with the rest of them divided by rivalries and cross-purposes, Scaglia's opinion could swing the decision. But his opinion must be nursed and nurtured. All this Marinetti explained, without rhetorical flourish, almost with an apologetic tone. He himself had been unable to secure a place on the panel, even after petitioning the Duce. No, he was told, the panel are selected by the Biennale committee and they alone can decide – despite the committee themselves being appointed by Mussolini, some pretence of autonomy must be maintained.

He may have lost the promised commission – Arturo tried not to think about that – but the Biennale competition was a chance to redeem his ambitions. Yet even seated within easy reach of Scaglia, he had been utterly unable to engage him in conversation. The man spoke only to Marinetti and Berardi, and so quietly that Arturo could not make out a word. It didn't help having Volpi sitting beside him, fidgeting and fussing as he launched a stream of barbed insinuations at Conti. And the dancer sitting on his other side, Adriana Giovene, was no help either.

There are two kinds of women in the world: those whom one could impress, and those whom one could not. So far, Signorina Giovene fell firmly into the latter category. Arturo had tried to be witty, tried to be amusing, but she had remained unmoved. Primly she sat in her grey dress, with her upright posture, eating very little of the food, dabbing at her lips with a napkin and smiling politely now and again at his sallies. She was engaged, Arturo had learned, to an army officer of some sort. She was born in Brescia but grew up in Milan. She had trained as a dancer at La Scala, where Marinetti had contacted her about the dance performance. She collaborated, it seemed, without any great enthusiasm. She was a professional and nothing more. It was hard to imagine that this remote and distracted young woman was the same fantastic creature that had danced on the stage downstairs. He praised her performance, but she appeared impermeable to flattery.

Her sober presence isolated him from the powerful trio of men at the end of the table. If only their places could be reversed! If he had been seated next to Berardi, he could have pitched into any conversation. Arturo drank heavily to cover his growing desperation, and tried to think of an opening gambit.

He wished Nina were with him instead. She knew Scaglia, after all – or her husband had. Arturo imagined her talking to him, charming him ... He cast a glance back over his shoulder, to where Nina sat talking to Moresco. She was too far away to help.

Frustrated, he regarded the plate of food before him. It was a thick, brown purée of mashed dates and bananas, drenched in sweet Marsala: the dessert course. Perched on top were intricate aircraft modelled from pastry, spread with coloured paste. Pistachio, tomato, mozzarella – they were Italian aircraft. The brown terrain must represent the north African desert. A desert of dessert!

"This reminds me," he said, too quietly for the words to carry, then louder. "Marinetti! This reminds me! Do you remember that first time I visited you?"

The men at the end of the table paused, interrupted mid-speech. He had spoken too loudly, almost shouted. Everyone was looking at him now.

"The first time we met," he went on, forcing the words, "in Rome, at your house in Piazza Adriana?"

"Yes?"

"Do you remember, I'd just returned from Africa? I was with the airforce in Tripolitania! Your food, your *formula* – it brings it all back to me!"

"Ah, yes, of course!" Marinetti exclaimed, with a look of relief. "Of course you were. I should have dedicated this dish in your honour! Our bold colonial adventurer!"

"You were in Africa?" Scaglia said. "Interesting …"

"Yes, I was based at Sirte, on the edge of the desert. Twelfth Caproni Squadron. I was only a wireless operator, but I got to know some of the airmen and one time they took me up for a flight."

"Did they indeed?"

Arturo nodded vigorously, the sound of his voice seeming to echo oddly in his ears. But he was warming to his theme, the scenario spinning out in his mind. "Yes, we flew out one night across the escarpment. I was up in the nacelle, you know, the gondola at the front of the plane. We flew down low over one of the rebel encampments and dropped flares on them …"

"Flares?" interrupted Mariagrazia. "But why flares? Shouldn't you have dropped *bombs* or something? I mean, they *were* the enemy, weren't they?"

"The bombs were in short supply at the time … The flares were to scare them." *Think, think.* Already the anecdote was going downhill. The Commendatore regarded him with doubtfully. As well he might, as the story was pure fiction. He had never managed to persuade anyone to let him go up in a plane, just watched them disappearing off over the dunes. The flares were real though, and the ammunition shortage: he had overheard the pilots complaining about it over dinner one night.

"But the sensation of flight," he said, with a sweeping gesture, "out there over the immensity of the desert, was something awesome. All I could hear was the roar of the engines behind me and the whine of the wind …"

How long could he keep this up? The truth intruded in his mind. The endless, exhausting days on the drab airfield, sitting over a hot wireless set in the shade of a tin hut. The reek of petrol rising through the sweat and the dirt. In summer, the great dust storms, the *ghibli*, swept in from the desert and blotted out the sky, turning everything murk-brown. Fine-blown sand seeped in everywhere like a viscous fluid, gritting between teeth, clogging the switches of the electrical equipment. Sand that reddened the eyes and coarsened the food, that pooled in sediment at the bottom of every drained cup, that worked its way into every orifice of the body – beneath fingernails, inside ears, under foreskins. And in winter, cold like a slow death.

"I remember once," Arturo said, "one of our planes came down at a village twenty kilometres inland, and we had to go out and salvage whatever we could find. We went out in lorries, big Fiats with sand tyres, all of us in sun helmets and goggles, choking on dust …"

The silence expanded around him, everyone at the table listening to his story. They dug the pastry planes into the purée mud, scooping up dark sticky lumps.

"We drove through the night and got to the village just after dawn. Not much was left of the plane, and the crew were all dead. And the place was deserted – everyone had just run off. Afraid of reprisals. Just a straggle of huts around a knot of palm trees. Dogs, scorpions, not much else. I realised then that all these places are like that, just squalid little encampments, and all the glorious battles we hear about are just dirty little skirmishes in the desert …"

He fell silent. Nobody seemed to want to look at him.

"Well, I don't know about that," said Scaglia. There was a collective slow exhalation.

"My fiancé's in Africa!" announced Adriana Giovene. "He's a lieutenant in the Second Blackshirt Legion. He ought to have have been made a captain but, well, promotions are so slow …"

"Is that so?" said Scaglia with heavy emphasis. He reached

into his breast pocket and took out a small spiral-bound notebook. "Tell me his name," he said crisply, "and the name of his commanding officer. I'll look into the matter."

And that, Arturo thought with a drab sense of futility, *is how it's done.*

More courses: tangerine segments arranged in a spiral, covered in a light cheese sauce; mounds of diced pineapple, adorned with deep-fried roses …

Surely it would stop soon, Emilio thought; it was already near midnight. He regarded the food with queasy indifference. His stomach was full, loaded with a rich stew: sweet and savoury, wines and meats. He felt hotly ill and quite drunk. He also needed to go to the toilet, with a steady urgency, but didn't want to leave the table before the meal reached its conclusion.

The room was too bright, the competing voices too loud. He wanted to slide down in his chair, to subside gently beneath the silver tablecloth into the muffled twilight below the table. As a child he had enjoyed hiding beneath the table at family dinners; now he could lie full length on the floor beneath the table, between the ranks of legs, the odd arrangements of feet, silken calves and shining shoes, trouser-hems raised to reveal elastic sock-suspenders on thin white shins. A sunken, secret world.

But he was no longer a child. The voices intruded again, talking about the war. Emilio kept quiet, hoping that nobody would ask him anything.

"I volunteered at the commencement of hostilities," Rossi was saying, "but sadly I was too old for front line duties." *The commencement of hostilities*, Emilio thought. The phrase was ridiculous.

"The same for me," said Osvaldi. "They put me in the pay corps!"

"And you, Signor Moresco," the journalist, Assanti, asked, "you surely fought?"

Moresco just shrugged. "I don't remember."

"Of course he did! No false modesty, please, Moresco."

"I was in the Montebello Lancers," Moresco said, and sipped his wine.

"With a gold medal for valour," Osvaldi added. "And what else?"

"I joined the air corps in '18. Made six kills before the armistice."

"You amaze me!" Fosca exclaimed with a look of delight. "Practically an air ace! But how did you become an artist after that?"

"I was in the hospital just after the war. Some of the others there knew Marinetti, and they signed me up for something called the Futurist Aerial Theatre. We flew a sort of aerobatic display over Milan, dropping manifesto leaflets."

"I saw that," Nina said quietly. "I was there, I saw you."

"Not that it seemed very artistic at the time. Most of the leaflets ended up caught in the rigging wires, or wrapped around the tailplane. We were lucky none got trapped in the air intakes or the exhausts; that could have made things difficult."

"I *saw* you," Nina said again, a hand on his arm. "I was there in Milan that day, with my father. We were down in Piazza Cordusio and saw everything. Which plane was yours?"

"I was flying a red and blue Nieuport, as I recall. But it was a long time ago. Feels like a different life."

"My brothers all fought in the war," Nina told him. "My eldest brother was killed. He won two silver medals, but he died at Caporetto. He was a captain in the Eighty-Seventh Infantry."

"The Friuli Brigade. They got hit badly by gas."

"Yes. That was what we were told."

"He was lucky then, in a way. A lot of the officers were shot by their own men during the retreat, or by the military police afterwards."

"They deserved to be!" Volpi cried. "No Italian officer should retreat in the face of battle."

"And what do you know about the face of battle?" Moresco said.

"What did you know about the war at all, Volpi?" added Conti. "You spent the whole time in a factory."

"I did more than you!" Volpi shouted, leaping up from his chair. "I fought the Communists during the revolution! You were never in the army, Conti! You spent the war hiding out in Switzerland, sucking off your German architect friends!" He stuck his finger in his mouth and sucked it, leering.

"That's a lie! Take that back!"

They were both standing now, glaring across the table. Others rose to grab their shoulders and restrain.

"It's lucky we don't have cutlery," whispered Rossi to Emilio, "I'm sure somebody would have stuck a fork in that young man by now."

"Ladies and gentlemen!" Marinetti announced from the head of the table, rising to his feet. "To the food technicians!" He lifted his glass in salute. From the other end of the room, two dour-looking men in tall white hats appeared from the stairs. The waiters stood ranked to either side.

The applause was immediate and generous, a release from disaster. Greco the majordomo bowed stiffly, while the two chefs nodded gravely.

"And here's to Marinetti!" declared Assanti, his voice pitched high above the clamour, "and the new Futurist cuisine!"

Another burst of congratulation, Marinetti beaming from the heart of it. The applause died away in a smattering of claps and coughs. Everyone remained standing, the waiters and chefs in their neat formation under the steady glare of the chandelier. There was another cough.

"To the roof terrace, everyone!" Mariagrazia cried. "Up the stairs to the roof terrace!"

And the guests were swept up into the funnel of the stairs, leaving the gleaming cloth, the smeared glasses, the muddied plates and the crumpled napkins. The waiters stood idle until the last of them had gone. Then their work began.

17th March 1929

It was Sunday, a clear morning washed fresh by night rain, and the sky was huge and blue above Emilio as he cycled north towards his uncle's house. He passed factory ditches and high, blank walls, rows of poplars and cypress and little clutches of houses. The road was long and straight, almost empty of traffic, and Emilio rode fast, breathing deeply the clean, cold air. He had travelled this road every day, in the years when he lived with his uncle, and even after he moved in with Arturo, these Sunday visits were a regular ritual. Recently he had been coming less often: first the weeks became fortnights, then months. It had become an obligation, more onerous with every passing year. But still he returned.

Away from the fumes and dust of the city, cycling was a joy. The air flowed around and through him, his muscles moving smoothly against the brace of the steel frame and the gears. The only sounds were the thin hiss of the tyres on the tarmac, and the noise of his own breath in his ears. Now and then a solitary suburban tram went by, white and clanking on its track. In the sky overhead, a slim, silver monoplane flew slanting upwards from the direction of the aerodrome.

Emilio had started cycling as a child, on the advice of the family doctor, who believed that the exercise of the lungs would be good for his asthma. Growing up in a multitude of different cities, cut off from firm and lasting friendships, he would find a solitary pleasure in long cross-country cycle expeditions in the winter fogs and stinging drizzle of the northern plains, or the parched heat and grinding hill-climbs of the south. When he lived with his uncle, after the deaths of his parents, he would ride for hours along these straight suburban roads, through Baranzate, Bresso, Monza, Crescenzago, tracing the web of highways around the city of Milan. Since then the city had reached steadily outwards, seeping across the surrounding countryside, and the tracks that Emilio had ridden as a youth were now tarmac roads, studded with housing developments, bracketed by factories.

He took a long curve to the right, off the main road and onto a dusty side street lined with bare trees. At the end he dismounted, took off his cap and cycle-clips, and paused to brush his hair and straighten his tie before pushing the bicycle the last few metres to his uncle's gate.

The house was square and solid, standing back from the street behind a wall and iron railings. It was one of several in the area built just before the war, each in its plot of garden: little patches of prosperity out here on the city's furthest fringe. Inside, the rooms were airy and plain, with a spartan lack of adornment that seemed to reflect a calm and orderly mind. In the gloomy hallway was a tiny, tidy atrium, one wall hung with photographic portraits. The names were written beneath the pictures: Matteotti, Amendola and Gobetti, Natale Gaiba and Don Giovanni Minzoni, Antonio Piccinini. They were by no means all socialists, but a rosette of red bunting hung beneath each framed picture. A gallery of resistance, Emilio's uncle called it: the martyrs of the anti-Fascist struggle. The austerity of this house did not, in fact, reflect an inner peace but rather the intense frustration of a mind painfully attuned to a harsh truth.

Emilio's uncle Renato was a short, heavy man in his fifties. He had the chesty swagger of a labourer, but his black hair shone with oil and his moustache was neatly clipped. Over the years Emilio had grown accustomed to his uncle's perpetual, frowning ill humour.

"So they tell me I'm a loudmouth," he said over the dinner table, as the housekeeper came and went from the kitchen, bringing soup tureen and dishes, bread and wine, "and I'll get myself in trouble. Well, I've kept my head on my shoulders so far, haven't I? They want to get rid of me, want to shuffle me off. Early retirement, nice pension. You know what I told them? *When the fox gets too old the chickens shit on his head!* I'm not that old yet, is what I said."

A lifelong bachelor, Uncle Renato worked as an engineer at the Breda aircraft factory. Emilio's father had discovered truth in the science of chemistry; Renato found it in mechanics.

"You know the trouble with this country?" he said, warming to his theme.

"What?" Emilio replied. A familiar guilt rose inside him, and he tried to swallow it down.

"We've never had any faith in politics," his uncle said, pouring his soup into a saucer to cool it. "We *expect* all our governments to be corrupt, all our politicians to be liars. The possibility that any government might do something genuine for the working man is treated like a joke! So now we get the current situation, with this theatrical buffoon in charge, and nobody sees anything wrong with it. We gave up our last hope for a just and equal society in exchange for a heap of songs and parades and uniforms, and everyone thinks that's just fine!"

"It's not that bad, is it? I mean ..."

"Oh? Oh, what's this now? Surely you aren't joining the chorus of approval? You're going to tell me about the trains, eh? The *battle for grain*? Eh?"

"Please don't shout, Signore," said the housekeeper, coming through from the kitchen with the roast chicken. "I'm sure Signor Emilio knows your views very well by now!" She set the platter down in the centre of the table, and Emilio's uncle began to carve.

"So how's work?" he said, spearing a slice of meat and passing it across the table.

"Not bad," Emilio told him. "I sold two paintings last month. One for seventy lire, the other for one hundred." His uncle made a kissing sound against his teeth.

"You can't live on that," he said. "You could do much better if you painted pictures that ordinary people liked. You just do this modern, abstract stuff, and all you get is handouts from rich bohemians."

Emilio had heard all this before. He gave a light cough.

"I know," his uncle said, his mouth full. "I know you think I'm a philistine. I'm not, though, I'm a populist. I believe in art for the masses. I saw those moving-picture posters you used to paint. I saw the people standing in the picture-house foyer enjoying them too. Now *they* were good. But you have to sneer at anything popular, I suppose."

"But look at Russia," Emilio interrupted. "That's a socialist country, but they have modern art there. The state commissions it."

"Ah, phoo!" his uncle said, waving a hand dismissively. "That's a passing trend."

They continued eating, the tall English clock in the corner regulating the silence between them. "I see," Emilio's uncle said, after a few minutes, "that your friend Marinetti has been selected for the new Royal Academy of Italy. Personal recommendation of the Duce!"

"He's not a friend," Emilio said. "I've never met him."

"Well, you know what I mean. Amusing, isn't it? He used to make himself out to be a revolutionary. Enemy of the monarchist priest-loving bourgeoisie, et cetera. Now he'll be bowing to His Majesty in a feathered hat and cape."

"I doubt that. As far as I know, he hasn't accepted the place yet."

"Oh, he will. These rich dilettantes are all the same. They

play at being rebels, but when they're offered a chance to dress up and parade about with the aristocracy, they grab it with both hands. What is he, anyway? Mussolini's court fool. His mascot."

Emilio kept silent, trying to look as if he didn't care. He had seen the story in the morning paper, but hadn't decided what he thought about it.

"Oh, the great New Italy," his uncle went on, scowling as he wiped his plate clean. "This wonderful nation, peaceful and prosperous, united behind the glorious Catholic Church at last, that can even bestow honours on madcap poets and turn them into pillars of the establishment!"

"Signore!" the housekeeper called from the kitchen door. "Enough! Please!"

After coffee the two men went out to the garage behind the house, where the boxy little Diatto coupé stood polished and gleaming. One side of the bonnet was folded up to reveal the engine beneath, and on the workbench nearby were arrayed rows of shining steel machine parts and tools. The air smelled of metallic oil. On a small table near the back of the garage was a portable gramophone. Emilio knew of his uncle's secret love for the music of Mahler, and it quietly amused him to imagine Renato in here, working on his engines, elbow deep in the grease and the steel, humming under his breath to stern Germanic cadences.

His uncle ran a cloth over the exposed engine, applied oil from a can, then dropped the bonnet back into place.

"Right then," he said, "let's get started."

Renato had first taken it upon himself to teach his nephew to drive the previous summer: partly, Emilio suspected, as a means to ensure his regular Sunday visits, but also as a last attempt to impart a worthwhile, practical skill. His uncle had always made it clear that he regarded Emilio as having squandered most of the opportunities and responsibilities of life. Perhaps if he could drive he might be saved.

But sitting in the passenger seat as his uncle steered the Diatto out onto the road to the aerodrome, Emilio already felt a deep sense of hopelessness about the task ahead. The truth was that he was simply not meant to drive a car. He disliked automobiles in general – noisy dangerous devices, hazardous to the cyclist, filling the air with stinking exhaust that grabbed at his throat and stopped his breath. His attempts so far to learn the basic skills, under his uncle's despairing gaze, had met with utter failure. But he dreamed regularly about driving, and had discovered that in his sleep he was perfectly competent.

"Now," his uncle said, as the car stood parked on the long empty perimeter road of the aerodrome, "let's try and do a little better than last time, shall we?"

The leather squeaked beneath him as Emilio shifted across to the driving seat. He gritted his teeth, placing his feet tentatively over the pedals. His uncle, climbing back into the passenger seat, was already seething with irritation. *Starter, clutch, gears,* Emilio thought – no, what have I forgotten? Choke ... *Choke, starter, clutch, gears* ... A memory from his awkward adolescence came to him: attempting to dance a waltz with a girl called Margherita, and treading all over her toes and the hem of her dress.

"Relax," his uncle said. "You look terrified. The steering wheel isn't going to explode in your hands, you know."

Nodding grimly, Emilio eased out the choke, then thumbed the starter button. The engine whined and coughed. He pressed the button again, harder this time. Another cough, and the engine died.

"Congratulations," his uncle said, addressing the sky outside. "You've managed to flood the carburettor."

Half an hour later, after several false starts and a slow and tentative progress along several hundred metres of road, Emilio stalled the car while trying to change gear.

"Well, it's not easy, mastering the double declutch," his uncle said, with weary resignation. "You'll get the hang of it, with practice."

They sat together in silence, the engine ticking gently beneath the bonnet. Outside, the day had turned grey and overcast. Across the field the vast aircraft hangars stood in rows, the control tower rising beyond. Renato tapped his fingers on the window frame, deep in contemplation.

"Tell me something," he said, a tense note in his voice. He turned to Emilio, reached over to grip his arm. "Have you joined?"

"Joined?" Emilio replied, baffled for a moment. "Joined the Party?"

His uncle nodded.

"No, no, I haven't."

"But you've joined this Syndicate of theirs, I suppose?"

"Well, yes, but it's not the same thing."

"It amounts to the same thing," his uncle said, with savage emphasis. He thumped his fist against the dashboard. Staring out over the field at the distant hangars, the muscles of his jaw clenched. "That's the way they work, isn't it?" he went on. "You don't need to sign up for their Party, wear their badge, even vote in their so-called elections. You just have to join their clubs, their syndicates. Sing their songs, march in their parades. That's all the legitimacy they need. And meanwhile their thugs go about beating people half to death, killing people if they want to, making people drink oil and petrol, mocking them, murdering them. Can you stand for that?"

"But you voted in the election last week didn't you … the plebiscite?"

"The election! Two voting slips, a tricolour one for *yes* and a blank one for *no*, and one of their thugs standing beside the ballot box checking off the names! How did you like it, eh? Of course I voted, but you know what I did? I took one of the tricolour slips, wrote *SHIT* right across it and put it in the box! How many 'spoiled' votes do you think they counted?"

"But you have to be careful ... They'll be watching you!"

"I'd be ashamed of myself if they weren't!" He turned to face Emilio again, his face red with fury. "They shot that schoolteacher recently, did you hear about that? They beat him till he shat himself, then shot him six times in the head, right in front of his wife and kids. Can you accept that? What had he done? Dared to teach the truth about what's happening in this country, instead of filling children's heads with rubbish. Can you stand for that? Can you?"

Emilio shook his head. He could not speak.

"If you weren't a blood relative, I wouldn't allow you in my house," his uncle said.

They sat in the car without speaking. Outside, the silver plane that Emilio saw earlier was droning across the sky towards the landing strip. A few drops of rain pricked at the windscreen.

"I'm sorry," Renato said. "I'm sorry I lost my temper with you. These things are not your fault, I know. I just get so angry with the way things are going." He slapped a palm onto Emilio's shoulder, gave it a brief squeeze. "We'd better get back to the house," he said. "I'll drive."

The rain passed over quickly, but the afternoon was polluted by bitterness. As he waited with his bicycle by the front steps of the house, Emilio tried to summon a farewell warmth, but without much success. His uncle hovered on the porch, ill at ease, then came down to stand beside him.

"Listen," he said, "do you need any money? I mean, it doesn't sound like you're surviving on much."

"I'm fine," Emilio said.

But his uncle was already reaching into his waistcoat. He drew out his pocketbook and passed Emilio a fifty-lire note.

"Take it, take it," he insisted, then slipped the money into the pocket of Emilio's jacket. "Families should stand by each other," he said gravely. "And I'm the only family you've got left."

"Thanks," Emilio said. Stiffly clumsy, his uncle stepped around the rear wheel of the bicycle and clasped him in a tight embrace. He kissed him firmly on both cheeks, then stepped back and nodded.

"Look after yourself," he said.

"And you," Emilio said. *And you.*

9

10th May 1930

The music met him as he climbed the stairs: a whine of horns and a rattle of drums, the tight snap and toot, the smooth syncopation. Arturo stepped out onto the roof terrace and saw everyone gathered under the artificial constellation. Furniture had been brought up from the house: chairs, couches and tables, with the central area left clear for dancing. Marinetti was seated on a huge wicker throne, his bald head gleaming like a planet under the electric bulbs. The gramophone stood on a side table. Its black horn, angled up into the night, was spilling out elegant dance tunes, but nobody was dancing. Smoke from the cigars and cigarettes formed a glowing haze.

Arturo stalked across the open space of the terrace, scanning the crowd. He overheard the journalist, Assanti, holding forth to the group clustered around Marinetti: "Certainly we should welcome tourists to our country. But we shouldn't be exhibiting the dead monuments of antiquity, not any more! Instead we should proudly display the technological achievements of Italian genius: the wireless and telephone, the aeroplane, the automatic carbine …"

"But surely, Signor Assanti," Mariagrazia broke in, "the aeroplane was invented by an American, Signor Wright-Brothers, was it not?"

"The aeroplane," Assanti declared, raising a proud finger, "was invented by an Italian, Leonardo Da Vinci, in the fifteenth century!"

Arturo spied Commendatore Scaglia, standing with Adriana Giovene at the far end of the terrace, beside the curve of the parapet. He slid closer, trying to look unobtrusive. If he could join in their conversation, or catch Scaglia alone, he could mention the Biennale …

"Hallo there," said Nina, taking his arm. "So you've decided to join us under the stars?" She gestured at the overhead bulbs.

"Clearly the place to be," Arturo replied. His mood lifted: the conjunction of Nina and the Commendatore was perfect. All he had to do was bring them together.

"Did you manage to speak to Marinetti at dinner?" Nina asked quietly, moving closer. She slipped her fingers into his palm. Her breath was warm on his cheek.

"No, no I didn't really get the chance. Listen, Nina, could you …"

She cut him off, speaking quickly. "I'm feeling rather tired, actually, Arturo. I wondered if perhaps we could leave? Things seem to be drawing to a close here, and if we go now, we could be back in Milan by dawn."

"Leave now? Are you mad?" Arturo said. "The bags are upstairs, and Emilio's disappeared …" By the parapet, Scaglia nodded to the dancer, then turned and walked towards him.

Nina caught the direction of his eye; she tensed, drawing away and pulling at his arm. "Then let's dance!" she exclaimed, her voice rising. "Nobody's dancing at all, and I'm quite in the mood!"

Scaglia was directly behind her now, moving towards Marinetti's group. Arturo took a long step forward, sweeping Nina along with him. "Commendatore!" he called out.

"Yes?" Scaglia said, halted mid pace. There was annoyance in his expression.

"Commendatore, I hear you've been selected for the Biennale competition jury?" Arturo began. He was talking too fast. "I wondered if you'd met Signora Della Torre? In fact, I believe the two of you are old friends?"

He felt Nina flinch, as though she wanted to hide behind him.

Scaglia looked baffled. "Have we met, Signora?" he asked.

"No, we haven't," Nina replied, as if she'd somehow been offended. "I don't know you at all."

"Oh. Then your friend is mistaken. Good evening," the Commendatore said with evident ill humour, and moved off again.

Nina was trembling as if she had been struck. Arturo seized her wrist, turning to shield her from the crowd. "What was that all about?" he hissed. "Of course you know him, Emilio told me … And even if you didn't, there was no need to be rude!"

"Let go of me."

Still gripping her wrist, he began marching her towards the stairs. Every few steps he turned his head, grinning absurdly, but nobody was watching. Nina stumbled, dragging against him, but he pulled her onwards.

"Arturo, you're hurting me! What are you doing?"

Marinetti's voice loomed behind them. "Why we have to listen to this anaemic American music I have no idea!" he said. "We should have Italian music!"

As he reached the stairs, Arturo saw Mariagrazia flourishing the cardboard sleeve of the record: it displayed the name of the Carlo Minari Hot Dance Orchestra. "Italian, Marinetti!" she declared. "Italian jazz music!"

"Well, the *style* is American," Marinetti said, as Mariagrazia laughed. "Or so they say. No genuine Negro would listen to it, I'm sure …"

Emilio pulled the chain and stood up as the waters crashed beneath him. Braced against the washbasin, he surveyed himself in the mirror: his eyes were pouched and sunken, his face pale.

He moved along the upstairs corridor, the thick carpet muffling his tread. Being alone after so long in close and noisy company warmed his spirits, and he slowed his steps as he emerged onto the well-lit mezzanine above the gallery. His glass of wine was still on the side table where he had left it. This was the exact place, he remembered, where Berardi had first told him about Scaglia and the commission, only a few hours ago.

He stared at the white wall and tried to imagine his picture, the *commission*, growing there, but it remained mockingly unclear. He felt at once alive with the glamour of talent and disgusted with himself. He felt like leaping out of his skin. Turning, he paced rapidly across the mezzanine. The lights were hot now, the high space above the gallery packed with stale air. A door opened onto a balcony, and the promise of a breeze. Carrying his glass, Emilio went outside. The night wrapped him with quiet noise: the steady reverberation of insects in the gardens, the tinny melody of a dance tune drifting down from the roof above the dining room.

The moon sailed near-full over the mountains, casting a warped reflection in the invisible waters of the lake. As he leaned on the balcony, Emilio became aware of the voices below him. First Arturo, then Nina, hushed as they passed from the house out through the French doors to the garden terrace directly below him. Emilio took a step away from the parapet, then another, and found the wall at his back. He listened intently. Their voices carried more clearly now. For a moment, the words were indistinct; then Arturo's voice rose up to him.

"Of course it was deliberate! How could it not be deliberate? The one man in this whole place I needed to take me seriously and you make me look like a damned idiot!"

Nina's reply was inaudible.

"Then why be so rude to him?" Arturo said abruptly. "You might as well have spat in his face!"

The voices fell to whispers, drowned by the throb of crickets from the garden. Emilio took a sip of his wine.

"You wanted me to talk to Marinetti for you," Nina said, louder. "Fine, I did it. Not that it helped you much, but is that my fault? At least I *like* Marinetti. At least he's good company. Unlike that other one, that odious reptile."

"Keep your voice down!" Arturo said, a tense hiss. "How can you say that about a man you've supposedly never met? You must know him!"

"I know *of* him," Nina said. Sound of her heels on the paving stones as she moved a few steps away. "My husband knew him."

"Oh, your husband. I see."

Emilio heard a match struck. Arturo was speaking quietly now: a conciliatory voice, a petitioning voice. A thin plume of rising cigarette smoke caught the light at the level of the balcony. He craned forward to hear what they were saying.

"Anyway, you were sitting opposite the man for hours and didn't manage to say whatever it was you needed to say." Nina's voice was flat and emotionless. "What good do you think I could have done?"

"You just needed to catch his attention, introduce me, then I could've spoken to him."

"So I'm a lure?" she said, suddenly loud and reckless. "That's why I'm here. I'm just something you can use to dazzle important men. You know what that makes you? A pimp!"

"Stop getting hysterical."

"I'm not hysterical!"

"Why are we shouting at each other?" Arturo said. "Is this necessary? I thought you understood. I thought you knew how important this was to me."

"Oh, certainly. The very important things in your life. I'm

very aware of all of them. I'm aware, for example, that I'm not one of them."

"You really don't see, do you? This is just a bit of fun for you. You don't have to take it seriously. You've got enough money to do whatever you want, whenever you want!"

"That's …"

"Let me finish. Your family and your husband have given you everything. Art is just a pastime for you, isn't it? You just do it for fun!" There was a pause, then: "I suppose you put Emilio up to asking for that commission, too."

"Oh, you really are insane! He never asked for it. It was offered to him. And why would I need to *put him up to it* anyway?"

"But you told him he should take it, am I right? You knew what it meant to me … But how tedious this must be for you, how vulgar! I suppose to you I'm just a vulgar grasping tradesman like all the others now … Oh, what's this? Tears?"

Silence. Emilio felt like he was listening in on a telephone conversation, with the muffled crackle of distant connections.

"There are things you don't know about me, Arturo," Nina said. "If there are people I choose to avoid, that's my business."

"Oh, I see! That's why you pretended not to know him! He's an old lover of yours, is he? Is that it?"

"*Him*? My God, I never knew you had such a low opinion of me!"

"Well, why not? You could've gone to bed with him for all I know! Why else would you be so rude to him? He's only a politician, not a fucking abortionist!"

Emilio, breath held tight, leaned out against the balcony rail.

"Bastard," Nina said. "You know what that means to me."

The stem of Emilio's glass slipped between his fingers; he made a clumsy grab, but only knocked it out of his hand altogether. The glass fell, a thin arc of red tracing from it. Emilio pressed himself back against the wall. A second later the glass shattered against the stone paving below.

"What was that?" Arturo said.

"They're throwing things at us now. See how popular we've become?"

A long silence. Nina exhaled – an exasperated noise – then Arturo spoke again.

"I never had a chance with you, did I? Not a real chance."

Nina said something, too quiet for Emilio to catch. It was almost like a sob.

"No, it's no good. Arturo, I can't talk to you."

"Where are you going?"

"Indoors. Actually I might go back up to the roof terrace with the others. This is a party, isn't it? I intend to enjoy myself."

"Oh God."

"Yes, I intend to dance and maybe sing. Hopefully I'll embarrass you enormously."

Crouched on the balcony, Emilio heard her steps pass beneath him and into the house. He stood up and leaned out over the parapet again, watching the thin white line of Arturo's collar diminishing as he walked away, then snuffing out in the darkness of the garden.

At the edge of the lawn, Arturo stood with legs braced, gazing back at the house. Black shapes of leaves and spiky branches stuck up from the bushes in front of him, a fantastic forest. Above them he saw the shapes of people up on the roof, illuminated under the strings of electric bulbs. A jolt of anger ran through him. *Bastards*, he thought. I'll show them. He held his penis with one hand, swaying back on his heels – imagined the house blasted by artillery, shells arcing down from the distant batteries on the far side of the lake, high explosive shattering the white shell and smashing it to dust, smashing them all to dust.

His piss spattered through the leaves of the bushes. His mind was empty. He whistled a tune through his teeth: the march from *Aida*. Where did he remember that from? He buttoned his trousers, took a step back, crunching onto gravel. What had happened just now? He had been sure of himself while he was talking to Nina, but now the sense of his own words had deserted him. Only the memory of hers remained.

He felt the effects of the wine reeling in his head, and the ground lurched beneath him. Oh God, Jesus, he thought, what have I done? He sniffed back the remorse, wiped his face, shrugged. You do what you have to do, he told himself. If nobody understands, it makes no difference, because you do what you have to do. He turned, lost his footing and fell onto the gravel path with a dull crunch.

Hauling himself up, grit in his palms, he saw the pale lines of the steps nearby. Carefully, tugging his jacket back into place and straightening his tie, he moved towards them. He stumbled against the bottom step, then sat heavily. A scrap of colour caught his eye – a crumpled cigarette packet stuck behind a statue. He had put it there himself, he remembered, only a few hours ago when he walked here with Nina. So long ago, it seemed.

A figure was coming towards him, vast in silhouette against the lit house.

"Arturo?"

"Emilio! What are you doing out here? Hunting for lions?"

"Lions?" Emilio said, sitting down beside him.

"All sorts of wildlife in those bushes, I'll bet," Arturo said, nudging his friend's shoulder. "Let's go and hunt lions together, eh?"

"Maybe another time."

Arturo patted his pocket, reached inside his jacket and

found nothing. "You don't have a cigarette, do you?" he asked. "Oh, no, sorry. Of course you don't."

"No, I don't," Emilio said.

Beyond the lawn, Arturo saw the lights of the house reflected on the lake, making little shivers as the water met the shore. He threw his arm over Emilio's shoulders and gripped him tightly.

"Talk to me, Emilio," he said. "Talk about something."

"Talk about what?"

"Let's talk about art. About painting, like we used to do. Do you remember? We used to talk for hours about it. We used to tell each other that art was a war, painting was an attack on mediocrity and … and somnolence. *Art should be an alcohol, not a balm.* Wasn't that it?"

"I'm going to take Scaglia's offer," Emilio cut in. "I'm going to take the commission. But not for the reasons you think."

"Oh," Arturo replied. "Good for you." He shrugged himself away. He heard Emilio telling him something about his uncle, about hospitals and police tribunals, but he could hardly force himself to listen.

"And Scaglia can help him," Emilio concluded, "if I do what he wants."

Emilio's uncle. The socialist. Arturo had met him once: a small, fussy man with a bristling moustache, who had clearly disapproved of him. Why did Emilio have such a bond with him anyway? Some sentimental fondness for the concept of family. Arturo had no time for his relations. He contacted his own parents once a month: a picture postcard of Milan with a scrawled message – *Still here!*

Emilio was waiting for him to speak. He wanted some word of acceptance, of understanding. Arturo could summon nothing.

"I have to try, Arturo," Emilio went on. "It's only one

painting, and afterwards I can go back to what we were doing before. You know, making art for the people."

Arturo laughed bitterly. "I'm sure your uncle will thank you! Imagine how proud he'll be of you!" His anger was gaining force again, spilling into vindictiveness. "I had high hopes for you once, I really did. I used to think … I used to think you were *better than me*! That you had an integrity I could never possess. Where's it gone now, eh?"

"I'm doing it to help my uncle. That's the only reason."

Arturo rocked back on the stone step. "You really think so!" He struck his brow, feigning sudden realisation. "I get it! They're buying you – buying your allegiance! Ha! And you're so very willing to sell yourself …" Even to himself he sounded demented.

"I heard those things you said to Nina," Emilio said. "You shouldn't have spoken like that to her."

"Nina? What do you know about me and Nina? You don't know anything!"

"Arturo, I care for Nina very much. Even if you don't any more."

"Oh, I see," Arturo said, and his words were sick with contempt. He hated himself, but could not hold back. "So that's why you want the commission! All this balls about your uncle! You're just trying to impress Nina!"

Emilio was scrambling to his feet now. Arturo lurched upright, his head spinning. The two men faced each other, perched on the top step.

"It won't work, you know. She's leaving."

"Leaving?"

"Yes, leaving," he said, revelling in his cruelty. "Going abroad to live with her husband. She just told me. You're too late."

"Where is she?" Emilio demanded. He was looking about wildly, as if he might spot her somewhere in the garden, racing away from him.

"Don't ask me. I'm nothing to do with her any more."

Emilio took a swift step forward and lashed out with an open hand, striking Arturo in the centre of his chest. Arturo staggered backwards, then found empty space beneath his feet. The lawn swung up to meet him as he collapsed down the steps, and he landed flat on his back, spread-eagled, all the breath rushing from him.

When he opened his eyes, Emilio was gone.

There was no sign of Nina among the crowd on the roof terrace. As Arturo threaded between the guests, Volpi bounded towards him, grinning with all his teeth. He moved to step aside, but Volpi blocked him, thwacking two fingers against his lapel. An unnatural zest gleamed from his face.

"Well, well," Volpi declared, his breath sour and metallic. "It seems I'll be entering the Biennale competition at Venice!"

"Will you?" Arturo replied, with a dull churn of dread.

"Yes, indeed! Commendatore Scaglia personally suggested it! He's a great admirer of my work, so he says. Imagine that! Forty-thousand lire in prize money! I bet you could do with forty-thousand lire, eh, Gallo? Ha ha!"

Off he bounded, with a skip in his step. Arturo shrugged, the energy pouring from him. Adrift, he wandered towards the cleared area at the centre: Fosca had pressed Osvaldi into dancing with her, and the two of them were stumbling around together.

"Signor Gallo!" exclaimed Mariagrazia, swooping down on him. "Surely you must know all the latest dance steps?" She grabbed him by the hand, drawing him dumbly onto the desert of the dance floor. "Can you dance Hot Jazz?"

"Why not?" Arturo said. Mariagrazia, locked in the hook of his arm, began to jerk rhythmically. He carried her, backstepping, his soles clicking on the concrete as the music tooted and skirled. His palm rested on the pivot of her hipbone. Other dancers had moved onto the floor now: Assanti and his wife in her harem outfit; Martino Rossi, performing a restrained solo shuffle. Mariagrazia's taut face beamed up at Arturo as he piloted her around between the other couples. A horn wailed; she threw herself backwards in a fake swoon, arching over the support of his arm, kicking up one leg.

Arturo remembered his soundless dance with Nina beside the pool earlier that day. He remembered also another day, a Sunday in the autumn of last year, when the two of them had driven out in her little Fiat along the Novara road, through the last suburbs to a dusty country taverna: a yard under a vine-hung trellis, jugs of white wine on the tables and a gypsy band reeling out fast, loose music. They had danced under the vines, ignoring the crowd that gathered to watch them, alone in the abandon of the afternoon. Would there ever be days like that again?

He kept moving, pulling his hostess about like a mannequin as she vainly attempted to keep up with the tempo.

"My, you dance well!" Mariagrazia exhaled. "I suppose you must have had a lot of practice. I just wish I had the time."

The song came to an end with a last dab of the cymbals, and the record crackled emptily from the gramophone. Mariagrazia made off to select a new disc, leaving Arturo momentarily alone in the middle of the terrace. Then the gramophone began to pop and hiss, and a new tune spilled forth. Arturo saw Adriana Giovene standing vacantly to one side of the terrace, and with a single swift movement he snatched her hand and pulled her to him, leading her into the dance before she could protest.

For a few beats she resisted, but he clung onto her until she began to move, almost automatically, to the music. It was a fast jogging number, full of drums and snorting saxophones.

The night was thickening around them, seeming to attain a form of its own – not just the absence of light but something palpable, massing and feverish. He gripped the girl, pulling her body tight against him, the muscles at the base of her spine hard under his palm. She moved with a mechanical vigour, bland and sexless, with fixed frigidity. Her face was small and neat: perfect nose, perfect mouth, a perfect clockwork body, diamond-cut under the sheen of grey silk.

Arturo had a sudden desire to hurt her, to break her, crack open the shell of her flesh and find what soft thing might live inside. He surged at her, quickstepping her backwards towards a group of servants. Shards of broken glass burst and crackled under their feet. He was enjoying himself now. Their dance had become a slow stylised combat, their bodies locked in competition as the spilled glass ground beneath their soles. What would she do, Arturo wondered, if I kissed her now, full on the lips? Would she even notice? Would she care?

When the song ended, the girl walked away from him without a word. Arturo moved to the parapet. He took a cigarette from a dish on a side-table. Somewhere below him, bushes rustled and sighed. The vague arousal he had felt while he danced with Adriana dissipated; he felt hollowed out. He breathed out smoke.

This was where the future ended, he thought. Beyond this there was nothing. No last erotic imaginations to stir the mind. Nothing more to dream or to say. He should find Emilio and apologise ... He should find Nina ... Where had she gone?

Arturo became aware that something was wrong. Something was happening, too fast for his blurred senses to catch: an eruption of motion from the group sitting to his left, a surprised yell and the sound of a glass smashing, men leaping up in confusion, chairs tumbling. Behind him a woman was saying, "Somebody should do something! They can't let him carry on like this! Is he drunk? Is he ill?"

At the centre of the disturbance was the figure of Bruno Moresco, still seated on the cane sofa. He leaned forward, his face waxy and brilliant, his body at once relaxed and tensed. The journalist Assanti crouched on the floor opposite him, his face and the front of his shirt streaming with what looked for a moment like blood.

"He threw his drink over Assanti!" Fosca said behind her hand. "Then he threw the glass at him! A good thing he missed …"

"My dear fellow," Assanti stuttered, wiping his face, "I assure you I meant no offence, I really had no idea!"

"I don't care what you say," Moresco replied. "You expect me to listen to shitty little comments about Jewish conspiracies and not react? I am a Jew – does that make me any less of an Italian? I am an Italian, a Fascist and a Jew, in that order! I fought for my country, and for the revolution, which is more than you can say, prick of a journalist!"

"Bruno, please," said Rossi, standing at his side. "Please be calm. Signor Assanti meant nothing by what he said."

"Nothing? *The Jews are conspiring with the corrupt Protestant democracies against Catholic Italy*? Is that nothing?" Moresco's forehead was sheened with sweat, and his body trembled. "If you were a man," he went on, jabbing a finger at the journalist, "you wouldn't be apologising now. You'd challenge me for that insult. You'd challenge me and I'd fight you, any time you like, with pistols, blades, fists – anything. But you're scared, aren't you? You're scared of *action*. All you know about is *words*!"

The journalist's wife threw her arms around her husband, as if to shield him with her body from Moresco's threatened assault.

Beyond them, Marinetti sat calmly in his throne,

squinting through the smoke of a cigarette. "Control yourself, Moresco," he said. "Have you lost all sense of reality?"

"All sense of reality ..." Moresco slumped back in his seat, chuckling under his breath. He seemed about to subside back into inertia. Fosca had her hand to her mouth, and Mariagrazia clinging to her arm; Berardi stood stiffly, with pained gravity, like the captain on the bridge of a sinking ship. Only Scaglia seemed unmoved.

The pause lasted only a moment, then Moresco again leapt to his feet. He stood towering above them.

"What's your sense of reality, Marinetti?" he demanded. Around him, men readied themselves to move, to grapple. "What does *His Excellency* really think?"

"I have not the faintest idea what you're talking about," Marinetti said calmly. The dome of his head glowed, and he held the cigarette burning between his fingers.

"Look at us!" Moresco declared. "We're all rotting from the inside. We should be dead! What do you say, Marinetti? You said once that by the time you were forty the youth of the future would despise you, that they would trample you underfoot! What do you say about that now?"

"Can't somebody make him stop?" Fosca whispered. "This is really too much!"

"Nobody should be held responsible for the ideas of their youth," Marinetti said, the anger barely held in his voice. "Even so, I stand by what I wrote. It was a different world then! Now Italy is a young country, reborn on the battlefields of Vittorio Veneto and the Piave – battles in which both you and I fought, Moresco! Have you forgotten that?"

Moresco snapped his fingers contemptuously.

"Do you deny it? That's damned close to treason, Moresco. We made this world, and it belongs to us. The *future* belongs to us. When I see the Italy of today, I feel the pride of a father, truly I do. Perhaps it's you who has grown too old to appreciate it? Perhaps your brains are clogged with the old macaroni! I still have good red Italian blood in my veins. About you I'm not so sure …"

"What do you mean by that?" Moresco said, slow and loaded. "What the hell are you implying by that?"

"Calm down, please, Bruno," said Martino Rossi, taking him by the sleeve. "Not now! Perhaps you should go inside for a while. Lie down until you feel better. I'm sorry, Signor Moresco hasn't been well lately."

"Is that so?" said Marinetti, raising an eyebrow.

Moresco shrugged himself free from Rossi's grasp, stumbled around the sofa and began to walk towards the stairs. When he reached the open space in the centre of the terrace he stopped dead, turning with his arms outspread to address them all.

"We stand upon the last promontory of the centuries!" he declared. "We're all dead, and we don't even know it!" Then he turned and walked away.

A nervous quiet followed his exit, punctuated by the hiss and click of the record revolving on the gramophone. Fosca lifted the needle from the disc: a single harsh scratch.

"A shame," Marinetti said. "I really used to think highly of that man."

13th September 1929

In the tearoom of the Pasticceria Marchesi, Nina sat at her usual table by the window, the curling gold calligraphy on the glass cutting her view of the street into arcs. The table was spread with a crisp white cloth and set with china coffee cups, a pot of warm milk, a silver dish with little amaretto biscuits and a single pink hibiscus in a neat white jar. Nina took her coffee French-style, the cup broad and brimming, the milk in a frothed spiral. Outside, the city passed: the clatter and bang of the trams along Corso Magenta, the weaving cycles and the grunting motor-lorries, the high sun lighting the cornices of the buildings against a late-summer sky. The shop awnings hung heavily over the pavements, like hat brims pulled down low, and the people moved beneath them in lanes of blue shade. The door to the café opened, ringing a tiny bell and letting in a swell of street noise, then closed and the calm returned.

The Marchesi was one of the oldest cafés in the city. It was panelled in heavy wood, its tables crowded close under the fringed lampshades, its fantastically ornamental cakes displayed under glass. It breathed the atmosphere of the lost Viennese dominion, of the *ancien régime*. Nina came here often, enjoying the quiet anonymity of the place. In the deepest recess, a private alcove, was the artists' table, with framed sketches displayed around it. She recognised most of the men that gathered there now, knew some of their names. They were neo-classicists, surrealists, members of the Novecento movement; they drank sweet wine and brandy, smoked cigars, doodled sketches on the tablecloth and argued loudly over their newspapers and magazines.

Nina had no wish to sit at the artists' table, even if she were invited. If they ever noticed her – and a few of them might glance in her direction, blowing a smoke ring – they would take her for some ordinary businessman's wife, no doubt. Young, wealthy, beautiful – but no artist. It amused her to remain apart from them, to observe them from a distance. The artists' table was a long-standing fixture at the Marchesi; its occupants tipped grandly when they were in funds, and were given credit when they were not. They came and went, old faces fading into unfashionable obscurity, new ones arriving to take their places; the staff treated them with condescending politeness. Marinetti had never come here, even when he lived in Milan. The Futurists had alternative rendezvous.

On the far side of the table, across the coffee cups, the milk jug, the pink flower and the tray of little biscuits, Nina's youngest brother Giuseppe sat and toyed with a polished brass cigarette lighter. The noises of the street filtered in through the glass.

"Well?" she asked.

Her brother was in Milan only for a few hours. He'd left Brescia by train before dawn, and had to be home in Turin before sunset in time for the Sabbath. A brief stopover in his business routine. Nina had not seen him for two months.

"The letter reached me last week," he said. He was a well-presented man, no longer quite young but still with a sharpness to him. His suit was spotless charcoal; his wristwatch gleamed from under a starched cuff. He gave the impression he was sitting for his own portrait. On his lapel, the tiny gold star of the Italian Jewish Business Association was pinned beside the tricolour Fascist Party badge. His long fingers shifted the brass lighter on the tablecloth, nudging it from side to side.

"And it was from Buenos Aires?"

"Yes, it was postmarked Buenos Aires. He didn't say exactly where he was living, nor where he was going next. He said very little …"

"I suppose he asked you to tell me."

Her brother nodded, his fingers twitching at the brass. He looked more weary than uncomfortable. It seemed to cost him a physical effort to raise his eyes. "I should apologise, I know," he said. "I was sworn to secrecy about the whole affair, and he is my brother-in-law."

"And I am your sister. But I understand."

Giuseppe nodded. Nearly a year had passed since Nina's husband had left – since he had disappeared. More than six months since she had returned from Paris, and that whole summer had been lost in a hellish, poisoned bliss of forgetfulness. Clear-headed now, clear-thinking, Nina sat, considering.

"He wrote about Marco," Giuseppe said. "He asked me to ensure that the boy is well and happy. I realise that you may find that somewhat offensive. He's gone now, I take it?"

"Yes, he's back in Switzerland. I was there with him for two months. It seemed easier than having him here over the summer with Amedeo gone."

Nina had taken rooms in the Hotel Bellevue et Belvedere at Glion. They had ridden the little funicular railway up the mountainside from Montreux, with Marco pressed up against the glass of the picture window as their compartment rose smoothly through the trees and the lake spread itself before them in the immaculate blue of the Swiss sunshine. They had eaten ice creams, listened to the hotel band playing waltzes, and taken the white paddle steamer across to Vevey. Marco had told her about his school, his friends, all departed now for the summer to their families in France and Sweden and the United States. His best friend, he'd told her, was an American boy called Tomato. He had seemed happy.

He did not ask where his Papa had gone, and when he might return. His indifference, his apparent contentment, had shocked her. It had also disappointed her: she had feared them, but she had wanted her son's questions. Yet they had made him this way, she and Amedeo between them. How could he miss what he had never experienced?

"It's a shame we don't see very much of him," Giuseppe said. "The children are growing up without knowing him. And of course Irena misses him. You should bring him with you next time you visit Turin."

"Perhaps," Nina said, stirring her coffee in her cup. The sediment lifted, black grains in the milk. Her brother's wife Irena had never much cared for her. But that was not the issue.

"Perhaps you could visit us for Yom Kippur," Giuseppe said. "It's still a month away – you could fetch Marco from school. It's good to be with your family then, with your own people. Actually, we were thinking, Irena and I were thinking, that you might consider moving back to Turin. You could sell Amedeo's apartment and come back to live with us. Marco could attend school there, rather than growing up in a foreign country. It would be better for you both, Nina. What is there left for you here?"

"Have you forgotten that I've lived in Milan for six years?" said Nina. "This is my home, Giuseppe. My friends are here. Even when Amedeo and I were … Even before he disappeared, that is, we lived very separate lives. His leaving has made little difference to me."

"But don't you see how your situation must appear to others? Don't you see how badly it reflects upon the rest of us?"

Nina's hand shook as she held her coffee cup. She tried to keep the anger from her voice. "I have done nothing wrong," she said. "Why should I be ashamed? Do you think I should be? Am I shameful to you, Giuseppe? I have been a good wife, a good mother. It wasn't me who ran away."

"It reflects badly," her brother said again. The lighter slipped from his fingers and clattered on the tabletop. "He deserted you. You can see what people might think."

"Why should I care?" Nina said. "I have done nothing wrong. Nothing!" With great care she lifted the cup and took a sip of coffee. Her eyes felt moist, and she blinked back the tears. To cry now would be to admit defeat. "I won't leave Milan," she said. "This is my home, and I like it here. I'm only twenty-six. I'm not going to retreat from the world when I've done nothing to deserve it."

Her brother was glancing around the room. His irritation was evident: the set of his jaw, the bunched muscle.

"All my life," Nina said, with hushed ferocity, "I've obeyed the wishes of others. The wishes of men. Father, Amedeo, you … I've done exactly what was required of me, and I've never argued. I've never suggested that I might want something different. I married Amedeo because Father required it. It was a business transaction, nothing more. I played the role of the good wife, the good mother, because it was required of me. I took lovers, because my husband wanted me to, because it was *useful* …"

"Nina, please!"

"You know it's true, Giuseppe. I obeyed. I did what was asked of me. And now, for the first time in my life, I don't have to obey anyone. For the first time, I can act how I choose."

"So," he said with effort, "what will you do?"

"I will live here," Nina replied. "I lead a very amusing existence, you know. I've just bought a car, in fact – a little Fiat. You never know, I might crash and you'll be rid of me."

"Nina, for God's sake!" Giuseppe said, slamming his hand down on the table. His face was lit with pain. For the first time, Nina saw how much this was grieving him.

"I'm sorry," she said.

A few of the other patrons of the tearoom were looking at them now. Nina turned her face to the window again, towards the heedless street. "I've been working on my photography a lot recently," she said. "I've got an exhibition at the moment, in fact."

"Photography?" Giuseppe said. "I'd assumed that was a passing interest."

"It's in a different café, the exhibition I mean," Nina continued. "The Craja, over behind the Scala. The pictures are just studies, really. I hoped you might have time to come and look at it."

"Now? No, I'm sorry. I'm late as it is." Her brother moved his wrist from under a cuff, frowning at his watch. He drummed his fingers on the tabletop, regarding blankly the pink flower in its little jar. He looked like he wanted to run out into the street.

"Tell me why Amedeo left," Nina said. "I know it's a secret, but tell me."

"You know I can't," he replied. "And even if I could, this is hardly the place to discuss it. I need to go now."

Outside, the air was charged with dust, exhaust hanging thickly, churned by the moving traffic. Together they walked to the tram stop on Via Meravigli to stand and wait in a patch of sun. Behind them, a big shop window had a display of winter furs.

"Will you at least consider visiting us next month?" Giuseppe said.

"I might," Nina told him. "I'll have to see." Away down the street, the yellow tram was moving across the junction towards them. Giuseppe stood holding his hat. Abruptly he took Nina's arm and drew her into the shade of the shop awning.

"Your husband …" he began, speaking quietly and very fast, watching the approaching tram. "Your husband was … Nina, Amedeo is a *homosexual.*" He whispered the word through his teeth. The look of pained disgust on his face was suddenly hilarious.

"Oh, Giuseppe, of course I knew that!"

"You did?" He blinked at her, turning the brim of his hat slowly between his fingers.

"What of it?"

"Nina, he became compromised, and that was why he had to leave. He wanted to protect you, even to the extent of hiding what he had done."

"Done what? Giuseppe, what did Amedeo do?"

Her brother looked at her, incomprehension in his eyes. The tram was close behind him now. "Does it matter?" he said. "He was in danger. He didn't want you to get involved with the mess he'd made. He didn't want you to know. I can tell you no more."

"Then he's not coming back?"

"He *can't* come back."

Nina pulled her brother into a tight embrace. Then he drew away, put on his hat and stepped aboard the tram.

"Loyalty is important, Nina," he said, turning for a moment. "To *show* loyalty is important. Now more than ever."

Heat buoyed her, carried her forward; she moved through the thick scents of the late-summer street without feeling the ground beneath her, from umber shade to bright sunlight and back. She heard the sound of church bells, black, medieval ringing over the clamour of the street, announcing noon. Passing the windows of shops, she saw herself in the glass amongst the cakes and the shoes and the clothes. In the air was the promise of autumn, her favourite season; the metropolis was awakening from the long, slow insomnia of summer, the mosquito-haunted nights and the days of solid heat, waking to freshness and clean breezes again. It was in autumn that Nina had first moved to Milan, wedding-fresh and unknowing. Six years ago, she had first seen the ranks of chestnut trees in the public gardens burst into colour from under their coating of dust.

Nina turned the corner into Via Dante. Far away the spires of the Duomo rose against a hazy sky. This last year she had lived in suspended uncertainty. Amedeo's disappearance, the mystery of it, had stilled something in her heart. She understood that she had been waiting for him to reappear, to step back into her life and resume control. But now it was clear that he was gone: truly gone and far away.

It was here, at the end of Via Dante, that she had climbed from her father's motor-car that day, more than ten years ago, and watched the aeroplanes above the city. She remembered the feeling, that breathless sensation of release. She felt it again now.

Profound happiness rose through her as she crossed the street, quick over the tramlines, to the central island with its newspaper kiosk and cluster of drab trees. The traffic was singing to her: the bark and whine of the tramcars, the heavy revving of the automobiles, the horn of a delivery dray. She almost wanted to dance, right here in the middle of Piazza Cordusio, to quickstep through the crowd beside the newspaper kiosk, around the base of the sombre statue.

All the confusion and madness of the last year – the trip to Paris, the abortion, the injections – all of it was slipping from her and leaving her ... Free, she thought. I am free.

On a wall high up, stencilled in repeat pattern, the frowning face of the dictator glared down at her. The pictures dated from the time of the public vote in the spring, but nobody had dared to paint over them. Beneath, in bold black type, the words repeated in sequence:

DUCE YES DUCE YES DUCE YES DUCE YES DUCE YES DUCE YES DUCE YES DUCE YES DUCE YES

And beneath that, daubed in dripping red brushstrokes:

MUSSOLINI IS ALWAYS RIGHT

Nina remembered the day of his victory back in March: the parades and the cheering in the streets, the cars driving wildly with flags streaming behind them. A ninety-nine per cent vote for the regime: who could argue with that? Yes Duce yes Duce yes Duce yes yes yes yes.

She turned on her heel, pressing her fingers to her temples. She was free, and she was safe. She was safe with the things she loved: a fast car, the swirl of milk in coffee, the snip of a camera shutter biting off a slice of the world. Safe beneath the frowning gaze of the dictator, who was always right.

Nina walked on into the great piazza of the Duomo. The huge façade rose before her, its swarming detail lost in the haze of midday. The tram carousel that used to circle the open space had gone now, and the piazza was abandoned to the pedestrians and the milling pigeons.

Beside the Vittorio Emmanuelle monument she paused, distracted. There was something happening that evening, she remembered – a party. She had been given an invitation at the opening of her exhibition in the Craja café, but had thought nothing of it then. Reaching into her handbag, she found the small card. *You are invited to an unseasonal party at the studios of Sig. Umberto Viventi, Sculptor, Piazza della Vetra, San Lorenzo, Milan. Friday 13th September 1929. 9.30PM. Fancy dress obligatory.*

Here was freedom! Here was life! She tucked the card back into her bag, already planning the disguise she would wear.

10

10th May 1930

Two lines traced on glass with the razor's edge: she followed them to the end, then picked up the last grains on a wetted finger, polishing her gums. She felt the cold burn at the back of her throat and in her sinuses, then the spreading numbness from the root of her tongue. Getting up, she stretched on her toes, arms spread, reeling, the drug rushing through her. She had needed this. The anxiety and the creeping dread, the sense of unknown threat, all of it was burning away now, eclipsed by white.

A jug of water was on the side table. She poured herself a glass and drank it down, then poured another. She watched herself in the mirror, her throat jogging as she swallowed. She wanted music: a string quartet to waltz her round the room in the arms of an invisible partner. Her scalp tingled as her body responded to its fuel, complex chemistry working beneath the skin.

She wanted to join the party again, but that would mean seeing Arturo. How would she react if she saw him? She might laugh in his face, burst into tears, slap him . Every shift in her emotions felt amplified. She needed him, didn't need him. She didn't want him, needed nobody … She wanted …

Falling back onto the mattress, she kicked off first one shoe and then the other, then lay full length as the burning in her throat eased to a slow heat that spread through her. She stared at the pulse of the ceiling. The room's quiet was electrified; the soft tungsten of the lamp on its tall stand fizzing with the rhythm of her blood. She pressed her palms to her eyes and felt the beating in her head, saw the redness through her closed fingers.

She rose up from the bed and paced to the window on stockinged feet. Opening the shutters, she threw back the windows and let the night glide over her, felt the thrill of the warm breeze on her face and arms. In the lit window, she clasped the rail of the little iron balcony. She felt illuminated, flung out like a beacon at the distant shore.

Sounds rose through her mind. They scattered and dashed, mixed and blurred, before focusing into memories of words and scraps of conversation. Arturo's voice, close against her ear as they lay together in his bed. For all these months, she realised now, she had been using him as a shield, a block against all that her past life contained. His face, his voice, the refuge of the days they made together, of the nights in his apartment in the big brass bed with the old springs that sighed and popped beneath them, with the rain battering the windows and gushing into the gutters outside …

Arturo was an outsider, like the other men she had loved – like Bianchi, like poor Tadeusz. Not – certainly not – like Amedeo, with his cool control, at home in the world, owning the world. Arturo was her santuary from all that: without him she would be left naked and exposed to all that pressed down upon her. Could she leave him? Could she run away to be with Amedeo, to live in the new world that Amedeo had created for her?

Lucidity was soaking through her, sharpening her mind. If Arturo were here now, she could explain her feelings to him, so that he would be forced to understand. She could talk to him about art and about love; tell him how much she had cherished the sincerity he had once possessed, how rare and how rich it had been after the emptiness and pretence of her life with Amedeo. It would be easy to tell him now: the words were formed in her mind, clear and perfect, like the pearls in the necklace that she ran through her fingers. Why had she not told him these things already? Why could he not have understood?

We only talk about these things, she thought, these most important things, when we are too angry to express ourselves. The thought seemed profound, and she decided to remember it … But already it was gone …

She remembered grabbing Moresco's hand at dinner. Moresco had known her husband. He knew what her husband had done, why he had to disappear. Nina herself did not know, had never wanted to know. It was amazing to her that she had managed to live for so long in ignorance; *willed* ignorance as well, a deliberate avoidance of the truth. As if awareness of her husband's crimes would contaminate her and destroy her sense of freedom. Now she felt a hungry desire for the truth. She needed to know, although knowing terrified her. What would she do, how could she react, if everything was exposed?

She thought of the gun under Berardi's pillow. She imagined her palm closing around the grip; saw herself advancing across the darkness of the garden; saw Scaglia turning slowly at her approach, his dawning horror as she raised the pistol and fired. She would do that to protect herself and her son. If she could believe that killing the man would kill all that he represented, she would do it. But it was a desperate idea, like all fantasies of the powerless. The first rush of the drug was burning out of her, and she felt suddenly frightened and very alone. What had she been thinking?

Returning to the dressing table, she stooped again over the little mirror. Another two lines on the glass, the last residue of the silver box. She perched on the edge of the bed, breathing hard. Fluid streamed from her nose. She sneezed suddenly, and felt the explosion in her head.

For a few seconds she could barely focus her vision. It had been months since she had taken this much cocaine. She was trembling, close to panic. She closed her eyes, and images flashed and collided; opened them, and the walls throbbed back at her. She remembered flying with Bianchi, the long moment of descent in the sky above Milan, feeling herself deserted and falling. She remembered the white room in Paris – she had almost wiped it from her memory – the bearded doctor and the stern-faced nurse, the confused slide beneath the sedatives. It was all a mistake. She had changed her mind, she wanted them to stop … *Détendez-vous, Madame. Détendez-vous,, et vous ne sentirez rien. Tout sera bientôt fini …*

She lay down on the bed. Other voices came to her now, echoing and distorted: her son Marco, telling her about his school and his friends. His best friend, Tomato. *Don't worry, Mama. I know Tomato isn't a real boy.* They were on the steamer coming back from Vevey; she had gripped the rail and tried not to cry. She searched desperately for a happier memory to counter it, something she could tolerate … An evening in the car, returning from some trip into the country. An open road, a racing breeze. Arturo leaning across to speak to her, telling her to pull over to the verge. Silence dropping around them as the engine died, and he drew her into his embrace. "Let's not hurry home so quickly," he said. Birds singing, trees sighing over the road, his voice and his kiss …

The memory of his touch was so keen, he could almost have been there in the room. But no, not him. Not Arturo … She tried to banish him from her mind. She remembered the hands of Moresco as he sat beside her at dinner. Outside the open window the night was solid as a wall. On the bed, Nina rode out the dizziness, the voluptuous spin. She wished she could turn out the lamp without moving.

The knock at the door startled her. She lay still. The knock again. The idea that it might be Arturo was dreadful to her. She could bear to see him now. But the idea that it might be Scaglia was worse. Then the voice, Emilio's voice, quiet and muffled through the door panel, calling her name.

She got up, tugged the hem of her dress straight and crossed to the door with her legs dead beneath her. The pulse was heavy in her neck. Heat radiated from her face. A quick glance at the dressing table, but there was no evidence of what she had been doing.

"Nina," he said to her as she let him in. "You've been crying."

She shook her head, stepping away from his hand, from his clumsy, consoling movement towards her. Looking in the mirror again, she saw herself clearly: the mascara streaked and blurred where she'd wiped at it. He handed her a tissue.

"Pour me a glass of water, would you?" she asked, her voice sounding as high and clear as a ringing bell. Sitting at the dresser again, she swabbed her face clean. His hand with the glass, setting it down beside her. She wanted to keep clear of him. He had no place in this room now.

"I heard you talking to Arturo earlier," he was saying. "I understand everything."

"Understand?" she heard herself reply. "What is there to understand?" Her voice was still high-pitched, near hilarious. She felt the laughter jumping in the pit of her throat. Behind her, Emilio had settled himself on the edge of the bed. He would try to touch her, to embrace her; she could not stand that.

On her feet again, she circled the room and he followed, dumbly tracking her. It was a chase in slow motion. Her body was full of wild energy, but there was nowhere to leap. She felt like running from the room and away across the hills.

"Nina," he kept saying, his face warped with concern. "Nina, please don't leave him. If you left him I wouldn't see you any more, would I?"

"Leave him?" she was saying. "Ha! Leave him?" *He left me*, she wanted to say. *He left me. He became someone else. I'm still here!*

Their slow chase had led back to the bed, the only place where he could not corner her. She knelt on it and tumbled sideways, sprawled over the pillows. Emilio was advancing over the end of the bed. Don't come closer, she wanted to say. I don't want you here. I don't want to be touched. I don't want to be consoled.

"Emilio," she said, raising an open palm. "Emilio, I ..." He reached for her hand, thinking she wanted him to take it –

All of a sudden the lights went out – no dull pop of dying filament, no flash, just total blackness. Silence for a moment, without sensation. The bulb, she thought, but knew almost at once that it was more than that. All the power had gone, in a blink, and left them submerged in electricless, unmodern dark.

"Emilio?" she said again, her open hand reaching out. "Emilio, are you there?"

28th February 1930

Crack-kneed, Emilio squatted before the fireplace, feeding sticks to the flame. Coal dust crunched beneath his feet, and the edge of the rug was crusty with splinters. Behind him loomed the cold emptiness of the studio. It was night, the shutters rattled and the wind spat rain at the windows. Emilio held his spread palms over the fire, but still he shivered. From the hall came the sound of Nina's voice. The bathroom door clattered in its frame.

They had a new routine now, he and Arturo. During the day they painted, as they had always done, with the wintry grey light through the windows and the sky outside stacked heavy with cloud. But in the evenings, when once they would have continued working by the yellow chandelier bulbs, or gone out to one of the neighbourhood bars, or just roamed the streets, walking quickly and talking together – now Nina's presence had come between them.

She would arrive shortly after dusk, filling the apartment with her voice, stirring the dead air into motion. Sometimes she stayed for the evening, and she and Arturo listened to music before retreating to his room. Her coat left draped over a chair, her scent lingering. Other times, she took him away to a restaurant or a dance; at first they had invited Emilio to come with them, but he always refused, not wanting to feel the constraint his presence imposed on them. Now they no longer asked. Alone in the apartment, Emilio would move from room to room, feeling the cold masses of air shifting around him, void of warmth and company. He tried to paint; his work got smaller and more complex, turned in upon itself.

It was not long before Nina had colonised the apartment and made it her own – not long before it seemed empty without her. When she was not there, Arturo would stalk the rooms in a fury of impatience, bitter at his own desire for her, primed for the raucous shrill of the doorbell that would announce her arrival. The nights when she never came were the worst: Arturo in a seething rage, sitting in the kitchen drinking coffee after coffee, fantasising grimly about where she might be, and with whom.

"She's driving me insane," he said. "I know she's seeing somebody else. Probably several others, who knows! Half the time she won't even tell me what she's doing. Why did I ever get involved with a married woman?"

"Didn't her husband leave her months ago?" Emilio asked.

"More than a year ago. Now she's free to do what she wants. You know, she told me she even had an affair with another woman once! What can you think about somebody like that? She could do anything! Sometimes I suspect she doesn't even *like* men …"

Emilio could only shrug. There was nothing to be said. They would go out to a bar, walk the streets as they used to do, but the topic of conversation would remain the same.

"You know the worst of it?" Arturo said. "You know why she always comes here to the apartment? She won't let me stay at her place because she doesn't want the maids to know about me! Isn't that the filthiest bourgeois hypocrisy?"

Arturo alone was allowed to criticise his lover. And as soon as she arrived, he would be illuminated by her presence, filled with the joy of her. This had been going on for over five months now.

Emilio stood in the hall. Light came from under the bathroom door, and the sound of splashing water. Arturo's low chuckle, then whispered words too low to hear. Emilio loitered. A squeaking sound, flesh against the bath enamel, then the slap of water spilled out onto the bathroom floor. The glow from under the door was soft and wavering – they were bathing by candlelight again.

Emilio went back into the studio, rubbing his hands for warmth, and sat before the easel again, wishing he could lose himself in his work. By the door Arturo's big empty canvas waited, idle. For weeks he'd been battering at it, sketching shapes onto the fabric and then scrubbing them out, whitewashing it back to blankness. He wanted it to be his great work, yet he was paralysed by the grandeur of his own ambition.

Pinned across the far wall were his sketches: drawings in charcoal and crayon, rough paint daubs, colour swipes. Amongst them were several nudes that he had done six months ago. The later ones were abstracted and artificial, the shapes of the naked body broken down into formal constructions, cylinders and spheres, an assemblage of machined parts – the stomach a stretched ovoid, the breasts perfect cones, the face a neat arrangement of interlocking triangles. The earlier ones, though, drawn from life, were clearly portraits of Nina. Arturo had finally worked them up into a painting, which Emilio found bland and formulaic after all the preparations that had gone into it. Nina herself had seemed less than fully convinced by the finished piece, her transmogrified form rendered as arcs of peachy flesh-tone against a billowing sky, shot through with machine-motifs.

But it was the sketches that captivated Emilio. The figure stood, her body half turned, arm raised and bent above her head, the volume of flesh described in only a few fluid lines, captured perfectly. Even with her face in profile, Emilio could recognise her – the shape of the body beneath the clothes, that he had imagined so guiltily, so often. It was the same woman, the one he had once tried to imagine and to set down on paper: the woman of his fantasies.

Emilio heard the bathroom door opening and emitting its warmth and steam, as the two of them, towel-wrapped no doubt, shuttled along the hall and into Arturo's room. Sound carried through the connecting doors: the low wail of the bedsprings, Arturo's yodel, Nina's shriek of hilarity. Emilio picked up an old newspaper, sat in the armchair and tried to read, but the words squirmed and he couldn't concentrate. From the grate, the fire cracked and smoked at him.

He felt himself waiting, conscious of his heart beating loudly in his ears. Did they talk about him when they were in bed together? Did they joke about him, imagine him listening at the door? He had, once, listened at the door, and he still suspected that they knew. It had made him feel greasy in his soul, but he could not help himself. He was fascinated; he was possessed.

Out, then. Out, and leave them to their private world. In the lobby he took his coat from the stand, pulled his cap on. He could smell her perfume on the fur stole looped on the peg. Closing the door quietly behind him, Emilio rattled down the stairs. Inside the black mesh of the lift shaft, the heavy counterweight fell smoothly past him; a moment later the lift itself came gliding up, the woman from the flat downstairs glaring from behind the diagonal lattice. The lift sailed on upwards, and Emilio reached the gloomy, stone-flagged passageway at the bottom of the stairs. His bicycle was there, propped with several others against the wall, but this evening he needed the slower rhythm of walking.

The night was funeral black. The wind had died away, but the rain still fell as a slow mist, fizzing around the globes of the streetlights and gleaming off the tarmac. At the corner, Emilio paused and gazed up at the windows of the apartment, picking out Arturo's room high above him. The shutters were closed. Emilio crossed, quick with his coat flapping, and turned along the avenue of trees that lined the public gardens. Anger put a clip in his stride; he hated them both, hated them for their selfishness. But lovers are always selfish, wrapped in the drama of each other. Arturo was still his best friend, and Nina … Nina was something else altogether.

Once, back in the autumn, he had sat with her in the Parco Sempione. The day was bright with the last of the summer sun, and they had been eating ice cream and waiting for Arturo to join them. Emilio had hardly known her then – it might even have been the first time he had been alone with her – and they spoke mainly about his work: she politely questioning, he self-effacing. He asked her about the bracelet she wore, with the strange symbol on the gold disc. A Hebrew character, she told him: *Shaddai*, meaning *Almighty*. One of the names of God. She had told him that the bracelet had belonged to her mother, and she wore it for luck.

"*He* doesn't like it though," she said. "He thinks it seems religious, and therefore … I don't know … somehow sordid. Perhaps I just wear it to annoy him." A smile, her slender fingers turning the gold chain on her wrist.

"What's it like," Emilio had asked her, "being Jewish? I've never met a Jew, you see."

"You probably have, but you just didn't know it. We're much the same as anyone else. It's just a family thing. Like being a socialist, I suppose. Arturo seems to think you're a socialist, by the way."

"Arturo thinks a lot of things," Emilio had said, and she laughed.

"What are his family like? Have you met his father?"

"I spoke to him once on the telephone. Arturo doesn't talk about his parents much. He seems a bit embarrassed by the notion that he has a family – probably prefers the idea that he formed himself out of primal matter. They live near Treviso somewhere. His father's a doctor, I think."

"My father was a lawyer," Nina said. "He's dead now."

"Mine too," Emilio told her. He was conscious that the tone of their conversation had changed, gaining a sense of complicity, a shared warmth.

But then there was Arturo, bounding towards them across the gravel path with his hat in his hand, grinning wildly, to catch her up in his arms and kiss her on the mouth and place himself back between them so no further intimacies could pass.

Emilio walked, head down, the gardens to his right a dimmed mass in hazy rain. Raindrops fell from the bare trees, an irregular wet spatter. To his left now was Piazza Oberdan, the sleeping trams drawn up in their sidings. A cart passed along the street, the horse shuddering in its traces, hooves ringing dull on the wet asphalt. Indistinct through the trees, he could see the flickering lights of a fair: canvas tarpaulins drawn over a carousel, a few wooden hutches with dripping awnings, figures of men huddled beneath, smoking wetly. Smell of roasting chestnuts, charcoal smoke and horse dung, the fumes of a petrol generator, all soaked together. It had started really raining now. Already the shoulders of his coat were heavy with it.

He passed the Porta Venezia gates. The rain formed a fine spray around the wheels of the cars and motor-lorries. The few figures around the junction were strafed by the circling headlamps. Emilio crossed the street and walked on, realising now where he wanted to go: the lit shops and the people on the Corso Buenos Aires. He needed a crowd to lose himself in. He could go to a bar, but that would mean the possibility of meeting somebody, of having to talk to some stranger. He didn't want to talk – just to walk and be alone and feel the rain pouring down over him. He tipped back his head and felt the water rushing over his face. Cold, but good, washing him.

Between the rows of cars and the windows of the shops, people were moving quickly, heads down. Emilio watched them, studied each of them as they passed: men in hats with their collars turned up; men with streaming umbrellas; women, in pairs or alone, their heels battering the pavement, hat-brims soaked and sagging over faces screwed up against the wet. The people walked fast, not noticing Emilio, as he passed among them noticing everything, like a spy.

They used to say, he and Arturo on their nocturnal walks, that the city was an entity in itself. Not a projection of the individual self but a force of its own, possessed of a logic beyond human rationality. It was a creed of sorts: the city as machine, with a machine-soul, a machine-consciousness. Great Milan the mighty engine, and themselves merely technicians working within it, trying to define its mechanism, learn its codes, express its purpose. The concept would not work if Nina was involved though: she made everything around her a mere backdrop. The concept did not work for love, and love's inescapable egotism.

He remembered meeting Nina in the kitchen one morning, soon after the beginning of the affair. Arturo was still in bed, or perhaps out buying cigarettes, and she was sitting at the table drinking coffee, the bowl cupped in her hands. She wore one of Arturo's shirts, and her hair was still unkempt from the bed. Emilio sat with her, watched her eating pastries, gulping them down as if she had not eaten in days. The cream smeared at the corners of her mouth, and a curl of black hair hung forward over her face. She smelled of sex, salty sweet. Or perhaps he had just imagined that. Her bare legs were crossed beneath the table, the hem of the shirt bunched between her thighs. She grinned at him as she ate, knowing and shameless.

"What are you thinking about?" she said, her voice sly and low. He said nothing, and she reached across the table and dabbed cream on the end of his nose.

He remembered the scene exactly – the pitch of her voice, the angle of her legs, the scent and the warmth. These were the things that told against grand notions; these were the things that defeated abstract ideals. That made love real. That turned the rest of the world into a pale projection.

But the street was real too, and the night was real. As he stepped away from the kerb to let a car pass, something dog-shaped leapt up from the gutter. Emilio started back, and a gush of water soaked his trouser leg. Sodden-footed, he crossed the side street and carried on up the broad pavement, under the damp brick arches of the railway bridge. A train passed overhead, shrieking through the rain, steam hanging ghostly high over the traffic in the street before the rain beat it down. He shuddered, the cold driving an ache up his spine.

Ahead of him were the open doors of a cinema, the space under the jutting awning packed with bodies sheltering from the rain, hunched shoulders in overcoats, fuming cigarettes. Emilio slipped in amongst them and the relief was immediate: the rain had been battering at him. Walking under the awning was like entering a crowded room. He shunted his way through the people at the door and into the foyer of the cinema. There were puddles on the red linoleum floor, dripping from coats and grounded umbrellas. Emilio paced across the lobby, looked at the posters around the walls. From one, the face of Augusto Bandini glowered manfully back at him, above a swooning female figure – *Vein of Gold*, the picture was called. Then there were the two clowns, Stanlio and Ollio, while on the opposite wall, Maciste, "The Italian Hercules", wrestled a serpent. The late feature was called *The Woman in the Moon*: the poster showed a huge rocketship looming, phallic, over the lunar plains.

A woman stood by the poster, facing the side door and leaning forward a little as she touched up her make-up in the glass. She turned towards Emilio as he drew closer.

"Signor Calvi?" Her face was wide and pretty, her lipstick smudged slightly. Emilio recognised her, and felt a dull thud deep in his bowels.

"Maddelena?" Dazed, he removed his hat, bowed from the neck.

"I thought it was you!" she said, brightening. She was still attractive. A little short, wide-hipped and large-breasted … but still the same. He wanted to touch her.

"You remember me, don't you?" she said, with a lopsided smile.

"Of course," Emilio said. She was putting her make-up case back into her handbag, a nervous flutter in her movements. A stray loop of hair had escaped from under her hat and was stuck to her forehead.

"How are you now?" she was saying, not quite looking at him. "And how is your friend Signor Gallo?"

"He's very well," Emilio said. "So am I, as you see."

"And are you still … Are you still doing your painting? But of course you must be! How is it? The work, I mean."

"Well, it's well," Emilio said. Maddalena's face looked a little blotchy, the powder matted and streaked by the rain.

"That's good, that's good," she said. Lipstick on her teeth. Perhaps he could go with her now to a bar or a café, and they could sit indoors out of the rain and repeat these drab, cosy phrases to each other. They could go together to her room in a lodging house, she still nicely unsure of herself. They could kiss again under a naked bulb, which she would then turn off to undress. There would be the stove and a water heater in the corner and her clothes draped, drying, over the chair beside the window, and they would have sex, just as they had those two or three times before, years ago. He would wake to the paleness of her back turned towards him, the delicate ridges of her spine in morning light through the thin drape. Then there would be her confusion and misgivings. And he would leave and walk to the tram stop in the morning rain, and go home to find Nina in the warm kitchen eating pastries, and none of it would have meant anything.

But they stood and gazed at one another, and there was nothing else for them to say. She shrugged, smiled, nodded her head a few times. "That's good," she said again. "Good to hear. Well, do tell your friend you saw me, won't you? And your uncle too – I remember him so well … Such a sweet, kind man. Good to have met you again."

"Yes, good," Emilio said, and Maddalena backed away from him, glancing back to check if the rain had stopped, then giving a quick wave.

"Goodbye then, Emilio," she said, and was gone.

The auditorium was thick with the stink of cigarettes, of wet woollens, of breath. Picking his way down the aisle, throat clenched, Emilio saw that most of the audience were solitary men. The tiny coals of their cigarettes glowed in the gloom, and the smoke churned in the beam from the projector.

He found a seat near the front, empty places to either side and the screen huge above him. The pianist beat out a spidery tune as the newsreels played. The screen showed a desert landscape, harsh white sands bleached by the sun, black serrated palms. A title card flashed up: *More Victories of Our Army in Africa.* Troops on the march through the white plains, passing ragged walls of mudbrick. A line of armoured cars drawn up, etched black in the heat. Emilio remembered Arturo telling stories of the desert. Postcards from Tripoli. A white city on a desert shore, with the jagged shadows of the palm leaves. *General Graziani Surveys the Rebel Position.* A staff-car with a dust-caked windscreen, a man in a peaked cap striding beside it. Soldiers in groups, their faces black beneath their domed sun-helmets. Then the Arabs, in headscarves and long robes, posed behind a head-high fence of barbed wire. The camera panned across them, as they stared back, impassive, immobilised by defeat. Heaps of antique-looking rifles spread on the sand.

Emilio remembered sitting in cinemas like this with Maddalena, her hand clasped warm in his own, as they waited for the main feature to begin. He remembered her face lit by the screen, her lips moving as she read the caption cards to herself. He could have been married to her by now. They could have had children together. Church on Sundays, a nursemaid pushing a perambulator, her firm hands kneading his tired shoulders when he returned from work; trips to the lakes in summer, or even the lido at Rimini … He could have all that by now, if he had wanted it. He pushed the thought from his mind. That sort of existence seemed distant to him now – more distant than those Arabs, crushed by modernity out in the desert. Compared to the promise of the future, what pleasure could mere happiness hold?

On the screen appeared a huge modern building in the mountains, dignitaries in regalia drawn up on the steps. *The Duce Visits the New Hydroelectric Plant At Cardano*: Mussolini, in Blackshirt militia uniform, climbed the steps of the building, trailed by his staff. In the huge turbine hall he stood with hands on hips, dwarfed by the massive machines. The Cardano facility, the title card said, would produce more electricity than any other power station in Europe. A few cheers from the men at the back of the auditorium; a brief burst of applause.

Now there were hordes of children in the picture: children in rows, children in prams, children riding a miniature carousel. A woman from Naples was being awarded a medal for having more than twelve babies. Someone whistled from the back of the auditorium. Emilio slid down in his seat, the damp collars of his coat riding up around his ears.

The screen flickered, black then white, the pianist breaking out a sequence of grandiose chords as the main feature began. Emilio felt himself drifting, not towards sleep but into a strange trance-like state. Motion filled the screen, pictures moving, telling a story, but he had no interest in it. There was a hero and a villain. A mad professor of some sort. A woman who was loved. The title cards explained things, but Emilio preferred not to read them. Instead he let the images carry him, ghost shapes forming in the smoky beam of the projector.

Now there was a huge hangar at night, lit by searchlights. The moon dangled above it, a white disc snipped from the black cloth of sky. The hangar doors opened and the huge rocketship emerged. Angled, daunting, towering over the tiny figures that gathered below it, the rocket slid from the darkness. This was the future, Emilio thought. This could be real. He remembered the other film by the same director – they'd watched it a year ago, he and Arturo, in this same cinema. The future city, the city of machines, skyscraper buildings rising above canyon streets. Then the woman: machine-woman, future-woman, wreathed in sparks, born of electricity. The origin, Emilio realised, of the portrait that Arturo had painted, based on his sketches of Nina.

The rocketship rose before the painted sky. The numbers counted down, launching themselves at the screen. A detonation, then infernal gusts of steam and smoke as the machine surged upwards. In the row behind Emilio somebody was snoring, the sound deep and resonant like a revving motor. The rocket sailed across the sky, showering sparks, pitched straight at the unwary moon.

Emilio watched, transfixed, but too soon the story re-emerged, the actors in their silver suits, in their silver rooms.

He didn't want the story. He wanted the rocket, remorselessly advancing, blasting and surging upwards, annihilating everything.

Before the final reel, he got up and picked his way along the aisle to the doors. Over his shoulder, the moon-explorers were trekking across white plains, white as the deserts of Africa, with the rocket rearing up huge behind them. Emilio passed through the swing doors into the lobby.

Outside, the rain was pouring.

11

10th May 1930

Night filled the house like a substance, a tide moving too fast for human senses to perceive, submerging the rooms, the stairs and the corridors. In the kitchens, loud until a moment ago with the noise of plates and trays, the gush of water and steam, there was now silence and stillness, everyone paused mid-pace, unwilling to take a step or set down whatever they were holding, the familiar space made alien.

On the roof terrace, the guests stood ambushed by night. When the lights died, a few had cried out – *oh!* and *ah!* – but then all were silent in the vastness of the sky and the surrounding landscape.

"Is this some new stunt of yours, Marinetti?" a bold voice asked.

"Oh, look at the stars!" said Adriana, gesturing upwards.

"They look almost as if they're mocking us, don't they?"

"No matter," Marinetti pronounced. "Our electric stars will burn twice as brightly when the power returns."

Berardi flung his dead cigar over the parapet. All along the valley shore he saw no glimmer from the scattered villages; the power cut must be wide-ranging. His gut churned and seethed, and he felt tiredness soaking through him.

"Might I ask," he said loudly, "that everyone remain here? The staff will no doubt bring lamps soon." His guests looked, he noticed as he picked out their faces, rather unnerved to find themselves so exposed under the naked sky. The noise of the insects rose from the gardens, sounding louder than before. Had they fallen silent too, for a moment, when the power vanished? He hadn't noticed.

Walking with care, the guests were finding chairs and sitting down, anchoring themselves. There were amused now, their voices ringing, buoyed up like children by the threat and the mischievous promise of night.

"Maurizio?" His wife's voice, then her figure, spectral. "Maurizio, could you perhaps go and ask Greco to hurry along the lamps? We really can't just sit here in the dark!"

"Yes, yes of course." He needed to fetch the peppermint tablets from his room anyway, to ease the burning of his stomach. As he turned from his wife he felt the world reel slightly, the concrete beneath him uncertain. He felt as though he were leaning on a slope, and with every step he tried to correct himself, only to feel the tilt beneath him growing steeper.

He was almost at the stairhead when he sensed a thickening of the shadow ahead of him: the form of a man blocked his way.

"Well, this is really *most* inconvenient, isn't it?" The distaste in Scaglia's voice massed in the air between them, loaded with a palpable accusation. As if he, Berardi, had arranged the electricity failure personally, to vex the Commendatore. "I have a very important engagement in Milan tomorrow," the man was saying, "and it is already very late. This disruption looks set to continue for some time, wouldn't you say?"

Berardi felt a violent annoyance flare in his body, all the trapped irritation of the evening finding focus. He wanted to snarl at Scaglia, or shove him roughly aside. But that would never do: he was a guest, a most important guest. His willpower ebbed from him. If only the lights would return, the world once more assume shape and proportion, he would be able to think clearly. Then he noticed something else about the Commendatore, a kind of nervous agitation beneath the scorn. Was he perhaps afraid of the dark? He gripped the man's shoulder.

"Wait here a little longer," he said, keeping his voice low and calm. "I'm sure that power will be restored very soon."

He took one step, then another towards the stairs. Bracing his hands in the doorway of the stairhead, he began to lower himself clumsily downwards.

Emilio paced along the corridor, his left hand stretched out to trace the wall and his right hand gripping Nina's wrist. His fingers brushed across the panels of closed doors, set a picture swinging in its frame. Nina, carrying her shoes dangling between them, felt her way along the opposite wall, and the two of them advanced towards the upper landing.

At the end of the corridor a faint radiance fell from the diamond panes of the skylight. Beneath it the stairs were a misty grey, the banisters a fretwork of black, a composition in ink and ashes. "It's like a haunted house," Nina said. "Or something in a dream."

Her voice sounded both distant and very close. Emilio felt that if he let go of her wrist she might fade away completely. The drug was propelling her, he knew. Arturo had told him that she had been taking cocaine more and more often these last few months. Emilio could only guess at what the effects might be. He feared what she might be compelled to do.

"Here, sit here," he said, guiding her to the top of the stairs. "We can wait here until the electricity comes back."

"Yes, until it comes back," she said, seating herself beside him on the top step. She giggled a little, trembling as he released her wrist, then clasped her hands in her lap. The diffuse light made her skin pearl-pale against the black silk of her dress: her face a white smudge, lips a dark swipe, her eyes charcoal. The house was silent.

Emilio imagined the other guests looking for them, moving through the chambers like explorers roped together in a deep cavern, feeling their way, calling out. A memory came to him: sitting at the top of the stairs in his parents' house, many years ago, before the war, listening to the sound of a dinner party below him. His parents and their friends talking together, voices muffled, the scents of the food and the cigar smoke rising up to him, alone on the upper landing.

"You should put your shoes back on," he said.

Nina leaned forward to slip first one foot and then the other into her shoes. "I can't do it," she whispered. "My hands are shaking. The buckles ..."

"Here, let me." He took her shoulder and eased her up. He felt assured now, at ease with touching her. He lifted her ankle to see the strap and the tiny silver buckle, while she let her weight drop onto his shoulder, hair pooling in the hollow of his neck. He fiddled the straps into place, feeling silk and leather, brocade under his fingers, the slim construction of her ankles, the arch of her foot. The sensation of her body against his was something profound, real in this unreal place – the intimacy increased by the stillness and the gloom. He had never been so close to her.

Carefully, as if she were sleeping and not to be woken, he slid his arm around her shoulders and drew her closer. She shifted to fit herself more comfortably against him. His arm smoothed the bare skin of her shoulder, and her body was warm and soft to the touch, alive in the grey shade.

But she shifted again, away from him, her head dropping forward into the cradle of her folded arms. His hand lay between the ridges of her shoulder blades, idle now and unwanted.

"I prefer it like this," she said, looking up into the gloom above the stairs. "Without lights, I mean. It seems ... kinder. Easier to believe in things. Like in the Middle Ages.

Everything lit by candles, surrounded by mystery. People believed in so much more then."

"I suppose so," Emilio said. He felt unsure of himself now. Just as he had begun to ease into the situation, the mood had shifted: Nina transformed from passive resignation to unexpected loquacity.

"Do you remember at dinner, when Fosca said you looked like a medieval monk?" Emilio could hear the smile in her words.

"Yes, I remember."

"She was right, wasn't she? You have that capacity for belief. You really *want* to believe, don't you?" She gripped his shoulder, her face close to his. "No, it's not a criticism! It's a good thing! I wish I could believe as well. But so much of what I've known in my life has been false, so much that I see around me seems ridiculous. People's shallowness. People's unending need to fit in, to be rewarded. I've become cynical. But you … you still have a purity about you. You still believe the world can be made *right*, don't you?"

Emilio took her hand. "Nina," he said. "Nina, listen."

"Yes, I'm listening," she said.

"I meant what I said to you in your room," he said. "I'm in love with you."

"Oh, Emilio, I know you are," she said, squeezing his hand. "I know you are, but it's no good."

"I'm in love with you, and you're in love with Arturo."

"You really think so?" She threw back her head and let out a cry of amusement.

"Nina, be serious, please …"

"I am being serious," she said, and stopped laughing. Her expression was impossible to make out.

"How can you …?" he began, but she silenced him with a finger to his lips.

"Shh. Listen to me. I loved a man once, truly loved him.

This was two years ago. I loved him, but he died. He died, and I was going to have his child. If my husband had still been there he would have claimed the child was his own and it would have been fine, but he was gone … He was gone and I had no support. I wanted to be free of everything. So I killed the child, Emilio. I had an abortion."

Emilio drew away from her, unnerved by her composure.

"You had to," he said.

"It was like killing the love inside of me. Can you understand that? Either the love died or I died. After that, I wanted no more of it, do you see? Maybe that's why I chose Arturo. I knew he would never fall in love with me, and never need me to love him in return. And you mustn't love me either, Emilio. I don't want you to."

"I can't help it," he said. He wanted to tell her that he could no more stop loving her than he could stop the rapid pulse of his blood, the heat rising to his face, the sweat that formed at the nape of his neck as she held him. His arms were around her, embracing her, and he kissed the hand she held to his mouth.

"I love my son," she said. "… but that's a different sort of love." Her head dropped back, the light filtering from above illuminating her.

"There's a man here," she went on, "Federico Scaglia. My husband knew him. I'm not sure, but I think he was responsible for Amedeo having to leave."

"The Commendatore? But …" Emilio caught the pale glint of tears on Nina's face.

"If it wasn't for him, Amedeo wouldn't have left. I wouldn't have needed to go to Paris and kill Bianchi's child … But he's here, and everyone's fawning over him their servile way. There are so many men like him. Powerful men who do nothing but ruin others' lives. Who feel nothing and love nothing, but everyone queues to kiss their hands. Why are *they* never hurt? I can't stand it, Emilio. I have to get away from this country."

"Nina, I'm not like that. I don't respect him … But I need to do this work for him. I have good reasons."

She said nothing, still gazing upwards into the pale light. Emilio began telling her about his uncle, and as he spoke he found a new strength entering his voice. He told her about the hospital; about Scaglia's oblique offer of assistance on the terrace. He liked the sound of his words. There was an authority to them, as though they were spoken by somebody else. He did not tell her about the promise he had made to his uncle, as he knelt on the greasy tiles beside his hospital bed. He did not want to think about that now.

"So you see, I have to take the commission." He fell silent and glanced at Nina. She seemed to be no longer listening, and to be floating in distant self-scrutiny.

"Emilio, don't fall into this," she said. "He won't help you. I know this man. I know his type. He'll use you, then throw you aside. Everything he told you – it's all a trap, nothing more. And you'd be losing the most valuable thing you possess."

Emilio let his arm drop from the last physical suggestion of their embrace.

"But didn't you say I should take it? … When we spoke about it earlier, on the roof terrace?"

"Did I? I don't remember … But I didn't know enough about it then." Nina swayed back to lean against the banister. Her face was a pale oval. "And now I'm going away. I'm going away, and I'm going to Argentina, never to return …" There was a sing-song lilt to her words.

"Don't," Emilio said. "Don't go."

"Candles!" she exclaimed suddenly. "I remember where I saw some, in Berardi's room!"

Already she was getting to her feet. Emilio stood too,

his legs weak beneath him. Nina shoved the hair back from her forehead, shook herself as if to wake from a stupor, and started across the landing towards the corridor. Her figure dissolved into the mosaic of shadows, the pearls around her neck gleaming as she passed beneath the skylight, then vanishing.

The question of what Nina had been doing in Berardi's bedroom only occurred to Emilio as they stood before the door. Was this quite right? But already she was opening it and slipping through. Emilio made out her movements by the disturbances in the still air, sensing like a cat. He followed her into the room, easing the door closed again behind him.

"Can you see anything?" Her voice was moving away from him. Emilio advanced a step from the door, then another. Nina's hand found his, and she led him forward.

"Over here somewhere," she said. "There should be a sideboard ..."

Something scuffed and tumbled, bumping onto the carpet. Nina whispered a curse. Emilio's free hand, reaching blind, found a wooden surface. He stroked along it, fearing sharp glass, needles, razors, until his fingers found the heavy brass base.

"Here it is," he whispered, running a hand up the fluted stem to the wax. He was able to distinguish shapes a little now: the forms of bed and bookcase, chairs and a side-table.

"I left my handbag back in my room," she said. "I don't have a match."

But there was something on the sideboard beside the tall candlestick: a squat round cigar-lighter in polished ormolu. Emilio flicked the catch, and a brilliant blue and orange flame leapt from the nozzle.

There were three candles. He lit them, holding the heavy lighter awkwardly, the flame hissing close to the end of his thumb. The wicks spluttered, then caught, the smell of the burning wax and the curls of black smoke rising.

Behind him, the room was revealed: the big bed, the Persian rug, the scattered books. His host's chamber. He reached for the candlestick, to take it quickly and make an escape. But Nina stopped him, taking his hand in hers. The look on her face was different now, softened and tender in the weaving light.

"I'm sorry I was harsh," she said quietly, drawing closer. "I don't want you to get hurt."

"It's all right," he said, his palm finding her hip now, their bodies closing. "I understand." They embraced, her breath against his neck. He could feel the touch of her lips. His arm circled her, his grasp firming, his face buried in her hair. Her body was lithe and real to his touch. Together they made the few steps to the bed, the dimness seeming granular, full of charged particles. It seemed almost as if the room was moving and not them, bringing the bed across to meet them, to bump against their shins, to tip them, toppling in each other's arms, onto the yielding mattress.

Feather-filled quilts rose around them, their legs still dangling over the floor. Emilio's hand was on her thigh now, tracing upwards along the smoothness of silk. He kissed the back of her neck, her cheek, then his lips found her mouth. He felt possessed; he willed himself to calm.

Nina made no sound as he kissed her. She dropped her head back, one hand on Emilio's neck to draw him down with her. He sucked her bottom lip, biting lightly, tasting her, his palm moving above the lace of her garter onto the bare flesh of her thigh, rucking the hem of her skirt.

She shifted, twisted. Emilio pulled the straps of dress and chemise from her left shoulder, dragging against the bunched fabric. She grabbed his hand and stopped him before he tore the dress. The pearls around her neck clattered on their string. Emilio dipped his head to kiss her exposed shoulder, the swell of her breast.

"What are we doing?" she said, her body rigid now.

"What?" Emilio said, hardly daring to look up. His penis pressed against her thigh.

"Look," she demanded. "Look at me." He raised his head. She was aiming the barrel of a gun straight at his face.

Nina's hand was trembling. "Don't worry, I won't shoot you," she said, stroking his face with the cold muzzle of the gun. "I told you I don't want to hurt you, didn't I?"

"Nina, put it down," Emilio was saying, his throat locked with dread. "Put it back where you found it. Is it loaded?"

"Who knows? I think so."

Carefully, he raised his hand and closed it around the gun, easing it away from her. Her grip began to slacken, but then she tensed. She drew the gun up to her own head, its muzzle to her temple, pulling Emilio's hand with it.

"Or perhaps you want to hurt me?" she whispered. "I wouldn't blame you. I wouldn't blame you if you hated me. Here, your finger's on the trigger now – shoot if you like. I give you permission."

Up off the bed in violent recoil, Emilio strode away from her. His forehead was burning, and sweat poured down his spine. His movement guttered the candle flames. He grasped his hair with both hands: an extravagant gesture, but he couldn't help himself.

"What were you doing?" he said, his back to her. "*What did you think you were doing*?" In the oval dressing-mirror on the bureau he saw her reflected, sprawled on the bed, black on the whiteness of the quilt. The gun dangled from her hand.

"Oh, I don't know," she said wearily. "I can't say."

"You led me on!" He turned on his heel and stabbed a finger at her. "What were you thinking? Did you hide that gun here on purpose, or were you just going to lie there and let me rape you?"

"Darling, women don't *let* men rape them." Nina studied the pistol in her hand, as if she had no idea how she came to be holding it. "They're forced. There is a difference. And if I thought there was any danger of that I really would have shot you. Not in the head. Maybe in the leg, or the shoulder. Then you and Arturo could have compared gunshot scars!"

"This isn't a joke!" Emilio shouted. His fists were clenched at his sides. Nina tossed the pistol down onto the bed; it lay beside her, black and crooked on the quilt. She was laughing. She's out of her mind, he thought. Deranged. But the thought didn't calm him. He stood hunched, his arms braced against the back of a chair. She rose from the bed and crossed the floor to stand behind him. Her hand on his shoulder, caressing the locked muscles of his back.

"I know you too well, Emilio," she said, her voice softening, "and you don't know me half well enough."

His anger was contained, held clenched within him. He had no wish to touch her.

"I need to leave you now," she said, keeping her hands on his shoulders, as if to steady herself.

"Yes," Emilio said.

In the mirror he watched her cross the room and take a candle. He heard the sound of the door closing behind her, and sagged against his braced arms. Her lipstick was smeared over his mouth and chin; he took a tissue from the dressing table and wiped it off. His ambitions, those proud fantasies he entertained over dinner, had been burned away. All of them empty without love. His love for Nina – he still believed in it – had been the solid centre to his imagined future. What a fool he had been!

Her words on the stairs returned to him. What she said about Scaglia appeared all too true, all too wounding. He felt stupid, foolish, ridiculously led. The anger that she had summoned was still there, gaining focus now. He felt charged with a terrible potential.

Emilio scooped the gun from the mattress. He stood before the mirror, the gun at his side, then raised it, stiff-armed, to aim at his own reflection. His lips compressed breath into the whisper of a gunshot – *pshhh!* – and he saw himself fall back, reeling, clutching his heart.

There was a sound at the door – the handle turning, the door opening. Emilio spun around, the gun held concealed. Berardi stood in the doorway, bulky and surprised.

"Excuse me!" Emilio said, lifting his hand to slip the gun into the pocket of his jacket. "I was just looking for a candle. I didn't think that this was your room!"

"Oh, I see," Berardi said, moving from the door. He sounded perplexed. "I myself was just looking for my peppermint pills. A touch of indigestion …"

Emilio released the gun, and its weight dropped into his pocket. "Well, I should leave you to your privacy."

"Oh, no matter, no matter," Berardi said.

On the bed, the quilt was crushed down by the weight of bodies and the pillows misplaced. But Berardi appeared not to notice as he sat down on the bed and opened the cabinet beside it. Emilio took a candle and moved swiftly to the door.

"I do hope you feel better shortly."

"Yes, and perhaps soon the power will return, eh?"

A nod of agreement, and Emilio slipped out of the room. The corridor was clear, but far away along the line of closed doors he saw the dim star of Nina's candle. He paced quickly in the other direction. In his pocket was the gun, swinging heavily with every step.

10th May 1930: 5.30 p.m.

From the window she watched him stalking up the afternoon street from the tram stop, his hunched stride unmistakeable. If he looked up he might see her standing there, framed in the tall window behind the railing of the first-floor balcony. But he kept his head down, hat jammed on the back of his skull, hands deep in his pockets. She could read the resentment in him already.

A sound from the room behind her, and Nina turned. The maid was waiting in the doorway of the salon, hands clasped at her waist.

"Will there be anything else, Signora?"

"No," Nina said. "You can go for today. I won't be home tonight, but be sure to return here by noon tomorrow."

"Very good, Signora." She made a curtsy and turned to go.

"Oh, Maria, there's a man outside. Do let him in as you leave."

"Yes, Signora."

The letter lay on the marble-topped side table. Nina picked it up, ran a pinched finger and thumb down the crease. She thought about hiding it somewhere – she should have destroyed it, as the letter itself requested. It didn't matter: either Arturo discovered what the letter contained or he did not, and it would be Nina's decision. She heard the sound of the door downstairs, the voice of the maid. His footsteps on the stairs, heavy tread on stone steps. She slipped the letter into her bag.

A brief knock at the lobby door, then Arturo came sidling into the apartment. He stood in the doorway, hat still on his head, hands still in pockets.

"Well?" he said. "Are we going?"

"You assumed I would agree, then. I don't remember actually doing so. You've left it a bit late to get to the house by yourself."

Arturo gave a slow blink. He would already have seen her overnight cases packed in the hall. "Of course we're going. Signor Berardi will be expecting us. You wouldn't want to disappoint him, eh?"

A long breath held, then slowly released. Nina nodded.

"Good," he said briskly. He wore his victory lightly, with a springy satisfaction. "Emilio's waiting for us, I told him we'd be there with the car in twenty minutes. We're late as it is." She moved past him into the lobby, and he stopped her with his hands on her shoulders.

"Don't I get a kiss, by the way?"

She gave him a peck, lips pursed, but he drew her closer. At first she held herself back, keeping up the front, then yielded.

"We've got a few minutes, you know," he breathed, kissing her neck. "We could … "

"Not here," she said, and peeled his arms from her. "And there's no time to spare, is there?"

"Not here, never here …" Arturo said under his breath, and then stooped to snatch up her cases.

She would never let him make love to her here, in her own bed, in this apartment filled with the memories of her husband and her son. Something that she tried to explain to him, but which he could not understand.

In her bedroom, the door closed against him, Nina took the letter from her bag again, unfolded it and read it quickly. The words moved her with the same unfocused panic as when she had first read them. Outside, she could hear Arturo coming back for the last of the cases. Downstairs the car was waiting. They would collect Emilio and drive to Berardi's house beside the lake; there would be a party with many guests. And somewhere in the mazes of the night there was her decision, waiting for her to discover it.

She imagined Buenos Aires, a city of palm trees and guitars and long siesta afternoons. Imagined herself there, walking arm in arm with Amedeo beneath white Spanish colonnades, while their son ran before them through the stipple of light and shade. A fantasy, but just for a moment it felt more substantial than the life she now inhabited. One last adventure then, she thought. One final night before I make my choice.

There was knocking at the door behind her, and Arturo's voice from the hall outside: "Come on! Are you ready yet?"

"Just a minute more," she called.

Two steps to the bureau beside the bed, and she took the slim silver mirror-case from the drawer and slipped it into her evening bag with the letter. A glance in the mirror, a hand to smooth her hair, and she was ready.

12

10th May 1930

The darkness was full of sensation, strange effects of touch and feeling. Nina paused at the door of the bathroom, her palm against the wall to steady herself. She breathed deeply, waiting for the vertigo to subside. Her body was racing, the drug bursting starshells in her head. Everything that had happened seemed remote now: the conversation on the stairs, the scene in Berardi's room. She had intended none of it. I must be insane, she told herself. *Insane.* She leaned hard against the wall while the tremors ran through her.

She could still taste Emilio's kisses, feel the pressure of his body pressing onto her. His grim, inexpert fumblings had left a tracery of discomfort. The gun had seemed to slip into her hand without her consciously reaching for it, and after that she had felt no control over her actions.

The candle stem in her hand was warm now, the flame guttering. Too easy to hold it still and be drawn to it, to the steady quiet glow. But she needed clean running water and a locked door, time to focus and reclaim herself. She turned the handle, shielding the flame from the shove of air as the door opened.

She was halfway through the door before she sensed the presence inside the room.

"Come in," a voice said with a hollow echo. "Come in and bring the light with you, but be careful where you step."

It was Moresco. Nina felt a thrill of fear. Somehow she had known it would be him.

He lay full length in the dry bathtub. His jacket was tossed in a corner, and he wore his shirt collar unbuttoned, sleeves rolled up. Nina took in the scene: the necktie bound above Moresco's elbow, the stub of a candle on the floor, the dab of wax on the cistern where he had tried to fix it upright. His face was appalling, slimy with sweat and tensed rigid.

"It's you," he said. "That's good. I thought it might be one of those bastards from upstairs, come to hunt me down. I hope you're not shocked by my condition."

"No," Nina said as she closed the door behind her. Moresco's right arm, the one without the tourniquet, dangled from the bath, fingers flexing weakly.

"My hands were shaking and I knocked the candle over ... Be careful where you step. I couldn't find it, you see ... Please hold your light a little more this way ..."

"I can see it," Nina said. "It's all right. Stay where you are."

She set her candle down carefully above the sink. The fallen syringe was by her feet, jabbed diagonally into a mat of thick fibre beside the bath. Neatly, finger and thumb, she plucked it free. Moresco made a swiping grab, but she pulled away.

"Give," he said, with a snap of his fingers. "*Please* ..."

"It's no good," Nina said, holding the syringe closer to the candle. "The needle's bent at the tip. Do you have another?"

"In my jacket pocket," Moresco groaned. His body was limp in the white coffin of the bath, but the tendons in his neck were like cables.

The case was small and black, a leather wallet. Nina fished it from the crumpled jacket and folded it open. Inside, bright ampoules and polished steel were secured neatly in leather bands. Her fingers tingled just looking at it all. How long had it been since she had done this? And would she ...? But this was not cocaine. Moresco did not have the look that Tadeusz used to have, all those months ago in Paris. His hunger was for something even more insidious. Quickly, her fingers remembering the movements, Nina held the syringe upright and unscrewed the bent needle. She selected a fresh needle and fixed it in place. A brisk tap-tap with her fingernail, and the slightest pressure on the plunger to bring the wink of fluid to the needle's tip, then she passed it carefully across to him. Already his head was crushed down into his shoulder, the strap of the tourniquet gripped in his teeth. Nina looked away as he injected himself.

She heard the long gasp, then the sigh. Moresco shifted in the bath, porcelain squeaking.

"Thank you my dear," he said a while later. "That was neatly done. Now tell me that you were a very young volunteer nurse during the war."

"I'm afraid not," she said. She looked back at him: already the change was apparent; the drug was beginning to smooth him out. His body shuddered, long, slow ripples running through him.

"That was where they gave it to me first," he said. "In the field hospital at Treviglio. You reminded me just then: the nurses would come to us with lamps to give us our medicine every evening. It's not just medals you get in wartime, you know."

"Morphine. I suspected it was."

"Morphine and amphetamine," Moresco said. "A royal combination, I find. And hopelessly addictive. Yours is cocaine, I suppose? Not injected though, I hope. Tut tut."

"Not any more," Nina said.

He seized her hand – a sudden and startling movement – and held it tight. Nina felt the sweat of his palm, the tremors running up his arm. Just as at dinner, they sat holding hands, the candle between them.

"Stay with me a while," he said. "I need you here." His smile was disconcerting, the grip of his hand too firm to be friendly. "We have things in common, you and I. You're young, but you understand things, don't you? Maybe you think I'm disgusting, maybe you think that ..."

"I don't think that, no."

"Well, maybe you're a liar too. But you *understand* ... You're shaking. Why?"

"I'm not. It's you that's shaking."

"I'm sorry if I'm upsetting you. I have so little control over myself these days."

"It's not that," Nina said with difficulty. "I *do* understand. I don't condemn you at all. I respect you ..." But the grip of his hand was repellent, and as Moresco returned to some sort of life, so all the dread and the poison that filled him seemed to be passing through his touch into her. Nina swallowed thickly, her mouth dry, and tried to concentrate.

"*Respect*, yes," Moresco said. He was no longer speaking directly to her, but casting words out into space, into a bleak void. "Easy to win respect. All too easy. You just need to do what's expected of you. Harder to *respect* oneself, though."

"You use the word as if it were an insult," Nina said. "You have nothing to be ashamed of." Why, she thought, do I have to be here with him? Did I choose this?

"Your man, though, Signor Gallo, he wants respect, doesn't he? He'll get it, I'm sure. He does the right sort of things to earn it. If he saw me here now it might not seem so glamorous, but I doubt he'd understand."

"Oh, he understands," Nina said. "I think he does." Moresco's face was lit up, unearthly, the flickering reflected glow of the candle shifting across his features. She remembered the exhibition of his work at the Galleria Pesaro – she had gone there with Arturo and Emilio last autumn. The greatest painter of our day, Emilio had called him.

But more than that, this was the man who had piloted the aeroplane she had seen all those years ago, dancing in the sky above Milan. He had been there, high in his wind-blasted cockpit above the swirl of the city as she, fifteen, terrified and ecstatic, had gazed up from the street below. He could have no idea what that experience had meant for her, or what it had come to mean since, through the prism of memory. On that day, it had seemed to Nina, the future was created, all the muffled, unspoken anguish of the past swept clean away and the new world, the new life revealed.

"What are we doing here, you and I?" Moresco said, squeezing her hand tighter. "What are we doing in this place, with all these dead people? Are we dead ourselves and just don't know it?"

"Don't talk of death, please," Nina said. "Nobody's dead."

"It was different once," Moresco went on, seeming not to have heard her, seeming barely aware of her presence save for the grip of his hand. "You should have seen him then, or heard him. Marinetti, I mean. Those years after the war, he was a dynamo! A genius, truly. Perhaps he still is, but it's all fouled up inside. *His Excellency*, as he likes to call himself now …" He made a dry spitting noise between pursed lips.

"Please …" Nina said. "You have to excuse me …" She needed quiet and comfort, somewhere to relax. She wanted to be where Moresco lay now, in a bath, but naked and submerged in hot soapy water, scented oils, perfume. She wanted wash herself clean of everything. She wanted light. More light …

"Before the war," Moresco went on, ignoring her, "I raced automobiles. During and after it I flew planes, then I became a painter. All of it *action*, all of it forward motion – forward, and sweeping all before me. We believed that we were building the future, creating it. Marinetti was greater than God in those days. He was *my* God …"

It was true: there was something religious about Moresco's expression as he spoke. A look of holy awe.

"The Fascist revolution, the Futurist dream. I loved all of that." His voice gained strength and volume. "I believed all of that. I still do, you see, and that's the tragedy. But what is this future we are creating? Just more of everything. More cars, more electric trains and telephones and aeroplanes and nice hats and shoes and immorality and idiots. More *fucking idiots.* Day by day we get more and more cynical, until the future itself is old and buried and we don't know what we want any more. But still we have to believe in it and salute it and applaud it. Just like Marinetti. He gets the prizes, but I gave my life for it, for Futurism, for Fascism. I still believe it all. *But nobody else does!*"

His grip slackened, and Nina pulled her hand free. Moresco subsided, his body slipping down further into the bathtub.

"Please, I need to use the bathroom," she said, fighting down the stabs of panic.

"Of course, of course," he said, and made an attempt to sit. "You'll have to help me up, I'm afraid."

Nina stooped over him, taking him by the shoulders. His legs scissored in the polished tub, shoes sliding for purchase; his body felt heavy and iron-hard to her touch, and sweat prickled under her arms as she lifted him. Together they swayed upright, and he sagged down at once onto the rim of the bath. His arms were embracing her, his face turned away from hers.

"I'm sorry to have burdened you," he said, muttering. "I'm quite ashamed of myself. It's not your fault."

"No, no, don't apologise," she said. Quite unexpectedly, she felt a surge of tenderness rise through her. He seemed a wounded creature – or a damaged machine. She found herself stroking his forehead, caressing his back. His body shook, trembling in fits, tension escaping from him like released heat.

"That man Scaglia," he said suddenly. "Have you spoken to him?"

"No … I was introduced, but I don't think he remembers me."

"He ought to have recognised the name." The savagery had returned. "Your husband knows enough about Scaglia to destroy him."

Nina tried to speak but could not. *Here it is*, she thought.

"Oh yes, he has information on our friend the Commendatore. They were partners once, as you surely know, in certain activities … certain potentially treasonable dealings."

"Tell me," she whispered. They were close, almost embracing, and she could almost feel the violence of his pulse.

"Five or six years ago, Scaglia was with the Ministry of the Interior. Your husband worked for him, in an unofficial capacity. There were certain dissident groups in Switzerland and France, and your husband … involved himself with them."

Nina nodded. The business trips Amedeo had made so often. Even some of the foreign holidays they had taken together.

"… and all the while he was reporting back to Scaglia. They had a *very close* working relationship."

Nina refused to rise to the insinuation. "And then?" she asked.

"Around the time that the Vatican pact was being discussed, there was a plot … a conspiracy. A group of radicals within the regime. Scaglia was part of it. Each acted from different motives: some wanted power; others believed the ideals of the revolution were being betrayed … The idea was to stage an assassination attempt on Mussolini. Conservative elements in the government would be implicated. Catholics, monarchists, military men. It would be the spur for change. Your husband was brought into it. Scaglia wanted him to use his dissident contacts and arrange a suitable group of assassins, paid for covertly by the Ministry."

It was not so hard to imagine Amedeo involved in such a scheme. Behind his easy calm, he had always been a gambler. He would have done it for the sense of risk.

"They were discovered?"

"Not exactly. Scaglia lost his nerve. He exposed the plot himself, and sacrificed a few of the less important members to save his skin. Maybe he'd always planned it that way, to gain favour with the regime. Anyway, your husband was left in a difficult position. He had no choice but to run. If he'd gone before a tribunal he could have taken Scaglia down with him, but he had you to consider, didn't he? His wife, his child. So he forced Scaglia to protect him, guarantee his assets here in Italy, keep him financially secure in exile ... Keep his family safe."

This had been her life, and she had known nothing of it. All these months, oblivious.

"And for a while, Scaglia did just that. But then, with his new appointment, he must have thought nothing could touch him. *The Institute of Fascist Culture!* Surely with something like that behind him, he could rid himself of any lingering inconveniences?"

"But now he's being investigated, you said?"

"The regime has its uses for compromised men. Men with too much to lose. They've probably had him under surveillance for years. Now they're putting the heat on him, seeing how much he sweats."

"And Amedeo?"

"Scaglia could do nothing to him, not any more. If your husband were accused and brought to trial, Scaglia would be ruined. In fact, I wouldn't be surprised if this current investigation hadn't been sparked by rumours coming from across the ocean …"

Nina pictured Amedeo, far away in Argentina. My husband is a traitor, she thought, a spy and a traitor. But she was free, that was the important thing; she was free and Marco was safe. The sense of release was dizzying.

"And what about you? Were you involved with this plot as well?"

"Oh, not really," Moresco said, with a long grin. "I'm not important. I'm a small man, insignificant. Scaglia commissioned some work from me, years ago when he was with the Ministry. But it was Marinetti who told me about the plot. He knew about it from the start."

He swayed back from her, drawing himself upright. He was no longer trembling now, no longer sick.

"I can trust you with these things, can't I?" Moresco said. He stood up, picking his jacket from the floor. She nodded. "I knew I could." He took the case of syringes and slipped it back into his pocket, took the stub of his candle from the cistern, and stood in the centre of the room, not looking directly at her. Nina reached out and touched his cheek, a brief caress. A human look stole across his face, rising from somewhere inside him, then he turned, opened the door and was gone.

Nina fell back onto the seat of the toilet, the silence like a symphony in her ears. She sat slackly, arms dangling. Turning the tap, she bathed her face in cold running water, and felt cleansed of all the anxieties of the night, all that had pressed upon her. So she was safe. But she still had to find Scaglia – yes, she needed that. Find him, and confront him with her knowledge that she was untouchable to him, impermeable to any threat. *Safe,* she thought, but couldn't quite believe it.

Marinetti sat in his great cane chair. His face shone, pale bronze under the great dome of his head. He looked, Arturo thought, like a statue of the Buddha. Or like some heavy-browed frowning idol of the Indies, some great Oriental despot. He was talking to Martino Rossi about an art show they had both visited recently in Rome – an exhibition of Japanese paintings. Arturo had lost the desire to talk, even to pay attention to the talk of others.

Four oil lamps stood on the low table between them, and all those remaining on the roof terrace had drawn together now, grouping themselves in the circle of lamplight around the clustered chairs with their backs to the great emptiness outside. It was late, but nobody mentioned going to bed. Better to stay here, with everyone else, in the steady ebb of the dying party.

Berardi had departed, and his earlier injunction about remaining on the terrace seemed to have lapsed. Neither Emilio nor Nina had returned, and Arturo suspected that they would not. The dish of cigarettes on the table was almost empty, and he seemed to have smoked most of them himself. The back of his throat felt scorched, and he took another swig of whatever bitter green fluid was in his glass to ease it.

He caught himself thinking about Nina, reminiscing as if she had been gone for days, months, a lifetime. Careless, he summoned the memory of her body. She lay face down on his bed, hair tousled black on the pillow, and he stroked her slow and warm, the nape of her neck down to the hollow of her back, the rise of her buttocks. Her legs were clasped together, and he parted them with his palm. Her sigh against the pillow, the murmur of assent. The smell of her, taste of her. He felt a slow warmth spreading from his groin. But she was gone now, and there would be no more of that. Or was that really true? If he could find and speak to her …

"What are you working on at the moment?" Marinetti said. To him, to Arturo. "I meant to ask earlier but there wasn't time."

He found it almost physically difficult to speak after so long. "Well, it's a portrait. A form of portrait. For the Biennale competition."

"Oh, that," Marinetti said, his brow lowering.

"It's very Futurist in conception. More a portrait of a state of mind, a state of being …"

"A portrait of … somebody?"

"Oh yes, naturally. Well, it's a portrait of Mussolini, of the Duce. But rather, you see, it's a portrait of his will. Based on your own writings, in part. That piece you wrote about him a few years ago: *his ultramagnetic eyes dart with the speed of automobiles* … Is that right? … *his baldness shines like an electric lamp, his will splits the crowd like a fast torpedo boat, an exploding bomb* … " Arturo thought of the great ravaged canvas propped in his studio, the scar where Nina had gouged at it still visible through the cakey glaze of paint, the smudged and scrubbed disaster of lost inspirations. "It's taken me some time," he said, "but I needed to get it right. I wanted to make it the very best piece I could possibly produce, so … "

"About the competition," Marinetti interrupted, dropping his head and leaning closer to speak in a low tone. "I wouldn't, ah … I wouldn't hope for too much. Matters have not turned out as I might have wished. I expected a more forward-thinking jury, to be plain about it. Argued for it very passionately, in fact, and at the highest levels. The very highest levels. But my hands are tied, unfortunately. In the event, Signor Scaglia is the best amongst them, which is why I invited him tonight. Even he, though, seems sadly corrupted by passéism … Hardly the Futurist sensibility we had all hoped for. So, as I say, please don't expect too much. I apologise if I once suggested otherwise."

"Think nothing of it," Arturo said. "I understand completely."

"You are a very talented artist, Arturo," Marinetti went on. "A very skilled artist, and I believe in you. You have a sharp eye, a revolutionary perception. I want to help you in any way I can. But sometimes you have to trust in yourself alone. Sometimes, you have to make your own future."

"Of course," Arturo said.

"Cigarette?"

"Thanks." He took a cigarette from Marinetti's case and leant to the flame of a match. So it was all over. *Thank Christ for that*, he thought.

Emilio sat on the bottom step on the staircase with the candle burning low beside him. A sound was creeping through the darkened house: the clear, quiet notes of a piano. The music seemed to be coming from the air, gathered by the night, formed from nothing. A slow, sad melody, the notes stepped carefully along the halls and across the deep rooms. The candle guttered and went out. Emilio got up and began to walk.

He crossed the lobby and entered the mazes of the salon, the geometries of colour rendered now in dim monochrome, the burst of lilies over the fireplace a ghostly smudge. Reaching into his pocket, he fingered the gun. He drew it out and carried it as he walked, pacing across the carpeted floor with the weapon held at his side. If he saw a shape, a human form, he would raise the gun and fire. He dared himself to do that.

The thought that he might have accepted Scaglia's commission sickened him now. The Commendatore's bargain was merely part of the wider scheme: the roping and securing of the spirit. His uncle had always understood that; he had always known the temptations that Emilio faced. Who was Scaglia anyway? He was nothing, a mere effusion of a greater power – the same power whose distant appendage was the hand that cracks the whip, the voice that shouts the commands. Emilio rejected it, as he rejected the aspirations that had so briefly possessed him.

The figure of a man appeared. Emilio raised his arm, the gun extended, finger on trigger; through the thunder of his blood he saw his own reflection, a dim shade in a long mirror. He lowered his arm and placed the gun safely back in his pocket. His image seemed hardly to move.

He would refuse Scaglia, but he would do it publicly. He would do it in front of everyone, so Nina and Arturo and all the rest could see it. Not in some discreet private conference but right in the faces of them all.

Emilio passed into the gallery, the high-ceilinged space above him full of the moon. From the open door of the auditorium, he heard the sound of the music. Across the gallery, he walked through the door. At the end of the room, before the low stage, the pianist sat behind the piano. He was intent on his music, not caring who listened. Other people were there, vague forms around the light of a single candle, but Emilio ignored them. He paused beside Osvaldi's noise machine, dead and soundless now in its box. He recognised the tune: Chopin, one of the Preludes. His mother had played it on the piano at home when he was a child.

In the warm, still air the music was all-encompassing, ecstatic and despairing. The face of the pianist, lit by thecandle, seemed to become the flame itself. Notes hammered and crashed, slid away trilling into nothing before bursting out again, the strange melody running through it all like a pulse.

Breath sighing out of him. Emilio felt caught on the verge of a great detonation. He sensed the steady quiet ticking of the explosive charge, the all-annihilating force held, barely, at the instant before release. He felt his thoughts accelerating, his mind sharpening to a purpose.

The last chord had been struck, and was fading now,

claimed by the silence. For a long while the sound still lingered, a resonance in the air. For a minute, two minutes, Emilio and all those unseen others in the auditorium held that sound between them, the memory of it, letting it throb silently. Then the pianist raised his head, almost apologetic, and creaked down the lid of the piano.

Far away, along the upstairs corridor, Berardi sat in an armchair in the corner of his bedroom. He felt much better now, his stomach cooled by two peppermint pills and as much water as he could drink. More than anything, he was tired. He would have loved to remain here in his room, to go to bed and wake again to find everything swept away by the clean light of dawn. But the guests would miss him; his wife would miss him, and send somebody to find him. He could not escape so easily.

How long had he been here? Twenty minutes? Half an hour, maybe. He had dozed a little, slumped in the armchair. At some point he would have to grope his way back up to the terrace – to all those people younger than himself, whom he found so difficult to comprehend. And all the while he would watching for the sight of his wife dancing with Conti, talking with him in tones of hushed affection, embracing him, sneaking away with him to the gardens or the furthest reaches of the house … It was intolerable. When had he suddenly become an old man? It was foolish of him to have hoped that a new, modern building would make him a new and modern person.

He stirred himself and struggled to stand, feeling the weight of his years pooled inside him. Swaying above the armchair, light-headed with the rush of blood, he felt a sudden sharp stabbing pain high in his chest. Oh God, he thought. *Madonna*, is this it? He caught the arm of the chair to steady himself, forcing himself to breathe slowly. The pain throbbed, and he grabbed for the lamp-stand. He saw himself sprawled on the carpet, pasty-faced and ridiculous. Was there no dignity?

With leaden steps he crossed to the bed and slumped down again. He swallowed heavily, and the pain eased slightly. Indigestion, he realised with a dull pang of relief: a last flare of acid bile. He snorted a sigh, smiled to himself.

As he eased himself back onto the bed, he saw that the pillow was lying askew. Annoyed – the maids should have tidied the room earlier – he bent to straighten it. The covers were rumpled too, as if somebody had been lying there. His mind awoke to a sudden realisation. Across the room, he saw a framed photograph lying on the floor, dislodged from the sideboard. He reached quickly across the bed and felt beneath the pillow. The gun was not there.

Up off the bed, he began pulling open the drawers of the cabinets, scrabbling in the dark amongst the documents, the pill bottles, the ties and socks and handkerchiefs. Perhaps he had moved the gun somewhere else … But no, he was certain the weapon had been under his pillow earlier that day. His wife must have removed it! His nerves jumped, and he squeezed his brow. But there was still the study, along the hall from his bedroom. Had he left the gun there?

Along the corridor, candle raised like a sceptre before him, he approached the study. A faint bleed of lamplight came from the part-opened door. Perhaps Greco had gone there to look for something and left the lamp burning on the desk? Apprehensive, he prowled closer. At the door he paused. The low cone of orange lamplight illuminated his desk with its green leather top, his neatly stacked papers. The rest of the room seemed to be empty, lost in murky shade. Berardi exhaled, stepped across the threshold and placed his own candle on the desk before picking up the lamp. Then he turned, and let out a low grunt of surprise.

On the chaise just behind the door, a couple lay entwined. He glanced hastily away, the image still printed on his retina: a woman's naked thighs, the rumple and twist of clothing, the man's aghast expression.

"Oh, excuse me!" he said. "I'm very sorry!" He placed the lamp quickly back on the desk and walked smartly out of the room. From the corridor he heard the quick whispers, the stifled giggle. The woman had been Signora Assanti, the journalist's wife, he realised. And the man ... Surely not? But yes – the man was the architect, Conti.

Empty-handed now, dazed, Berardi wandered towards the mezzanine. The things one found in one's own house! One's own study! He should have been outraged; he could have snatched up his malacca cane and flogged them both down the stairs! But ... If Conti was the lover of Signora Assanti, he surely could not be his own wife's lover as well. What had happened, what obscure mysteries of disentanglement and connection, while he had not noticed? Then, blinking in the dark, he suddenly understood everything. He had been mistaken all along. There had been no affair with his wife, no outrage, no insult. All thoughts of the missing gun vanished from his mind. He walked out onto the mezzanine, high above the empty gallery, with a sense of tired awakening after a long, fevered sleep.

There was a soft, liquid cough from somewhere away to his left. Berardi stared, but at first could only see the white gleam of the bust set in the alcove: Mussolini, with his tireless frown.

"Signor Berardi," a voice said, as the man emerged from the gloom.

"Commendatore! I've been attempting to telephone somebody about this power failure, but without success, I'm afraid." His voice surprised him; he sounded skittish and startled, as if he were about to burst into nervous laughter.

"But why are you up here? You should be on the terrace upstairs, surely?"

Scaglia cleared his throat, sidling closer. "To be honest," he said, "I was starting to find the antics of some of your guests slightly trying."

"Oh, I see," Berardi said, feeling a stir of fresh annoyance. Was Scaglia's comment not an implied insult? The man was insufferable. His carapace of authority would not permit the slightest crack. "Did you speak to Signor Calvi about the commission?" he asked.

"I did," Scaglia said. "But I found him perhaps a little flimsy. Not entirely to be relied upon. He lacked, one might say, *zeal.*"

"I'm sorry to hear that," Berardi said, slowly and without emphasis.

"And between you and me," the Commendatore went on, "I don't know if all this sort of thing is quite healthy these days."

"This sort of thing?"

"This sort of experimentation, I mean. This *avante-gardism.* Not quite appropriate for these difficult times. We've humoured Signor Marinetti and his associates for quite some time, but really now his games are beginning to seem … a little *unsound* perhaps. Would you not agree?"

Berardi could only nod. All his plans and ambitions, his voice on the Grand Council, all of it was stealing away, swallowed up by the stale aura of the man beside him. He felt a sudden deep contempt for Scaglia, and for all the others like him; something close to loathing for their gracelessness, their ignoble grasping for promotion, their unearned sense of superiority. How could power reside in such unimpressive men, such drab souls? I am not like him, Berardi thought. For all my faults, I am a greater man than he. But it was criminal that he, Maurizio Berardi, should need to seek favours from the likes of Scaglia. And not only Berardi himself, but even Marinetti, a flawed but rare and glittering intellect. Rage filled him. He was glad of the darkness. He wanted to grab Scaglia and crush him between his fists, crumple him into a ball and toss him away over the railing of the mezzanine.

The Commendatore had fallen silent. From the corridor, a star was approaching. Growing closer, wavering as it moved, it formed into the flame of a candle. The tapping of heels as the candle-bearer moved from the carpeted corridor onto the harder floor of the mezzanine, then Berardi saw the face in the globe of flickering light.

"Signora," he said. "Are you searching for something?"

"No, no," Nina replied. "I merely had to visit the bathroom." She raised the candle between them, illuminating Scaglia. She was smiling, inscrutable.

"Perhaps you haven't met before?" Berardi asked. "May I present the Commendatore Federico …"

"Oh, I know Signor Scaglia … But perhaps he's forgotten me? It's been a long time!" There was something suggestive in her voice, a hint of a giggle, almost flirtatious. But surely not, Berardi thought. What was happening now?

"The Commendatore was friends with my husband, Amedeo Sorani. One might even say partners, isn't that right, Commendatore? How strange that I heard from Amedeo only this morning! He *will* be surprised to hear that we've met."

"This morning?" Scaglia said thickly. "He's here? In Italy?"

"Oh, not exactly. But he's very well, you'll be glad to know."

Scaglia, Berardi saw, looked almost queasy now, jaundiced in the yellow candlelight.

"But I'm sure," Nina went on, "that he won't want to disturb you. I mean, you have so many responsibilities now! I know you were close once, but that was a long time ago, wasn't it?"

"Indeed," Scaglia said, with obvious effort.

"And I very much doubt you'll be wanting to disturb him either, will you?"

"Certainly not, Signora. As you say, these things are in the past and … should be forgotten."

Berardi caught the heady breath of scandal, sensed the strange, malevolent currents of disgrace. He felt a dazed elation. Was this unexpected justice?

"I need some fresh air, I think," the Commendatore announced, then turned and paced decisively towards the stairs that led to the roof terrace. Nina inhaled sharply, then shuddered. For a moment she and Berardi stood silently together. The distant whirr of the insects came from outside.

"I wanted to thank you," she said. "It has been a splendid evening."

Splendid? Berardi felt the word flower inside him. It had been Mariagrazia's work, not his own, and all this time he had been lost in sour fantasies about her. He should find her. He would go up to the terrace and find her and embrace her, thank her for all she had done. Perhaps they would dance together, under the moon.

"We should go upstairs and join the others." He raised an elbow. "Shall we?"

"Thank you." Nina took his arm, and together they walked slowly around the mezzanine.

With the gentle pressure of her hand upon his sleeve, Berardi felt himself grow in stature. He felt the years sliding from him, the knots of loathing and frustration unravel and slip away. The old man, the finished man he had feared himself to be, was gone, and the relief was a tonic to his spirits.

The sound of their steps echoed in the gulf of the gallery below them. They reached the stairs, and Berardi moved aside and gestured for Nina to go up before him. The candle raised – a beacon – she climbed.

Everyone was gathering now. All those who had been scattered throughout the house were congregated once more on the wide roof terrace, waiting for the end. Beside the stairhead, a group of tired waiters lounged on the parapet, yawning, smoking weary cigarettes, checking their watches by the faint lamplight: 1 a.m., and a Sunday morning.

Nina came from the stairhead, with Berardi following her. She scanned the faces in the congregation, searching for her friends. She saw Arturo, sitting with Marinetti, saw him notice her and haul himself upright. She saw Moresco too, alone beside the wall. There was no sign of Emilio, but he would return soon; he would return and they would talk and he would forgive her. Now there would be time for that, for talk and forgiveness. Mariagrazia and Fosca were winding up the gramophone again – then the music started, the same neutered jazz as before, a tinny echo of something that was alive once in America, but the sound was fitting to this night, to this slow decline.

"Nina," Arturo said, taking her hand. "I want to apologise, I want … I missed you." The words did not come easily to him. Nina kissed him softly on the cheek.

"Not now," she said. "We'll talk later. There are things we need to talk about, but I want to enjoy myself for a while first. Don't worry."

She felt contentment wrapping her, even a kind of bliss: the afterwash of her anguish and anxiety. There was no need to decide anything, no need to care about anything now. To stay with Arturo or to leave him, to remain in Italy or to cross the ocean to America: all of that seemed immaterial. She had understood so little of the danger she had been in; understood so little now of her deliverance.

"Shall we dance?" she said. "I've been wanting to dance all evening."

She took Arturo's hand, laid a palm on his shoulder and

began to sway gently. He shuffled his feet, and they danced, a slow and measured step, barely moving at all. A suggestion of a dance, but enough. True, the music was silly, crackling and jumping, but its silliness was unimportant. Nina felt sublime.

Nearby, Berardi and his wife were dancing too, Mariagrazia's dress swirling. Marinetti was talking, his voice rolling out over the music: he was making another speech, but Nina could not make out who he was talking to.

"... and so it falls to me," he was saying, gesturing from his chair, "to draw this evening to a close. Futuristically, of course, as tomorrow morning has already begun! What I propose is that we should remain here and salute the dawn when it rises, in the true spirit of our irrepressible, irresponsible, ever-youthful hearts!"

Nina kept dancing. Briefly, she caught sight of the solitary figure at the far end of the roof terrace: Scaglia, alone and staring into the night.

"... because, as must be clear to all here tonight, we remain always at the vanguard of the race towards tomorrow. We, the Futurists of Italy, must never slacken or admit defeat. Perhaps we must never sleep. There are those, I know, who say that we have grown old and no longer have the spirit of youth within us. To those people I say, look around you now! Are we not surrounded by youth? I see with us here the brilliant painter Arturo Gallo, the revolutionary sculptor Arnaldo Volpi, the superb and ever-vivacious photographer and aviatrix Signora Della Torre, the dazzlingly talented dancer Adriana Giovene, not to mention young Emilio Calvi" – he paused, looking around in vain for Emilio – "whose work promises so much. Faced with such talent, who could claim that Futurism is not vital in its blood? Rather, I would say, Futurism is only now beginning to live!"

There was scattered applause from the dimness. Marinetti

beamed, gesturing for all to stand with him. Nina suddenly became aware that Arturo had frozen. The music crackled and jumped, but her feet were locked to the paving. Somebody was shouting, standing and shouting, and everyone was turning to look.

"Emilio, what are you doing?" Arturo said.

By the stairhead, Emilio was standing with a gun in his hand: Berardi's small black Beretta. His arm shook visibly, the muzzle of the pistol weaving, and his face was taut with fear.

"Listen to me," he yelled, his words staccato and high pitched. "Listen to me, all of you!"

"You're being very stupid," Marinetti said, pointing back at Emilio. The gun was trained on him, but Emilio shook so violently that everyone was included in the arc of potential fire. People shifted to one side or the other. Somebody laughed.

"That's my gun," said Berardi. "He's got my gun!"

The music was still playing, a jaunty number, full of tootling horns. No longer locked by surprise, Nina urged herself towards Emilio.

"Stay away, all of you," Emilio said, darting the gun from side to side. "I'm serious. I'm very serious. I want you all to understand. You all have to understand that this is over."

"The party's over?" somebody said. "I think we knew that!"

"Everything … everything's over." The expression on his face was one of rising panic. Clearly he no longer knew what he was doing. The pistol was now trained upon the Commendatore.

"Emilio, don't …" said Nina.

"Stay away from me!" Emilio cried out, his whole body quivering.

Nina's hand was clamped over her mouth, but she was

unable to move. Then, almost casually, Moresco strolled across the paving and placed his hand over the gun.

"Give it to me," he said. "Give it to me and sit down."

Emilio sobbed, his body falling slack, as if Moresco's touch had released him from an unwanted compulsion. He turned, hiding his face, as Moresco took the gun from his hand.

"You couldn't have shot anybody with this," he said. "The safety catch is still on." He flicked off the catch. Then, in one smooth motion, he turned on his heel, jutted out his arm and fired.

In that instant Nina saw everything with startling clarity: the flash and jerk of the pistol, the cartridge ejected to arc and fall, ringing, to the paving; she saw the bullet striking the gramophone and staggering it back on its table, splintering it into shards and extinguishing with violent authority the strains of "My Cutie's Due at Two to Two" …

Silence ballooned outwards from the sound of the gunshot.

"Now," said Moresco, swinging the levelled gun to indict them all. "I believe our young friend had a valid point to make, but was unable to express himself clearly."

"Bruno, there's no need for this," said Rossi quietly.

"No need? Oh, I'd say there is a very pressing need! A need to introduce some real violence to proceedings. Isn't that the sort of thing you admire, Marinetti? How about you, Commendatore?"

Moresco's presence was commanding. He stood over them all, bulky in his heavy suit. There was a terrible sobriety about him. An awful murder in his voice.

"What I think we need," Moresco said, "is a sacrifice. Don't you think? How else can we prove that we're alive? Are we all too complacent, though? Don't any of you want to volunteer? What is it that our great leader, our Duce, says? *Better one day as a lion than a hundred years as a sheep*!"

"Out of your mind," Marinetti was saying, shaking his head. "You're completely out of your mind." People were turning to look at him, as if wanting to look anywhere, at anyone, rather than face Moresco's savage smile. Unnervingly, on Marinetti's face there was also a flicker of amusement, a twitch of the lips. Could this be a performance? Surely not, Nina thought. Surely the whole thing could not be a charade, arranged beforehand by Moresco and Marinetti? What about Emilio? The scene in the bathroom? For an instant Nina disbelieved everything. All of it, unreal ...

Then Moresco fired another shot, loud as a whipcrack splitting the air just over their heads. Nina grabbed Arturo's lapels, her head hunched down. At the moment of the shot, everyone seemed to move at once, then freeze at once. A game, Nina thought, it was all a stupid game.

"Let's stop pretending, shall we?" Moresco said. "Let's admit our defeat, our total defeat. What are we doing here? What exactly are we all doing here? We have lived our days as lions, Marinetti, and no one can deny that. We have lived ... but now ..." His voice cracked, his arm wavered. Suddenly he seemed far less imposing, but a lot more dangerous.

"Might I suggest," Marinetti said, "that you cease this display, Moresco? I'm not impressed, you know."

"I'm not trying to fucking impress you," Moresco said quietly. "I'm not trying to impress anybody. All I wanted was a moment of truth. Just one moment of honest truth, that's all." He raised the gun, arm crooked, and placed the muzzle against his temple.

"No, don't ..." Nina had time to say.

And at that instant, with a jolt, all the lights in the house, all the lamps in the bedrooms and the chandeliers in the salon and the tiny bulbs strung around the roof terrace, burst into violent white illumination; at that instant too, simultaneously, Moresco pulled the trigger. The flat crack of the shot and the brilliance of electric fire came at once, then the bright red streak that lanced from Moresco's head. His body wavered and swayed, collapsing into the pit of its own shadow, the blood trailing after him to spatter a vivid design on the concrete floor.

Emilio plunged corkscrewing down the spiral stairs, and every footstep was a gunshot echoing above him. His head rang with the light, the sudden saturating light from the electric bulbs. His face was hot, flecked by the blood spray, and he wanted to tear it off. He heard screams, the sound of a woman crying, men shouting. His name: they were shouting his name.

At the bottom of the stairs the floor raced up to meet him; he stumbled forward and almost fell, then crashed through the door and out onto the gravel of the drive. Every window of the house threw a searching beam, stretching his running silhouette. As though he were fleeing in a dream, his steps did not carry him anywhere; he was digging himself steadily into the earth.

Ahead of him, Emilio saw the line of cars drawn up in front of the garages. He stumbled against a polished metal flank, grabbed at a mudguard. Breath thudded at the back of his throat, and he felt he might be sick. He ran his palm along the side of the car – a red car, Marinetti's Alfa Romeo. The soft top was still folded down. Emilio swung himself into the driving seat. The long jutting snout of the car gleamed. Emilio's feet were on the pedals, and he groped for the brake lever. Running shapes moved against the blaze of the house.

As though in a dream, he ran through the sequence of movements. Choke out, thumb on the starter button. Key ignition, he realised, through his panic. He turned the key, and the motor fired. A bang, and the car came to life. *Gears, brake pedal, accelerator.*

The guests spilled from the house. They heard the noise of the engine, then saw the car surging across the gravel. Over the front lawn, churning the turf from its tyres, the sleek red Alfa Romeo curved past them, gathering speed. A wide swerve and the car swept away. A moment later it appeared again, lit by its own headlights between the tall hedges lining the drive.

"Isn't that my car?" Marinetti said as he came out onto the porch. From the kitchen door his chauffeur was running, yelling furiously. Away across the grass others were running too: Nina, holding her shoes in one hand, with Arturo close behind her.

"Stay here," Nina called back to him. "Stay here and let me go after him."

She swung an arm back at him, the heel of one shoe catching his shoulder, and Arturo stumbled, tripping on the rutted grass. Ahead of him, Nina reached her car and opened the door.

"Nina, wait!" he called out. He heard the engine of the Fiat. The twin headlights blinded him, then the car moved, kicking a spray of grit.

Back in the house, Arturo slowly climbed to the roof terrace. Downstairs, Mariagrazia had been tapping at the telephone, trying to get a connection, while the others sat in the salon under the burning chandeliers, waiting for Greco to bring them cups of strong coffee. None would sleep tonight.

On the terrace the body still lay where it fell, the pool of blood beginning to coagulate, turning to a deep crimson gloss. Under the steady rain of light it looked striking, deliberately composed. The shattered face was turned to the concrete.

"Well, that was quite a show," Arturo said to the corpse. He took a cigarette from the table. Then he shrugged off his jacket and spread it over Moresco – one sleeve lay in the lake of blood, turning slowly black with it. Staring down at the body, Arturo felt a brief stab of jealousy, then a swell of nausea. *It should have been me*, he thought.

"And now what?" he said to himself. "And now nothing," he replied. The night was absolute, with no possibility of dawn. He wanted it all to end, right here: today and all future days to be extinguished, only the blank white flicker of a cinema film clattering empty at the end of its reel. Far off along the lake he could still see the headlights of the two cars, blinking in and out of sight. He remembered the famous paintings by Boccioni, from the *States of Mind* triptych: *Those Who Go*, speeding into the future, and *Those Who Stay*, receding behind the bars of a rainy obscurity. He should have gone, one way or the other, but he had not. He could not.

He took a last long pull on his cigarette, then flicked it out over the parapet.

11th May 1930

Ahead, the twin beams of the speeding car opened the night, snatching objects out of nothing – trees, rocks, roadside hedges – and flinging them aside. Emilio felt almost motionless, as though the hungry car were sucking the road into its polished muzzle – but the steering wheel of the Alfa Romeo bucked and wrenched in his grip, the chassis hammered beneath him and the howl of the wind and the supercharged engine was loud in his ears. He dared not glance down at the speedometer, nor take his eyes off the road ahead, the converging V of light that the car threw ahead of itself, that the car launched itself into, unstoppable.

A village appeared, stone walls rearing up on either side of the road and then tumbling away. Somewhere ahead was the Swiss border. By dawn he could be safe in another country. But Emilio knew that it would not happen, that Switzerland no longer truly existed, as the dawn no longer existed, and the house that he had left behind and everyone in it had ceased to exist. Driving was easy now, just as it was in his dreams; he kept his foot on the accelerator, shifted gear effortlessly. Nothing that he could do to this machine would affect it. He was no longer truly in control of it.

Back at the house he had killed a man – or handed him the gun to blow out his brains. He had never intended to point the gun at anybody, or even to take it from his pocket. He had been compelled by a momentum not his own. He had intended none of it, yet it was done.

Moresco's blood still flecked his face, and there were traces of it on his sleeve and the front of his shirt. Taking a hand from the wheel, Emilio wrestled the knot of his tie down from his neck, dragging the noose over his head and flinging it aside. He loosed an arm from his jacket, changed hands and freed himself of it completely. His shirt was damp with sweat, chilled now by the wind. He ripped the collar away, scattering studs, then tore loose the cheap fabric. Emilio felt the wind clean on his bare skin, the engine a hot roar through his whole body. Am I mad now? he thought. He could not tell. He felt lucid, everything reduced to this speeding darkness, the proximity of death, out here on the dirt roads, racing towards that all-extinguishing second.

The Alfa Romeo was almost obscured by the dust kicked up by its wheels, dust that billowed pale as smoke in the headlights of Nina's Fiat. Nina eased off the accelerator, dropped back and the car ahead vanished utterly, swallowed by its own fog, only the single burning red tail-light still visible. She edged up closer again until her own lights flooded the rear of the red car, the spare wheel on the back a glowing disc in its white cover. *Stupid stupid stupid* she said to herself as she fought the wheel, a grim repeated prayer. *Maniac, maniac, insane, insane, INSANE.*

She weaved in Emilio's wake, stabbing at the horn button. She had wanted to overtake him, swerve out around him as he slowed to negotiate a curve, pull ahead and force him to a halt. But there was no chance of that. The road was too narrow and winding, and Emilio was driving too fast. Where had he learned to drive like that? From within her fury, Nina tried to reach out to him, to the living being in the car ahead. She willed him to slow down, to give up and draw to a halt, but knew that he would not. She knew his need for escape, even felt grateful to him for giving her reason to go after him, to escape the house and its horrors.

The road followed the curve of the lakeshore. To one side

the mountain slope rose steeply, to the other the ground fell away through the trees to the water's edge. Nina could see nothing of it, just the pines zipping past in the dusty glare, thrown back at her by the car ahead. The road was a funnel, and she was plummeting down it

In the square mirror mounted above the dashboard, Emilio saw the flash of the pursuing car. He wanted to drive faster, but felt an awful sense of awakening. He had slipped out of his dream and found himself at the wheel of a speeding car, a steel torpedo bursting the night. The tyres clipped the rocks at the verge of the road, and ahead he saw only meaningless racing shapes. Terror gripped him suddenly, and he lifted his foot from the accelerator.

Too late. He saw the sweep of road ahead eaten into black, the curve too tight to take. He hauled at the wheel, his toe finding the brake pedal and pressing down hard. In the pit of his stomach he felt the loss of control, the car beginning to slide. A noise like tearing steel, and the wind coursing against him, first from one side and then the other. *Not this,* Emilio said to himself, *not this now.* But already he was lost inside the vortex of the car as it spun. A solid thud as the front wheels struck the roadside verge and then crashed over it. Emptiness, the wrenching sensation of falling. He felt a blow like a vast fist punching every part of his body at once. Then nothing.

An hour remained until daybreak, but the sky was lightening, the mountains already visible on the far shore. At a bend in the road, where the trees broke to allow a view out over the water, the Fiat stood pulled up at the verge. Nina leaned back against the car door, staring into the slow grey opening of the dawn. A flight of birds passed low in the distance.

In the passenger seat, Emilio lay hunched in a tartan

travelling blanket, mumbling in fitful sleep. His face was bloody, his forehead bruised from the collision with the steering wheel, his skin lacerated by splintered glass, his ribs possibly broken. But he was alive, at least, and conscious. Hours had passed since Nina had dragged him from the wreckage.

She had seen the crash, the glare of the headlights as the Alfa Romeo swung and plunged from the road. Running from her own car, stockings ripped and feet cut on the gravel of the roadway, she had scrambled down to the wrecked machine crumpled against the base of a tree. Steam rose from the buckled radiator, lit by the beams from the Fiat on the road above. Nina barely remembered hauling Emilio from the driving seat, forcing him up through the crushed undergrowth and back onto the road. She had knelt with his head cradled in her lap, shaking and crying. The only sound had been the ticking of the cooling engines, the hiss of the radiator and the steady creaking of the pines.

The crash site was only a kilometre back along the road. She should have driven further, but her nerves were so battered that she could hardy drive at all, crawling the car along so slowly that she had stalled the engine twice. In the morning, when she was calmer, she would take Emilio to a hospital. Then she would return to the house, though the idea was almost inconceivable. Was the Villa Berardi still standing? Was anyone there still alive?

A crucifix stood at the roadside. A crucifix at this lonely place, with a carved figure of Christ hanging, agonised, on the cross. In the car, Emilio was stirring in his blanket.

"Where are we?"

"Heaven." She gestured towards Jesus nailed up on his cross. "Can't you see?"

The last of the night was fading now, draining from the air and revealing the contours of the land, the surface of the water sheened with mist, the distant shore and the pines ranked on either side. Colour was beginning to rise from the monochrome – the lake a deep oceanic blue. Nina let its stillness soak through her, loving this moment, the shapes of things not quite formed. But she knew the dawn would show her the same world – show it beautifully, in the clarity of early sunrise on the mountains.

Across the water the birds were flying, in a loose chevron formation, wings beating silently, effortlessly. Nina imagined herself flying. She remembered the sensations of piloting an aircraft, the rush of the cutting breeze and the slow wheeling of the ground far below, the limitless sense of freedom. From above, the world was an abstraction, a perfectible place. From a plane she could see everything as an architect might, surveying a perfect model future laid out on a tabletop.

"What are we going to do?" Emilio said, his voice stretched tight. "What are we going to do now?"

"I don't know," Nina told him with a shrug. Let the night last a little longer, she thought. Let me live a while more in unknowing.

"I suppose," Emilio said, struggling to sit up, "tomorrow everything might make more sense."

Nina shook her head. In the far distance, the highest peaks of the mountains were beginning to glow with the sun.

"It's tomorrow already," she said.